Wegener's Jigsaw

Clare Dudman

Wegener's Jigsaw

SCEPTRE

copyright © 2003 by Clare Dudman

First published in Great Britain in 2003 by Hodder and Stoughton
A division of Hodder Headline

The right of Clare Dudman to be identified as the Author of the Work has
been asserted by her in accordance with the Copyright, Designs and Patents
Act 1988.

A Sceptre Book

1 3 5 7 9 10 8 6 4 2

A CIP catalogue record for this title is available from the British Library

ISBN 0 340 82304 6

Typeset in Sabon by Palimpsest Book Production Limited,
Polmont, Stirlingshire

Printed and bound in Great Britain by
Selwood Printing Ltd. West Sussex

Hodder and Stoughton
A division of Hodder Headline
338 Euston Road
London NW1 3BH

To CCD
With all my love

Contents

Acknowledgments

I am indebted to the Arts Council of England for their Writers' Award, which enabled me to visit Germany, Denmark and Greenland.

I am most grateful to the following people:

In Germany, Professor Jörn Thiede, Jutta Voss-Diestelkamp and Karin Leiding of the Alfred Wegener Polar and Marine Institute in Bremerhaven; to Anja Sauer, librarian at the Humbolt University in Berlin, and to Hauptmann Groh of the Militärgeschichtliches Forschungsamt.

In Denmark, Professor Minik Rosing of the Geological Museum in Copenhagen and Grete Dalum-Tilds of the Dansk Polar Centre.

In Greenland, Lucia Ludvigsen, curator of the museum in Ummannaq, her husband Niels Mønsted, and to Jean-Michel Huctin, Lucia's assistant at the museum.

In England, Dr Alan Bowden of the Liverpool Museum, and the staff of the British Library.

In Chester, Jan Bengree, Gladys Mary Coles, Dilys Dowswell, Pat Land, Irene Matthewson, Mike McGuigan, Sheila Parry, Ravi Raizada and the other members of Chester Writers, and also Alison Hollindale for relentlessly keeping up my stamina in her aerobics group.

Many thanks also to my agent, Rupert Heath, for his long-term faith and support of the project, my editor at Sceptre, Helen Garnons-Williams, who is responsible for all the bits I like the most, and my editor at Viking, Paul Slovak, who sharpened up my style.

Clare Dudman

And most of all my thanks to my husband and mother, who both patiently read the many versions of the script, and the rest of my family.

Preface

Let me tell you about ice. There are a few things you should know: firstly, it's not white. Usually it's blue, almost a turquoise, almost warmly Mediterranean. Sometimes it's not even blue, but yellow or maybe orange. That's when the sun is setting. Sometimes it seems that the sun is always on the point of setting up here. It's not, of course. It's just that often it is so low that all the light is scattered, and for a small while, just a few seconds, it is so beautiful you could forget to breathe. Stupid to forget to breathe, I know, but it happens. You forget to breathe and then you have to take a great mouthful of air and gasp at the coldness of it.

Now I shall tell you how ice sounds. For it is never silent. Just placing one foot on it can cause it to groan for thousands of metres. And ice can carry sound. It is most proficient: a loud cry for help may seem close but the mouth will be out of sight; and a whispering laugh may tickle your ear but the jokers will be lost in distant rumbles.

Of course, ice is cold too. Always cold, but when you live in it for days and days, coldness becomes relative. There is a new scale: at the top it is zero degrees Centigrade and at the bottom it is . . . well, there is no bottom. So there is just cold ice and cold cold ice, and, like the Inuit, we have names for the different sorts. I will tell you them later. Just now I want you to consider this: just cold ice can be melted with a man's skate, but cold cold ice cannot. Just cold ice melts under pressure and allows the blade to glide, but cold cold ice doesn't melt, it has to be pushed through. It breaks like sand and then solidifies into a mass again. Just cold ice is white and young; the old is suffused with blue, oxygen and cold.

And once ice is old, really old – even, you might say, prehistoric – it is ready to become young again. It is ready to start again, around and around in a cycle that defies age. How it goes is this: water evaporates, even here it evaporates, rises up, cools and forms clouds. Unique clouds. Cirrus bands and haloes. Even the clouds are different up here. And it's in the clouds that tiny ice crystals start to grow. Oh, and the way they grow, almost as if they're living, each arm extending in perfect sixfold symmetry. Eventually they become too heavy to stay there, and so they fall down on to the ice cap, down on to this Greenlandic basin within its circlet of mountain chains. Then more snow, year upon year. And all the time it's falling and collecting, man is moving, inventing, coveting the land and the ocean. Puny flags and shelters declare their temporary ownership. But the snow keeps falling, inscrutably, covering and burying, and soon it is ice, deep ice.

Now let me tell you something marvellous. Ice is schizophrenic. Even though it is a solid, it flows like something liquid. Like the medieval windows in Graz cathedral, it obeys gravity and moves. Most solids flow if something big enough presses against them for long enough – rocks, for example, fold into mountains. That's another incredible thing . . . But that comes later. Now I am telling you about ice, Greenlandic ice. This Pleistocene ice flows, down from the ice cap in the middle of the island, outwards, down and down, until it reaches the mountain chain by the coast. Then it can't move. Where can it go? Like all liquids it finds gaps. Now it flicks through, like a tongue, licks slowly down the side of the mountain, scours the rock beneath it, grinds it into flour, and then melts. Small rivulets find channels, coalesce into streams, force themselves through moraine until they reach the sweet water of the sea. You see, it comes full circle. All this Pleistocene ice, the remnants of an ice age, after tens of thousands of years reaches the sea again.

All this ancient ice holds its ancient secrets before turning into water again and flowing out to sea. That's another thing about ice. It can hold secrets. It can tell you about the weather. It can tell you which year was good and which was bad, by the quantities of microscopic pollen fossils. One day men will be able to read the ice like tree rings, they will be able to search for warm years and cold and the ice will tell them. Have you ever seen inside a hailstone? It holds its own history in its rings, its flight up and down the cumulus cloud, how fast, how long, all that melting and refreezing. Ice is good at telling tales when it wishes, and holding them, preserving them, an efficient embalmer. It is not only pollen grains it preserves but mothers and sons, even a baby; a mummy from an Inuit boating trip, his sweet face pinched in the ice.

Maybe one day the ice will reveal all its dead. Maybe as it flows downwards and outwards, everything it contains will be expelled too. Maybe it will reveal individuals from each time, each race that tried and failed to conquer this most lifeless place on earth. There would be a Saqaq hunter, with a huge dog and a bow and arrow. Then an old woman from the Dorset people found with a broken harpoon and shells for trade. Then maybe a little girl from the sea people who had crept away from the winter house and followed the northern lights in play. Then the ice would reveal the men in boats: from the north a woman and a baby in a umiak, and from the east a ship full of people. The woman would be small and dark and her baby would have a blue mark at the base of its back. She will wear furs and will be fat and strong. The people in the longboat would be tall with long, thin faces. The ice will reveal their relatives: all of them thin and ill, their clothes made from cloth and in their stomachs scraps of scrawny mutton. They had died astonished, as if they had thought they had been living somewhere else.

Sometimes the ice has good years. Distant events, like a volcano erupting or a meteorite impacting perhaps, will mask the sun and make the earth go cold. Then the ice grows. It covers the sea and obscures the land, as if it is hiding something. So men come searching. They come for what they can see: whales or walrus or just a passage to Indian treasure. Sometimes they come just to see what is there. The ice plays with them then: it crushes their ships, and lures them on to itself before losing interest and slowly crumbling away.

There used to be stories: inside the ice were oases of life. There was a paradise with animals and plants living undisturbed. Maybe there were people; the tall people with the cloth clothes and stone houses. Maybe the ice hadn't claimed all of them, and some of them had escaped the cold and were hiding in their own paradise.

Little by little men started to nibble at the ice and make inroads. Peary pushed forward a hundred miles and found just snow. Then, two years later, in 1888, Nansen bludgeoned his way through on snowshoes. There were no oases, no benign areas; instead the ice bulged into a mountain of nearly three thousand metres, and the place was a barren cold desert.

Now the ice became a training ground, a place to prove intent. Peary, the defiant, crossed it again and again before veering ever more northwards to the Pole. Mikkelsen van-quished the north-east, Rasmussen the north and Garde the south. De Quervain crossed it from the west coast to the east, while Koch and Wegener crossed it from the east. Scientists measured glaciers and winds on the margins. Complacently, men assumed they had won.

But they had not. The ice, jealous of its sterility, tried to dispel any disturbances. It covered up. It snuffed out. It suffocated and drowned. Even graves were obliterated. Even the graves of its lovers.

It is the twelfth of May 1930, 118 miles inland on Greenland's ice sheet. There, in the ice, are three objects, black and strange against the snow: two upturned skis, about three yards apart, and a broken ski stick halfway between. Around the broken ski there is a depression, betraying the fact that someone has been there recently and dug. Even though only six days have passed the wind and snow have already smoothed the hole into just a shallow cavity.

The diggers return. Small dots on the horizon become smears of movement, then there are shouting, cries and whistles as seven dog sledges come to a halt beside the skis. For a brief moment they stand in silence, and then there is movement again. Spades and shovels materialise from beneath furs on the sledges and they dig again in the space between the skis. They are silent, intent; even the dogs are quiet as they burrow into the snow and shelter their faces from the prevailing wind.

Suddenly one of the diggers, smaller than the rest, gives a small shout and the others crowd round to see. It is a small thing, insignificant to an onlooker – a fragment of hair. Yet it causes the diggers to return to their task with increased intent. Now something larger is exposed, a piece of animal skin, then something with more shape, something that would fit a man. This is laid on top of the snow and they pause to look at this in silence. One of the larger men turns, squats down and turns it over.

'It's his,' he says, dully. He turns and grips the shoulders of the man next to him. 'Keep digging, Johan.'

They turn to dig again. Their movements are slower now, as if they are tired, or maybe as if they are afraid of what they will find.

Part I
Die Einleitung

I

My first memory is this. I am looking at water. It must be water; there are bright patches of light, and I am watching them come and go. Suddenly I know that if I go forward a little I can capture one of these bright patches in my hand and I shall know how it feels to hold light. But there is a problem with this. My hands are already full. At one side of me is my long sister Tony and at the other my long brother Willy, and they have strict instructions not to let me go. Of course, I don't know this just then. It is something I find out later. So I give them a little test. Just how firmly are they holding me? The little test is to pull forward sharply and suddenly, and it turns out they are not holding me firmly at all. So I run towards the bright patches, but as I run towards them they change. The bright patches disappear and what is left is something dark, almost black. Even though this is disappointing I don't stop. I keep running into it, because if I get close enough the light will surely return.

Of course, it does not. Instead of light there is just the red-black of my eyelids; instead of heat, the coldness of a Berlin canal; and instead of a comfortable satisfaction, a blink of terror which is another sort of satisfaction, but a satisfaction all the same.

I can't remember what happens next. Some memories are like that. Single photographs. Disconnected. Bright beads on a string with long dull patches between. Other memories are not just single beads, but sequences, arranged in patterns, sometimes vague; just the way the string is twisted upon itself in the box. The memories I have of Father's school are like this. The faces of the boys I knew have merged and become just one face, bland and without character. The memories have superimposed themselves one upon the other, developing and changing through time until it is impossible to tell them apart.

We shared out home with other boys and so we had to share our parents too. My father, aloof and strict, was easy to share, my mother not so easy. Yet it was my mother they all came to, my mother with her placid humour and comfortable lap, and she welcomed them until it was time for them to leave. They were all poor boys, she said, poor boys without mothers and fathers, all alone in the big uncomfortable world, and then she would sigh and say she knew how that felt.

Orphans. For a long time they were all I knew. Sometimes it seemed strange to be endowed with not just one parent, but two. Sometimes I thought that this was just a temporary state of things, and that one day I too would wake to find them gone. Nothing would change very much, I thought. Willy, Kurt and I would sleep with the other boys, and there would be a new sir and a new ma'am to replace the ones that had left. Tony and Käte worried me, however. Where would they go? For Käte the answer came quickly; Käte would go to heaven, but what about Tony? Maybe she could cut her hair short and turn into a boy. Until that time came, though, we were special. We had our rooms separate from the rest; we were allowed to call 'sir' Father, and 'ma'am' Mother; we were allowed to have sisters; and, when the vacations came, we were allowed to go to our house in Zechlinerhütte, when Mother would become Mamma and Father Papa, and they would be all ours, without interruption. But Papa only acquired our house in Zechlinerhütte when I was six, and until then I had to make do with the Berlin suburbs.

I am watching the canal again. Now that I am older I am allowed to do this without anyone holding on to my hands, but no doubt someone is watching. It is probably my mother. Now that she has lost Käte she has become wary, and I am her youngest child, her most precious. She loves me because we look at the world through the same-shaped eyes. Today I have walked the short distance from the front door of the orphanage to the railings at the side of the canal, and I have noticed that there is a set of steps from the pavement to the edge of the water. I look around. I know that what I am about to do is wicked but I am going to do it anyway. At the bottom of the steps, just a short jump over the water, is a rather interesting-looking boat. On the boat there is something covered with tarpaulin, and a few minutes ago the edge of the tarpaulin twitched on its own.

I move slowly. It is something I have learnt. Slow, careful movement attracts less attention. It has been raining. In the middle of the smile of each step there is a crescent of water. I tread at the edges, downwards, until I am at the bottom-most step and I have to make my leap. But next to the water the gap seems almost impossibly large. I decide how I'm going to do it. I take note of all the places I could cling on to if I miss. I shut my eyes. I tense up the muscles in my legs.

'Alfred?'

She can't see me. I hold my breath. If I don't breathe she won't see me.

'Where are you?'

The edge of the tarpaulin is twitching again. I think I see the end of a tiny white tail.

Maybe I don't have to jump. Maybe if I just lean forward.

'Alfred!'

My hand is almost reaching the edge of the boat, but the boat keeps moving.

'Don't move. I'm coming down.'

The tarpaulin moves again. I can see a head. Definitely a head. It has pale brown fur and a long pointed chin. It looks a lot like my brother, Kurt. I stretch out a little more, but it is difficult to balance.

'Stay still, Alfred.' My mother has trouble squeezing through the railings, but at last she pops out like a cork from a gun. I look at the boat and I look at my mother. The boat looks safer.

'Got you!' she says, grabbing my arm. The face of little Kurt disappears and I stare after it. Three eyelets at the blunt back of the boat. I shall return later.

I can't remember now if I did. Probably something stopped me. Perhaps it was school. School interrupted all my real studies. My school was the Collnischen Gymnasium, which was a little distance away. It would have been easier for Willy, Kurt and me simply to follow the orphans to the school where my father taught. But of course we did not. The Gymnasium zum Graunen Kloster was a famous one. It cultivated leaders and men of power. It had provided von Bismarck with a few ideas and no doubt would have provided us with many more. It would have been a privilege to have gone there. But we were our father's sons, and our father had principles, and one of those principles was that we should not take advantage. We were to make our own mark with our own labours. We were to be honourable. So, every morning Willy, Kurt and I set off for one school, Tony for another, while my father silently packed his books for yet another. But school was just as annoyance, an insignificant aspect of life. We really couldn't wait to be rid of it.

I am running alongside the canal. My breath is gushing from me, great white jets of water vapour adding to the opacity of the air. Beside me the masts and chimneys of the barges are set into an eccentric stillness because last night the water of the canal froze. People are walking across it, making black footprints in the snow that fell at lunch-time. All day I

have waited and watched. Would the sun break through
the freezing fog? Would a warm wind come? But the only
thing that has happened is that it has snowed. Through the
transparent tops of the school windows I had seen fat flakes
fall, and felt my imprisonment even more strongly than ever.
News of the snow had hissed around the classroom until we
were all looking, following individual flakes downwards until
they were obscured by the etched glass below. A cough from
our teacher had returned us to our books, but even so the
afternoon had dragged. Numbers had piled up in my book
and become incomprehensible. There was only the snow, only
the ice.

It is still here. I can feel it chilling my feet into numbness.
Everything is bright. The light is reflected by the whiteness
so that even the undersides of ledges and faces are lit. Ahead
of me is Kurt. He has an awkward lolloping run, but still I
can't catch him up. I call out. He turns around, waves, and
waits for me. We exchange smiles. I notice the blueness of
his eyes made more intense by the light. There is no need to
talk, we know what we will do. We had lined up our skates
last night: Willy's, Tony's, Kurt's, a small space and then
mine. For a few seconds we had all looked at them. Mamma
had sighed because of the gap, but I had liked the way they
looked, smaller and smaller pairs until there was mine.

We lace up our skates at the side of the canal. Kurt is away
first. A few seconds to remember how it feels and then he is
off. His long body is bent stiffly at the waist and his feet flash
backwards, right, left, right, left, as regular as the piston on
a motor. At first I am a little slower, but gradually my body
remembers how to balance, my legs remember how to push
forward, and soon I am as fearless as Kurt, shouting at him
on the other side of the canal, challenging him to a race to
the footbridge. Soon there are three of us. Our big brother
Willy has at last escaped from his studies and is leading us
towards the centre of town. We do everything he tells us. We

see how long we can skate on one leg. We see who can make the tightest turn. We see who can skate the most quickly, the most slowly, the most crookedly. He plans a course and we take it in turns to negotiate it.

At last it is properly dark. The lamps have been lit, but their light is paltry. We have to skate back. We go together: Willy one side of me, Kurt the other. We are moving slowly now, talking, taking our time, not wanting it to end. I was quicker than Kurt on the obstacle course, but he was quicker than me on the flat. Willy says that when I skate it looks as if I had been born on the ice, as if I'd been doing it all my life, and it is hard to believe that this is only my first pair of skates. When he says this I am so happy that I have to hug my arms to my chest to stop my heart escaping.

From time to time a street light illuminates Willy's face, and when he notices me looking he smiles.

'We are the great Wegener brothers,' he says, as we sit down outside the orphanage. 'We will do great things.'

'Three musketeers.' Kurt says.

'Or adventurers,'

'Or explorers.'

'Or scientists.'

'Yes,' says Willy, 'scientists. Great scientists.'

Willy was a scientist already. Sometimes he showed us his experiments. He would take vinegar and baking powder from Mamma's kitchen and make small explosions on the pavement. It seemed miraculous and Kurt and I would beg to learn the secret. Now I know there is no secret, but then he seemed to us to be a magician. Powder would froth and bubble in a white volcano, cans would expel their lids and contents, and small white parcels would explode into shards. One bang brought Father out of his study. He said nothing, just slowly allowed his eyes to travel up from the mess on the pavement to my face, then Kurt's and then Willy's.

'I'll clear it up now, sir.'

My father nodded, his face without expression. But when Willy had gone for a brush and Kurt for a bucket I saw my father turn away. Even though the sun was in my eyes I was sure that he was smiling. Then I realised: in spite of his almost surly silence and his humourless reprimands, my father was proud of his eldest son.

'Is Willy going to be a scientist, Papa?' I asked, venturing to break into my father's quiet.

'I believe so, Alfred. Maybe a great one. But please don't tell him so. It is our secret.'

It is getting dark. Mamma is lighting the lamps. I can hear a quiet his as the gas escapes and a small thud as the mantle lights. She moves slowly. Her footsteps make the boards creak one after the other as she heaves herself around the room. It would be better to let the dark stay. Then we wouldn't see. The long table is set with just five places. But slowly we all sit. My father at one end, Mamma at the other, then Tony to the left, Kurt and I to the right. We all sit around the too-large table, as if we are waiting, but nothing comes.

It is something that haunts me; why did I mourn the passing of Willy but not the passing of Käte? Why did I miss him with an ache that kept me awake night after night? Why does the pain of his absence still hit me at the most unexpected moments? But it was Käte's passing which first caused my parents to become old. Before her death I have vague memories of my mother dancing, but after Käte's death she became worn and joyless. The apartment became quiet and dark, the shutters drawn as if opening them would reveal too much sorrow. Maybe it was because of all this that my father decided to buy the house of the old glass foundry's manager in Zechlinerhütte. Zechlinerhütte was my mother's birthplace, a place of lakes and wooded hills, and at last we found a place to breathe.

2

It is my first nocturnal expedition. My new notebook is jammed full with small writing. My planning has been quite thorough, but already I have discovered that I have made an important mistake: next time I shall leave Kurt at home. He charges through the undergrowth like a clumsy truffle-hog, and now we have stopped he is making the short snorts of a small pig.

'Can you see anything?' he whispers, too loudly.

I shake my head, put my finger to my lips, and sink lower. I move carefully and slowly, making sure that that I disturb as little as possible. Kurt, on the other hand, causes a small rainfall of leaves as he crouches, grunts when he finds himself sitting on something a little prickly, and then rummages around in his pockets until he finds his notebook. Once he is still the notebook is the only thing I can see – a pale rhombus from this direction – reflecting moonlight into his face. He has thought of something to report, and I can hear his pencil rasp at the paper.

I shut my eyes. At the moment there is little point in keeping them open. When my eyes are shut it seems to me that I can hear and smell more clearly. I become something wild, my other senses heightened. First there is that smell that always comes from damp places. Later I shall discover it is a single chemical with a single name, but now it just reminds me of wet black earth. Then there is the feel of that earth. At the moment it is covered with a thick layer of slimy leaves, but even so I am aware of it moving slightly to accommodate me, the grains of earth shifting then being pressed together to form an impression of me beneath. I shift a little to avoid roots and low-lying branches, and then I am comfortable. The leaves are warming under my body, and I have a seat moulded to fit. Kurt should be comfortable too but he is not. I can hear his every movement: a quiet creak as a branch shifts, a squelching sound as he presses his foot into a water-sodden patch of peat, and then the not-quite-silent hiss of inhalation as he no doubt stabs himself again on an inconvenient twig.

But there is another sound. I open my eyes. Incredibly, given Kurt's blunderings, there is something moving ahead of us. I incline my head slightly. It is all that is necessary. Even in the light of this gibbous moon I can see that Kurt's eyes have followed mine, and he can see what I see: a small striped head nuzzling at the ground.

Now even Kurt is silent and motionless. I follow the badger intently, forming words in my head, repeating them to myself so that later my observations will be detailed and accurate. He makes four movements with his snout to the right, and then repeats this to the left. He shuffles forward a little and repeats the whole process again. Abruptly he stops. My breath pauses in my lungs. Has he smelt us? Heard us? No, he has found something under the leaves. Now his snout is skewering the ground. Leaves are being thrown up and crackling like paper. He grunts and pulls. Something white is pulled away, there is a glimpse of something hairy, a root or a small gourd, and the badger turns away.

His back has another beauty, understand but still there: the smoothness of the fur, the graceful curvature of the rump, the uniformity of the grey, and too soon it disappears. We peer after it. Now it is possible to pick out a small hole in the bank ahead of us. I take out my notebook, write down my memorised words, then I look around me. Why did the badger choose to make his home just here? I decide it is mainly by accident: the hole could be natural, the result of a large root implanted in a steep bank; but this is also a place where the badger can find food while remaining undisturbed and sheltered. I put all this down in my notebook and then look at Kurt. He smiles at me across the gloom.

'You were right, Alfred,' he says. 'It's the obvious place.'

And I forgive him. I forgive him his clumsiness and noise. 'Shall we examine the den?'

Kurt nods vigorously.

I point with my finger to the hole and we creep forward.

He gasps his excitement. 'I think there's something in there! Look, eyes. This is amazing, Alfred, wonderful!'

I look at his face, his eyes as shiny as the ones we can dimly see ahead of us. He is here and has seen all of this, because of me. I want to be acknowledged, thanked for my perseverance. But instead he just peers into the hole in silence. The badger's eyes disappear. We shift position and peer in again, but all we can see now is darkness.

'Maybe it's his young. Maybe we'd better leave them,' he says, and we turn away.

I wait for him to speak again but he says nothing.

'I was right about the den, then, wasn't I?'

Again I wait, and again I am disappointed.

As we reach a clearing he straightens up. 'I think we should come back in the daylight, Alfred. Maybe we'll see more then.'

Gradually we came to know the map of Zechlinerhütte. We drew it on paper, but more importantly we began to carry it in our heads. We worked hard to accomplish what every Inuit achieves with ease: an indelible map drawn inside the head. Every hillock, every lake, every valley is plotted and remembered, assigned spirits and demons, so that it is impossible for them ever to become lost, even when winter brings the anonymity of snow.

Each season in Zechlinerhütte had its charm: in the summer Father taught us to swim, and then, convinced he had done all he could to ensure our safety, allowed us the freedom to sail or row. The lakes seemed to be miniature seas, with small sandy bays, tiny rippling waves, and the water going on and on until interrupted by hills and trees. But it was winter that was my favourite season. Then the lakes became icing rinks, the hills surrounding them sledging tracks, and all at once it seemed that the landscape had returned to its Pleistocene origin. Once I stood at the highest place I could find and imagined it all: great ice sheets scouring out giant hollows for lakes, sealing the edges with impervious clay, then dumping bits of out-of-place rocks to form minor mountains. Winter was also the time when we could guarantee that we would be alone. There would be no surprise guests from the orphanage taking up space in the loft, and Mamma and Papa would be all ours.

But in the end there was always the return journey to Berlin, school and our apartment at the orphanage.

Kurt and I are standing at the threshold of the kitchen. We are a little in the way, but that is part of our intention. Tony is fussing with something; making some sort of elaborate tart and becoming cross in the process.

'What are you doing there?' she demands, brushing hair away from her face with a floury hand. 'You're in the way. Go away, little beasts.'

'Why are you in such a hurry, Tony?' Kurt asks slyly. Then he sniffs. 'Is something burning?'

He nudges me as she dives towards the stove. Her best skirt, the noisy black one, is smeared at the back with flour. She is trying to impress someone. When she opens the stove door there is just a rich complicated smell of sweet and savoury things cooking together, no burning at all. She slams the door shut and turns back to Kurt and me, her eyes shining with temper.

'You made that up, didn't you, little vermin?'

Tony is nineteen and at the height of her beauty. Of course, I don't know this then. To me she just seems old, tall, thin and not quite straight. Her arms are awkward levers, unoiled and slightly unresponsive, and, as she works, they make exaggeratedly obtuse angles at her sides. Like Kurt she always seems to take up too much room. At the moment, though, her long face is as balanced as it ever will be, with youthful soft cheeks, and eyes that still seem characterful rather than drained. Her air of expectation has a frantic edge, as if she knows that she will have little time and will have to make the most of every opportunity. Today there is someone coming to tea, one of the pallid young men from the Lutheran church, and once again she will be too attentive, too eager to laugh and try to change herself into something she is not, and the suitor will hurry away oppressed and slightly preoccupied.

But now it is Tony's turn to be preoccupied. When my mother enters she screeches with annoyance.

'Can't something be done about them, Mamma?'

Kurt puts his elbow on the door frame and leans against it. I follow suit on the other side. We both grin, competing with each other to show the most teeth.

'Look, Mamma. Little beasts. They're just doing it to annoy me. Please, Mamma. I haven't got long. I need to concentrate. Why are they just standing there like that?'

'We're bored.'

'Oh, make them go, Mamma, please.'

'We need somewhere to do our experiments.'

'We want to use that chemistry book Papa bought us.'

'We thought maybe that old laundry room.'

'No one uses it much.'

'We could go in there and not be any trouble to anyone.'

'Oh, let them, please, Mamma.'

'I don't know. Helga sometimes needs it.'

'Hardly ever.'

'It would be ideal. A sink, a place to put our stuff.'

'What stuff?'

'The stuff we're going to buy.'

'Chemicals. Test tubes. Burners. Proper experiments.'

'Like Willy.'

My words make the world stop. Tony is looking up from her bowl, the spoon pausing in the space above, viscous mixture slowly flowing downwards, collecting into a mass until it is heavy enough to fall. I want to eat back my words, swallow them whole, make them unsaid, but of course I can't. I am too young yet to realise the value of silence and careful thought.

'Yes, just like Willy,' Mamma says. Her shoulders sink a little. She takes a couple of steps towards the table and looks in Tony's large earthenware bowl.

'That's looking good, Tony.'

Tony gives a tight little smile. 'Thank you. Mamma, could you beat the eggs?'

Mamma reaches for her apron, which is hanging up behind the door. With slow deliberate movements she wraps it around herself. Kurt glares at me. My big mouth has destroyed all our plans. Now we will not be allowed to do anything. We may as well just go. His disapproval and disappointment hurt far more than his anger, and I can't bear to lift my eyes to his. Instead I examine the tiles of the floor and allow him to nudge me through the doorway into the corridor. I watch the tiles turn to wood and then the wood into matting, but stop when Mamma's voice calls after us. 'I suppose it will be all right. I'll have a word with Helga. But just be careful, will you?'

We run up the stairs. We have not forgotten Willy. He is part of everything we do. Now he is going to be involved even more closely. In a deep cupboard built into the wall of our bedroom is a small wooden box. It used to be Willy's. It is roughly made and stained with spillages of different colours. Large blots describe continents on a sea of light wood. Where they overlap some of them have become black, and at the edges of one of the stains is a fine crystalline border which glistens when we bring it out into the daylight. We know how it will smell when we open it: a bit like the cupboard where Papa keeps all the medicines, but cleaner and more intense. It is the smell of science, Willy's science.

The smell of Willy's science came to fill the small laundry room. Sometimes it even escaped from there and forced our maid, Helga, out of her kitchen with yells of complaint and much flapping of her aprons, but sometimes it faded away altogether and was replaced by bangs and sparks. In the end all of our pocket money was literally burnt away, but it was a glorious burning, with a full musical accompaniment.

We are standing side by side. It is a competition. We have learnt how to make hydrogen, and now we are seeing who can make the most. The way we are going to do this is to take a fine dust of metal and watch it dissolve in a special liquid. The man in the hardware shop called this liquid 'spirit of salts', but Kurt and I know it by a different name: 'hydrochloric acid'. Hold it too close and you will shed sanitised tears. We roll the test tubes around in our hands. Does it move more slowly than water or faster or the same? It is impossible to tell. Bored at last with this, we put the test tubes in their racks and assemble everything else. It is important to be quick, important to cover the end of the test tube with a thumb when the reaction starts. So we arrange a pile of iron filings each, a spoon to ladle them in, and then, next to this, outwards like the cutlery for an elaborate meal of many courses, our tapers with the spirit burner between. At last everything is in place. Our eyes lock.

'Ready?' Kurt asks.

I nod, my arms and shoulders tense.

It is Kurt who counts down: 'Three, two, one – *go*.'

His hands are trembling; his first dose of filings misses the test tube and litters the table between us, but mine goes in. The bubbling starts at once. I touch the side of the test tube: it is hot, almost too hot to touch, but at the top, where I put my thumb, it is cool. My thumb is shorter than Kurt's but fatter. It forms a satisfying seal around the top and I watch while Kurt fumbles with his second spoonful of filings. Now I have a test tube of hydrogen, just a very small amount. Later I shall be making more, much more, sufficient to fill a balloon large enough to take me and Kurt over half a continent and a bit of an ocean. But now I have to be careful to keep the scrap that I have made from escaping: the smallest gap and it will rise away, undetected, to the edge of the atmosphere and beyond. Not even gravity can hold it down. So, keeping our thumbs on the top of the test tubes we reach for our tapers. They light quickly and the smoky flames quiver with excitement.

'Ready?' Kurt asks again.

I nod. He is the orchestrator and I am happy to be led. It is necessary to get the timing correct; to remove the thumb just as the splint enters the test tube.

Two satisfying squeals. Mine higher pitched, but Kurt's lasting a little longer. The squeal has extinguished the flame, and around the inside of the test tube is a fine spray of water.

'I won,' Kurt says.

There will be no dispute.

'But your squeal was very loud too.'

I smile at his generosity.

'But I won.'

I smile and nod.

'I am the eldest.'

I nod again. It is only fair that the eldest wins. But my squeal was louder. Much louder.

3

It is the thirteenth of October, three months before the twentieth century begins. At the end of today I shall be a student. This transition will only happen once and I want to remember it. Today I am determined to be aware of everything I see and taste and do, and burn it all into my memory.

I start, as usual, from the orphanage. I look back; today I shall really see it, concentrate on each small part, so that it will stay with me as it is now. There, for instance, above the mock colonnades, where the roof is raised to form two curved brows, are windows like the eyes of a tiny frong. So often I have looked out and imagined myself to be one of its pupils, flicking up and down Friedrichtsgracht, waiting patiently for my life to change. And now it is.

I head north beside the river towards the affluent sector of the Kaisers. There is not a scrap of soil or vegetation. A continual traffic of barges feeds the Prince's palace and makes it fat. The squat medieval halls have sprouted domes, baroque architraves and triumphal arches. As I approach, masonry hammers ring on an embellishment to a vestibule.

I walk quickly. One building merges into the next, massive façades of light stone unexpectedly giving way now and again to intimate-looking courtyards. The one I enter is guarded with statues. I go closer to inspect the names: Wilhelm and Alexander Humboldt. Alexander Humbolt. I look at his calm face contemplating the world. If he were here now what would he make of these crowds of people, all this

24

hurrying and frantic activity? I look round. Kurt is supposed to be here, waiting for me. Where is he?

I pause for a short while before attempting to march onwards, past the privet hedges and into the courtyard of people. Where is Kurt? Maybe he is among this crowd of people. As I look for his long, thin head balancing on his long, thin body I am pressed into the mass of bodies. My direction is decided for me. I am shoved into line, forced through a set of inadequate double doors and into an entrance hall. There is nothing much to see, just chocolate-coloured marble pillars, and, rising up at the back of the room, an over-grand stairway in the same stone. Brown is everywhere: in the cloth of the jacket of the man in front of me, and in the hair on his head which I am forced to examine minutely whenever I look forward. Where is Kurt? Even if he is here he won't see me in this tight crowd of people. Behind me, someone treads on my heel. I haven't even got room enough to bend down to coax the pain away. We move relentlessly forward again. It is a flowing movement no one can control or stop, and we are all carried along within it, detritus, moving in bands, slower at the edges where the walls cause drag.

Then the memory fades. In spite of all my intentions that morning I remember nothing about what happened next. Maybe I don't want to remember. Maybe I felt a panic. Maybe I tried to calm myself with thoughts of Zechlinerhütte and memories of open spaces. Eventually I must have reached a desk with an official, chosen my lectures and found Kurt. But I don't remember that. All I remember is that squeezing of people and a sudden disillusionment. There were thousands of us cramming the university halls that day and I was as unimportant as the next. In order to rise above it all I would have to work hard.

I am in the undergraduate's chemical laboratory of the

Friedrichs-Wilhelms University, staring at the samples in front of me: five small jars of powder. One powder is green, one a brick red and the other three are white.

Why am I not excited? Surely I am, at last, a scientist. But I am not enthralled. I am a little bored, a little restless.

The laboratory is crowded. Four of us are crammed along this small bench, constantly apologising for our accidental nudges and inadvertent kicks. We are watching each other carefully, looking for clues on how to proceed. Even though we have attended the lecture we remember very little about what we have to do. Eventually we all decide to try the Bunsen burner first, and now we are standing in a line along the bench, waiting while our wire hoops burn clean.

'And what are you doing, sir?'

I stand up a little straighter. My piece of wire darts out of the flame. I glance over my shoulder.

'Trying to burn off impurities, sir.'

'And what will you do then?'

By the time I have drawn in enough breath to reply, Professor Fischer has gone. I watch as he moves rapidly through the laboratory: a neat figure with small movements. He pauses to stop at each bench, asks a question and then moves rapidly on.

What will I do then? I try to answer his question. No more of this, I decide, looking around at the crowded laboratory. I need something that requires room and space to breathe. Professor Fischer reaches the end of the room. He glances round, his eyes behind his pincenez checking that all seems to be in order. Does he catch my eye? Can he see that I am longing to defect? But I can think of nothing to do instead; at the moment all my ideas are raw and badly formed. They come and go like spots before the eyes, moving too quickly for me to know they are really there. So as Professor Fischer leaves the room, I return to my investigation. I wet the wire with acid, pick up a little of the green powder and poke it into the small fire above the Bunsen: an almost invisible flame is transformed into the layered one of copper, a green tongue within the blue. Malachite. The green powder is malachite: a moment of satisfaction that lasts only as long as the flame.

My life at university was little different from my life at school. At the end of each day I would take the same walk home to the orphanage and my parents. Even though I was in Berlin, one of the most dynamic cities in Europe, I lived quietly. Close around me great cultural centres were being formed: museums, churches, a cathedral, even new banks and department stores. But it was not part of my world. I tried to keep it away.

Tony would come back chattering about what she'd seen: a huge shop containing everything you'd ever want, four floors in glass and stone, or a glass-roofed courtyard with chandeliers and golden walls where everything could be seen and touched, or a garden filled with statues.

'I went to the Tiergarten today.' Tony pauses, waiting for someone to say something. But no one does.

'At each statue there's a bench, and at each bench a great crowd of people.'

I stare hard at the numbers in front of me, trying to make them line up and make sense.

'Such great art.' She sits back and sighs affectedly. 'So moving, so beautiful, so inspiring.' She sighs again.

'And so much rubbish.'

'Oh.' Her voice is a quiet, hurt. 'Have you seen them too, Papa?'

'In here.' He flaps his newspaper. 'I've never seen such melodramatic tat. You really need to learn to judge these things for yourself, Tony.'

Tony exchanges a glance with our mother, then silently reaches down into a basket beside her for her sewing. She is twenty-seven and already her face is set into a frown.

I stand up. This room is like the rest of Berlin; too small and too densely packed. When I open the door of my room Kurt is there, leaning over the desk, taking up space, breathing too loudly.

I need to escape. I make my plans in secret; I decide that for the final term of my first year I will swap universities and taste the distant delights of Heidelberg.

4

This is my escape: a dark and noisy room in Heidelberg with sawdust on the floor and beer in my hand. Every few minutes a man called Heinrich emphasises what he is saying with a slap on my back. I am trying to time my sips of beer to coincide with lulls in his diatribe. I don't always succeed, and evidence of my failure lies in the long dark streaks down the front of my waistcoat. I am telling myself that this is freedom and happiness, but my strongest emotion, if I think about it, and I'm trying not to, is anxiety. Some time ago Heinrich had begun to explain the difference between a girl from the north and his female of choice, a woman from the Black Forest, but he now seems to have lost track of his argument.

'Berlin women are not flat chested.' A thin man in a suit juts his beard towards Heinrich's face.

'Yes they are. Like a blackboard.' Heinrich rocks back in his chair with a hoot of laughter.

'And fat too? Impossible. You are talking with the mouth of an idiot, my friend.'

'Ah, your life is too sheltered, Fritz, you need to go out into the world.' Heinrich shakes his head with mock sadness and then sits back, spreading himself in his chair so the rest of us have to squeeze back into our own. 'Scatter yourself around, test the waters. Berlin women, now, if you came across them, you'd learn to avoid them. Each one of them is fat, flat . . .' He grips on my arm as he searches for the word. '. . . supercilious, dim and . . . what else? Dreary!'

Heinrich slaps my back to enhance his enjoyment of his

words. I inhale a nostrilful of beer. Heinrich laughs at my spluttering and beats my back again.

'In Heidelberg, my young friend, we drink our beer like this, with our mouths.' Heinrich takes a mouthful to demonstrate, then continues, 'Not through our noses. We drink . . .' He drinks again. 'And inhale.' He wheezes in. 'Drink . . . and inhale. It takes practice, like most important things in life. Lots of practice.'

'And he has had more than most!'

There are more wails of laughter, and again my beer forms great foamy globules over my chest.

'And what do you think?' asks Fritz, his beard now pointing in my direction. 'You should know, you're from those parts, aren't you? Surely there must be a few with decent figures.'

'Big women, great big women, you can really grab – with both hands.' Heinrich roars, his hands supporting imaginary flesh in front of him.

I think about the women I have met – very few. In that city of close to two million souls, I can only remember about half a dozen women, all of them Tony's friends, from either the Lutheran church or her schooldays. But apart from a general impression of their build (and they all seemed to fall into one of two main varieties – either very ample or very mean), I cannot remember the details of their form, where they jutted out and in, and whether it was a gentle curve or more like planes and angles. It was just something I hadn't ever bothered to notice. Yet to everyone else here the rump and breast in the female seem to be of paramount importance. Maybe I have spent too long at my studies, too long staring at pages of algebra or the movements of the stars. I need to broaden my studies a little. I decide to start at once. 'Heinrich has a point,' I say, trying to sound knowledgeable.

'More than one point – two!' Heinrich rises from his seat to demonstrate, his jacket partly drawn over his hands, which are arranged over his chest. To a chorus of whoops and whistles he attempts to mince around the tables and then resumes his seat, but not before he has given me another whack across my shoulders.

This time I keep drinking. I follow his instructions, gulping and breathing my way through the entire glass. At the end of it I feel as though something has fallen from me.

'Certainly they never appealed to me,' I say, truthfully.

'Ha, you see, Fritz, I'm right.' Heinrich stands up again, swaying to some tune that I am beginning to hear too. 'Another jug, I think.' He turns towards the bar and yells at a woman who is leaning there. 'Mathilde, you little beauty, another one of these, if you please.'

Obediently the woman fills her large earthenware jug and approaches the table. Four pairs of eyes follow her with silent appreciation. I am looking too, inspecting, taking note. It is something more I have to learn. Her light brown hair is braided into two ammonites above her ears. Her blouse is white with lacy edges finishing just below the elbows. But it is the rest I was supposed to be noticing and appreciating: the way her bodice curves out above her waist, the way it is so tight that it is possible to follow the movement of her lungs beneath, the way the bodice ends and her blouse billows out again, revealing little but suggesting more, the way the bottom of her throat forms a hollow at the base of her neck, and the way this hollow rises and then fills in again as she swallows.

'Mathilde, I think you have an admirer.'

She follows their smirks back to me. I have got it wrong again, examined her for too long and drawn attention to myself. We gaze at each other for a few seconds. She has a small face, her nose, eyes and mouth squashed together as if there is insufficient room. When she smiles her mouth barely opens, but even so I glimpse teeth; white, tiny and perfect like those of a field mouse. I smile back and look quickly down again.

'Ah, Mathilde, if you play your cards right you could have a Berliner falling at your feet.'

I don't look up. There is more beer in front of me, it seems darker than before. In desperation I take a gulp, and another and another, and suddenly Mathilde is forgotten, fades away, a spectre with a jug, and all that is left is the richness of my beer.

I must have drunk then, drunk soundly, I suppose. I remember vaguely women swaying between us, sometimes Mathilde, sometimes an older woman. But then I forgot to notice. I became distracted. I was concentrating on something else, something even more important and profound: freedom. It seemed to me that night that I was losing my skins, shedding layers and layers of useless epidermis that had held the real me, constrained and anxious to be released. I felt that if I looked down I would see them there on the sawdust-sprinkled floor, yellow and translucent, maybe even retaining the shape of what they had once been: a left shoulder with the imprint of my father's hand as he guided my study, my mother's gentler hand print on the other shoulder, reminding me to work hard, and Tony's hand like a slap on my leg commanding me to be quiet. I shed them all that night. All at once they had turned from reassurance to threat, from protection to suffocation. I needed them no longer. But Kurt's arm, with its firm friendly hold, stayed for now. Its impression, a furrow across my back, was too deep to be slewed away so readily.

Heinrich is standing over me. He is telling me to do something, but it is not making much sense.

'She's waiting.'

Who is waiting? I feel I ought to know, as if I've been only half listening to a lecture and have now been caught out. He leans forward and makes fresh imprints on my new and tender skin.

'Go on. Now. She won't wait long.'

I get up, just to rid myself of his hands, which already seem to be gripping more securely than those I have just shed. I wade forward, pushing against chairs and tables. With my new freedom I do not need to walk around them. It is easier to make them fall, satisfying and right that they should crash against the tables. It doesn't matter that glasses fall, that beer forms small tides along the rough surface of the table, that one glass smashes in front of me and my feet grind the pieces into powder.

Then there is light, lots of bright light, and there is Mathilde and her small perfect teeth, slightly parted, waiting for me.

'Go on,' says Heinrich, giving me a shove.

I fall into the room. I hear the door shut behind me, and his hands are gone.

There is no need to move. In fact I have landed in a rather comfortable position with the rug beneath my legs, my back against the quilt of Mathilde's bed, and the gas light giving a warm, comfortable glow. And there is Mathilde's face next to mine, her head dangling over the edge of her bed, while mine lolls against the counterpane. She moves slightly forward while I move back. We gaze at each other for a few seconds, then she jumps lightly to the floor.

Now she is sitting by me. She has taken my raw hand and pressed it between hers. It is burning under her touch. She strokes my exfoliated cheek. Although her touch is soft it is also acidic. I flinch away.

She frowns. I smile. She bites her bottom lip. I shut my eyes.

I think I slept a little: a dreamless sleep or maybe just a faint, certainly a period of unconsciousness. I woke feeling thirsty and with a full bladder. I needed to move urgently to empty it but instead I found myself apparently set into a slumped position beside a bed.

*   *   *

I open my eyes. There is little difference; only a faint filament of moonlight from the window. When I move my flesh sticks, it seems to tear a little before parting from whatever was supporting my back. Gradually, with little interest, I realise that I am naked. It seems a natural extension of my shedding of my skins, but I am fairly sure that I am not responsible. It takes me a little time to form the word 'Mathilde' in my head and remember the frown and the biting of her lip. Without hope I feel around the floor for my clothes, but there is only rug and then, to my dull delight, the coldness of pot. My relief is painful but exquisite.

I am just returning the pot to its place under the bed when I hear footsteps. Their owner is wearing boots rather than shoes and there is no rustle of skirt or petticoat. I casually pull at the bed. It is resolutely made, with a heavy quilt and blankets fastened into position with determined folding. At last I reveal the sheet. I pull and for a few seconds it hovers like a spectre in the bluey darkness. As I take a corner and throw it over my shoulder, I cry out at the coldness of it and the door opens.

It is Fritz and he is holding a tray with two glasses of beer.

'I hear Mathilde is not to your taste,' he says, slamming the tray on the small cupboard beside the bed and then sitting on the floor beside me. I fasten the sheet around me with knots. Now that it is secure I rather like it. I feel like an ancient king.

'She's pretty mad. Mainly at Heinrich, but she's not being too complimentary about cold Berliners either.'

He reaches for the glasses and passes one down to me. '*Prost!*' he says, and we follow Heinrich's advice to the bottom of the glass.

It was Heinrich who decided that we were Romans; suitable judgment on his behalf because he was much too corpulent to belong to any other epoch. Soon there were four of us dressed in sheets: Heinrich, Fritz and one other I can't remember, heading through the Heidelberg streets towards the river. We almost reached the market square.

At first I don't notice that the rest are quiet. I am at the front, leading them onwards. There are few streetlamps, but the moon is full, and by its light I have noticed that there is a woman leaning from a window. She is probably a Vandal, but no matter. 'We are of the twentieth legion, heading north to unexplored territories,' I tell her. 'Will you give us alms?'

She giggles. Even though she is quite old, about thirty, she giggles.

'I said, will you give us alms?'

I look up at her. She could be beautiful, but it is difficult to see. Her hair is dark, part of it has escaped from her little white cap, and she is smiling. She is wearing something light, probably a sleeping gown.

'Why should I?' she asks. 'I mean, you'd have woken me up, if I'd been asleep.'

We are quite close now, and I can see that even though she is no longer a maiden she is indeed fairly beautiful, with square, even features. There is not one aspect of her that reminds me of a rodent. Instead she reminds me of all the skins I have lost this night and of the freedom that is now tugging at my toga.

'Come away with me,' I say suddenly. They don't seem like my words, but now I've said them I feel quite proud of them.

'Hmm, I'll have to see. Maybe after I've asked my husband.' She giggles again.

I remember a map I saw yesterday. It showed Nansen's single crossing of Greenland, the top of the island fuzzy, still unmapped. 'We could explore the uncharted territory of the north.' I squint upwards, trying to see whether she's interested. 'No one would follow us. We could . . .'

Before I can tell her more she is distracted by something behind me. She puts a finger to her lips and abruptly closes the window. I stare after her.

It is a closed window that I shall come to know well, one I shall inspect every time I pass. Behind that closed window the hidden woman will become ever more beautiful and desirable, her nose straighter, her eyes larger, her wisps of hair arranged in an ever more elaborate and pleasing framing of her face. She will grow so lovely in my mind that one day, when she passes me in the street, a small, solidly built woman, I will not recognise her. It is only when she giggles that I shall stop and look. Her hair is a mousy brown, her eyes are hazel and rather small, and across her cheeks are the pits of an old adolescent scourge of acne. Her eyes will slide from mine without recognition and we shall both continue on our ways, only one of us disillusioned and puzzled.

But now, as I gaze at the newly shuttered window, my dreams are interrupted. A gloved hand is placed roughly on the knot at my shoulder. I look around. Apart from a university policeman I am alone on the street. Heinrich, Fritz and the other have vanished. The policeman flicks open a small notebook and asks for my name.

I wasted Hiedelberg. I suppose that much is obvious now. I wasted it on Heinrich, Fritz, young men I can hardly remember and a woman with a bad complexion. I was so proud of my new skin. I flaunted it. My punishment for disturbing the peace was a small fine, which I paid without embarrassment. In truth it would have served me better to languish a little in the student jail, not a very harsh option then, with release each day for lectures, but at least I would have been forced to think. Was this new skin really so much better than the old? I wish now I could take the foolish youth that was me then and shake some sense into him. I would mention the Königstuhl observatory and suggest a visit, I would point out the privilege of being taught by Professor Wolf, I would tell him to listen to his lectures instead of just attending them.

The man behind the rostrum is talking excitedly. Languidly I take notes. It is warm, and getting warmer. It is hard to concentrate on the stars when there is so much of greater interest close at hand. He points up, his fingers describing orbits, and I follow them on the ceiling. But when his hand drops my eyes remain looking upwards. For a short time they follow Wolf's meteors, but then they wander off on their own path along the scrolls and curlicues of the stucco on the ceiling. There is a woman's hand there, and an arm.

Listen, o most foolish young man. Life is short. It goes so quickly, flows away until you are left old and cheated. Listen to the words around you. They seep from these ancient walls. They are telling you the same thing: time must not be wasted, but you are too young yet to believe them.

I allow my eyes to drift back to his face. There is no hurry. My pen follows the voice I hear. He talks about dark bodies among the stars, and I pause a little. It distracts me a few minutes imagining what they could be, imagining seeing them, clouds of smoke between the stars, doing nothing, just being there. But now he is talking of other things. His voice is breaking at the injustice of it all: a nova appearing in the sky just before the invention of the telescope. Tycho Brahe measuring, observing, yet unable to really see. But the nova is gone now, disappeared without any apparent trace. It is God laughing at his creation. Almost as if He doesn't want us to know. My pencil breaks. I stoop for another. Outside, the sun shines. Outside, the river waits and Fritz has hired a boat. He said last night that he might invite a few girls to join us. Was Tycho's nova a new star or the explosive end of an old one? Maybe, while it burned, it seemed to Tycho that there was another sun in the sky. Did he know it would be temporary or did he think it would go on for ever: a glorious new world lit by two suns? I wish I could see it now. I wish my woman had come from her window, left her husband snoring in his bed and followed me to the land of the Inuit. I can see her face, shining, framed by fur and lit by the two suns reflecting off the snow. There's lots of time, she says. So I stand and wait. And the nova burns and burns, but like Tycho Brahe I can't really see.

5

In Berlin that year it was easy to believe that God was indeed dead. Away from the summer light of Heidelberg everything seemed darker, dirtier, contaminated with something I couldn't identify. It evolved with the blow of the demolition hammer and was sent around the city in a dry choking wind. It settled on the newly arranged statues, was swept up by the busy mason's trowel and then set into the foundations of each piece of vainglorious architecture. Inevitably it began to settle on me too. I could feel it collecting where my new skin creased, filling in pores until I was caked with an unwanted covering. I began to take walks outwards, away from the centre, looking again for escape.

Later I will see this place in a painting. Instead of a young man with a well-fitting suit there will be a railwayman and his wife. Instead of a hopeful face searching the horizon for space, their two faces will be downcast, pallid with exhaustion. Behind them, behind me, the lights of the city pollute the darkness and hide the stars. Even at this time of night the incessant clanging and roars of locomotive engines intrude into our every thought until they become just twitches of consciousness. But beyond the railway tracks, beyond the monochrome outlines of chimneys and roofs, there is something real and important. The middle-aged couple knew this once but are too resigned to remember now. But my eyes are still keen, I can see it; the place where the red-grey of the sky is mixed with blue, where air becomes less solid and the ground rises up with exciting unpredictability. I come here to remember how it was and how it shall be again soon.

Heidelberg had made me restless, but as the dust of Berlin settled around me my memories turned into something as uncertain as dreams. My subjects were more real and applied now, those of the open air: meteorology, astronomy and navigation. At night I perfected the art of dreaming. If I sat alone in my room I could make it open out around me into a vast cold space, the voices of my parents and sister blending together to form the wind. When Kurt came home he entered my dreams too and we schemed of escape. We could not, we decided, bear another semester in Berlin. Our joints were becoming set in place and our muscles atrophied. But we had to have an excuse to leave. That much was obvious. In the Wegener household there always had to be a good reason to do anything; something to improve the mind as well as the body.

A few days into 1901 Kurt came home with a smile even he could not contain. He covered the notes on my desk with a newly acquired map. The shading was so deep and plentiful that the smooth paper seemed crumpled, and beneath the colours we could see that the contour lines merged together to indicate precipitous cliffs and edges. Kurt jabbed a finger at the centre of the map: the Leopold Franzens University in Innsbruck. He had overheard someone talking about it at a seminar. Lots of students went there in the summer. It was ideal. There were academic excursions and field trips, as many as you could wish for. Strong geology and botany departments. And forests. And rivers. And mountains. Just like Zechlinerhütte but better. Real mountains this time, with twisted rocks and precarious vegetation. Unmarked routes. Remote and lonely places. We could climb and take long expeditions to the summits. We could inspect glaciers. We could . . . At last he ran out of words and inspected my face.

What did I think? Should we go there? I looked at the map.
I could feel the bitter air on my face, cold and exhilarating.
I couldn't answer.

'Well?' asked Kurt, a little impatient now.

I looked up, my smile, I think, matching his.

'Good,' he said, 'I'll start making arrangements.'

I am watching the river. It is so extraordinarily white that it
fascinates me. Something that is so opaque should not flow
so quickly. But it tumbles down, giggling over the rocks and
gurgling through self-made tunnels.

'Are you ready?' Kurt says, already hurling his haversack
on to his back. He disappears into the woods.

When did the woods stop? It is something that always
puzzles me. I never notice the last tree. Is it because there
is never a last tree? Is it because tree turns into bush and
bush into stunted shrub and shrub into scraps of vegetation
clinging to the ground? Maybe the process is so gradual it
is impossible to tell: this is where the woodland stops and
the meadow begins. There are no trees now, not even a
desperately clinging Scots pine. I look around. There are
few plants of any sort, just patches of dark green that are
probably heather or reindeer moss, and an occasional patch
of fiery red from a scrawny rhododendron bush. Ahead of us
is the mountain, streaked in purple, grey and white, but before
that is a steep slope of scree. Kurt stops at the bottom.

'This way?' he asks.

There seems to be no other.

The sun has heated up the black rock and turned it into a
griddle.

'We could fry eggs on this,' I say to Kurt, touching it lightly
with my bare hands.

He touches it too, holding his hand there slightly longer
before he also draws it away.

'Almost,' he says. 'Not quite.'

I look away so that Kurt cannot see my smile. Sometimes Kurt's lack of humour is, in itself, amusing. The slab of rock stretches above us, almost vertical, almost smooth, without any obvious handhold.

Kurt frowns. 'I think we could do it,' he says. 'That way, look.' He traces out a zigzag across the face.

Sometimes my foot slips. Sometimes I don't think it will go in at all. But I am following Kurt, and where Kurt's foot has gone so mine must follow. But his stretches are longer than mine and there are places where I have to make two moves to his one; places where I have to scramble a little to grab hold; and once I found myself terrified, with both feet displaced, holding on to a ledge with my fingertips. But now, mysteriously, I have overtaken him. I look down and all I can see is the flatness of the top of his hat. How has this happened? How have I stopped following in my brother's footsteps and taken the lead?

I have no idea how we are going to continue. I am in a shallow cave halfway up the rock face. From a distance I expect it looks a lot like a small unsmiling mouth. The roof above me has a full set of teeth: an array of small stalacites, and the floor below holds a blunter set of stalagmites and a tongue of loose flat rocks. The back of this mouth is criss-crossed by mineral veins, which I suppose could be the vocal cords, but that would really be taking this simile too far. As I wait for Kurt to lever himself on to the sill beside me I break off a piece of the mineral and hold it to the light. It is translucent. And white. And when I scratch it against the rock of the floor it leaves a narrow furrow: so it is hard. What else? My fingers tell me it is smooth and, I suppose, crystalline. I try to remember my classes. I could smell it. It has no smell. I could taste it. I lick one of its flat surfaces and hope it tastes of nothing. It does, except, I suppose, of cold. Not really a taste. What else could I do? Measure the crystal angles? Classify them according to the system of Miller or Weiss?

Kurt's head appears above the sill. 'Quartz,' he says. 'Nice specimen.'

Of course it is quartz: he doesn't know how I laboured to come up with no answer. I throw it back on to the floor with disgust and consider a more immediate problem.

'Do you think you could reach that ledge?' I ask him, pointing to the nose that protrudes above this mouth. Kurt stretches out. His hands test the rock, and his feet follow. Soon he is up there, dangling from a nostril. When he is sure it is safe he gestures for me to follow. Soon we have ascended the whole face and we are sitting on the grass hair of the head.

'Look at that,' I say, pointing.

Kurt groans: a quiet bellow without words.

Beside us there is a valley with rocks at regular intervals. It forms a natural stairway; but we are coming up the hard way. Now we have a choice: we either continue on our route, which will take us almost on to the edge of the knife-sharp arêtes, or we can slither down to the valley and the steps. We know which will be easier but we both know which we will choose.

My hands are cut and my legs are trembling with exhaustion. Now we are nearly at the top where the valley, with its easy steps, and our path merge.

'It would have been so easy.' Kurt groans again, looking down at the steps.

But I am looking ahead. 'Look, we're almost there.'

The sun is on our side of the mountain, lighting the diagonal stripes of snow on the summit above us. Why are there stripes? I squint through the light. It is just possible to see the layers: rough or colder rock where the snow is stuck and unmelted, and then the lighter rock between. All of the peaks seem to have these stripes, except farther down it is possible to see where the layers have been pushed into elaborate and remarkable-looking curves. I pick a particularly dark band and try to follow its meanderings, but I lose it at a break. What great force has caused these dips and folds? What colossal thing pushed and pushed until the earth rose up and then snapped?

Without speaking, we clamber up the last few feet to the summit. The sun burns brashly without interruption. We are above the clouds. I look down on them, trying to make out shapes, but all I can see is an ocean of whiteness, and the tops of the mountains protruding like islands. It is another whiteness, as fascinating as the river. Kurt removes his haversack, unpacks some wurst and bread, while I take a flagon of water from mine. We sit on our bags in silence. It is too disrespectful to speak. Any sound would unsettle the mountains and disturb the clouds, and anyway all the words that I can think of – 'beautiful', 'wonderful' or 'magnificent' – seem inadequate long before they even form in my mouth. But we can't stay here long. The sun will soon start its slow descent and we are anxious to reach the valley before it sets. I look around, committing it all to memory: the stripes with their ancient twisting and the clouds that swirl still. Everything, it seems, is moving, some of it slowly, and some of it fast enough to see: the grains in the rock, the ice crystals in the air and the flour of limestone in the white river. So much change. And so much to know, understand and discover.

6

Now some more beads, small, jammed together on the string, impossible to remove: each one precisely made, brightly coloured, the edges square and tidy, clacking against the next with the sound of a pair of army boots. Ah, those months of military service; they contained such tedious pointless tasks that sometimes I felt my mind was emptying. But maybe, sometimes, it is good for the mind to be emptied. Maybe an empty mind is a more receptive one.

When I enter the lecture theatre now I make sure I sit at the front. I want to hear everything, see everything, absorb it all. No longer do I let my eyes stray to the ceiling, or allow my mind to wander into an empty space. There is no need. There is enough here in front of me. The chalk rasps on the blackboard and I follow each line, take it all down on the paper in front of me: an H for heat, a G for energy, and then, the thing I find most absorbing, an S to show disorder. Disorder, Professor Planck tells us, is always increasing. He tells us to think about the universe expanding or maybe to think about something smaller – this glass of water, for instance, on his bench. If he knocks it over – and he does; the audience gasps – the disorder increases. Now we are all staring at the disorder, looking at the water as if we can see the molecules wilfully becoming more disorganised. This disorder is so important it has been given a name, and can anyone tell him what this is? Well, the word entropy is a very recent one, he says, but he expects us all to become acquainted with it as soon as possible, and once again the chalk stabs at the board. 'Entropy'. I roll the word around on my tongue. I like the way it sounds. At last, I feel, I am entering the boundary between what is known and what is yet to be discovered. I am becoming a scientist.

Berlin became exciting to me, even the crowds of people became part of the vibrancy of the place. The university, I realise now, was bursting with ideas: Max Planck with his black box and quantum theory, Emil Fischer with his sugars and proteins, and Wilhelm Dilthey with his ideas on the importance of culture and history. There was a general infectious enthusiasm that I was anxious to catch too.

On the wall are pictures so bright that they catch my eyes. Each one shows light from a star that has been passed through a prism and separated into a rainbow. There is a different rainbow for each star; some stars have more blue, some more red and some more yellow. But there is something else that distinguishes them too: across each rainbow is a unique set of dark bars. These bars, like the light, have come from the stars. Each black-banded rainbow is called a spectrum and is the fingerprint of a star.

Professor Bauschinger taps his cane on the floor. When we are quiet he asks us to look at two of the spectra in front of us and compare one rainbow with another. He tells us that both spectra come from the same star and can anyone spot the difference? We all see at once: two bars in one spectrum, while there is only one in the other. He taps his cane again at the sudden babble of sound.

'Yes, two bands indicating two stars,' he says, 'where we thought there was just one. One moving away, while the other approaches. Yes, thank you, sir, a Doppler shift. But what is the important thing? The truly important thing we must learn from this?'

There is a short silence and then he answers for us.

'That you must look closely, gentlemen. Examine all the evidence. Muster up as much of it as you can, because only then can you hope to find some way to the truth.'

'Examine all the evidence': the words impressed me. I noted them down on the front of my workbook, and for a while they became my mantra.

Stars started to blaze in my mind: their fires seemed intense, beautiful, pure; their movements perfect and fascinating. To calculate the formula of a curve, and then to sketch its form, to admire its arc and then to compare it with the passage of a heavenly body, became, for me, an addictive satisfaction. Now I thought I knew my calling in life: to be an astronomer. I ignored my father's snort and applied for the post of student assistant at the 'Urania' observatory. I spent my spare time showing children and their parents the stars. Meanwhile, at the university, I began to learn more ancient skills: how to use quadrants, sextants, astrolabes and almanacs. I studied the astronomy of the Greeks, Arabs and medieval Europeans. I learnt that once the sun appeared to move around the earth in a strange off-centre circle.

I am a conjuror. My head and tall pointed hat are filled with stars. Around me a black velvet cloak glitters as I move. Asteroids flash at my shoulders and meteors become meteorites at my hem. I am repeating the work of medieval astronomers, and this is how I imagine these workers to be: bent like crows over desks, their eyes twinkling with the sly brightness of starlings, and their beaks of noses jerkily moving in the manner of birds, side to side, up and then down. They peer along the upper edges of a brightly polished brass quadrant, check the position and then check again. They read off the angles from the finely engraved scale at the bottom and then transfer their readings to the parchment on their desks. Observe, measure, note. Observe, measure, note.

Their disjointed movements unsettle the eyes. From time to time they seek out King Alfonso, who smiles, fatly, in red and purple from his throne, his face beaded with Spanish perspiration from the Sevillian heat.

Already I have discovered something new. There are no Arabic scholars here, only the savants of Israel and Christ. It is 1272 and at last Christendom is catching up with the ancient knowledge of the Muslims and Greeks. They are discovering how the planets move across the sky, how each one follows its own pattern and that this pattern can be written in tables: a table for each epoch, year, month, hour, minute, and second; and a set for each of the five planets, the moon, and the sun. From these tables it will be possible for King Alfonso to tell when Mars moves through Aquarius, when Venus will start to enter Aries, and their exact celestial longitude and latitude. The crows at their desks caw at each new triumph, flutter their tatters as they hop towards the king, and the king swallows each wriggling acquisition and calls it his own. In this way King Alfonso X of Castille, nominated emperor of the Holy Roman Empire by the German electors, will soon become a poet, a songwriter, an expert on the stars, the astrolabe, and various sorts of non-mechanical clocks. Unfortunately he will prove to be no statesman and will die twelve years later, deposed by his son, defeated and disowned.

But for now he is relishing the works of Ptolemy which he has recently commissioned to be translated into Spanish. He knows now that the planets, like the sun and the moon, go round the earth and the stars are motionless. He knows that there are laws called epicycles. If he shuts his eyes he can see the small circles his astronomers have drawn, and these explain why some of the planets appear to go back on themselves before continuing their passage across the stars. He has also heard of 'precession' and 'trepidation', which he might look into later. But there is one important thing that keeps his (nominated) imperial majesty awake with excitement: if he can predict the positions of the planets then surely he will be able to predict the future of everything else. The science of astronomy is still entangled with the witchcraft of astrology, and this king of Castille believes these new tables are his route to power over the future. But instead they will be his route to fame. Long after the folly of his taxation policy and the rebellion of his people have been forgotten the name of Alfonso will live on in his tables. A sexagesimal system will be invented to reduce the amount of copying, and then printing will take over from copying. In this form the tables will take over the Western world for two hundred and fifty years.

It is a printed copy I hold now, a late edition, the famous Parisian one of 1545. The paper is cream, thick, wizened with age, and the printing is imperfect – some of the curved Latin letters have bled a little from their moulded fonts – for this is a new art, not yet properly mastered. The owners of these tables have made notes, and with time the ink has become a gentle sepia, unobtrusive, part of the book. I too am adding part of myself to the pages: oils are leaking from the skin of my hands and molecules of fat are smearing themselves invisibly on its surface. Part of the book is also becoming part of me: some of the ink is leaching minutely from the paper and into my pores, and some of the grains of the paper are detaching themselves, floating into the air and being drawn irretrievably into my lungs. In these small ways we are blending together, the wizard and his book of spells.

From these old tables I am making something new. I am recalculating, finding mistakes and eradicating them. I am converting back from the ancient sexagesimal system into one consisting of years, months, days, hours and minutes. At the same time I am converting dates, incorporating the leap years of the Gregorian calendar and replacing the old astrological terminology of star constellations with modern stellar longitudes and latitudes. But I am using the same laws that Isaac ibn Sid used. As his hooked beak wrinkled in the sunlight, so my nose twitches now in the Berlin gloom. I am pretending that I too believe that the sun goes round the earth.

We are working together, Alfonso, Isaac ibn Sid and I, to predict the future. Only I know that this future will contain Copernicus with his eccentric orbits, perigees and apogees, and his ridiculous idea that the earth moves around the sun. It will also contain the new tables of Tycho Brahe, which will make our tables obsolete.

But I try not to think about this. If I do, all this work, all these intricate calculations, will seem worthless and of little point. The stars filling my head will smoulder and lose their brilliance. Like Alfonso I desire my piece of fame.

For some months I continued with my study. I became fascinated with those early times, how one set of tables had been adapted to produce the next. It became obvious to me how much men like to make their own mark: each edition was not just copied, but embellished in some way, so that each was different and could bear the mark of a new scholar. But soon it occurred to me that I was just another of these authors with nothing original to say. Instead of producing fresh ideas of my own I was summarising the work of others, remarking on precedence and inaccuracies. Later, in 1920, it provoked the then familiar taste of polemic; a man in Geneva disputing my conclusions. But by this time I had almost forgotten the Alfonsine tables. I would shrug off this Swiss criticism in a way that would soon become a reflex. My foray into astronomy had been a pointless academic exercise. I had no real love of mathematics, and no love of crouching crow-like over a desk. I needed something real, something that mattered.

So after I had completed my dissertation and the paper that

followed, I looked around me. Kurt, I noticed peevishly, was enjoying a life of adventure at the Lindenburg meteorological observatory, and when he remarked one evening that his professor was searching for another assistant I applied for the post the next day.

7

Now I shall teach you how to fly. Not the noisy flying that Kurt has recently grown to love, but that of our first flight together, which was almost silent, almost peaceful, and joined us together so completely that at last we had to pull apart.

It is the eleventh of May 1905, but the day is cold. In a field at Reinickendorf near Berlin there are men wrestling with a carcass of rubberised silk. They have checked the direction of the wind and now they are laying out the cloth cigar in a certain direction, downwind of the small wicker basket. Slowly it is inflating. Slowly it is possible to see it gather life, stir a little, collapse, and then stir again. It is men who are making this thing live. Men who are mixing one chemical with another and producing that same gas we made so long ago in my mother's washroom. Hydrogen. *Wasserstoff*. It is being fed through leather tubes and brass valves, hissing and expanding to fill the space, bouncing from the walls of the cloth, tumbling joyously in a new-found freedom. Hydrogen. Lighter than air. Light enough to escape the troposphere and whatever lies above. Light enough to defy gravity and search for the sun.

Now it is possible to see the gores of material sewn together. Each one meets the next like segments of an orange. Perfectly. A masterpiece of tapestry. At the top, which I shall call the north pole, is a circle. A hoop of wood. If you go closer you can see it is laminated, and has a polished beauty of its own. But it's not that I want you to notice. It is the flap of material stretched over this hoop which I want you to admire. The way it is fixed into position with a spring so that it stays shut and the hydrogen stays in. You can't see it now, but below there is a cord, my rip-cord. Our way down. Pull the cord and the flap opens. The hydrogen yelps at its release and we are able to descend. The down button. Easy.

There is something else. A fisherman's net. Now that the balloon is taking shape and becoming globular we can see that this net encircles the whole. It is a second outer balloon, and this mesh balloon ends at a hoop below the south pole. It is to this hoop that we now attach sandbags. It is a tedious business, but as we work it becomes clear why we strive to attach such a heavy fringe. The balloon is straining to escape. Already it has grown wild enough to desire freedom. But fortunately there are ropes. Ropes everywhere. Ropes to the basket from the ground, ropes from the basket to the hoops, ropes from the hoops to the sandbags. A complicated cat's cradle.

We receive a signal. We come forward to the basket. And it is just that: a basket. Except for scale it could be the sort of wicker work that Tony would take to market. In the side are small foot holes, but we ignore these for the present. Our supplies have to be loaded before we board ourselves: bags of food that are tossed quickly aboard, and more fragile items, like Marcuse's quadrant, which are stashed with care, either tied into place or firmly wedged into position.

Soon we are ready. With a final hiss the brass valves are turned and the tubing removed from the open base of the balloon. You might wonder why the gas does not escape, but it does not, not yet. Remember that *Wasserstoff* is lighter than air. It wants to go up. It has a preference. It will only escape through this open neck when it needs more room, when it has been heated by the sun and has become a little too excited to stay put, or if the cold air around it entices it out with promises of space.

We clamber in. It is surprisingly difficult; the wicker work shifts a little as we move, as though it is resisting us, and inside it is a little cramped, not at all as I was expecting. There are just two small seats woven into the sides, but they are slightly prickly.

'Ready?' Professor Berson asks.

I nod. My throat is too dry for me to speak.

'Cut us free,' he calls, and heaves a bag of ballast over the side.

The basket judders. It is an involuntary movement: to clutch at the sides, to reach for the ropes, to shut the eyes, to mutter words that only God can hear. And when I open my eyes and look towards Berson to see whether he has noticed my disquiet, I forget to inspect his face. My eyes are drawn past him: the ground has gone, instead there is just the air, rushing past my face, making it cold.

After ten hours we landed unremarkably at Gleiwitz. I suppose you might expect such an experienced pilot as Professor Berson to land with decorum, and so we did. He picked out a likely field and we landed precisely there. I think there was one gentle bounce. I remember having to adjust my hat a little before clambering over the basket sides. But everything was fine. Just like the sheep, the duck and the cock of the Montgolfiers' first live flight, we were undamaged by our experience, and happy to embark on another. In fact I was quite anxious to fly again. It was, after all, why I had joined Kurt at Lindenburg: the anticipation of adventure and the promise of flight.

For eight months I patiently sent up captive balloons and kites, took measurements and plotted results, but I became more and more restless. Kurt was feeling it too: we were, we decided, no longer satisfied by sailing or skating or skiing. We had become like the opium addicts the British had cultivated in China; but instead of the resin of poppies we needed the piquancy of danger. Our euphoria, Kurt said, came from the inhalation of peril, and we urgently needed to taste it again. So when we were offered a second-hand balloon, one that the airship battalion at Reinickendorf no longer needed, we grabbed the offer eagerly.

It is 7 a.m. on the fifth of April 1906. Our balloon, *Ziegler*, is the usual size, but it seems to be taking hours for its twelve hundred cubic metres to fill. After attaching all the sandbags there is little left to do, and so we just pace, and then check our plans, and then pace again. We both feel seasoned, ready. Apart from the official plan to check Marcuse's navigational method we have our own secret aspirations: we want to go high, and we want to go for as long as we can. We will beat records and test ourselves to the limit. It is something we do not even need to discuss; we know each other too well. We will keep going when all we want to do is stop. It is what we always do, in Zechlinerhütte, in Innsbruck, in the lakes around Berlin, and now again in this, our first flight together.

We ascend quickly, but not to any great height, and so for a time we hover over the ground, still connected to the world of man by smells and sounds. For a short while we indulge ourselves, reminding ourselves of what it is to be aloft, silent and drifting. Below us the world vacillates between dimensions: the two dimensions of a map, then, when we come closer, the three dimensions of a living, moving, breathing world. Objects explain themselves: why the church is just there, tucked in between an outcrop and a lake; why the road twists to avoid a sharp incline; why the house is turned away from the road, to avoid an area of marshland. It all has a logical beauty. It mesmerises me, and when Kurt suggests that we take a reading I wave his voice away. The observations must wait. He tuts a little but then becomes silent at my pointing finger. We will start soon, but just now we must watch a shoal of fish fighting the river flow, and the wind ruffling grass like hair. We hover silently. A mother duck marshals her ducklings into order and calmly takes to the water, a swan shifts on her nest revealing a white-blue flash of egg, a cat stretches, a hare lollops easily across a meadow. It is possible to shut your eyes and identify the colours: the rich heavy brown of newly turned mud, the green of cut grass, the multi-coloured hues of a field laid out to meadow. And we can see secrets: a woman stealing potatoes from a field, a man hiding on the top of a shed while his wife calls, and a small boy cutting open a dead cat.

As the balloon sinks, Kurt expertly discharges ballast and we begin to rise again. If hydrogen had a colour I would soon see it gushing from the open neck of the balloon as it endeavours to equilibrate with the sparseness of the air around us.

How do you control a balloon? You already know about the up and down, but what about the north and south, the east and west? For the last few months I had had many opportunities to observe how objects fly in the air. I had launched kites, and pilot balloons, even watched small scraps of paper take flight. I had noticed that often they had zigzagged: for some time they would rise in one direction, then, a little higher, they would come back on themselves, and then, higher still, change direction again. It seemed to me that if you could draw a profile through the layer of air above the earth showing the wind direction it would be like a herringbone. If this was the case then navigating a balloon should be straightforward: it should be just a case of choosing the correct layer. Of course, it proved to be a little more complicated than that. A balloon, I learnt, is never fully controllable. It has a mind of its own. You can suggest a way forward but whether you actually go that way depends on the whim of the balloon as well as luck, skill and knowledge.

At noon we encountered the Baltic sea and for the rest of the afternoon and evening we battled to keep control. If we became becalmed, we let out ballast; if the wind returned we let out a little hydrogen. All the time we drifted over the coast and its islands. At 8 p.m. the wind turned again and we were worried that we should be swept out to the North Sea. We decided to give up and started to look for a suitable landing site. Then the wind changed direction again and swept us inland towards Hamburg. Now at last we would be able to complete our work. We chose our stars and with the help of the chronometer and quadrant plotted our position twice. By the second night we had reached Hanover and made another two readings. That was ample. These results together with our abundant meteorological readings would keep the professor well satisfied. Now we could go home.

The sun is rising over Kassel. I suppose you could describe it as startling, brilliant and inspiring, but I fail to be inspired. I am cold, miserable, hungry. I want us to land, right now, right this second, but I am determined I am not going to be the one to suggest it.

Someone, and I am looking at him right now, forgot to pick up our coats from the ground, and the bag of blankets from the outbuilding. So we haven't slept for two days. It is impossible to sleep if you're very cold. You doze a little only to be woken by your own body, trembling and jerking to keep warm. I wrap my thin summer jacket around me and wish yet again it was my thicker winter one. If only I could stop shivering. We have also run out of food and drink. Another oversight. Kurt has blamed me. Apparently I was always the one making the plans, in Zechlinerhütte and Innsbruck, for instance, so why hadn't I made some for this little trip? What, I retorted, was I supposed to have planned for? The official experiment only required a few hours; how could I have justified food and equipment for the days and nights we have now been aloft?

I break the silence. 'How long now?'

Kurt glances not at his watch but at the chronometer. He really doesn't need to be that accurate.

'The nearest minute will do.' I sound irritable because I am.

'Forty-nine hours, fourteen minutes . . .' He pauses, pouts a little and then adds, just to annoy me '. . . and ten seconds.'

We have already beaten La Vaux's record by fourteen hours. Surely that will do. I don't feel glad or victorious, just fed up and eager to touch the ground. At this end, where Kurt has missed in his attempt to urinate over the side, the basket is beginning to acquire the stench of a Berlin alleyway. I shift a little and the cramp in the ball of my foot starts again. I extend my toes upwards in my boot in an attempt to make it subside.

Kurt stands upright, as if he's going somewhere. Out of the basket, I hope, but I don't mean that. 'Let's go up!' he says in a curiously high-pitched voice that is not really his. I look at him. He's obviously mad with fatigue. When he is tired his eyes sink even farther into his head. Now I can hardly see them. He is flapping around the basket in an attempt to grab hold of one of the sandbags, dislodging equipment and cursing when he does so. When he notices I am not joining him in this insane little jig he turns to me with a humourless smile that is half-question and half-challenge.

'What about our height? We've still got that one to beat.'

I sigh. It is something we discussed forty-eight hours ago when we were still feeling relatively comfortable and sane; even though we did not feel ready to attempt to beat the record of Berson, we did feel we could improve on our own individual records. I can't go back on this now. I couldn't bear to see and hear his contempt if I did. I stand up, trying not to let my reluctance show.

'This one,' Kurt says, pointing to a sandbag at his feet.

I cross the minuscule deck. I only have to pace once, maybe twice, but even so I slip. Kurt grabs me and we both collapse against the side, panting.

Kurt takes two swipes at the bag of ballast before he even touches it with his hand. He tugs at it but it doesn't move.

'Help me,' he says, using his high-pitched voice again.

We both kneel on the bottom of the basket and pull. The sandbag comes slowly. We press it against the side of the basket until it is almost halfway up, but then it slips a little back down again. We tug once more. This time it almost

k, Mylius-Erichsen proposed that there should also be
ll itinerary of scientific investigations: I was to be the
orologist, but Mylius-Erichsen also intended to find a
nist, a zoologist, a geologist and a surgeon. Even now
unds impressive, but twenty-five years ago it attracted
public attention that we were unable to prepare the
without interruption. For a short time we all felt like the
bits in a zoo. The publicity grew to a frenzy, culminating
visit from the Crown Prince of Denmark and one of
own German princes. Unfortunately it was only after a
icularly enthusiastic report on 'the brave men that were
ng their lives for science' that I decided to make a final
back to Berlin.

day afternoon. So quiet that the ticking of the clock above
mantelpiece feels as though it is chipping at my brain.
are all sitting around the table waiting. This is a familiar
generian tableau. Like my father, Kurt and Tony are sitting
ght, the undersides of their noses parallel with the table,
my mother's face is inclined, and in shadow, as though
does not want it to be seen. What is she thinking? Is it
usual anxiety about Tony's unmarried state? Or maybe
is looking at all three of her surviving children, not one
s with a consort. Maybe she is despairing of ever being
vided with grandchildren.

ly father rustles his paper: a signal for us all to take notice.
ccurs to me how much we are still like children, how we
wait for our father to provide instruction.
o, Alfred, this is where my money has gone.' He jabs at
paper with a finger.
Yes, sir,' I say happily, expecting his approval.
le sighs. 'That balloon escapade was bad enough, but
. . .'
A record-breaking flight, Father,' Kurt reminds him a little
lantly.

---

reaches the rim before it falls away. We try again and again,
but each time the sandbag rises a little less.

'It's no good, Kurt,' I say at last.

Then I realise that he has been waiting for me to say it. Even
though he tries to cajole me into making one more attempt, I
can tell that his conviction has disappeared. I say nothing in
reply but instead reach for the down cord and give it as firm a
tug as I can manage. The jolt flings us both on to the floor of
the basket, and for a few seconds we sit amongst our debris,
slightly winded. I recover first and stagger over to Kurt. I offer
him my arm but he doesn't take it. Instead he elbows his way
upwards using the basket sides, closes the valve a little so our
descent is moderated, and then turns at last to face me. There
is more than relief in his eyes. At first I think it is annoyance,
but then when his eyes slither away from mine I see that there
is something else.

'Well, we've done it,' Kurt says, in a dull voice now which
has returned to its correct pitch.

'The longest flight, ever.'

He turns to look at me, his thin lips drawn into a smile.
'We're record-breakers now, Alfred.'

I try to smile back but cannot. That look of his before we
began our slow controlled descent has numbed my face. There
is something wrong, and on the journey home it nags at me
so much that I am unable to think of anything else. At first I
think it might be my disquiet at the record claims. But then,
as Kurt and I are toasted and our eyes meet, I realise it is the
mixture of contempt and pity I can now see so clearly in my
brother's face: *I* was the one that gave up first and demanded
that we descend. Then, as I sip the bubbles from the surface
of my wine, my last skin begins to slip from me. It is dry with
age and crumbles into dust to be blown away by the wind. At
last my back is smooth and the furrow of my brother's hold,
which had begun to grip too hard, is gone. I sniff the wind. It
is cold and strangely alluring.

8

Just recently I have begun to long for parts of my former self. Myself, say, at twenty-five, half my lifetime ago. Sometimes, to amuse myself, I choose which parts I would take and which I would leave behind. The eyes I would snatch first, for at twenty-five they are still a clear blue, undamaged, able to see into the distance and then down on to a page instantly, each equally in focus. Then I would take some of the internal organs, the lungs maybe, and the heart. Perhaps I would take more care of them this time, listen to them when they ached and protect them from hurt. But then there are also parts I would leave: the moustache, for instance; at twenty-five it is still sparse, as though I am still just pretending to be a man, and then there is that rather dreamy expression. It belies an innocent idealism. I would not wish for that again; it is rather like a blown egg, hollow, empty and conspicuously vulnerable.

I expect I wore this face when I first greeted Mylius-Erichsen. I used words that matched his. He wanted to lift the 'uneven curtain over unknown countries', while I wanted to discover; he wanted to 'breathe new life into new areas', while I wanted to investigate and understand; he described an 'irresistible urge to explore unknown regions', and I said, simply, that I felt it too.

Now he stops and looks intently into my eyes. 'Do you think you could stand it, eh? The cold, the hunger, the months without light?'

I nod, keeping his eyes in line with mine.

'And you are fit, eh?'

I nod again, and it seems to me that in distant places.

'And can you keep going, on and on . . .

Still the eyes stare into mine, but now I an open white field.

'. . . until you feel you simply have to st on . . .'

And this whiteness stretches on until it grey sky.

'. . . a little more?'

Another nod. This time I hope it is m final. Mylius-Erichsen's moustache twitch wispy blond corners, the shaven gap belo the same blond hairs appearing again in am conscious that my fingers have strayed moustache.

'We are aiming to start in the early par says, and the snowfields melt and become

'Could you be ready then? I wonder. Yo on your own, eh? Wouldn't want me to know much about the wind and the rain an I don't like them.'

His voice is clipped, and ends in a strange laugh. Then he gives a curt bow and I bow surprised. I hadn't expected to be accepted This expedition is prestigious, there are ma allowed to come, and I am not Danish.

Mylius-Erichsen had been to Greenland t now he proposed to go there again. This to explore and map the north-east coast, cessible region, touched only fleetingly by before, and still represented on maps by a and question marks. Apart from this impor reaches the rim before it falls away. We try again and again, but each time the sandbag rises a little less.

'It's no good, Kurt,' I say at last.

Then I realise that he has been waiting for me to say it. Even though he tries to cajole me into making one more attempt, I can tell that his conviction has disappeared. I say nothing in reply but instead reach for the down cord and give it as firm a tug as I can manage. The jolt flings us both on to the floor of the basket, and for a few seconds we sit amongst our debris, slightly winded. I recover first and stagger over to Kurt. I offer him my arm but he doesn't take it. Instead he elbows his way upwards using the basket sides, closes the valve a little so our descent is moderated, and then turns at last to face me. There is more than relief in his eyes. At first I think it is annoyance, but then when his eyes slither away from mine I see that there is something else.

'Well, we've done it,' Kurt says, in a dull voice now which has returned to its correct pitch.

'The longest flight, ever.'

He turns to look at me, his thin lips drawn into a smile. 'We're record-breakers now, Alfred.'

I try to smile back but cannot. That look of his before we began our slow controlled descent has numbed my face. There is something wrong, and on the journey home it nags at me so much that I am unable to think of anything else. At first I think it might be my disquiet at the record claims. But then, as Kurt and I are toasted and our eyes meet, I realise it is the mixture of contempt and pity I can now see so clearly in my brother's face: *I* was the one that gave up first and demanded that we descend. Then, as I sip the bubbles from the surface of my wine, my last skin begins to slip from me. It is dry with age and crumbles into dust to be blown away by the wind. At last my back is smooth and the furrow of my brother's hold, which had begun to grip too hard, is gone. I sniff the wind. It is cold and strangely alluring.

8

Just recently I have begun to long for parts of my former self. Myself, say, at twenty-five, half my lifetime ago. Sometimes, to amuse myself, I choose which parts I would take and which I would leave behind. The eyes I would snatch first, for at twenty-five they are still a clear blue, undamaged, able to see into the distance and then down on to a page instantly, each equally in focus. Then I would take some of the internal organs, the lungs maybe, and the heart. Perhaps I would take more care of them this time, listen to them when they ached and protect them from hurt. But then there are also parts I would leave: the moustache, for instance; at twenty-five it is still sparse, as though I am still just pretending to be a man, and then there is that rather dreamy expression. It belies an innocent idealism. I would not wish for that again; it is rather like a blown egg, hollow, empty and conspicuously vulnerable.

I expect I wore this face when I first greeted Mylius-Erichsen. I used words that matched his. He wanted to lift the 'uneven curtain over unknown countries', while I wanted to discover; he wanted to 'breathe new life into new areas', while I wanted to investigate and understand; he described an 'irresistible urge to explore unknown regions', and I said, simply, that I felt it too.

Now he stops and looks intently into my eyes. 'Do you think you could stand it, eh? The cold, the hunger, the months without light?'

I nod, keeping his eyes in line with mine.

'And you are fit, eh?'

I nod again, and it seems to me that in his eyes I can see distant places.

'And can you keep going, on and on . . .'

Still the eyes stare into mine, but now I see what they see: an open white field.

'. . . until you feel you simply have to stop, but then carry on . . .'

And this whiteness stretches on until it merges with the grey sky.

'. . . a little more?'

Another nod. This time I hope it is more emphatic and final. Mylius-Erichsen's moustache twitches. I examine its wispy blond corners, the shaven gap below his mouth and the same blond hairs appearing again in a goatee beard. I am conscious that my fingers have strayed to my own sorry moustache.

'We are aiming to start in the early part of summer,' he says, and the snowfields melt and become eyes again.

'Could you be ready then? I wonder. You'd want to work on your own, eh? Wouldn't want me to interfere? I don't know much about the wind and the rain anyway, except that I don't like them.'

His voice is clipped, and ends in a strange coughing sort of laugh. Then he gives a curt bow and I bow back. I am a little surprised. I hadn't expected to be accepted quite so readily. This expedition is prestigious, there are many pressing to be allowed to come, and I am not Danish.

Mylius-Erichsen had been to Greenland twice before, and now he proposed to go there again. This time he intended to explore and map the north-east coast, an almost inaccessible region, touched only fleetingly by Peary six years before, and still represented on maps by a vague dashed line and question marks. Apart from this important cartographic work, Mylius-Erichsen proposed that there should also be a full itinerary of scientific investigations: I was to be the meteorologist, but Mylius-Erichsen also intended to find a botanist, a zoologist, a geologist and a surgeon. Even now it sounds impressive, but twenty-five years ago it attracted such public attention that we were unable to prepare the ship without interruption. For a short time we all felt like the exhibits in a zoo. The publicity grew to a frenzy, culminating in a visit from the Crown Prince of Denmark and one of our own German princes. Unfortunately it was only after a particularly enthusiastic report on 'the brave men that were risking their lives for science' that I decided to make a final visit back to Berlin.

Sunday afternoon. So quiet that the ticking of the clock above the mantelpiece feels as though it is chipping at my brain. We are all sitting around the table waiting. This is a familiar Wegenerian tableau. Like my father, Kurt and Tony are sitting upright, the undersides of their noses parallel with the table, but my mother's face is inclined, and in shadow, as though she does not want it to be seen. What is she thinking? Is it her usual anxiety about Tony's unmarried state? Or maybe she is looking at all three of her surviving children, not one of us with a consort. Maybe she is despairing of ever being provided with grandchildren.

My father rustles his paper: a signal for us all to take notice. It occurs to me how much we are still like children, how we still wait for our father to provide instruction.

'So, Alfred, this is where my money has gone.' He jabs at his paper with a finger.

'Yes, sir,' I say happily, expecting his approval.

He sighs. 'That balloon escapade was bad enough, but this . . .'

'A record-breaking flight, Father,' Kurt reminds him a little petulantly.

'Dangerous and foolhardy, that's what it was, and now I see this *Danmark* escapade is even worse.'

'Can I see, Franz?'

My father thrusts the paper to my mother. I watch as her face changes. Her eyes dart along the paper as her mouth forms the words in silence.

'You didn't say it would be two years, Alfred,' she says at last.

'At least that, I'd say.' Kurt's voice, too helpful.

'And the ice. It says here that sometimes it is so thick, so cold, no one can get through.' Suddenly she turns to Kurt. 'Why didn't *you* tell us? You knew, didn't you?'

'Not all the details.'

Kurt glances across at me. His eyes are suddenly unhooded, so bright that I can see everything. I have betrayed him. Now that I have steered ahead on my own, without his collaboration, he is confused and angry.

'Well, I think it's exciting.' Tony raises her chin in defiance. 'The Kaiser would be proud. A German explorer.'

'When do you go, Alfred?' my mother says quietly.

'Next month some time.'

I look from her face to Kurt's. I feel his hurt as though it is my own. Until now I had mistaken his smarting silence for his normal reticence. I had thought that I would regain his respect with my enterprise, but now I realise I have divided us more than ever.

'Well, don't look for us in the crowd,' my father says, drawing his mouth into a line. 'We won't be there.'

'You should have told us, Alfred,' my mother whispers.

But they came. For a few fleeting seconds I saw them, enough time for me to etch their small figures into my memory, and they were gone. I turned back to my tasks. As the *Danmark* at last slipped from Copenhagen on the twenty-fourth of June 1906 we were too busy with our inventories and our lists of missing items to worry too much about waving and smiling.

The *Danmark* possessed both masts and funnels, so we could steam along when the wind ran out. She was solid looking, tub-like. She rode the waves stoically rather than with grace. At under 500 tons, and less than 40 metres long, she was no huge vessel, and in truth she was hardly large enough to support the thirteen crew, the twelve scientists, and the additional three Greenlanders and hundred Greenland dogs that were crammed aboard at the Faeroes. But there was much to do: four hours' duty followed four hours' leisure, and there was little time in which to contemplate our overcrowding. Even my leisure time was busy: I had to learn to speak Danish as well as educate my assistant, Peter Freuchen, in the ways of the barometer, and the meterological kites and balloons.

It is the ninth of August, but it is not summer. Instead, outside the round porthole of the cabin, there is a beautiful permanent winter. The sky is intensely blue: a pure cobalt, undiluted, even at the horizon. Then there is the sea: also blue, this time an ultramarine, but just as intense as the sky. Then the sun: low down, yellow-red, possible to watch for minutes without blinking. But slicing through all these colours is the ice: jagged, dangerous. Sometimes it is a pure white, but most of the time, like now, it takes on the colours of the sea and the sun, changing them into intense secondaries. Last night I saw a violet, this morning a lime green, now an orange with shadows of purple. Even though I know it is just the light being bent by its passage through the ice it seems magical, as if I am a child noticing his first rainbow.

I am an easy sailor. The rock of the ship delights me when I am awake and lulls me to sleep. In the frequent storms I am often the only scientist who is not making sudden rushes for the ship's sides. Instead I relish the feeling of unease as the horizon of the ship slips away from the horizon of the sea and the sky. As one deck slope is replaced by another, as forty degrees upwards becomes forty degrees downwards, I keep going. I slither and lurch but still I keep going. I remember the Sees of Zechlinerhütte and the small but ferocious storms that swept across me there. The important thing is to keep going. When I feel that I must stop I conjure up Kurt's face in front of me. I can do this quite readily. It is important to keep his face smiling, then I know I am doing well. But now, as I go to sleep, the face disappears. There is no Kurt, no other German here, just me.

I wake incompletely. The ship is making only the merest movement from side to side. It is as though the ice has calmed the waves. I know this can't be true but I let the thought carry me back to sleep. The air smells of oil and fish. It is reassuring, reminds me of something long ago . . .

Am I dreaming? I can hear clinking, glasses hitting each other, chiming a little. '*Prost!*' I listen. Hard. No, it's not '*Prost*'. It's something else. Something strange. Voices that sing up and down as they speak. Words I know sometimes, if they're said slowly, carefully . . . I strain to hear. That clinking sound again. Like glass. Just like glass . . .

'Wegener! Wake up!'

I groan. All I want to do is sleep. When I open my eyes Koch is standing there. I smile. Koch's moustache puts Mylius-Erichsen's to shame. It is dense, oiled, the ends smoothed into large curves, and below the moustache is another goatee beard. Are they in competition, these two?

'Get up Wegener. Now.'

Koch's German is good, but he uses it little.

'Now?' I know I sound stupid.

'Yes. We have to get to the boats. Come now, quickly.'

I sit up, too suddenly, hit my head on the ceiling, then dazedly jump to the floor. Taking the blanket from my bunk, I follow Koch on to the deck. Behind Koch there is no light, so effectively does his body fill the space of the corridor in front of me. I catch up with him in the laboratory, but then he is gone again, up on deck before me. I blink in the sudden brightness, trying to take in the mayhem. The whole crew (and we all count as crew now) is above deck, each man taking up three times more space than normal. There are ropes being pulled, heavy objects being rolled around, packages being strapped together then thrown into the small lifeboats that are being lowered to the sea.

I am conscious of being still, inert, and that my pathetic blanket is dipping into the pools of water on deck.

'Take this.' Koch throws me a package. It appears to be more blankets, rolled up in tarpaulin.

I smile gratefully at him, hoping to catch his eye, but he is gone, reaching down into a hatch and hauling something up. I start to do what everyone else is doing and throw the package into a lifeboat. Following Koch, I find more bundles and throw them in with the others. All the time I listen and try to make out words. After a few minutes I make out the words: 'Go, go!'

And so we all go, down into the lifeboats where the towers of ice seem more magnificent and majestic than ever. What is going to happen now? Are we going to try to row back to Iceland around these cathedrals of ice?

Everyone is quiet now, looking around. The Greenlanders are beginning to smile. Captain Trolle looks at Mylius-Erichsen, who nods back. Slowly Trolle counts twenty-eight souls scattered among the four boats, then yells something at Mylius-Erichsen, who laughs back. I look around for someone who will be willing to explain, and see Freuchen's large head and open mouth.

'What's happening?' I ask, in Danish.

'A drill in case the ice hits. We'll go back on board again soon, I think.' The boy speaks slowly, considerate of my lack of fluency. He pauses, looks intently into my face, obviously anxious that I should have understood. As usual I feel the urge to reassure him, and lightly brush the floppy fringe of his hair with the palm of my hand.

'Yes. I see. Thank you.'

Everything I say is so stiff and restricted.

Freuchen smiles a little and then turns back towards the ship's hull as Trolle yells a hoarse command.

It is Mylius-Erichsen who clambers aboard first, and so it is he who sees them first: dogs. There are dogs everywhere, peering over the deck, urinating at every corner, howling, chewing, biting, eating, swallowing. And they have swallowed a lot: ropes, pieces of wood, cloth, anything that could be detached with a pair of greedy jaws. In the chaos of our disembarking the doors to their kennels have been left open and they have marauded through the ship.

When I reach my cabin I pause at the door. The place stinks of urine, and there, in the middle of Koch's bunk, is a neat mound of faeces. It is still warm. I tear out a few pages from my diary and begin to pick out the topmost piece with the paper. It is cylindrical, tapering at both ends, black, rather like a country wurst. And this thought, so trivial and inappropriate, seems suddenly to be the most amusing thought I have ever had in my life. I snigger, loudly, and then, as I see the turd enveloped in the paper, where it looks even more like the sort of wurst the street sellers offer for a snack, I begin to laugh more loudly. Soon it is beyond me to stop.

When Koch returns I am sitting on the edge of his bunk, weak and crying. He looks at the remains of the dog-mound and then at my hands holding the soiled paper, then he frowns as if he is puzzled.

'This is funny?'

I nod.

He shakes his head, and removes the paper from my loosened fingers.

'No, my friend, this is not funny. Not funny at all.'

My breath catches suddenly in my mouth. I close my lips. Not even a smile escapes now.

'I'm sorry. I didn't mean . . .'

'A bad business with these dogs. Lots of things gone, no use.'

I swallow. 'I'm sorry. I shouldn't have laughed.'

He doesn't disagree. He bends towards his bunk and removes the rest of the dirt with some fresh paper, then mumbles into the empty air beyond his nose, 'Thank you for trying to clean up.'

'Trying'. It seems I wasn't successful even in that. I feel wretched. I swing myself up on to my bunk above. The sun is setting and there is no moon. Soon the darkness will be complete.

A few days later we met what Freuchen called 'the big ice'. It annoyed me a little that my junior should be more knowledgeable than I in these matters, but Mylius-Erichsen had entrusted this nineteen-year-old, fresh from medical school in Copenhagen, to acquire our dogs from Greenland in the spring, and so he was already familiar with Greenlandic conditions. The more usual name for this ice is pack ice, but whatever it is called it is always difficult to penetrate. Time and time again the lookout on the crow's-nest would spot a lead through the ice, but by the time Captain Trolle had manoeuvred the ship around, the ice would have closed. For days we were frustratingly close to land; our ship in an isolated patch of open sea, surrounded on all sides by ice.

Koch sees it first: the ice moving, becoming bear. At his low whistle, we scramble for our guns and the starboard side of the ship suddenly bristles rifle barrels. It is the bacon which has attracted him, and now it draws him closer; the overpowering smell of meat and fat streaming out and then dissipating over the ice. Soon we all see him, a grey shape with long shadows, but he is still too far away to shoot.

We remain poised, our arm muscles straining to keep our guns aloft, waiting for the bear to enter our sights. There is little sound, just the slapping of small waves at the wooden bow of the ship, and the hissing of many bacon rashers on the cook's stove. The smell of the bacon is tantalising to men as well as bear; we are all hungry for meat.

There is a single crack. The bear-shaped grey pauses, but then seems to gather strength and moves forward again. But he is injured. Behind him the snow darkens. Later we will see his footprints, infilled, dark red. Now his movement is erratic. He steps to the side and then backwards into his own prints. He is coming closer, growing larger, head and then limbs becoming discernible from the mass of the body. For one terrifying second it seems he will be on us, too near for any of us to line up in the rifle sight, and too powerful for a knife or a spear, but then, in silence, he topples. Now a quiet sound, half moan, half roar, primeval and horrifying, issues from the ice. It grows in volume until the boards of the ship shake. It takes another shot to snuff it out; another shot and the ice is silent, shocked.

I look around. Only Koch's gun smells of gunpowder. He lowers it, makes it safe, then invites two Inuit to accompany him. I am glad he has not chosen me. The cry of the bear has sickened me. Later I will recover, tear at the flesh with everyone else, but just now it seems to me that the ice has been plundered and I feel a little ashamed of my species.

I'd forgotten the intimacy of ocean and small rowing boat, how the sea seems to claim the hull as part of itself. The water is so close; if I fell I would last five minutes. Five minutes to recover from the shock of the cold, force my limbs to swim, grab the nearest flotsam and struggle into the air. It is why the Inuit kayakers never learn to swim; it would be pointless, a wasted effort. Yet this water looks so much like ordinary water: the same mixtures of green and blue, the same hint of life, even the same familiar beat of waves at its surface. Everything is peaceful. If I shut my eyes I could be anywhere: on my brother's boat on the See at Zechlinerhütte; or on a pleasure boat with Tony in Berlin. But I am not. At last the ice has opened enough to allow a small part of us through and my eyes are open wide, anxious once more to take everything in.

Even though we are still several metres from the shore there is a sudden scraping sound on the keel. The two crewmen, Christian and Gustav Throstrup, swear at each other and stop rowing. After a quick discussion Christian begins again, a little gingerly, and the boat swings around. We enter the shore more closely. This time the boat is only a metre away from shore when the rasping begins again. We are near a bank of dark pebbles and I can hear some of them grinding beneath the boat.

'Are you ready, Dr Wegener?' Christian asks.

'Yes?' I am not sure what I am supposed to be ready for.

'Well, jump, then, man,' Gustav says, paddling at the water impatiently. 'Then you can pull the rest of us in.'

So I stand up slowly in the boat, wait until she steadies, and climb on to the plank seat at the stern: one foot, then the other. I bend my knees, breathe in, spring forward, close my eyes, and brace myself for the inrush of water into my boots.

But it doesn't come. I open my eyes. Pebbles shift beneath my feet: all of them a shiny black. I look around me. Farther up the beach the pebbles fade to grey, and beyond them are large boulders of the same rock. I smile at the ancient deceit: a place called Greenland even though all that anyone can see right now is shades of grey.

9

My first set of white beads. If only you could feel them as I do: cold, of course, but so beautifully shaped, they nestle in my hands and mostly they feel comfortable there. They are soapstone, the rock the Inuit engrave with patterns and carve into lamps, toys and charms. There is just one part where the blade has slipped, where the edges of the bead are sharp and dig into my hand. Even after twenty-four years it has not been worn smooth. It would jab at me if it could hear my thoughts. I shall tell you them soon. But for now I shall tell you about the beginning, when, by the light of a soapstone lamp, my forehead was still a smooth plane, unblemished by the Greenland sun.

So this is Danmarkshavn; two days ago it was just a small bay west of Cape Bismarck on the north-east Greenland coast, but now it has a name and an importance. From this day onwards, the fifteenth of August 1906, it will be our temporary home. There are features that make it a most desirable residence: a useful promontory; deep water essential for the ship; mountains all around us giving shelter; and a flat wide beach with flat wide pebbles, useful for the motor car. Did I mention the motor car?

I suspect it is Mylius-Erichsen's idea – it goes with his curled moustache; a little rakish, a little impractical. He has supervised its unloading with care, and now it stands on the beach, rather more incongruous than anything else we have brought. I suspect that its thin hard tyres will make any journey an uncomfortable experience, because although the beach looks flat from a distance, close inspection reveals that it is uneven, strewn with small hollows and large boulders.

'What are we going to do with that?' Koch mutters. His voice is hardly audible. Maybe he is talking to himself.

I decide to answer him anyway. 'I can think of something.'

'An unnecessary extravagance,' he continues, ignoring me. 'A complete waste of space.'

While Mylius-Erichsen took a team of nine men to hunt for dog fodder, the rest of us unloaded crates, assembled a hut, and started our scientific measurements. Within two days I had calibrated my instruments and begun my first set of thrice-daily weather readings. A fortnight later my first kite was ready to be launched into the Greenland air. The kite is Vladimir Köppen's. Later you will hear his name again and again, but for now I shall just tell you that he is one of the greatest meteorologists that has ever lived, and that he generously donated his expertise to me in the form of kites and instructions.

There is a mist over the sea, so that all the distant mountains are diffuse. Nearer, the ship is a clear silhouette. From here it seems grounded, the hull right next to the shore, and already there is a pathway as the pebbles on the beach have shifted to accommodate us as we pass from the hut to the ship and back again. In front of the ship is another silhouette. This one is of a human figure, Peter Freuchen, my assistant, his arms outstretched, his legs apart, his lean body converted into something a little more squat by layers of cloth. Above his head, with its odd little flat-topped cap, is the top 'box' of our kite; its partner, an identical box without top or bottom, is at his knees. The open framework joining these two boxes is invisible at this distance but has been made up to Köppen's precise instructions. If this kite flies it will be the first one ever flown in Greenland.

'Ready?' I have to yell above the sound of the car engine. Its chugging is familiar and comforting on the alien beach.

Peter's yes is drowned out, but I see his little cap tipping up and down. He is as eager I am to see whether it will work.

Here is my great idea. I will use the car to do my work. It will power the hoist with an improvised fan belt, and, if I've got this right, it will pull Greenland's first kite high into the air. I wave my hands and let the engine take the strain. There is a small change in pitch as the slack of the rope is pulled quickly taut.

'Now, Peter!'

Quickly the white material of the kite merges with the white of the sky. For a few seconds the numbers on the topmost box are distinct, and then these too are obscured by cloud. I stop the engine, and the rope remains taut. Above me the automatic instruments are recording the temperature and pressure. I concentrate on the rope and the winch, and then squint up to the sky to see whether I can detect anything. But something is disturbing my concentration: the sound of voices. I turn around. The remainder of the *Danmark*'s crew is clustered by the shed. They must have been cheering for some time because now their hands are beginning to drop and their mouths are beginning to close. Friis, one of the two expedition artists, runs forward with a piece of paper. It is a picture of me: a fat cartoon man with a stripy vest holding a kite on a string. But this kite is a trapezoid, with a trailing string of bows, the sort that children fly in parks. Friis is grinning, waiting. I can't decide whether he is laughing at me or with me. I take the paper and bow my thanks.

Friis laughs. 'My pleasure, Mr Meteorologist.'

Quickly our village grew: first with a winter residence, a hut called the Villa complete with paths and telephone lines to the ships, then an observatory and a meteorological station. Overhead, flocks of birds made curved and pointed letters in the sky as they flew south. Maybe they had smelt the coming of the snow. And soon it fell, and fell again, covering the sea and land with a uniform generosity. The ship was covered too, this time by Trolle's tarpaulin. The decks were enclosed, the wood greased, the heat trapped for winter. Now, with the sea and land a single homogeneous white, the ship looked incongruous. It seemed wedged there, without reason, the small boats huddled together on deck like frightened offspring, all now useless in the solid landscape. But the death of one sort of transport brought the birth of another.

Henrik, one of the Greenlanders, arranges my dogs. Each dog has a harness and to each harness is tied a trace. The traces, all of equal length, are tied to a ring and the ring fastened with more traces to the sledge. This is the Greenlandic way; democratic, every dog for himself. When they stand up they are supposed to form a fan, so that each dog pulls in a slightly different direction, so the sum of all these small pulls is one large pull forwards. That is the idea.

That is the idea, but now all the dogs are doing is sitting in front of the sledge refusing to budge. I whistle between my teeth, I call out, 'Hup, hup,' as close an imitation of the Inuit as I can make it, but nothing happens.

Henrik is grinning, his eyes two crescents drawn on his face with a fine pen. His face is long for a Greenlander, and his nose high bridged and crooked.

'The whip,' he says in Danish, pointing to my hand.

I raise it cautiously, high above the heads of the dogs, and lower it sharply, so it crackles like static. The dogs raise their heads languidly, but otherwise do not move.

'Lower.' Henrik motions with his hand.

The whip slaps down. I feel a quick resistance as leather meets fur. Now they rise, all at once, baying, shifting from position, shoving forward, howling, twisting, and giving short yelps.

Henrik cries out, a sharp repetitive 'Oy-oy-oy', and the dogs are immediately still.

We inspect the hopeless mess; the dogs are crammed together near the sledge with their traces twisted into knots. Henrik looks at me, still smiling. That crooked nose of his gives him a sly, slightly mocking expression. Then he leaps in among the dogs, his tiny body changing their scale, so that beside him they seem huge and dangerous. Later, years from now, there will be other dogs, larger still, and truly wild. They will come in the night and hunt Henrik down. They will rise in a pack, baying and panting. Later his hands will be too slow, but now, in his youth, they work quickly, undoing the traces from their hoop and then refastening them again. Later he will reach out and find nothing, but now he takes the whip and sits at the back of my sledge.

'Like this,' he says, raising his hand with the whip, 'one dog, then one again.'

Later their cousins, the wolves, will snarl and bite until Henrik is still, but these dogs rise mutely in sequence. I whistle my appreciation and Henrik's face widens in a grin as he hands me the whip.

My first white bead: so bright it would dazzle you if you kept looking at it for long enough. Your eyes would water, you'd have to narrow them, hunch up the skin around them just to keep out a little of this overwhelming light. You'd look away eventually, of course, there is no need to keep looking at a bead, but what if you had to keep staring, just to see where you were going? The Inuit have developed eye shields: pieces of bone with slits, and of course I had snow goggles, but neither of these can prevent snow-blindness. An Inuit blinded by the snow would be left behind in a doorless igloo, or led to the edge of a cliff, or hung by his eldest son at the end of a feast. For an Inuit blindness is also uselessness, and therefore the ending of life is the only logical alternative in the remorselessly practical Greenland society. But I am not blind, even now I am not blind, at least not in my eyes, even though my blue irises must have let in more light over their fifty years than the Inuit brown. My blindness, they say, lies in what some call my blinkered vision but I call the truth. Sometimes I feel that some of my contemporaries in science would love to leave me behind in a convenient snow hole or lead me to a cliff-edge and push. But I am not blind yet. I believe I still see more than most, even though my eyes ache and cause me pain.

If I close my eyes it sounds as though there are eight small watches ticking. Every second, each one ticks, but never all at the same time. There is another sound too, a hushed scraping, as if something were being swept away with a soft brush. Then there are smells: brief pungent whiffs of something animal, transient, leaving me as soon as I detect them. I open my eyes and see them – dogs, brown and black and white, tails arching over their backs, their breath escaping from them in eight sets of quiet pants. My dogs. Already they have become my dogs. I know their ways. I know which one will lead, which one would like to lead, which one is greedy, and which one needs a little coaxing with my whip. I have even given them new names. I try them out now, call them softly over the fan of leads in front of me and watch as their ears prick upwards. They know my voice. We have learnt much together. We know how to start and how to stop. They have learnt that I feed all of them equally but the most quiet is fed first. They have learnt that sometimes I have to be alone and they must carry their noise away from me.

Squinting ahead, I see Mylius-Erichsen's hood and back. It is October and he has asked me to accompany him on to the ice. Like me he is preserving his energy, letting the dogs carry the driver as well as the sledge now that we are on the flat and the snow is not too deep. In this way we can travel many miles with little effort. We are free to examine the scenery and to muse on whatever comes to mind. What, for instance, inspires the dogs to pull the sledge forward for hour after hour when their reward comes so much later? It must seem unconnected to them then, a magical result of allegiance to this two-legged god. Yet they keep on pulling, without rest, their only impulse, it seems, to pull and pull. I think of the Germans who came here before us thirty-five years ago, without dogs; how they had to pull their sledges alone, unaided; and how they must have toiled for days to make the same progress that we now make in hours. These Germans haunt me. I imagine the impossible; that they could see this same iceberg, that same snowdrift, as if this were a permanent landscape where nothing moves. But of course everything shifts here; snowdrifts creep infinitesimally along the ground with the wind, and icebergs are made afresh each summer by a distant glacier.

Mylius-Erichsen whoops at the dogs as he throws himself from his sledge. He runs alongside for a couple of minutes, keeping pace with the dogs, and then slows to a halt. He waits for me to perform a similar manoeuvre and then points ahead of us at an almost vertically sided iceberg in this immobile sea. As we reach the summit the dogs start their howls of despair at our absence. We squint to the horizon in all directions, looking for something: the meandering tracks of a bear, a glimpse of open sea, or just some clue that someone has been here before us. But there is nothing. For a short while we stare in silence, and then Mylius-Erichsen turns his head towards me so that his face looks into mine and the steam of our breaths mingles.

'You handle the dogs well, my friend.'

I mean to say something, maybe mention Henrik or my hours of practice, but quickly he interrupts me with a snigger and adds, 'A rather surprising talent for a German, eh?' Before I can ask him to explain himself he is gone, slithering down the sides of the ice mountain to where the dogs are clamouring for us.

On the second of November the sun disappeared for three months; the start of my first long arctic night. In some ways darkness makes travelling easier; the snow stays crisp, and the moon soothes the eyes. But of course the darkness also brings its own treachery, disguising crevasses, hiding uneven ground, and convincing the primitive parts of my brain that I should be asleep.

To my great joy and satisfaction Mylius-Erichsen again selected me to travel with him, but this time there were four others: Koch the cartographer (and my former cabin mate), Gustav Throstrup, Ring and the Greenlander Brønlund, Mylius-Erichsen's Inuit companion of old. The journey would be a long one, about six hundred kilometres to Shannon Island in the south-east, but would take only a month – the first such journey made by Europeans in complete darkness. Apart from investigating some old American food caches and depositing mail in a predetermined place for passing ships, Koch and I had our own private scientific objectives. For these we needed to travel farther south to Sabine Island, and so, on the twentieth of November, on the south-west corner of Shannon Island, we divided into two teams: Mylius-Erichsen, Brønlund and Ring heading eastwards to the depot, while Koch, Throstrup and I headed southwards over the frozen sea.

There is little moon, just a thin sliver, sufficient only to light up the ground a few metres ahead of us. It is so quiet, and I can see so little, that sometimes I become convinced that I am not moving at all, and I have to reassure myself by looking ahead to see the eight pairs of dog hind legs still flashing forward in front of me. Now that we have left the land the ice has taken on a new aspect. It is pressed up into troughs and high ridges by the tides beneath, and from time to time we have to dismount to help the dogs up the steep slopes. The dogs have changed too, from willing animals, impatient to proceed, to recalcitrant beasts urged on only by the whip. Koch remarks that they can detect our inexperience, but I think it is the difficulty of the terrain, or maybe they have become unsettled by the transparency of the ice. Whenever the moon is released from a cloud I look down, fascinated and yet a little appalled. We are so close to the water. I can see the shadow of a walrus as it searches for a way through to the air, the glitter of fishes, and the slow billowing dance of seaweed.

There is a shout ahead of me: it is Koch's voice, high pitched and urgent. As I lean forward, squinting through the darkness, trying to see, the dogs rush forward, as if Koch's shout has beckoned them. I grab the traces, trying to bring them about, but the leather rips through my hand. There is nothing I can do; the whip just makes them faster. I try all the slowing-down noises I know but nothing works. At last I see the tall back of Koch's sledge, dark grey in the moonlight, but all around it is the intense blackness of water. Koch has broken through the ice and his sledge is sinking. Ahead of it the pale heads of the dogs are bobbing in the water, and they are oddly silent, as if the cold has numbed away all sound. Where is Koch? I call out.

Now that my dogs have seen the danger they are attempting to stop, but it is too late. My sledge is starting to sink. I launch myself out of the sledge sideways, roll along a little and then encounter something soft: Koch.

Koch! I grip on to him. He is warm, dry. Even below his layers of fur I can feel the bulk of his torso, and the reassuring heaviness of his limbs.

'Thank God!'

He turns to face me, smiles a little, but then his smile disappears. 'Move, quick! Now!' He shoves me in front of him. 'Keep going, that way.'

Soon I feel why. The ice is collapsing beneath us; the coldness I had just thought was the snow is something more insinuating. It is the sea: liquid, penetrating and deadly.

Now, somehow, Koch is ahead of me. It is as if the sea is playing tricks with where we are.

I look again and he is above me, looking down. I feel colder than ever.

A hand reaches down. There is something familiar about the gesture. I can't seem to reach high enough, I need to kneel, somehow gain a purchase . . .

'Help me!' I shut my eyes, then I think I say, 'Kurt!'

'I am here, Alfred, just stretch . . . a little more, come on, a little more.'

Our fingers link. At first just the tips touch and then gradually one hand begins to curl round the other. My hand in a larger hand. It feels like Kurt's.

Our hands are joined by another. My body is pulled a little, stops and then is pulled again. Soon I am being drawn steadily out of the cold.

'You all right, Wegener?'

Koch is looking at me. The moon is catching his eyes but the rest of his face is in shadow. 'We almost lost you,' he says in German. 'If you hadn't managed to reach up that little bit more just then . . .'

'Thank you.'

'My pleasure.' His voice is smiling. 'Follow me,' he says, stepping lightly away over the ice. Just now I feel that if he asked me I would follow him to the ends of the earth.

It took the concerted effort of all three men and all twenty-four dogs to pull the sledges back on to the ice. Even then we were not safe: the ice was rotten all around us, and required us to make a considerable detour in order to safely reach Germaniahaven on Sabine Island.

Koch is looking at the stars. But this is not just an idle

whim. He is looking with the concentration I now know he applies to everything. He is sitting astride the meridian: that imaginary line that divides the night sky in half along the north–south axis, so that the middle of his moustache and the small telescope of his sextant are pointing due north.

First he finds our local time. He selects a star, one he knows will be in our tables, and searches meticulously through the sky. It is a clear night, with only a few clouds at the horizon. They don't bother us there. We choose that part of the sky which is overhead, where our view of the stars is least hindered by the thickness of the atmosphere, where the light of the stars is bent least so that the image we see is as true as we can make it.

'Ah.' His breath escapes, hangs opaquely for a moment in the air then quickly dissipates. Now he holds his sextant still and close. I know what he will see: through the eyepiece of the sextant a circle divided by a vertical line. On one side of the line is the star, on the other a piece of cloudy sky. Slowly he rotates the mirror. The cloudy sky gives way to sky and land. He keeps turning until the horizon and the star are matched. Now he lifts the sextant from him and finds the angle from the engraved brass scale at the base. From the angle we can find the altitude of the star. He turns to me, reads out the figure, and I note it down in my book. Then, using a sodden set of tables, I match the measurement to find the local time: 6 a.m.

I look around. Six o'clock. It is so dark, so still. Around me the ice has been moulded into huge strange cliffs that erupt abruptly from an undulating terrain. There are plenty of places in which to hide. Suddenly, unreasonably, I become convinced that we are not alone. I look around for eyes, but of course I can see nothing. The Inuit believe in ghosts; already I have been told more tales about these creatures of the ice than I care to know. There are stories of men who remove themselves inexplicably from the fold to inhabit the inland ice – the wild-men. Henrik has told me tales of how they acquire animal-like senses . . . how they roam the fringes of the settlements, spying, waiting for an opportunity . . . how they are difficult to kill and yet are desperate to die . . . how a wild-man must be trapped in a cave to be released from his misery of life . . . The ice sighs. I turn around. But there are no caves here, there is nothing but this strange ice and its grotesque out-of-scale shapes. Every man, Henrik says, has three souls: his name, his spirit and something else . . . It is the spirit which lurks after he dies . . . Maybe there are spirits here; maybe the spirits of my countrymen who came before me, who stood in this place and performed these same measurements that Koch performs now. Is that Koldeway's ghost causing the ice to creak? Is that his careful footstep on the snow? Is he coming back to warn his countryman about the wretchedness of this place? How easy it is to run out of food and die of exhaustion? How it is almost impossible to escape?

I look towards the horizon, lit up by the moon. Before it seemed rich with exotic ice, but now I see it is overwhelmingly barren. Koch's voice calls out to Throstrup, and Throstrup gives a short laugh back. It is some complicated Danish joke I can't understand. The laughter echoes off the cliff with a jeer. I feel so unbearably lonely . . . The wind is making my eyes smart with tears. It is so cold standing here, waiting.

Now Koch is looking at another star, lining it up by tilting the little mirror in the sextant, until it lies beside the image of the moon that he sees before him. It is a fine moon, big faced and clear. This time he reads off the angular distance – the angle made between the two lines of sight running from his eye to the moon and to the star. At last I have something to do. I write it down gratefully. Again I look in the tables: when will this same conjunction of moon and star be seen in Greenwich? About 7.12 a.m. – a rough calculation for now. At 7.12 in Berlin Father would be packing his bags, and Mother would be serving breakfast.

The wind blows again.

'Got it down?'

'Yes.'

'Good man.'

Maybe Tony will see it. Maybe she will look through her window a little over an hour from now and see this same moon, this same star. But now I must compare our times with Greenwich. I make the calculation: one and one-fifth of an hour is equal to eighteen degrees. So we must be something like eighteen degrees west of Greenwich – a little farther west from Berlin, of course . . . and my bed with its comfortable mattress.

'Wegener?'

Koch has come up to me, so close I can see the tiny crystals of ice on his beard. It is unkempt now, I notice, and smells of rotting fur.

'Are you all right? I've been trying to ask you something.'

I nod. It is too uncomfortable to speak.

'I was wondering if you could do a couple of these measurements. My results . . . they seem a little strange, too far west.'

Together we examine his results. They should be the same as Koldeway's thirty-five years ago, but they are not. We go through the measurements again and again but each time they come out too far west. Yet we are sure this is the correct place. This is Koldeway's cairn. I can almost see his imprint in the shape of the rocks.

I take the sextant and clamber to the cairn. I am anxious to continue now, to see whether my results match Koch's or Koldeway's. Koch flicks through the drenched ephemerides then sighs gratefully as he finds the right page.

'Ready?' he asks.

I look through the telescope and find the moon's familiar

face: it could be German or Danish or the round face of an Inuit. This simple vague impression of a mouth and eyes we all see in its shadows transcends time and nationality. What causes the shadows? Why are they there? 'Almost.' I shouldn't feel warm but now I do. Koch needs me, respects my opinion. Our demand to know is binding us together. It will hold us more securely and more tightly than anything else.

10

Koch always said he saw flames as the dogs' paws struck the
ice on the way back from Germaniahaven. He said it in his
flat, plain voice, so no one could tell whether he was smiling.
I didn't see flames, but I know we moved quickly: sixty-three
kilometres a day. It seems impossible now. Was it just because
the snow was crisp and the storms few or was it because we
were young and inspired by what we thought lay ahead of
us? Maybe if we had known then what would happen soon,
we would have been a little more circumspect.

It is Christmas day 1906 and I am waiting for the traditional
speeches to start. All day I've been waiting; I thought maybe
they'd start after lunch, but there is no after lunch. The eating
and drinking seem to be going on and on. I have my speech
already prepared; a quick, and modest, summary of all the
great things I have accomplished. I thought I'd start with the
rather successful meteorological station: all the instruments
are working well and with the willing and able help of
Freuchen I have succeeded in maintaining a round-the-clock
record of the weather since we started here on the seventeenth
of August. I would like them to acknowledge the diligent
work of Freuchen. Thanks to my expert training he is now
an accomplished meteorological assistant. In fact he can
set up and read the thermographs almost as well as his
teacher. It would be a pleasant thing to acknowledge this, and
motivating too. But there is no sign of anyone bringing anyone
else to order. Instead there is more eating and drinking, and
Mylius-Erichsen looks as deeply entrenched in this as the rest

of them. I would have thought, as leader, he would be the one who would call for toasts, tell us of future hopes and aspirations, but instead he merely seems to be dozing.

I could have reminded everyone about my kites and balloons, not that they need reminding, I suppose. No one can fail to be aware of the strange birds that have replaced the feathered ones that flew south months ago. But I could have told them all about my findings; only Koch and Freuchen have shown much interest so far. I could have told them about the quite fascinating temperature inversions and how this will be of importance to future aeronauts. I could have told them about the unexpectedly virulent Föhn winds and the dramatic effects these have on the air pressure. It is all such original and important work, they couldn't fail to be impressed. I would tell them of the great interest it will generate among the famous meteorologists around the world, especially, I imagine, my benevolent benefactor Vladimir Köppen.

They are singing now, some sort of Danish sea shanty. I think they are a little drunk. Surely the cook, Jensen, will soon bring out the coffee. When they are quiet again I think I might suggest to Mylius-Erichsen that someone begins. I might even suggest it be me. After all, I am quite well prepared. To add interest to my talk I have assembled some of my better photographs, including my recent innovative pictures of the northern lights. I am not sure everyone has seen these yet. Friis, the artist, has asked to see copies and I think he has shown them to some of the rest of the men, but it would do no harm for them to be admired again. They are rather beautiful, even in black and white. I am looking forward to being able to see them in full colour when we get back home to Europe. I wonder whether it will work: the three separate camera shots of the same view, each with a different colour filter, mixed together at home with the three coloured lights of the projector. Greenland in Berlin! Tony will be impressed. I wonder whether everyone here realises that this is the first time anyone has used colour photography on a scientific expedition? I am sure they would be interested to know.

I could finish my little talk with a quick description of our sledge journey to Sabine Island and describe the rather odd results. It is really rather important that we have found that this part of Greenland is, in fact, rather more west than has been thought up until now. Since we are quite convinced of the rigour of our measurements it must mean that Koldeway's were wrong – an uncomfortable conclusion since Koldeway himself was an accomplished navigator. I would leave it to Koch to go into detail about our method. I'm sure he would be grateful for the opportunity. He has grumbled to me recently about how little interest everyone is showing in everyone else's results.

The song has finished. Now is the time to approach Mylius-Erichsen with my suggestion. I stand up, but before I can move one centimetre across the deck there is a loud pig-like snort from Mylius-Erichsen's open mouth. The Inuit, Brønlund, smiles and nudges Hagen, who nudges Friis farther along the line. Taking up his pencil and sketch book, Friis starts to scribble. His subject is stretched back on his bunk, sleeping the sleep of a man with a full stomach. Brønlund and Hagen snigger as the sketch takes shape. I sigh. There is obviously no point in approaching him now. I had been hoping after all the toasts and speeches to press him into disclosing which of us will be making the great journey north with him to the unexplored territory. It has obviously been uppermost in everyone's mind for months, discussed in whispers whenever a pair of us find ourselves alone. It is, after all, the major task of the expedition: to map the part of Greenland's island which is still represented by dashes and question marks. It will complete the coastline, from the end of the solid line that marks our present position, to the other solid line made by Peary six years ago on the northern coast. It is the main reason we are here, and I am hoping to be part of it. To increase my chances of selection I have been attempting to improve my dog-driving skills in the flat stretch of snow beside the ship. Every time Mylius-Erichsen passes by I glance up to see whether he is noticing my efforts. But if he is impressed he never gives a sign: his only comment so far has been to ask whether any of the dogs are natural German-speakers.

I open the hatch to the deck with its tarpaulin cover. The Danes, I decide, have no sense of occasion. This is not how it should be. Everything should have been decided long before now. We shouldn't be kept waiting and wondering like this. I poke my head outside the canvas. My sledge tracks are being licked by the dogs. I have had to work so hard to master these hounds, it would be most unfair if I were not chosen.

Outside, the sea glitters, petrified into a beautiful rigidity. The ice begins to creak and groan with the incoming tide. Is it only the pulse of the sea which can penetrate this icy kingdom? Or will I too become its invader?

The impending journey to the north forced us to overcome the lethargy brought on by the three-month-long arctic night: Knudsen the carpenter produced sledges, one after the other, the slats of wood strapped together with sealskin thongs in the Greenland fashion; traces and whips were cut from fresh skins; and kamiks, clothes and sleeping bags were sewn together in a small production-line assembly. On the ninth of February the sun made its first brief appearance, and teams of dogs were sent out to establish caches of food up to Cape Bismarck.

In his own good time Mylius-Erichsen deigned to tell us. When the periods of daylight had grown long enough to be useful, he gathered us all together around the large table in the ship's laboratory. There was an expectant air, everyone listening intently to his words. I think he rather enjoyed it, and spun the whole thing out a little, much more than he needed to. That is something I vowed then never to do. It is important not to play with people. I could see that Mylius-Erichsen was teasing me. He kept giving me little glances, as if he was interested in my reaction. There would be four teams, he said. Everyone brightened; that would mean twelve of us would be going: good odds. Koch and Hagen, of course, as cartographers they'd have to go, and two of the Inuit. Everyone made calculations: seven places left. But two of the teams were going as support, making caches there and back. They'd go only so far and turn back. Mylius-Erichsen looked at me again. This time it wasn't a glance but a full thoughtful stare, as if he was still not sure. Now he began to rattle off names: in Mylius-Erichsen's team there would be his old trusted friends Hagen and Brønlund, and in Koch's team, for he was to be the other leader . . . I held my breath . . . they would need a Greenlander, Tobias Gabrielsen, and one more . . . this could be me . . . there was no reason for it not to be me. Surely I had earned my place. Now Mylius-Erichsen looked at me again, one of his long stares, then he smiled and spoke . . . Bertelsen. Bertelsen! I opened my mouth. Bertelsen was just another artist, a good artist, but even so I had so much more to offer; already I was an accomplished photographer, and a scientist . . . and besides, I was Koch's natural companion. We were a good team, surely even Mylius-Erichsen had noticed.

I remember I looked at Koch. I remember he was looking down as if trying to hide his face. I wanted to shout out, protest. What had I done wrong? Hadn't I proved myself with the dogs? Was it because I was German? But Mylius-Erichsen went on again, rapidly, as if he feared my outburst. The support teams would consist of two teams of two. Just two: there was a groan. I looked at the others, we exchanged frustrated glances. In one team Ring and Bistrup and in the other Gustav Throstrup and Dr Wegener.

Now Mylius-Erichsen looked at me and smiled. 'We'll keep you with us as long as possible, Wegener,' he said, as if that were sufficient compensation. 'And I'll be expecting you to do some exploratory work on the way back.' That was a little better, but not much.

It is the end of April, almost a month into our journey, and up to now the weather has not let up for a single hour; storms have swept away our tents, blizzards have left us shivering, and the deep snow has torn at our sledges again and again. It has become apparent to all of us that in spite of all our work we are ill prepared for this journey. But now the weather has become brighter, the ferocious winds have died away, and we are filled with a new enthusiasm. There is a general conviction that very soon now the coast will start to bend away to the west, and we shall encounter the fjords and capes that Peary described seven years ago. But for now the coast is stubbornly continuing to head north-eastwards and the going is difficult. We have been forced on to the sea ice but it grates and rumbles as we pass and threatens us with inundation. We scrabble quickly, as if that will save us, but eventually the ice gives way before us to a large wake and then the open sea. Now we head westwards around the wake, keeping our eyes on the headland to the north.

It must be another mirage. There cannot be cliffs this steep, this high. We have come across such mirages before; glaciers, for example, that appeared to be high and impassable but dissolved on our approach into something quite ordinary. The phenomenon is caused by the coldness of the air next to the ice and the warmer air above. This is the opposite of the usual way of things and is called a temperature inversion. It causes the light to bend in strange ways so that the eye is tricked. It has fooled men before but it will not fool us. I have recorded such trickery with my camera. We approach warily on the precarious ice, waiting for the top part of the cliff to suddenly waver and disappear. But it does not. Instead it becomes more firm, more certain. As we come closer still it changes character again. Now pieces appear to be breaking off and there is a roar that is not the sea. It is the cry of birds, thousands of them, wheeling and dipping from their nesting platforms, spattering the rocks below them with guano.

One by one we come to a halt before the cliffs. There is something sinister about this place. Maybe it is the way it seems so out of scale, the way the land seems to heave itself out of the ocean. Maybe it is the blank steepness of the rock or the way the seagulls seem to jeer at us with their calls.

'*Mallemukfelsen*,' Throstrup mutters darkly, fingering his pipe.

'A good name,' Mylius-Erichsen says, then translates it for me, although there is no need. 'Storm-seagull-rock.'

There seemed to be no way forward. The country behind the cliff rose steeply to a plateau, while to the east there was the frozen sea churned up into a series of gigantic ridges and furrows. In desperation we made camp, hoping the morning would bring a solution. Instead it brought a storm. In the gusts of a bitter wind we searched for a way through, vainly hoping that this promontory of rock was an island, but instead we found more cliffs and more high land. It was hopeless. In desperation Mylius-Erichsen ordered us back on to the sea to the east. We went timorously, one behind the other, squeezing our way through narrow passages in the rugged mountain of ice, breaking our sledges and exhausting our dogs, until at last we reached more gentle scenery. Now we looked back. Mallemukfelsen seemed to glower back at us, layer upon layer of horizontal rock cut off perpendicularly at the sea. Later Koch told me he was thinking it too: when the sea ice melted there would be no way back. The sea would thrash on the platforms of white-encrusted guano and there would be no passage home, narrow or otherwise. From now on the thought of Mallemukfelsen would be at the back of all our minds: a summer trap, a dark threat, to haunt our dreams.

After Mallemukfelsen Ring and Bistrup started their return journey to Danmarkshavn. They had helped bring supplies this far north, and now had to make further caches as they journeyed back to the south. Gustav Throstrup and I, however, were allowed to continue a little farther north.

Later we shall know this place as Eskimo Point. The views are good: on the other side of the fjord the coast veers north-eastwards in a series of bays. This is the last time that the coastline will edge eastwards; north of this the land will turn at last to the west. We have almost reached the north-east corner.

But we are not the first people here. There are the remains of others: curved outlines of houses in low walls, middens, pits filled with bones and then fragments of sledges, kayaks, spears and children's toys. Mylius-Erichsen is squatting in one of the curved-off rectangles, examining something he has just found on the ground. It is white, round, maybe a piece of bone carved into something. I watch his face. It is rapt, totally absorbed by the thing in his hand. He turns it round, feels the edges with his thumb, tries to fit it into something else, and then turns it again. I have never seen his face like this before: the thoughtful expression, his complete concentration on something so small.

Suddenly he becomes aware of me. I'm a little embarrassed because I've been caught staring. 'A tent-ring,' he says, holding it up so I can see the light shining through its centre. 'How did they come here, eh, Wegener? How could they live?'

His voice is quiet, wondrous, as if we are in some sacred place. He doesn't seem to want an answer. He has already found it anyway, lying in the kitchen middens: the bones of the caribou. Maybe they followed the caribou here to this desolate place and, once entrapped here, only then realised the foolishness of relying on one species for sustenance. Along with the caribou antlers there are the bones of dogs and men, sometimes scattered about the place, sometimes curled up in the shelter of a wall. They must have died of starvation.

'So many things disappear in Greenland, eh, Wegener? Where are the caribou now, eh?'

Only thirty-five years ago there were caribou. To Koldeway their antlers were like a moving forest, but now there are none.

Mylius-Erichsen stands up, watching Brønlund approach with a bag. 'So many puzzles. Where did they go, Jorgen? Eh?'

Brønlund shrugs and throws down the bag at Mylius-Erichsen's feet. 'Hunting no good. No musk ox.'

Now Mylius-Erichsen notices my bag, swinging from my arm. 'So what have you found, my friend?'

I show him my fossils: shells curled up on themselves in spirals, and bivalves like the hard toenails of an old man. Brønlund leans over too. 'Ah, sea creatures,' he says, 'from the flood.'

'No, Jorgen, Noah's flood was in a hot land, miles away from here.'

'No, another one, here. The old ones tell tales. A great flood. The creatures of the sea-woman carried up on to the kingdom of the land.'

Mylius-Erichsen and I look at each other. This information seems important to us both. Maybe Mylius-Erichsen is thinking about the origins of the Inuit people, a distant land inundated with water, or maybe he is thinking about these strange coincidences in the myths of men. I am thinking of more physical things: about the sea level rising and sinking, and how it must have happened recently to have entered the spoken record of an illiterate people. We each take a fossil, weigh them in our hands, turn them over, each of us fascinated for different reasons, then one by one we drop them

Clare Dudman

back into the bag. I carry it to my sledge and tie it in with the
rest. When I look back, Mylius-Erichsen is still turning the
tent-ring in his hand, but this time he is looking northwards
to where the land rises again.

I was eager to go as far north as possible, and Koch's killing
of a bear gave us another day's grace, but after a hunt for
musk oxen proved fruitless our return became inevitable: if
we stayed there would not be enough food for us all.

Maybe this is the farthest north any German has ever been.
I shall give you my location – the all-important degrees of
latitude north: 80 degrees 43 minutes. But I am going no
farther. I have exchanged my best pair of dogs for a pair
of mangier ones, and my sturdy sledge for Bertelsen's less
reliable one. In this way I am showing forgiveness: he is
going north with Koch and I am not. If I think about this
I still find it hard not to feel aggrieved. But as we toast each
other with coffee I try to think of a more positive thing, my
opportunity to map and explore as we return south, and I
find that I can look Mylius-Erichsen in the eye, and even
smile. But now it is time to go. We all know it. I get up. I
embrace each man in turn: Brønlund and Hagen, who are to
go with Mylius-Erichsen, then Bertelsen, Tobias Gabrielsen,
Mylius-Erichsen and finally Koch.
  'I wish . . .' I say to Koch, but do not finish. I don't need
to. He knows. I wish I were going too. I wish I were trudging
behind you, picking up the wisdom that you scatter around
you like the hairs of this caribou skin. I wish I were learning
more. I wish I were crossing the ice, making camps alongside
you, learning how to survive. Instead I crawl through the tent
flaps without looking back. I mount my sledge and cry at the
dogs. Only when Throstrup and I are moving off do I look
over my shoulder. Six silhouettes wave on the ice.

*   *   *

94

The journey back was full of discoveries and mapping: the Henrik-Kroyers Islands, for example, where I could see the open ocean just a few kilometres away; or the deep gorge of a river bed at the north of Ingolf fjord. Our passage by the ominous Mallemukfelsen was without serious incident (after all my forebodings) and we were even able to supply bear meat to the depot to the south. After circumnavigating Lynn Island in Hekla Sound I noticed that this fjord did not end in mountains but in an astonishing glacier: it was massive, a forty-kilometre ridge of ice. Since it seemed to provide a passage on to the inland ice it did not seem particularly foolhardly at the time to investigate it.

What should I advise this intent young man that was me? Look how he persuades the recalcitrant sailor Gustav Throstrup to climb on to the ice. Look how he convinces him that everything will work out when they arrive at the top, hungry and exhausted by effort. How can he know the way to proceed? Yet he marches with confidence. That glow to the south he knows, without any evidence, will be Lambert Land, with its life-saving depot and its easy way south. He knows all this with a certainty I feel no longer.

We climb by night and travel by night; then the ice is crisp and we are not blinded by the low sun. But in the morning, before we make camp, the sun lights everything and reveals the masterpieces of the ice: great columns rising up to form a wall of ridges, banks with horizontal layers of colour, twisting here and there like the folds in mountainsides, icicles longer than a house, and all flowing softly into rounded forms. I am amazed by it all, and thank Throstrup again and again for allowing me to see this splendour. He just shrugs as if it is nothing, but when he thinks I am not looking I notice he admires it too, pausing at odd times just to stand and look.

We reach the top of the ice sheet and far into the distance

there are just undulating ridges; the cold snow dunes of a lifeless desert. Again we travel by night. The light from the moon is diffuse, hidden by the clouds, but even so it reflects into our eyes, making them sore and swollen. But it is not our eyes which are giving us the most discomfort now but the emptiness of our bellies. We are desperate for food, so desperate it is impossible to sleep for long because of the screaming of our stomachs, so we break camp too early, and whip the famished and exhausted dogs into serving us yet again.

Throstrup says little, and when I say we must sleep he refuses now to stop, just keeps trudging slowly forward. When I say that the glow ahead of us is the sea and that if we march towards it we will find our depot, he shrugs. No doubt he is regretting our detour on to this ice and blaming me for what he thinks is our impending demise.

Throstrup stops. He is so abrupt that I have difficulty bringing the dogs around. Soon I see why. There is a break in the ice, with crevasses too wide to cross, and at the bottom we can see and hear the sea ice creaking with the tide. For a few minutes we examine the extent of the break, then Throstrup stiffens and points. 'Over there.'

He is pointing to where the ground sinks and there is a sparkle of sea ice.

'A mirage,' I say. It is too soon for Cape Bergendahl and the depot.

But we trudge towards it, and soon we find a way through the break, driving the dogs on to one thin isthmus and then another. I was wrong. It is Lambert Land, and the mirage is real. We are back on our way home. At last Throstrup smiles.

After the detour over the inland ice Throstrup would brook no unnecessary stoppages. I think he had been a little frightened by the experience on top of the glacier and was adamant that we should get back to Danmarkshavn as soon as possible. I saw so many ice forms and land forms tugging at my eyes and my camera that I begged to stop, but each time Throstrup ignored my requests. Would I be quite so frustrated now? Am I more patient? Would I still silently curse Throstrup's huddled back as I did then?

Something drops in front of me and the sledge swerves. I leap down on to the snow, and wrestle away the dogs to where the sick one lies. It is Gamle Ajungpok, Hagen's old decrepit dog. It is blind, deaf and toothless, and yet still it has padded alongside the others for mile after mile. I lay his tired old head on my lap and he stirs weakly. A shadow crosses mine: Throstrup.

'Shall we make camp?' he asks briskly.

'Yes.'

I feed the dog by hand, and let it lie by me in the tent, away from the others. In the night it seems to gather strength and the next day shows more interest in its pemmican.

I fasten Gamle behind the sledge so he no longer has to pull, but there is something in the dog which makes him remember his calling. Again and again he tries to overtake the sledge to achieve his position at the front, but each time he fails. At last I take him on the sledge alongside me, but still he hankers after the others, whimpering to be allowed to take his turn in pulling until, at last, he is silent.

I remember lowering the dog Gamle into the ice. I remember grieving over this creature which had spent its whole life in the service of man. Maybe I was weak with hunger, exhaustion and cold, but I couldn't leave his corpse to be scavenged by a bear or fox. I waited until we were by a crevasse and nudged his body inside. Later, when Throstrup was relating the tale to the others, it seemed sentimental, but at the time I felt an overpowering gratitude to that dog and his friends. It seemed to me we were working towards the same thing: exploration and discovery. The dog had wanted to help and impress me just as much as I had wanted to help and impress my colleagues. As I left the dog's body behind I felt we had both failed. As I approached Danmarkshavn the euphoria of homecoming was overwhelmed by a feeling of intense dissatisfaction. I had not, I thought, mapped, explored or investigated enough. Too easily I had allowed Throstrup to persuade me home. Kurt would have disapproved, I thought, and Koch, I was sure, would be disappointed.

II

Where were they? Uncertainty chafed at my mind that spring until I felt ill with anxiety. As soon as Throstrup and I began to unwrap our celebratory cigars on the deck of the *Danmark* I started to wonder. As we smoked and posed for our photograph among the lathes and canisters of petroleum I began to calculate: maybe a couple of weeks, that was all it would take for them to reach Peary's cairn at the top of Greenland. I decided they would be back by the fourteenth of April and waited with confidence.

Meanwhile spring came to Danmarkshavn. What was the first sign? I have to think hard to remember. Was it the birds returning, calling suddenly from some hidden place along the shore? Or was it the first small rivulet, heard before it was seen; the tantalising sound of running water gurgling beneath the snow? Maybe it was none of these. Maybe it was just an intangible expectancy that something was about to happen. The air seemed to crackle with something new: spring. Once it started it quickly gathered momentum. Rivulets became visible and turned rapidly into brooks before disappearing under the snow again to form subterranean rivers. Ice became pocked with holes which grew and grew until the ice was lacy and transparent and collapsed under the smallest pressure. The underground streams gurgled into the open, displaying beds of multi-coloured pebbles. On the sea the ice cracked suddenly and loudly. Crevasses opened out into leads and then into wakes. The *Danmark* became a ship again, free and mobile. The land and sea became distinguishable; two different kingdoms with an obvious border.

But Koch did not return. I lay without sleeping, listening for the sound of his feet on the ground outside, which now crunched again with pebbles. The morning of the fourteenth turned into afternoon and then into evening but still Koch did not come. Up until then I had mapped his movements in my head. Today, I had decided, he would be gathering some of the artefacts we had left behind at Eskimo Point. A couple of days later he would be negotiating the narrow passage outside Mallemukfelsen, then maybe taking the route inland past Lynn Island and Lambert Land. Today he would be making the final descent. Today he would be here. But he wasn't.

Now the chafing began in earnest. The images in my mind began to change. Instead of squeezing through the sea-ice ridges at Mallemukfelsen they had encountered open water. Instead of sledging steadily south they had had to go back to the north. Now they were hunting musk ox and bear in Peary Land and finding little. Now they were scrubbing around the nests of birds for eggs. Now the dogs were weak and the oldest had fallen like Gamle . . . I tried to shake away the pictures but in the night, as I lay on my bunk in 'the Villa', they returned in full colour.

For some reason, in those early days, the fate of Mylius-Erichsen didn't concern me. I think I had always expected him to return later. I had expected him to sniff around up there for a while, maybe check a few readings, maybe even follow a musk ox trail to the west. It was Koch I was expecting first, and then, suddenly one morning, it was Koch and his team who came.

I am inspecting the remains of my pilot balloon. The oiled cotton is in tatters; the intense cold has converted the pliable threads into something brittle and delicate. The balloons have not had the same success as the kites; they rise too slowly and so get swept away by the wind before they have had the chance to rise to the heights I require of them. Next time, if there is a next time . . . I decide to make some notes in my journal. I smooth down the page, ready to write . . .

'Still at those damned balloons, then?'

A familiar voice. A longed-for voice. I look up. I can barely pick out his features, they are so well hidden by whiskers, hood, goggles and shadows.

'Koch!'

I leap up. The diary drops on the snow. It doesn't matter. I throw out my arms, try to encircle his layers of skins and furs, but I can barely reach his arms.

'Thank God.'

It is so good to see the old bear again. Now he steps backwards, removes his goggles and growls at my face, 'We got there, Wegener. That's it. The whole coast's mapped.'

I am ashamed by my feelings. It will be some time before I can look and listen to Bertelsen without bitterness. Envy, my father would say, is a sin, but who does not feel it? *I should have been there with Koch*, completing the circuit around this icy island. *I should have been standing next to him at Peary's cairn*, placing our report next to his. I was so close, only twenty-five days away. It is infuriating, anyone would feel it. But now I listen to Koch and note every word: a private résumé of his adventures just for me before he has to tell them again to the rest. We sit, squashed between instruments and equipment, and he rumbles out his story, drawing maps in the snow. They had been the first to reach Peary's cairn, the first to explore the adjacent fjord, the first to measure the distance between Peary's last two cairns, the first to . . .

The records went on and on. Bertelsen revelled in them again and again when he took over the telling of the trip in the ship at night. I remember anchoring a smile on to my face to listen to the details of that visit to Peary's cairn: of the tears that coursed down Bertelsen's face and of his speechless wonderment at standing there in the same spot, just seven years later than the great man himself. Much more interesting to me, although Bertelsen just skipped over this part, was how they had become ill owing to eating half-cooked musk ox meat, and how they had encountered Mylius-Erichsen again, quite unexpectedly, on the shoreline of Wandel's Sea.

Later Koch described how he had tried to persuade Mylius-Erichsen to return with him then to the *Danmark*, but Mylius-Erichsen, as usual, had been cheerfully obstinate. He had wanted to find Peary's channel. It had become a holy grail to him, and, it turned out, equally bogus. He had declared they would be gone only a few days and that the best thing Koch could do now was to keep his opinions to himself and concentrate instead on ensuring that all the depots were in order for their return. So they had separated again; a rather grumpy Koch to the south and an equally grumpy Mylius-Erichsen to the west.

Now we waited again, waited until summer disappeared with the birds, until it was September and Mylius-Erichsen's team had still not appeared. All we could talk about now was what might have happened. Everyone had their own theory: maybe they had been stopped by Mallemukfelsen and were waiting for the autumn ice; maybe they had made an exciting find and were conducting a thorough investigation; maybe they had followed the musk oxen as far as the settlements on the western coast; or maybe they had discovered a lost Viking settlement and were living there safe and well, waiting for the return of the winter weather (this was Friis's idea after a couple of beers, and he denied it later). Of course, there was another possibility, the one nobody articulated; but it was the reason why Lindhard the physician was the first one chosen to join the rescue party.

There was nothing the rest of us could do while the rescue party prepared the sledge and began the mission northwards, and so, when Lindhard and Bertelsen came hurtling down to camp gabbling about a hole in the ice that just had to be investigated, we were grateful for the distraction.

The icicles dangle like the fringed edges of an Inuit's anorak. They pick out each ridge of the icy roof, layer after layer, as if they are hung from a hidden rope and the slightest wind would make them jangle. But they ping only if they are touched, snapping neatly into a fragile spike and a blunt partner. So we limbodance carefully under the low roof of the entrance, following the river under the glacier. Even Bertelsenis speechless. We have emerged into a cathedral, blue-lit not from the sky, but from the sun shining through the ice: cerulean blue and turquoise glance off every face and illuminate every crevasse. The sound of water mixes with its own echoes off the ceiling: gurglings and sudden rushes, quieter and then louder. A gasp from Koch is made into a whisper, as if there is someone listening and answering back.

When Bertelsen is released from his spell words fall from him as if he too is ice standing in the sun. He revels in his role of artist, as if it is only he who can appreciate such beauty. He moans about his lack of time, his lack of pigment, and, in silent answer. I set up the tripod of my camera and point it back through the entrance. I am practised now and quite accomplished. I frame my picture with a jagged oblique screen of icicles leading the eye to where the wide and sluggish river disappears under a crumpled tablecloth of snow.

As Bertelsen settles down on a flat rock on the river bed with his pad and pencils, Koch takes up my cause of the camera and together we penetrate more deeply into this place we call Gnipa Cave.

Koch stops. The next screen of icicles reaches almost to the floor. We edge through, and Koch points the camera back. Ice, snow, water and boulders – all of it glistens in this strange blue light.

'Why is it here?'

Koch looks at me. 'A river bed. The water has to go somewhere.'

'But why like this?'

Koch shrugs, then looks at me and smiles. 'You want to find out?'

I nod.

'Let's make a study, then. Map it, find out everything.'

It is exactly what I wanted. 'You don't mind?'

He swings his rucksack down from his shoulder, and, making sure I am watching, unloads it in front of me. He has everything we shall need. He looks up at me and smiles. 'It seems we were of a like mind, Dr Wegener.'

One mind. The thought fills me with pleasure. The same mind as Koch. Who could wish for anything more?

The light of the entrance is fading. It is becoming more difficult to see which is water-sculpted rock and which is water-sculpted ice: each have the same rounded edges, the same hollows and the same erratic shapes. But there is still enough light for a section of ice drapery to sparkle, and for an ice stalactite to glitter like an unlit chandelier. Beneath, its partner, the mound of an ice stalagmite, is lit with a jelly-like translucence, its globules of ice fused together like abandoned frog spawn.

Now we light our torches, the wavering flames emphasising our solitude.

'Look!' Koch has lit up a corner. In it there is another curtain of icicles, but these are showing off the plasticity of ice. Near the floor they are bent, almost at right angles. We look up nervously. Something has slowly bent this ice. Something is pressing down, slowly, determinedly. I measure the distance from floor to ceiling.

Later we will find this distance shrunk, proof that the ceiling is gradually closing in. We will also find the icicles transformed: their surfaces smoothed away by the wind into glass and their roots wizened away until they are held by lamella-like threads, ready to drop on us like sharpened spears.

But now we insert thermometers into the walls of ice, making our first recording of depth and temperature. I wonder whether Koch notices the way we work together, the way we fit our tasks around each other, as if we are part of the same mechanism. As we trudge farther along the brook's bed, I try to form the question I want to ask.

'What will you do after this?' I say eventually. 'Will you go on another expedition?'

'Maybe,' he replies shortly. I feel I am trespassing on some part of Koch he wants to keep to himself. But I am determined to know more.

'To Greenland again?'

'Maybe.'

'Or somewhere else? The Antarctic?'

'Maybe.'

He wants me to be quiet. Maybe he wants to listen. The sound of water is louder now and the character of the cave has changed. It has become more tunnel-like, and instead of pebbles the brook has a smooth, deep bed cut out of the rock. Above this the ice is curved into a tube which is clearly striped with colour. I hold up my lamp.

'Another photograph?'

By the bright white light of burning magnesium the tunnel takes on a new beauty. The layers form a regular pattern of colour: a translucent yellowish brown, a sharp boundary then blue clear ice gradually becoming more opaque and white before turning yellow again. Later we will work this out: the yellow snow is the autumn firn ice, porous and grainy, mixed in with the summer dust. The blue-turning-to-white layer is the winter snow that falls next, the blue caused by summer melt-water that freezes to a clear blue in the next frost.

As the last of the magnesium fizzles away we become aware

of a noise like faraway thunder. We hurry forward, pause to admire a confluence and then continue up the steepening incline. It is a little slippery now, and the going is hard. But the sound of roaring is becoming deafening. There is little point in talking.

I feel it before I see it. The air is so humid it seems to be condensing on my face. The sound of thundering water is so close I can feel the ground vibrating. It is a little unnerving in the semi-darkness. Koch holds up his lamp and we see it, just fleetingly: the spectacular smoothness of falling water giving way to frothy whiteness. Then the lamps blow out.

For a moment we stand, startled and breathless. But then we become aware of another light: gentle, diffuse, falling over the top of the waterfall. It is so beautiful we do not try to relight our lanterns but lean towards it, grope at the sides of the waterfall for handholds and move slowly upwards. We can smell the light. It is cold, moving exhilaratingly fast past our nostrils, and we strain towards it as if we are green and sap-filled. Koch's head reaches it first. I see his face, pale and blinking, a troglodyte coming into the open.

'Ah, now I see,' he says, his voice just audible above the water.

What does he see? I scramble towards him.

'Ah.' Now everything is clear. The mysterious pockmarks on the glacier we have seen from a distance are explained: they are just the potholes where the ice has given way above a cave.

At the edges of our pothole are boulders. We sit astride one of these and share out tobacco for our pipes.

'I wonder what Bertelsen's doing now.'

'I expect he's not even noticed we've gone.'

Koch laughs. 'We make a good team, Wegener, you and I.'

I nod, too vigorously, and agree too enthusiastically. Koch smiles and draws again on his pipe. Maybe he is thinking I am a young fool, too eager to please. If he is thinking that then it won't matter if I say this:

'If you do go to Antarctica, can I come too?'

'I don't think that's likely to be on the cards, my young friend. More likely I'll be enticed back to this place.'

'And you'd allow me to come?'

'Of course. I'd demand it.'

I lean back. The tobacco smoke escapes through my nose and is hurried away by the wind; it has never smelt sweeter.

I 2

The rescue team came back noiselessly in the dark. Lindhard the surgeon had nothing to report except that at Mallemukfelsen they had met open water. For some time they had tried to find a way through the high country but it had been all in vain. They had returned with nothing.

If only they had called out, maybe then Mylius-Erichsen would have heard them and shouted back his reply. Sometimes, in my dreams, they send their voices over the plateau behind Mallemukfelsen. They call high and clear and Mylius-Erichsen's dogs howl in recognition from the north.

'I am here,' he calls back. 'Come, help me.'

In my dreams Lindhard stretches out his hand. It becomes long, the fingers reaching out, feeling over the roughness of a single massive rock until they meet with Mylius-Erichsen's. And Mylius-Erichsen holds on. In my dreams they know that it is only this rock which separates them. They know that help will come soon. I wake up with a contentedness that is soon displaced with fresh despair as I realise my dream is not true.

And then it was our second long night of winter.

I finish my notes and look around. The balloon went off course again today. I lost sight of it quickly and it was difficult to winch back in the strong winds. The motor engine has not lived up to its earlier promise. I sit back, faintly feel the cold of the hut wall against my back, and listen. It is the usual topic: Mylius-Erichsen. Gradually the tense has changed – from an optimistic definite future to one that is more conditional, sometimes to one that is hopelessly past: when he comes back . . . if he comes back . . . he was a courageous leader . . . All they can do is talk. Everyone seems to be affected by the same lethargy. I begin to pace the small length of the hut, trying to find something useful to do.

'Sit down, Wegener. You're getting on my nerves, hovering like that.'

It is as if everyone's nerves have been rubbed raw. There is not enough to hear, not enough to see. Stepping outside seems to take me into something even smaller. It is as though I am stepping into the Gnipa Cave and the invisible ceiling is close to my head and dropping slowly closer.

'Sit down, Wegener, please.' There is an edge to Bertelsen's voice.

I sit and morosely doodle on a scrap of paper. There is not enough to do. In future expeditions, in the one I am planning in private with Koch, we will ensure that there is sufficient to keep the mind occupied over the winter months. A projector would be ideal – it would give us all a sense of space again. We could look at beautiful pictures of sunlit landscapes and feel a little happier.

At the end of February I looked up from my instruments to find that a certain colour and depth had returned to the landscape. To the south I could see the shape of mountains picked out in the faintest mauve. The sun was waking at last and our dark captivity would soon be ended.

Soon the ship was bustling with activity and ideas. Eventually Captain Trolle, the expedition's second-in-command, called a meeting. It was obvious to everyone that we could not go home without attempting once more to solve the mystery of Mylius-Erichsen's disappearance. Of course, Koch, the most experienced member of the expedition, should go. Trolle looked around. But only one person could accompany him because of the shortage of dogs, and of course that other person had to be an expert dog-handler, an Inuit. The captain's eye settled on Tobias Gabrielsen.

I remember waiting. I remember planning and making local expeditions of apparently little consequence, to Dronning Louise Land and the edge of the ice. Such desperate distractions; how I longed to squeeze away the images that formed in my mind: Koch crawling through the snow and Tobias Gabrielsen wandering homewards alone.

It is the third of April 1908 and we are returning to Danmarkshavn after a small excursion on to the inland ice. As we see the ship, still locked in the solid sea, we hear dogs. Dogs! Have they returned before us? Soon we will know. We begin to run and slip over the ice. We fall and rise again. We leave our traces and the sledge on the snow. Is Koch back? Are those his footprints beside the dogs'? Or maybe they're Gabrielsen's. Or maybe someone else's, maybe a ghost returned. The snow has disappeared in patches. We have to trudge through the drifts but we can move a little faster over the banks of pebbles. Is that Koch's sledge? Are those Tobias Gabrielsen's dogs? They run towards us, yelping, demanding food. We have none. I hold out my empty hands and the dogs scurry from me.

'Koch? Koch?'

Faces appear on the deck of the ship. Trolle, Friis, Henrik and now ... Koch. Yes, it's Koch. But no one else. No ghosts.

I slow down to a walk. I remember the sledge and think about retrieving it but Lindhard and Weinschenck are back there already, shooing away the dogs. Koch waits for us to board. Everyone is silent, treading carefully. Only Koch's eyes meet mine.

'We found Brønlund ...' His voice becomes so low, so gruff, I can't hear it.

Trolle continues for him. His eyes are glittering with anger. 'The poor bastard had dragged himself to the depot with Hagen's bloody map and a diary, half in Danish, half in Inuit – we're still trying to make sense of it.'

'He was prepared for death,' Koch says, finding a voice. 'Surrounded by unopened cans, he starved to death. I don't understand it. There was food all around him.' His voice fades away again. When I stretch my arm around his shoulder he doesn't flinch but allows himself to be guided down to the laboratory below deck where Tobias Gabrielsen sits, staring blankly.

Later we read the diaries and work out their journey to mortality. The snow gave out so it was impossible to travel by sledge. They lived on what they could hunt. The dogs started to die. A sledge was broken up for fuel. They lost their sewing kit so they could not repair their boots. Then they were stopped by the open water at Mallemukfelsen . . .

Now we checked the dates and shook our heads in disbelief: Lindhard had been just the other side of the rock, just a few miles away.

They climbed on to the inland ice in stockinged feet. It took four days, and at the end of it they had just four dogs left. They started to walk southwards on to the white waste.

'Do you think you could stand it, eh? The cold, the hunger, the months without light?'

I nod, keeping his eyes in line with mine.

'And you are fit, eh?'

I nod again, and it seems to me that in his eyes I can see distant places.

'And can you keep going, on and on and on . . .'

Still the eyes stare into mine, but now I see what they see: an open white field.

But it was dark. Their feet started to swell. The last of the dogs died. There was no moon. Frost bit at their feet. They walked.

'*On and on . . .*'

A fjord. Scrambling down. Exhaustion hitting them suddenly like the strongest of winds.

'*Until you feel you simply have to stop, but then carry on . . .*'

Hagen dropping, getting up, dropping, becoming still.

'*. . . but then carry on . . .*'

Brønlund creeping slowly. Mylius-Erichsen slower still. Colder than they could ever remember.

'*. . . a little more.*'

Mylius-Erichsen dropping, suddenly, finally. The wind howling. Brønlund inspecting the bags, selecting the diary, tucking it in beside Hagen's drawings. Creeping forward.

'*. . . a little more.*'

Then crawling. A dry cave. A depot. Filling a paper slowly with writing. A bottle to keep the paper dry. Clumsy hands making clumsy folds. Thinking. Arranging. Thinking. Arranging again.

'*. . . a little more.*'

Stopping. Eyes closing. Lying back. Waiting.

Part II
Die Hypothese

13

I remember the warmth of Copenhagen, the warmth of Berlin. A warmth that stuck to me, enveloped me in the dark until my bed became a damp, clinging poultice. I ached for the dry, clear air of Greenland. I longed for its coldness and quiet, but instead I was forced to become used again to the clamour of Europe and its insistence that I should talk and perform. But I ignored all offers except the one I couldn't refuse: an invitation to lecture at the German Meteorological Society at Hamburg from its chairman, Vladimir Köppen. The audience was bigger than I expected, and more varied. In among the shirts and ties I spotted the odd lacy collar and bow.

Later she tells me that it was my eyes: grey-blue, she says, I couldn't stop looking at them. Or maybe it was my face, or my skin, still sunburnt, she says, so brown it made everyone else look ill. Or maybe it was the eyes in the face, maybe the contrast, the way the eyes glowed, lit up even, or maybe the voice. You were so clear, she says, I could hear every word, I couldn't stop listening. Entrancing. Didn't I notice her being entranced? Didn't I notice her staring? Probably her mouth was open. She was near the back. She shouldn't have been there really, she says, and giggles, looks a little anxious, appears to be examining my face. I smile and she relaxes a little. I told Herr Möller, she says. I told him that I simply had to meet you and . . . She seems unable to finish.

'Would you like a little more soup?' I fill in the pause. I feel a little embarrassed. Why have I been placed next to this young girl? A child really.

'Thank you. Yes. I would. I mean, if there is any. There is enough, isn't there? I mean . . . It's one of his rules. Papa's, I mean. Not to be greedy. Enough for everyone, he says, if everyone is . . . Oh, thank you. That's enough. Really. Oh . . .'

We watch as the handle of her spoon disappears into her soup.

Using my fork, I extricate her spoon, wipe the handle and give it back to her. I smile but she doesn't see, just murmurs a thank-you and bows her head so far down that her hair forms a near-perfect curtain. Even so, through the strands I can see her face darken. Her hand is clenched so tightly around the handle of her spoon now that her knuckles shine. Before it reaches her mouth she gulps once, loudly. Alarmingly, at the edge of the hair-curtain, I can see her eyelashes quiver and then blink downwards as if they are forcing something away.

'I have some photographs,' I say quickly. 'They're quite interesting, I think. Kites and balloons. That sort of thing.'

'Like Papa's?' She looks up. I was right about the tears. Her eyes are a little too sparkly. She nods her head on the other side of the table. Köppen is watching us. When our eyes meet, he smiles. I stare at his white beard, and his old man's skin, browned in patches. How can this child be his daughter?

But she is waiting to see my photographs. When I hand them to her she examines them quietly, as if she is trying to memorise each one. Then I notice: his frown on her face, his fingers fluttering on her hands, and his words from her mouth: How did you? What if you'd? Have you ever? Could I? And so I answer her as if I am answering him, and forget that she is a child at all. There is just Köppen and this piping mouthpiece. Then, when she is called away, there is just Köppen with his own voice; volleying questions, arguing, listening. Gradually we sink into a place where there is just us and when we stop it is as if we have woken from the same dream: the gas lights

splutter, the room is cold, and around us is the silence of a
sleeping house.

Over the next two days I learnt the players in Köppen's household: a tiny wife, her widowed sister, the widowed sister's
daughter, a son, the son's friend, a housemaid, an assortment
of itinerant meteorologists squeezed into the house for the
conference, and of course his little mouthpiece. The house
was crowded. We were spread about the place on sofas, even
the floor. As I crept away from my nightly discussions with
Köppen I had to be careful how I moved; a step to the side
would cause a grunt, a shuffle backwards, a groan; an attempt
to lie flat would generate a cry that would set the others off
like dogs. Settled in a spot at last, I would hardly sleep, it was
too warm, the air moved only as far as the next mouth to be
drawn again into mine, humid and already spent. Even so I
was sorry to return to my parents' house in Berlin, where I
promptly succumbed to an infection.

It is strange to be ill. Strange to lie in a bed with nothing to
do. Strange to be indulged, to have my meals brought to me.
From time to time I glimpse my mother, passing the door, a
short, sharp look inside and then she hurries away. I know
what she is thinking; Kurt has told me, she's whispered it to
him in the kitchen. She thinks I have endangered myself. She
says that my heart has always been weak and now I have
weakened it some more with my exertions.

When she passes again I call out. I am pleased with the
way my voice fades away into a croak.

'What is it, Alfred?'

I ask her for paper and a pen. Her eyes narrow. 'What for?'

I flop back, allowing my arms to fall languidly across
the quilt.

'I need to put everything in order, Mother . . .' My throat
is so dry the words are hardly audible.

'Oh, Alfred!' She drops heavily at my side, grabs my nearest arm. 'Are you really feeling that bad?'

I nod weakly, sit still for a few seconds, and then sit quickly upright. 'Much too noisy!'

She leaps up, frowning and pouting. 'That's not at all funny!'

'Well, there's Papa with his noisy newspaper, you with your loud needles, and as for Tony . . .'

I shudder. 'The sound of that brush rasping across the canvas, day after day . . . No, it's no good.

I've just got to find somewhere more peaceful.'

'You are a wicked boy, Alfred. I thought . . .' She wipes her eyes, and guiltily I remember Käte and Willy.

'I'm sorry, Mother.' Her slight smile encourages me enough to add: 'Would you get me the paper?'

'No!' As she moves through the room her dress brushes both my bed and my chest of drawers at once. I lie back, listening to the swishing noise of the fabric.

'Please.'

'No.'

Nevertheless, a few minutes later the maid arrives with a new pen and paper.

'Madam says to not take too long.'

'I won't.'

I know what I am going to say and to whom I am going to say it: Marburg University is small, quiet and peaceful, and I am sure that they will find that they need me.

I started work on the seventh of May at six in the evening. I remember that the fat student in the front row had a noisy stomach and he bent forward and rustled his paper to cover up the noise of its rumbling. I remember a group in the back row groaning every time a new name was mentioned. I remember running out of breath and taking too long. It was a complicated topic: 'The development of the astronomical conception of the world,' and I think I spent a little too long on the Alfonsine tables. But in the end I began to enjoy the attention. I remembered how it was to be a student: how it is to know little and to be bombarded with unfamiliar symbols and words. I tried to make it simple and not dress everything up with equations just to make it sound more scientific. I used the language of the schoolroom rather than the undergraduate, and I noticed that my students grew happier and more relaxed: the fat boy at the front sat back, and the back row was vacated while the front rows filled. In the winter term I took them, still in their seats, to Sabine Island and looked at Koch's stars to find our position; while in the summer we merely looked outside to observe the physics of the atmosphere. In the nights I took small groups to the observatory to look into space.

He has come again to stare. Sometimes he seems to stare more at me than at the stars. He demands to see my photographs. It is as though he can't see them enough. He stares at the great ice cliffs at the edge of Dronning Louise Land. He traces the ridges with a finger hovering carefully above the page to make no mark. Then finally his eyes travel from the paper to me.

'Is that you?' he asks, knowing the answer.

'What was it like? What was it really like?'

'Cold,' someone says, but I am careful not to laugh.

'Yes, but sometimes a wind came off the ice that seemed almost warm.'

'A föhn wind?' he asks. He has a chin that doesn't jut out quite enough, and above it a sharply pointed nose. It gives him a rather peevish, weak expression, but his voice is strong.

I nod. 'That's good, very good. What is your name?'

'Johannes Georgi, sir,' he says, and clicks his heels together, staring at my face. He is on parade.

Ah yes, Georgi, he was such a peaceful companion then.

I remember he amused me by his almost constant presence: at night in my observatory staring at the stars and in the day examining my diagrams of air pressure, temperature and precipitation. And such questions; even then his interest was obvious and unusual. Sometimes I felt I couldn't help him. So little was known about meteorology then and there was so much that puzzled me. There were few experts but there was always Köppen: the generous sage of Hamburg, with his full replies and his generous invitations.

The house seems empty. Even the garden seems hushed. Winter has cleared away everything: the leaves from the trees, the garden benches, the flowers and the berries. Everything is gone or wrapped away or hidden or forgotten. Two summers ago this place seemed to spew out people from windows and doors, but now Köppen's family seem alone in their quiet occupation.

Their maid opens the door and invites me to enter. As I follow behind her I notice pictures: trees with odd, uniformly thick branches, portraits of children with uneven eyes, clumped houses in landscapes with opaque skies. No doubt Tony would cast her critical eye over them and tell me why my eyes are arrested. Upstairs a woman's voice begins a song and then stops quickly. It is a song I used to know and I want to hear more, but ahead of me the maid turns and gestures for me to go forward into the room ahead. It is a room I should recognise, but it seems larger than I remember and, in spite of the lateness of the season, more light. Behind the sliding door into the adjacent room I can hear a man's voice talking. The door opens and the voice is louder. It is Köppen.

He backs into the room, a small, light-footed man, still talking to the person beyond the door. 'But you must decide soon, Alexis, what it is to be . . .'

Köppen stops, turns, and at last he notices me. His eye-brows, eyelids and the top of his mouth move upwards and there is the whiteness of his eyes, the whiteness of his teeth. 'Ah, Wegener, my boy, so good to see you!' he says, then calls through the door, 'Alexis, come here and say hello to Dr Wegener.'

A slight young man enters. How much like his father he is: the same light way of walking, the same downward inclina-tion of the head. But whereas Köppen's head lifts frequently with a question or a glance, this boy's head remains tipped floorward as if there is something of great interest at his feet. When I hold out my hand he takes it and drops it quickly, murmuring something I cannot hear. He stands still for a minute, head still bowed, then abruptly turns to his father. 'I have to go now.'

Köppen tuts. 'If you must . . .' he says, then after the door shuts adds, 'Such an unsociable boy. You know, I think he'd much prefer it if he was one of the fish in his aquarium. It seems so much bother for him to speak.' He sighs, looks at the closed door for a second, then slaps me on the back and ushers me to a chair.

'Now that letter of yours . . . You say you've found more evidence for temperature anomalies . . .' Then he plunges in, quoting my readings, asking for details. At the mention of air boundaries he claps his hands, and breathes the words inversion and temperature as if they are hallowed. When I tell him of my plan to write a book he nods vigorously and tells me he can help with references and old papers. When I tell him that above all I want it to be understandable to the average student, with only as much maths as is absolutely necessary, he spreads his hands out wide to emphasise the excellence of my idea.

We don't notice the door close and then, an hour later, open again. Someone enters. I suppose I see a movement at the edge of my eyes, but I am following Köppen's pen tracing anticyclones on a map. I am not aware of the growing darkness but I do notice when I am suddenly able to see clearly again under the light of a lamp.

'Vladimir, have you asked the young man if he would like some supper?'

We look around at the voice, both of us slightly irritated to be interrupted. It is the tiny wife attired in an artist's smock, paint daubs in her hair; the artist, then.

I look around me. The curtains have been drawn and the lamps have been lit. Outside the room, quite close, someone is singing a song about gypsies and a countess.

'I suppose he's expecting some, he's staying the weekend after all.'

'Vladimir, you didn't tell me!'

'I'm sure I did.'

'You did not!'

I am embarrassed. I rise from my seat. I think the maid has my hat. Outside the room the singer begins a shrill chorus: the gypsies are enticing the lady from her castle. Maybe if I go now I could still catch a train to Berlin, or maybe I could find a room in the centre of the town. But Köppen's small hand pushes me back down into the chair with surprising strength. I grunt a little as my breath escapes.

'He's always doing this, don't worry, I'm used to it.' Frau Köppen smiles down at me – a round face with glasses.

'I am not.'

Mrs Köppen reaches the door. As she opens it the chorus of the gypsy song noisily enters the room.

'You are. Ask Else.'

The singing stops and a face appears at the door. It is the little mouthpiece, but now she has found words of her own: 'What are you all arguing about now?' She looks with mock irritation from one to the other, then smiles at me.

I smile back, but I can't think of anything to say. It is not like me to be tongue-tied.

'You're staying?' she asks.

'Of course he is,' answers Köppen.

'Good. I'll help Marthe make up a room, then.'

Köppen rubs his hands together and sits again. 'Now that that's all sorted out . . .'

Frau Köppen lets out a long sigh, then turns to me. 'It's a pleasure to see you again, Dr Wegener.' Then with a glare at her husband adds, 'I'd just like to have a little warning once in a while.'

Outside the room a new song rises up the stairs: the song about the Eskimo and his wife.

14

One day I would like to see the world again from a high balloon. Shall I ever go up there again now? I wonder. Is it too late? Am I too old? I would take oxygen, strap the mask firmly to my face, and go to where the air runs out and space begins. It would be so silent: an infinite roof of speckled indigo stretching out above, and below the precious opal of the earth, its cloudiness picking out cyclones and anticyclones. From such a viewpoint how could I fail to understand everything? I would see the masses of sand-laden air sweeping hotly from deserts; tropical storms coming quickly to life; and the complex pattern of circulating winds changing with the seasons. But in 1910, in Köppen's house in Hamburg, I could only describe what I knew from my experiments just a little way up from the ground.

I think Frau Köppen finds us amusing: the way we talk, the way we sit, one each side of Köppen's desk, every night into the early hours. I am talking through the book. It is so easy under Köppen's direction – just a nod from him and I can talk without stopping. I shall begin with the planets, just to give a little setting, and then move on to the physics of the atmosphere. Köppen agrees it is best to start with thermodynamics. So I shall concentrate on the gases of the atmosphere and review the ideal gas laws first. Köppen stops me. Wouldn't it be better to have something a little less esoteric first, something to fire the imagination, something everyone can see? What about the 'educated layman'; wouldn't he be a little frightened by so much maths so soon? We think for a few seconds. What exactly is 'the atmosphere' anyway? asks Köppen; wouldn't it be a good idea to describe that first? So we list the different layers and discuss how best to describe them, and for a while we are sidetracked on to our favourite subject of boundary layers, before we come round again to the book.

I don't know when she comes in. But she does. She moves so quietly, so deftly, that I don't notice her entrance. There is no thud of books, no rustle of paper; even the pen on her page makes little sound. But then, just as I stare into mid-distance while I consider one of Köppen's questions, she is there. Her face is looking into mine, and in it I can still see the remnants of that same adulation I saw two years ago. I am embarrassed, of course, but also more than a little flattered. No one has ever looked at me like this before. She doesn't try to hide her eyes; instead she seems to relish their view. Maybe she is not aware that her face is so expressive, but I suspect that she is.

Köppen, of course, notices nothing. I suppose it is natural to him that his daughter should come in here to work alongside us. The fire is warm, and although we are not quiet, neither are we strident. The pages of her work book keep pace with ours.

Now at last we can consider the gases. We imagine molecules and atoms. We become so small that we are in among them. There is no attraction, we are free to move independently without effect. If we are squashed together we huddle, if we are heated our dances require a bigger space, but still we avoid the touch of each other. We are ideal gases. We are independent. We do not touch unless we can help it.

Else laughs. She shoves my arm and for a few seconds her hand stays there on my sleeve.

Köppen peers over his glasses. He looks at Else and then at me. I see him notice what I've noticed already: her seat is shoved close to mine so the legs interlock, her books are spread open at my feet, her elbow is so close I can feel its warmth on the back of my hand. Across his face flickers an expression of interest and then satisfaction.

'Have you finished your work now, Else? Maybe you'd like to see if your mother has received a letter from Aline.'

As she leaves the room he leans over to me. 'We are going to become grandparents very soon, it's most exciting.'

I want to hear more. This house holds more than the living. There are ghosts, children that command sighs and long silences; a happy ghost and an unhappy one. The happy ghost is Otto, buried among flowers, like Willy, at the cusp of young adulthood. Later I will hear of the night of cold poultices, of botched diagnoses, of regrets and a poisonous appendix. The unhappy ghost is Max, who haunts more vociferously because he is alive. That much I know. Max is seldom mentioned, but when he is, usually in a sentence that remains unfinished, it is clear that he is considered to be still among the living. I am intrigued but not intrigued enough to enquire and cause hurt. Then there is Aline, the older sister, a nervous, shy creature who shocked everybody one day by announcing her secret engagement and her imminent departure with her man. Still waters, says Köppen, smiling and tapping the side of his nose, still waters.

Then there are two others, who are strong and living here still; Else, the trainee schoolteacher, and Alexis, who is still a schoolboy. These are the children of his old age, he says, then, leaning towards me, he advises me that fertility is a product of an active mind, and that the two enhance each other, and to partake myself of both as soon as possible.

Now we talk about other molecules, molecules that tend to follow the herd. The talk on ideal gases was just a preamble to the discussion on the behaviour of these far more interesting molecules. Water molecules, for instance, like to keep company; squash these and they will clump together a little, taking up much less space than expected. Provide a piece of salt and they will throw themselves at it, one after the other until they have formed a minute droplet.

Else has come in again. She has given up her pretence of doing her own work and is listening intently.

Köppen sits back, folds his arms, and asks me whether I am going to go farther with this, am I going to describe the formation of snow and rain? I pause, stare into the distance, and again I am conscious of Else's eyes on mine. I struggle to concentrate. I have an idea but I am not sure I am ready to share it quite yet, much less commit it to paper. Köppen speaks into the silence:

'It seems to me,' he says, stroking his small white beard, 'that all rain must first of all start as ice.'

He thinks so too! I nod, vigorously, waiting for him to continue, but nothing comes. Now I can't stop myself. 'Yes, that's exactly what I think. Rain must start at the tops of clouds.'

Else opens her mouth then closes it again. She wants to know something. I tell her that nimbus clouds produce rain. I tell her about the nimbostratus clouds of the middle layers, how they look grey and ragged, how, from a distance, it is possible to see the rain falling continuously from their base. She nods. She looks happy. She creeps closer. Her hand rests upon my knee. I feel it there, its warmth, its heaviness. I fight the urge to move, to shake it away . . . and to clasp it in mine.

But Köppen wants to know the rest, and if he sees Else's hand he gives no indication. So we enter the clouds together. We climb to the top of the anvil-shaped cumulonimbus, where it is so cold that there are just minute ice crystals and minute droplets of super-cooled water, both of them swirling around, too small to fall. We become smaller still. We step on the surface of the ice and on to the surface of the water. We are not so small that we fall through, but we can see molecules of water holding hands beneath us. In the ice they are dancing a slow jig, barely moving, but in the water they move a little more, and from time to time one of them escapes into the air above. We watch one of these molecules as it is swept away, and follow it to see where it will go. For a time it vacillates, as if it is considering, but then, suddenly, it seems to be drawn towards the ice. As it approaches we can see why; there is a space waiting for it in the side of an ice crystal, and its insertion will complete the sixfold symmetry. Now, as if this one molecule has shown the way, others follow, surging from the water droplet on to the ice, and the ice grows until it is a massive flake, too large to be held. And, since we are now on this huge crystal of ice, we fall too. As we meet other molecules we fall faster, and soon we are falling through the cloud, falling through the place where all ice must turn to water, and we have become a raindrop, heavy, fat, part of a population of millions.

I stop. Köppen is leaning back in his chair, smiling, his eyes shut.

'You really are a remarkable young man,' he murmurs.

I enjoy his praise, but I don't know how to respond. 'Thank you' would seem a conceited agreement. Instead I say nothing and stroke the warm brown head that has now joined the hand on my lap.

15

I settled in Köppen's household in Hamburg like a heavy
stone, every day becoming a little heavier thanks to the
copious amounts of food that were piled upon my plate.
At every meal Else was at my elbow, watching my dish,
obviously anxious that it should be full and then equally
anxious that it should be empty at the end. Her fussing
amused me and everyone else. Alexis, in particular, seemed
highly entertained, lifting his head slightly to point out any
shortcoming at once before tucking his chin back into his
collar with a grin: pork served without the correct amount
of crackling; a potato that was slightly undercooked; a plate
that was not quite warm . . . Else rose to remedy each defect
until her mother told her to sit still.

Our parting was tearful, at least on her part. She promised
that she would write and waited until I promised to do the
same. For some time she held both my hands in hers and
looked sorrowfully into my face. When I tried to speak she
told me to hush, that she was concentrating on my eyes so
that she could remember them and bring them to her mind
every night before she slept. Since this seemed to require so
much effort I suggested that I would send her a photograph
of both eyes, together with the rest of my face, if, in return, she
would send me a photograph of hers. This prospect seemed to
please her so much that she gave a small delighted smile.

On the way to the station I promised Köppen I would keep
him updated on the book, and send him further parts to read.
He seemed pleased at the prospect. So I returned to Marburg
fat and happy. I had much to do: my report on the *Danmark*

expedition was unfinished, there were lectures and magazine articles to write, and now there was the book. Köppen had convinced me that I had something important to say and now I felt eager to start. I soon became absorbed. I forgot to sleep, forgot to eat and worked into the night, fuelled only by cigars and coffee. By December the manuscript was finished and I could send it to the publisher.

As soon as the parcel of paper had been sent I felt bereft; now that my days of frantic activity were over I had a void to fill before Christmas. I had already bought Else a present – the account of the *Danmark* expedition by my friend Friis – but now I thought I would send her something else as well, something Alexis in particular would also appreciate. I wrapped it most carefully in a crate, then an old photographic box, then in two more boxes. Each layer held a note: the outside one said 'Do not unwrap before Christmas'. This, I guessed, would ensure they would waste no time in opening it. The next layer had 'Caution – open only in subdued light', which I thought would ensure a pause or a little hesitation. Maybe they would wait until dark, but I doubted that. I guessed they'd move it to a windowless cupboard and continue their frantic unwrapping in there. The next box had 'Most important – keep horizontal' and was tightly sealed and impossible to open without tipping. The final note said 'Wait for Christmas!' There would, of course, be nothing else. I was poor and penniless, after all. The preparation of this parcel preoccupied me for several days, but after I had sent it I immediately started to worry that it would cause offence. A letter from Else quickly reassured me that the reverse was the case. She had, she said, cried with happiness, even Alexis had laughed out loud, and the real present had almost been a disappointment in comparison. I wrote back to say that I would ensure that all future presents would consist of old cases and sticky tape, and then I talked a little about Christmas presents in general, and how my colleague and next-door neighbour, Dr Emil Take, had received a very interesting book indeed.

Is there a moment in everyone's life which changes everything for ever? I am not talking about the numerous little beads that gently nudge a life along, but the brightest, biggest bead; the bead that causes the string to fold in two and the necklace to hang low in the nape of the neck. Beside it all the other beads seem puny and incompletely formed. This is my bead. The one that hangs round my neck like a heavy amulet.

Emil Take places his Christmas present on the table in front of me. The atlas hits the desk with a satisfying thud. Several students look around, and then return to their work.

Did the sun break through then? I think it did. The way I remember it, it was a dark winter day in January. No sun at all. And then, just as Emil opened the pages, there must have been a gap in the clouds, and there was a beam of light hitting the maps, making the colours bright.

'Look,' he says, just that. 'Look.'
    The pages are so new I can still smell the ink. As I turn I remember other maps: a map with crumpled mountains; a map that wasn't a map, just the land seen from far above; and then Koch's map, drawn quickly in the snow, replacing question marks and dashes with boundaries. The pages flutter open, one country following the next until the book lies open at the page where Emil has just been looking.

Emil had already told me that in this atlas the seas too had been given their own mountains and valleys.

The Atlantic Ocean. I can see all of it, from Iceland to the capes of Good Hope and Horn. My eye can leap across in an instant. To the east the fussy European coast, and the elegant curve of Africa. To the west more smooth curves, more juttings in and out.

Emil was especially interested in the shape of the continental shelves, how in some places they are narrow while in others they stretch out from the coast for miles. In fact, he said, if you consider that they are just a submerged part of the land, things look entirely different . . .

A pale blue indicates the shallow parts of the sea. It is possible to follow a new outline. To the east is the concave platform of the Gulf of Guinea and then, across the water, the convex shelf of Brazil. They seem so close. The slightest push would bring them together . . .

Emil said later that I became still. I kept looking and looking, my eyes moving back and forth again and again.

. . . where they would interlock, almost perfectly. As if they had once been joined and had somehow been pulled apart.

'Look,' I say to Emil, repeating his word back to him, 'it's a jigsaw, it's just one big jigsaw,' and he sits beside me watching my fingers.

That night I wrote to Köppen. I wanted to know whether he too had ever noticed this fitting together of the pieces. Maybe, I said, not just America and Africa had been joined, but all the continents had once been part of a huge supercontinent . . . then I stopped. The vision of a continent splitting apart, and then these two enormous fragments drifting away from each other over thousands of miles across the sea, suddenly seemed too fantastic. I put my pen down. I imagined Köppen's face. It looked puzzled and concerned. It was a ridiculous notion.

I decided to dismiss it from my mind. There was more important work to be done, after all; more proofs of my book had arrived that morning and I had not yet opened them. But the idea would not go away. I went to sleep with the shapes of the continents outlined in white on the blackness of my eyelids.

So my bead lay by the string, the hole through the middle incompletely bored, too crude yet to bother me. Besides, there were other beads, so many that I sometimes felt I was in danger of losing them. There were my lectures, requests came from all over Germany on a variety of topics, and then there were balloon flights, book proofs to correct, as well as some experimentation on the brightness of clouds. And then, one day, there was Koch, looking more like a Viking chief than ever.

How easy it was then to become something else; a meteorologist one day, talking about the air, and the next a glaciologist, talking about the ice. When things are new it is easy to find out all there is to know to become an expert. After a few hours together Koch and I decided we were expert glaciologists. A few hours later we decided we needed to record our expert knowledge in a substantial account for a Danish journal, and a few hours later still we decided that someone, an expert, obviously, needed to conduct another field trip to find out more.

'Tell me, Wegener, do you remember the Gnipa Cave?' Koch sits back. He is more than slightly flushed, but I think this has less to do with the warmth of this early spring day and more to do with the empty beer glass in his hand.

I smile. Of course I remember the Gnipa Cave. We have spent most of the afternoon considering how we will describe it in our paper.

'Do you remember the top, Wegener, do you remember what you asked?'

I lean forward, nodding. Is he going to say what I have been longing for him to say for so long?

'Well, I've been thinking. How does next year sound?'

He wants me to go with him back to Greenland.

'Wegener? I thought you'd be delighted.'

'I am, I am.' But I am not as joyful as I thought I would be. I have so much to do just now, I am feeling a little over-whelmed. The *Danmark* expedition is not fully written up yet, and the thermodynamics book is still not corrected, and the thought of not seeing Köppen or the rest of his household for so long is already making me feel a little bereft.

'Do you remember our plan? The one we made with Freuchen?'

That long polar night. The hours of dark. There was nothing to do sometimes but sit and talk and make plans. I think it was Freuchen who suggested that we overwinter on the ice sheet. Now Koch was proposing something else, something more interesting.

'We could cross from east to west,' he is saying, then he snorts a little. 'It would give us a reason to keep on going.'

I laugh too, a dry little laugh like Koch's. In contrast to the east coast, the west coast of Greenland is inhabited. If we crossed in this direction we would be lured forwards by the promise of human company.

'I would use ponies. I've used them on Iceland. They're very sturdy little animals. Better than dogs.'

A strange idea. I open my mouth to argue, but Koch continues.

'And I'd like to start on that odd piece of land you investigated, you know, that large nunatak, what was it called?'

'Dronning Louise Land?' I shut my eyes, remembering the way the ice finished in enormous cliffs, the way the land loomed up, sliced by valleys and frozen lakes. It was so unusual, so fascinating, and now I so much want to go back.

'Of course, that would mean we would be crossing at the widest part. But that in itself would be useful, I think, to a meteorologist?'

He stops. I open my eyes. He is looking at me, smiling. He knows me too well.

'Well, Wegener, what do you say? Lundager says he'd be interested, and I know an Icelandic farmer who is an expert with the ponies.'

'Lundager? The *Danmark* botanist?'

Koch nods. 'He sounds quite keen.'

'I don't know if I can raise the money,' I say.

'Oh, don't worry about that. I have some ideas.'

'But I must pay my way.'

Koch tuts, looks at my face then shrugs. 'If you must.'

'Yes. Otherwise I couldn't go.'

'You've changed, my boy.'

Had I changed? I suppose I had. After I had said goodbye to Koch I began to wonder. Maybe I had become more contemplative, more anxious to do well and settle down. As my father reminded me on my infrequent visits to Berlin, I had no secure work, no real home. Everything in my life was still uncertain. I was too much like my brother and sister, he said. It was his favourite subject and he could go on for hours at a time. None of us had settled down: there was Kurt in Samoa (why Samoa? he asked, but he didn't really want to know), and Tony still unmarried, claiming to be an artist, and now me, living this precarious life as a private lecturer, never knowing where the next mark would come from. Why couldn't any of us find normal things to do?

Köppen added his voice to my father's. He too seemed to think that it was important I have a reliable income. Recently he had been hinting that there might be work for me in Hamburg, maybe something permanent, soon.

And then there was Else. Ah yes, Else, the little mouthpiece. Since February, when she had taken her final teaching exam, she had had nothing much to do. As a consequence her letters to me had become longer and more frequent. I had come to expect them, even look forward to them, and of course it had been only polite to write back. When I told her about my balloon journeys and my passengers she asked whether she could come too. When I told her it cost a hundred marks she sent her booking and cheque by return of post. When the journey was set for Whitsun she wrote excitedly, one letter after the other: How far would we go? How high? Would I take readings? Could she make some? Should we have a picnic? Who were the other passengers? The other passengers were a man and his wife, and when the wife was taken ill they cancelled. I knew Else would be devastated. It seemed too cold just to write, so I made the journey to Hamburg to break it to her in person.

When I get up to go it is Frau Köppen who says I am to stay. Everyone seems happy that I am here, especially Köppen. It seems that we are merely resuming the conversation we had just an hour ago rather than taking up the subject of our last correspondence. But after dinner his behaviour is odd. He does not lead me to our normal place by his desk. Instead he suggests that Else and I might like to take a walk. It is such a balmy night, he says, the result probably of a high-pressure system establishing itself over central Europe. Everyone nods solemnly in agreement, except for Alexis, who appears to be sneezing as he leaves the room. So Frau Köppen fetches Else's shawl and we begin our walk through the Hamburg suburb of Grossborstel.

The moon is bright, Else keeps saying, so bright it is almost like day. I tell her that in Greenland I used to long for the moon. Tell me about it, she says, linking my arm with hers. So I do. I tell her everything. I tell her more than I have told anyone else in my life before. I can't seem to find the will to stop, it is too easy to keep going. And Else listens. Like her father, she listens. I tell her too much. I tell her about my expedition with Koch. And when I tell her it seems that I have already decided to go, that there is no uncertainty. I tell her about the ponies and the distance and what I expect to see. And when I have finished we are back in their garden, and she leads me to a seat. I can see her face clearly, a pale oval in the moonlight. For a time she seems to be thinking, but then she speaks and her voice sounds so small and frightened that I want to hold her.

'But you must go,' she says, as if she knows my doubts. 'I shall hate it, but you must go.' Her face dips and disappears. I want it to return. My hand reaches forward and gently lifts her chin. It shifts under my hand as she speaks.

'It would be quite wrong of me to stop you, but remember this . . .'

Her head twists slightly so my hand drops away. When her voice returns it is determined and strong. 'I shall count each day until you are back.'

Now she rises, suddenly. I grab her arm. She doesn't try to pull it away. When I draw her back towards me she comes easily. I can feel the warmth of her, the softness of her, the smallness of her back, and I can smell the peppery scent of her skin. Now her moonlit oval is close to mine. The features are fuzzy, too close to be in focus. I pull her closer still. I pull her so close that our faces meet.

16

Else often says she would like to have 1911 again. She says she didn't relish it enough the first time. Next time she has 1911, she says, she will look more at everything else, not just at me.

I decided at Grossborstel that night that since Else was so adamant that she would be waiting for me, for ever, if necessary, the obvious thing to do would be to ask her to marry me. I think I can confidently say that the Köppen household was delighted. At Whitsun I asked her to come with me to Zechlinerhütte; I was anxious that my parents appreciate this first sign that one of their children was perhaps going to settle down into domesticity.

Else is talking, all the time talking. She is really rather like an excited child; exclaiming at the view outside the train one minute, commenting on our other passengers the next in a voice that is scarcely quieter. I can see that Kurt is bemused. He is looking from my face to hers. This is my nineteen-year-old bride-to-be and she is noisy. Maybe he is wondering how I can stand all this chatter. Maybe he is wondering whether it will last. But now she has asked him a question and it is his turn to speak. He is telling her about Samoa, and at once she has become the thoughtful, listening Else, and it is my turn to look at him.

Kurt looks tired; underneath the intensity of his tan there is a bloodless pallor. When he reaches into his jacket to find his ticket the hand that is withdrawn shakes and fumbles with the fastening on his wallet. He can't be nervous, not of Else. Outside the train the familiar view rolls out before us: tenement housing giving way to suburbs and suburbs to the weekend chalets of the more wealthy Berliners. Soon we are in the country and there are fields and woods and sandy banks. Else settles beside me. Even though our seat is wide and there is plenty of room, she tucks herself close by me so I can feel her leg through her skirt and my trousers. From time to time she allows her head to rest on my shoulder, as though listening to Kurt is tiring work. As he describes the difficulties of working in such a warm climate, his problems with the bureaucrats and workers and the tedium of his journey home, I have to fight to keep my eyes open. It is such a warm day.

I am disturbed from my doze by Else. 'Look,' she says, 'water.'

It is a sign we have almost reached Rheinsberg: a lake that looks like a sea, complete with beaches and boats. We dive into woods again and pass through small villages. Else remarks that everyone here seems to be on holiday. I look and see it through her eyes; the tents, the men and boys in shorts and long socks and the women in light cotton dresses. They smile at the train and wave. We wave back.

'I'm so happy,' Else whispers to me, squeezing my arm. 'Aren't you?'

Tony is waiting for us at the station with a car. After greeting us, she and Else eye each other for a few seconds and I am startled at the contrast. Tony seems so old now; her hair is grey and she has cut it very short, almost as short as a man's, and her face seems to have withered into an expression of pure bitterness. Else ends the silence with a laugh and chatter which only Kurt and I join. As we drive through the wide cobbled streets of Rheinsberg and into more woods, Tony speaks little and gradually we all become quiet. Beside me I feel Else pull herself close to my arm and stiffen. She has seen the sign for Zechlinerhütte.

As Tony draws up outside the old house I feel quite proud

of the place: around the entrance the rose is in flower and the sun is lighting the lake, making it shine through the trees. As we step out, I smell lilac and hear the gossip of ducks on the water.

'Oh, Alfred, you didn't tell me, it's so pretty,'

Tony frowns and swats away mosquitoes, while Kurt fusses at the boot, sighing when it won't open. Impatiently Tony tuts, nudges him out of the way and then opens it for him. When Else steps forward to help, Tony tells her gruffly not to bother. Else's head bows. I put my arm around her shoulder. This is not a good start.

'How's the painting going?' I ask Tony.

But she doesn't have time to reply. With cries of greeting my father and then my mother are hurrying from the house, and soon they are taking Else from me with hugs and handshakes.

After Tony has refused her help three times, Else sits. My mother is busy with the maid in the kitchen and Tony's job is to bring in the dishes, one after the other. She brings in each one with a sigh, and, with each sigh, Else stiffens.

'She hates me,' Else says, when I take her to watch the deer feeding at the edge of the lake.

'No she doesn't.' But my words do not convince even myself.

'Why does she not talk, then? Why does she turn away every time I approach?'

'It's difficult for her.'

'Why?'

'I suppose because you are young and happy and she is neither.'

'Has she never been loved?'

'Only by us.'

Else is silent then. I lead her on to the boat and row her across to where there is a small wooded island, and still she does not talk. Only when we are lying on its sandy bank does she roll over to me and rest her head on my chest.

Ah, the warm parts of Else. How I wish I could feel them now.

She props herself up on her elbow, looks at my face, traces a finger around each of my eyes and then down the length of my nose. No one has ever owned me like this. I don't ever remember feeling quite so warm, quite so happy. I reach up, feel the springiness of her hair, pull at the clips that hold handfuls of curls to her head.

We were quite alone then, young, at least one of us impassioned. What was it that held us apart?

Her elbow gives. I feel . . . what? That triangle of soft flesh? An overwhelming urge to pull her closer to me? But she draws away, restores her prop, smiles at me, wipes her forehead with the back of her hand. Her lips, now that they are shaded, are the colour of plums. When they move it takes me a second to understand what they say.

'Do you think I could ever make her like me?'

Do I frown? In spite of the sun I feel than a shadow has passed over me and I am suddenly cold.

Tony. She's still thinking about Tony. Never has my sister been such a source of irritation.

'Well, do you think I could?'

'No.'

She cuffs me on my arm.

'Well, I've never found a way,' I say, and rub pointedly at where she has struck, as if I am hurt.

For the next few days Tony became Else's preoccupation. She paid her compliments, she did her little favours, she even gave her presents, but Tony seemed to ignore each overture.

It is time to go. My mother and father stand together by their door, framed in flowers. They exchange happy smiles with Kurt, with me, with Else. But there is no sign of Tony and Kurt is becoming restless.

'We're going to miss it,' he says, 'and there won't be another for an hour.'

From the back of the house our driver emerges. She is carrying a small package, wrapped in brown paper.

'For you,' she says to Else, and thrusts it into her arms.

On the train back to Berlin we unwrap it. It is a small pen-and-ink sketch of Else standing beneath a tree. In the picture she has a slight coy smile; a contrast to the smug grin she is bestowing on me now.

I resumed my work. This time my lecture course was about the optical appearances of the atmosphere, and it drew quite a substantial crowd for such a small university. Even other members of staff attended, attracted, I think, by my photographs and illustrations from the *Danmark* expedition.

The Inuit would say that this halo is the moon's hood. He has drawn it around himself in grief because he mourns his own kind; somewhere a male child has died or a girl child has been born. He greets each of these calamities by drawing away in the night. But I would say that the moon wears not a hood but a veil, and that this faint white ring that surrounds him is a gauze of delicate ice crystals. When the moon shines his covering shimmers; each unique crystal bending his light to form a tiny rainbow, each rainbow merging together again to form a hazy circle of light. If the crystals are flat, the ring will be broad, if the crystals are longer, more like flat-ended prisms, then the ring will be tighter, drawn more closely around the moon's head. Perhaps not a single male death, but the birth of twin girls, two rosy faces in their mother's arms.

But when the sun rises she will celebrate: two new sisters! As her brother the moon fades away from the sky she will search for her earrings. Such strange earrings, like small versions of herself, one either side of her face. My audience nod and murmur their appreciation. Sometimes they are called sun dogs or mock suns, but I prefer to give them a more beautiful name: parhelia. As with the halo there must be a translucent cloud of ice, but here the crystals are falling, slowly, their large flat surfaces facing groundwards. They bend the sunlight in the same direction, concentrating it into two bright spots, moving as the sun moves, until she becomes tired of celebrating and sheds them.

The final photographs showed mirages. It surprised my audience, I think, to discover that it is possible to have mirages in the cold as well as in the heat. But all that is necessary for a mirage is for the light to bend through air of different temperatures. At the poles the air near the frozen ground is often colder than the air above, and light travelling through this lower air slows and is bent downwards. The eye sees light that is coming down and so follows the image back up to its apparent source: a hill becomes a mountain, a dog a monster, an Inuit child a giant. 'Fata Morgana,' I told them, rolling the words on my tongue. Do you remember Morgana, the witch-like sister of the English king Arthur? She too could conjure up castles from empty air.

The images seemed to haunt everyone, even the non-specialists. I used them to illustrate my book *The Thermodynamics of the Atmosphere*, which was reviewed very positively, except by one. Unfortunately that one was Professor Exner from Vienna.

Ha, Professor Exner: how different things would have been

if he had welcomed my book along with everyone else. How I raged, how I spluttered; he seemed to be missing the point of my book with a wilful obstinacy. But there was nothing I could do. His one critical review caused my career in meteorology to stall, and because it stalled I suppose I felt more at liberty to look around me, to let my mind creep elsewhere.

The library is empty. Since I have a little time to spare this afternoon I have not gone directly to the shelves on astronomy but am lingering by the shelves on other disciplines along the way. I am inspecting titles and dates, feeling slightly decadent and also furtive. This is not my realm. I should not be here. My finger runs along the spines of the books. It stops. One book is sticking out more than the rest; it is a pleasing dark maroon. I try to shove it back into line, but it won't go. It seems to be a little too big to fit in with the rest. I smile; maybe it is a self-important book, and this is just a ploy it has to get itself read. I remove it from the shelf and inspect the contents. It seems to be a compendium on fossils. Not very interesting after all. I am just going to put it back into its space on the shelf when I notice the two words 'Africa' and 'Brazil' close together again and again. Then the words 'land bridge'. This could be interesting after all. I take the book to an adjacent desk. It is just a list of fossils from Brazil and Africa. Africa and Brazil. A continent and a country. The pairing sounds strangely familiar.

   The fossils are the same age and identical and yet they come from either side of an ocean. Why are they the same? Brazil and Africa. There is something I should remember. Maybe the book will tell me. But it does not. Instead it tells me something that I know quite instinctively must be wrong. When these animals lived, it says, there was a gigantic bridge of land joining the two areas. I shake my head. There is another explanation, fuzzy and unformed in the back of my mind, but I can't reach it yet. I flick backwards and forwards in the book trying to find out more. I pull out the work book I always keep in my pocket and start to make notes: in order to pull something apart it is always best to know how it is sewn together.

The land bridge sank under the ocean after the fossils were formed. There was one underneath the North Atlantic, and this, says the revered Austrian geologist Suess, is the origin of the story of Atlantis, and so Atlantis is what he calls this ancient vast tract of land. He also identifies one farther south, the supercontinent he calls Gondwanaland, which encompasses Argentina, the South Atlantic Ocean, parts of Africa, Arabia and India. This is really an enormous supercontinent encompassing a third of the globe.

I stop. My pen blots the page. I watch the ink spreading through the paper. I shut my eyes. There is another way to form a supercontinent. Behind my eyelids the white outlines of the continents slide together to form one unbroken jigsaw. This idea of land bridges is an unnecessary complication. It is much simpler just to assume that the land masses have moved. It explains the fossil similarities just as well. I know it is right.

Who is it that threads the beads upon this string of my life? As I sat in the library that autumnal day this necklace-maker was busy. He licked the end of the string, drew it into a point and began to direct the spittle-stiffened cord into the bore of the bead that was waiting.

My pen continues below the blot. I make numbered points under the words 'Sinking Land Bridge Theory'.

1. The land bridges sank because the earth is shrinking.
2. The earth is shrinking because it is cooling down.

Now I need to explain each of these in turn. In the beginning the earth was a molten ball. Once it was left to its own devices, spinning at a regular distance from the sun, it began to cool. As it cooled it began to settle out. Suess's earth now formed three layers, a little like those in an apple: there was a spherical core, then around this the flesh, which he calls the 'sima', and then the apple skin, the 'sal' (but which I prefer to call the 'sial'). This much I have no argument with, it is what comes next that to me seems wrong; Suess assumes the earth kept cooling, and so, like an apple kept too long in the cold, it began to shrivel. As the flesh shrank the skin formed ruckles and dips on the surface. These ruckles, Suess says, are mountain chains and the dips are the land bridges falling below the surface of the ocean.

I look up. The library is still empty, but outside it is becoming dark. I look at my watch. I have been here for two hours. But I can't stop now. Underneath my notes I draw a line and then underneath that write 'Arguments Against'. It is easy. Again a series of points.

1. The earth is not cooling down any more.

2. Since it is not cooling down it can't be contracting.

3. Since it is not contracting there can have been no sinking land bridges.

The Curies and Becquerel have demolished the cooling earth theory quite categorically with their measurements of radiogenic heat; even if the earth contains just a small amount of radioactive material it would be enough to ensure that it stays warm. Of course, it is easy to forgive Suess for not mentioning radioactivity; radioactivity is a new discovery and he is an old man. The rest of what he says is true, and serves to support my modern jigsaw theory just as effectively as his outmoded theory of contraction.

I put down my pen. It is quite dark. Someone has lit the lamps and there is a comfortable warm glow.

Now I needed to develop my theory further. I began with Suess's idea of the structure of the earth consisting of the flesh of sima and the skin of sial. Like Suess I considered that the sial floated on the sima, but, unlike Suess's, my sial did not stretch over the entire planet's surface. Instead it was clumped up into continental islands, the space in between being the oceanic basins of exposed sima. The sialic continents floated on the sima like icebergs, and like icebergs they could break up, move, and when they collided could gradually be squeezed into great mounds or mountain ranges. Like icebergs these mountains had 'roots', a hidden subterranean depth of sial extending as far down into the sima as the root of an iceberg descends into the sea. The geophysicists already had a word to describe how icebergs of various heights float in the sea, a certain visible fraction always betraying the hidden portion beneath: 'isostasy'. It is an obvious thing, a child observing different sizes of ice floating in a bowl can see it; for each portion of ice visible above the water there is a bigger portion beneath.

In my mind I travel to places I have never seen, to times I have never known. I creep in amongst a party of British surveyors taking gravimetric readings on the Ganges plain at Kaliana. Beside them is the start of the Himalayan massif. All they have is a piece of lead at the end of a string, but with this they are going to find out something astonishing. They look at the mountains and allow the string to dangle. Such a large mountain! They expect the lead to be attracted by such a massive amount of rock; it should not fall vertically downwards but should swing a little towards the mountain. But it does not, at least not as much as they expect. It is as if the mountain is hollow. They look at each other and try again. Like Koch and I on Sabine Island they ask each other to check. But the mountain remains apparently hollow. Now I move among them but they cannot see me. I am not of their time. They stand quite still, staring at the swinging lead and the mountain. I whisper the answer but they cannot hear. Airy, the Astronomer Royal, will tell them the answer soon:

the rock of the mountain is like an iceberg floating on the denser rock of the mantle. Its low density ensures that the plumb line is little affected. Isostasy, I whisper, but it is a word no one yet knows. Isostasy: it sounds a little like the wind shaking up dry leaves.

Now I travel to where there are geologists mapping the Alps. In Berlin my brothers and sisters are quarrelling over toys but I am as yet two pieces, unjoined, waiting for my moment to be. The geologists have found places where the rock has been folded into great waves. A five-mile length has been squeezed so that it now fits into a space just one mile long. The geologists sit down, just as I sat down next to Kurt in Austria, and look at the great contortions before them. If the earth has shrunk, how can it have shrunk so much? There is a fold before them, quite obvious on this side of the slope. Is it really possible the earth was once five times as big? No, I tell them, but they can't hear. There is no need for the earth to have shrunk. Instead the continents have jostled for position. They have pushed together and rifted apart. Where they have pushed they have squeezed the surface sediments into folds and nappes. One of the men rises, then stoops to hack out part of the rock beneath him. Listen to me, I tell him, but his tapping is too loud. Is it not obvious that these folds are the result of two great forces, one against the other? But he just shrugs and concentrates on extracting the small things he will have to look through a microscope to see: minute molluscs that have been stretched on the outside curves of folds, and crystals that have fractured under pressure.

I couldn't sleep. Every night I thought of new ideas and new evidence. I practised ways of telling, ways of agreeing and disagreeing. The geophysicists were right: the continents were permanent but they were not static, they could shift position. The geologists too were right: the supercontinents had become divided, not by the land sinking but by it moving thousands of miles. It was obvious. I was sure that it would satisfy everyone. They would all sigh in realisation. At last a theory that explained everything. I couldn't see how anyone could disagree. So, four months after I first came across the compendium of fossils in the library, I persuaded the chairman of the newly formed Geological Association to allow me to give my first address on the subject in Frankfurt am Main.

Ha. This younger edition of me. Is there anything much to admire? Already he thinks he knows all there is to know. He is fearless for the worst of reasons. He thinks his bead is so fine, so strong. If only he would wait. If only I could stop him and make him look, but I know he wouldn't listen. The bead, I would tell him, is still unfinished. But he opens his mouth. He speaks and he expects the world to listen. A young man before a room full of experts. For unlike meteorology this is not a young science. The experts in this room have earned their position through years of study of received wisdom. So they distrust insight. And they distrust youth. And they hate change.

It is the usual sort of auditorium; a lectern, a blackboard, and in front of me a sloping floor of seats. It is well attended, as if they know they are about to hear something important. They receive me warmly, smiling and clapping after I am introduced, and when I start to speak it is obvious that most of them are listening: a middle-aged man at the back sits forward on his chair; in the middle a group of young women make notes; and at the front an elderly man cups his face in his hand, his eyes fixed on my face. While I recount the fossil evidence he remains benign, and even nods a little. It is only when I start to explain the idea of isostasy that his stare becomes less friendly.

*   *   *

How does a gaze change into a glare? Is it just the eyes becoming set, the eyelids motionless? Or is it the forehead becoming paralysed into a frown, or the mouth becoming taut, or the teeth clenching together? In that first audience of geologists I saw all of these changes. The middle-aged man at the back sighed and then drummed his fingers, the older man at the front glared, while the women in the middle exchanged glances, and began to whisper, threading their words through gaps in my own.

The unrest disturbed me. I began to talk more quickly. I decided to abandon some of what I was going to say and left some of my diagrams in my files. While the women's chatter increased the men's silence seemed like something clenched.

At last I stopped. There was a couple of seconds' silence and then the middle-aged man began a question: 'Did I then refute the conclusions of Suess's recent masterpiece . . . ?'

At once I nodded, anxious to respond, but my words were submerged. A wave of sound swept from the back of the auditorium, everyone talking at once. The middle-aged man protested loudly from the back, the young women huddled together, and the old man at the front stood up and glared at the audience until it was again quiet. Then he turned again in order to switch his glare to me. 'This balderdash,' he said, spitting out the words as if they were sour, 'does not deserve the dignity of rhetoric.' Then, removing his hat and cane from an adjacent seat, he walked stiffly from the auditorium, slamming the door behind him.

I spoke quickly into the silence that followed. 'I am sure that if Suess had been able to consider radioactivity . . .' but I was not allowed to finish. The middle-aged man at the back stood up. 'I think, Dr Wegener, we have all heard enough about your moving continents for now.'

'And for ever more,' someone at the front whispered loudly, and the young women giggled.

'Don't you see,' I said, my voice becoming a little higher,

'it's the only possible explanation. How else can we explain the distribution of the fossils, the geophysical evidence, the folding of the Alps? I know I have to do a little more work on some of the details, but surely the concept deserves your serious consideration?'

'Dr Wegener, I'm afraid I'm going to have to ask you to finish just there,' the middle-aged man said. 'I'm sure everyone will think very carefully about what you've said.' He spoke as though talking to a wilful child. After pointedly brief applause the meeting was declared closed.

My reception at Marburg four days later was kinder but just as contentious. I was astonished. There seemed to be no one that was happy to learn the truth.

Köppen glances from my face to Else's as he speaks. 'It is always better to stick with what you know,' he says.

'But I do know.'

'Not enough.' He pauses to look at me full in the face. 'Isn't there enough to do in meteorology? Why not concentrate your skills in one place, where they are needed the most?'

'I can do that too, later.'

'You are damaging yourself, your reputation, your career, your future.'

I want to stand to add force to my words. I begin to rise, but Else's hand on my arm clenches in warning.

'But this theory is important.'

Why can't anyone see?

'It answers so much, Köppen.' I try to speak evenly and quietly. 'It doesn't make sense to stick to the old theory when there is something so much simpler that works so much better.' He is listening again. I take heart. 'The old theory of sinking land bridges, it must be overturned. It is just a matter of time. How can the rock of continents sink below the oceans when it is composed of materials so much lighter? Why should it be able to float during one epoch but then sink during the next?'

Köppen is stroking his beard. A good sign.

'I am right, Köppen. Another ten years and everyone will see.'

Ha, such arrogance. And such certainty. Why does Köppen continue to stand there listening to such pomposity?

Else glances hurriedly at her father and then at me. 'Is there much to do before Professor Langham has his paper?' she asks.

'You're not publishing all this?'

'I'm bequeathing it, in three parts.'

Else is squeezing my arm. 'He has to, Father. Because of Greenland. Just in case. Nothing will happen, I'm sure, but . . .'

'So you've decided to go after all?' He sits and allows his head to sink. 'It's all madness. You're almost a married man.'

Why is he doubting me so much? 'I can't believe you think we won't make it!' There is Else's hand again, but it fails to calm me this time. 'I can't understand your pessimism. Do you have no faith in me at all? We can't afford to even think like that. We will keep going. We have to. We can't afford to consider any other possibility.'

There is a silence where there has never been one before. Else's hand has left my arm. Am I deserting both of them? But now going again to Greenland seems the only sensible thing to do.

Koch had managed to raise enough money for a departure in June. There was just enough time to put everything in order at the university and for me to take Else for her much-anticipated balloon flight.

*　　*　　*

Tony stands erect and a little stiff. It was Else's idea to insist that she come, and now Tony clutches on to the ropes with such an expression of extreme forbearance that there is something in me that wants to laugh out loud. She is wearing a hat chosen for her by Else, and its frivolous decoration of pale flowers emphasises the funereal black of the rest of her dress. Else in contrast is dressed in pale coloured cotton for this perfect day of summer. She holds on to the basket rim, but not tightly, and she watches everything that is going on with interest. Kurt and I are taking it in turns to command; his presence was Else's idea too. Now she turns round to smile at everyone, captures each face one by one, and they grin back, even Tony, with a reflected radiance.

We rise quickly, passing birds and scraps of cloud, into quiet. Tony continues to grip, smiles grimly at Else whenever she asks a question, and looks steadily beyond her. It is a stance I've seen before, a paralysis brought on by terror. Else, however, leans so far over the side I have to warn her to be careful. She exclaims so frequently about the peace and quiet that I feel obliged to comment on her noise. She giggles. I smile back. Kurt has the aloofness of Tony. They both stand with the resignation of pillars.

At twelve o'clock Else announces that she is hungry and pulls up parcels of food she has stored in one of the basket containers woven into the side.

'Ham,' she says. 'Anyone care for some ham?'

Parcel after parcel appears until I am surprised that we managed to take off at all. Soon we each have a seat at the corners of the basket, eating whatever Else shoves into our hands. There is little sound. From time to time a church bell chimes faintly to tell us we are passing over people, but mostly there is nothing. The air is cool, a pleasant antidote to the sun which has shone down on us all day without respite.

'I can smell the sea!' Else exclaims, and tips the basket to look.

Beyond the green strips of field there is the line of a pale yellow beach cutting abruptly across. Bordering this is the white line of the surf. As usual it seems still, just another line.

'Why can't we see it move?' Else asks, leaning again over the side.

'Too far away,' Kurt says. He is scrutinising the ground, looking for a place to land. He takes us in smoothly, low over an avenue of trees so that Else whoops in mock fear, and then skirts a telegraph wire. The meadow is flat, without even a mole hill. Tony sways, grips tighter and then stands rigid. When I gesture for her to bend her knees with the rest of us she does so, tentatively. Kurt throws over the trail rope and then the grapnel. There is the slightest of jolts and we are down.

Else and I clap and cheer our pilot, then, after stinging me by giving Kurt a light kiss on his cheek, she scrambles on to her seat and then up over the side. While Else jumps and whoops at the solidity of the field, Tony doesn't move. She continues just to stand and blink. I hold out my hand to her so she can climb up on to the seat.

'Are you glad you came?' I ask as she moves cautiously forward.

'It makes a change.' Her careful neutral voice, giving nothing away.

After saying goodbye to Kurt and Tony in a beer cellar in Bremen, Else and I made our way to Hamburg. It was there that I first began to taste the responses of the world to my drift theory. Semper's was particularly acidic: he advised me not to honour geology with my presence any longer, but to go and make trouble in some other unsuspecting and innocent discipline.

The peace of Greenland seemed more attractive than ever.

17

Copenhagen. It has everything I hate in a city: a sprawl of tenements, life teeming beside them, and a flatness I find particularly depressing. It purports to have beaches and even a sea, but it has nothing of the kind. It is beside the lake of the Baltic: no waves, little tide, neatly ordered parks beside the jetties, and boats. No sense of wilderness, no grandiose storms. Everything is quiet and tidy. Even the division between land and sea is tidy; a line of sandiness of uniform width as if it has been regulated by some mighty bureaucratic hand. There is nothing to recommend Copenhagen, and yet the thought of the place causes me to catch my breath and stop. Copenhagen is the start and end of adventure. A place where dreams begin.

Else has resigned from her teaching post. After just a year she has become restless. If her sister Aline can travel, she says, so can she. She wants to see the world a little, while she can, she says, looking at me, and has some vague idea that she would like to visit Scandinavia. So she has come with me to Copenhagen. Prim, little, standing beside the *Godthaab* with a clipboard, she checks everything on and off. Nothing passes by her. She is quite unafraid to stop anyone, to demand that crates be opened and checked. She taps the side of the pemmican cans to see whether they're full, dips her hand into the cereal to test for dampness, sniffs at the pony's fodder, and demands that petrol canisters be weighed and labelled. No one complains. But I can see that Koch is amused by her, asks her questions he knows she will answer rather too fully, and then strokes his beard to cover his smile as she answers. When he compliments her on her efficiency she smiles and stretches her neck a little so her chin juts out, then turns quickly away as if there is no time to lose.

Else was right, as she's always right – there was no time to lose. We were due to sail on the first day of June and our cargo had to be ready. We packed everything in horse-loads so that they would be ready to transport when we arrived in Iceland. Iceland was another of Koch's ideas: it was to be a practice ground, where we could experiment driving the ponies. Koch insisted that we practise everything: in a field outside Copenhagen we even practised building our hut.

'Well, gentlemen, I think we can perform this task in four hours. What do you say?'

Koch loves to challenge us. Lundager and I look at the pile of wooden boards before us. On one side of each board there is a painted number, and this number corresponds to a wall or a roof or a floor in the diagram in front of us. The diagram is on a large piece of draughtman's paper held down on the grass by a pebble at each corner. I try to imagine this same piece of paper in Greenland. There will be no grass there, just the bare rock of Dronning Louise Land.

'Four hours?' says Lundager. 'I think we can be a little quicker than that.' He grins quickly at me and advances to the topmost board. Lundager is forty-four years old, but moves like someone at least twenty years older. Every step is measured, every hand gesture a deliberate movement thought out in advance.

'Trivial, don't you think?' He smiles at me again, then notices a flower trapped beneath the board. He shifts it gently so that it springs free, then slowly stoops to stroke its petals.

'Ready, gentlemen?' Koch says loudly as if to rouse us. He is looking at his watch.

'And waiting,' I say. I am impatient to start. Impatient to see how it will look, how we are to live.

'Go.'

We work without stopping. At first our roles are differentiated: I am the board-shifter, walking them over from the pile on the ground according to Koch's instructions, while Lundager holds them in place and Koch hammers. Soon we take over each other's tasks: I shift and hammer, Lundager holds and barks out instructions, and Koch hammers and holds and stands back and examines the plan and smiles.

When Koch announces the four-hour deadline we all stop and stand back to admire our progress. We are not alone. Frau Koch and Else have arrived together by car, and behind them have come a group of loud journalists. One of them has set up a small easel and is drawing furiously. I stand behind him to see what he sees. There is the blank-faced hut, its roof rising to a shallow apex, two small windows centrally placed, and on the other side a narrow door.

Now Frau Koch passes in front of us with a bottle of cheap wine.

'Is it time?' she demands of her husband, brandishing the bottle a little in the air. She has a sharp, slightly strident voice that causes everyone to stop and look.

'Yes, it is time,' Koch says slowly and a little dramatically. He looks around at the small collection of people, checking that they are paying attention.

Unexpectedly Frau Koch giggles. It is loud and breathless and, like most giggles, infectious. The journalists smile.

'I've been so looking forward to this. Where shall I smash it? Just here? Or here?'

Koch directs her with his arm.

'And what are we calling it? Have we decided? I need to have a name, Johan.'

Koch leans forward and whispers something in her ear.

She giggles again and, as if in reply, someone giggles back. I think it is Else. It is stifled quickly.

'Shall I start, then? Is that all right? Shall I stand here? Can you see me?'

Koch steers her into position, moves in among the audience, ensuring we can all see, then nods to his wife.

She seems suddenly overcome with embarrassment. She smashes the bottle against the wall a little too violently and then her words come out suddenly, joined together as if the sentence is just one word.

'I-name-this-hut . . . Is that what it's called, Johan? A hut?' Another giggle and then, 'I name this hut . . . "Borg". I hope it will prove to be a warm and safe dwelling and . . .' Now her voice becomes more quiet and slow. '. . . our men come back to tell us so.'

Everyone is quiet now. The sound of the artist's charcoal can be heard clearly rasping on the paper. Frau Koch giggles again, but now it seems a deliberate, determined sort of sound.

'Can we go in now, Johan? I promised Else that we could. Is it safe? It won't collapse, will it?'

Koch motions Else forward. She comes a little uncertainly and stands next to me. I put my arm on her shoulder and nudge her towards the door. She moves so slowly that my hand sinks down her arm and is soon around her. She leans slightly towards me but then leaves me again as we separate to go through the door. It is dark and warm inside the hut. I can smell the resin of the wood and the tang of turpentine. It seems quite large, but then it is unfurnished and the interior walls are missing. Koch points out how it will be. His arms describe shapes in the shadows. Just here will be the stables, a large space, enough for about six horses.

Else murmurs a sigh, and loops her arm through mine. She looks at the place where the stove will be as though it is already there.

'It is of military construction, the doors seal hermetically. Probably the best house ever constructed for an arctic expedition.'

Now she looks at Koch, a look of utter trust, and then squeezes my arm.

'It's good, isn't it, Alfred? You're going to be all right?' And then she waits for me to agree, but I don't. How can I know? How can I lie? How can I give her false assurances?

So we walk onwards, through the space for the stores and then out to where the journalists are waiting. The artist begs us to stand still, just for a minute, while the rest ask questions: When do we depart? What do we hope to achieve? How long do we expect to be away? Is it true we shall be using ponies? And as Koch answers I can feel Else becoming smaller by my side, as if by hiding she will no longer hear.

Before we left I gave her errands. It seemed the best thing to do. She seemed to enjoy being part of the process of preparation, and when she was busy she seemed more cheerful and less anxious. I was soon reminded she was her father's daughter. She seemed to understand immediately the importance of contacting Kurt at Spitzbergen, and even became excited with me as I pointed out that Kurt and I would be seeing the same northern lights but hundreds of miles apart. She said she would watch too. How? I asked, and she smiled and said she had been waiting to tell me. I was not the only traveller; her father had secured her a place as a German teacher to the family of a meteorological acquaintance in Christiana. Then she made me promise that when I saw the lights I would think at least a little of her as well as Kurt, and I assured her that I would. Then she said that when she saw them I would be all that she thought of: my eyes, my face, my nose, my arms, my legs . . . and then her voice faded. So I turned to my diary again and started to read out the dates to cover her embarrassment, but then my voice faded too and it was some time before either of us dared speak again.

The *Godthaab* is just one of the larger ships anchored alongside the canal. There is a pleasing array of masts, stretching down the dockside, each one threaded through with lines at an identical slant, like the components of some gigantic loom. Usually it is quiet here, but now there is a complicated mixture of sound: clanging, many people talking, crying and shouting, the roar of engines and horns, hooves clipping paving, and above it all Else's voice, saying something I can't hear. Her mouth is opening and shutting, and when I bend down I can feel her breath warming my ear. But I can only catch single words: 'miss', 'write', 'wait', 'love'. I shake my head. It's no good, I mouth back, then shout, 'I have to go,' and point to the *Godthaab*.

Now Else looks up, her eyes searching mine. A sudden movement behind her presses her into my chest, but still she keeps her eyes on my face. There is another shove and her hands flail out, meet behind me, and squeeze so tightly that I think she might hurt herself on the fastening of my bag. There is no time for this. I dislodge her gently and shout that the rest of the crew are aboard and waiting. When I start to shift away her face contorts, and for a few seconds she struggles, gradually winning the battle for composure, until her face is so calm and naked and vulnerable that I want to hide it away in my arms. Instead I bend down and kiss it once on its salty cheek. Her look of gratitude is too much to bear. I turn away and begin to force my way through the mass of bodies to the *Godthaab*. The wind is stinging my eyes. I can't look back. Instead I watch the ground change: stone, metal, wood. I can't look up. To wipe my eyes would give the wrong impression, but they are smarting so badly it is almost impossible to resist. I wait until I am hidden by the mast.

Then there is her voice, high above everything else, finding a pitch nothing can match:

'Alfred?'

I have no voice to reply. And as the master of the *Godthaab* begins to haul the anchor I feel Koch's hand on my shoulder lift away slightly then come down again with a reassuring grip. We are on our way to Iceland.

18

Shut your eyes. Imagine a Nordic longboat, captained not by a blond ancestor of Koch, but by a thin red-haired Celt. He is so thin it is part of his name: Helgi the Lean. But he holds himself well. Even though he almost starved to death in his Orkney childhood he is now thriving and, through a mixture of fighting and fortunate deaths, has become noble. For this he thanks his god, Thor, and it is for Thor's blessing he now stands at the the bow of his ship, roars and throws a piece of wood into the sea. Everyone watches it go. Eager eyes follow it to shore. This is no ordinary wood. It would be inconvenient if it were lost or sank or otherwise disappeared from sight. This is Helgi's sacred 'high-seat pillar', and the gods will direct its voyage. Where it is washed ashore will be the site of the homestead, and they are hoping that the gods are feeling kind. One man hopes for a meadow, another man for a dependable stream, while Helgi just prays for shelter from this unending rain.

It rains now, over a thousand years later, as we approach the quay at Akureyri. It is a persistent rain which has given anyone going on deck a through soaking. Helgi's wooden pillar came ashore a couple of miles south of here. A pity. Akureyri is the obvious place for a settlement: flat but sheltered by a backdrop of snow-covered peaks. It is on the north coast of Iceland but a long fjord has led us southward so now we are sheltered on either side by land. It is a small place, whose inhabitants, Lundager informs us excitedly, have a fasciantion with plants.

Later the sun will shine and we will see and smell their window boxes, their gardens, their borders, all filled with the most colourful flowers, and Lundager will marvel at it all, so close to the Arctic Circle. But for now we are occupied with unloading supplies off the *Godthaab* and locating possible ponies and handlers.

Koch had allowed us just over two weeks to cross the island to Vatnajökull, Iceland's miniature ice cap. By Greenlandic standards it is merely a large glacier, but even so, when we crossed it that summer, it was still little explored. We went with twenty-six ponies, and three farmers that we picked up on the way.

Another ice cave, another Gnipa, but here there is not the quiet gurgle of melt-water, but the roar of something more powerful. What is this water? It is something more than just melted ice. It has the smell of some hellish place, a yellowish silt mixed in with what the glacier offers. And it boils. Like some type of viscous soup; bubbles of gas escape and then the mud flops back on itself in crater-like rings. It is so strange, this mixture of ice and heat. A contradiction that doesn't fit.

For a while we sit and watch. There is so much to fascinate: the way steam swirls above the water, the way the same swirls pattern the ice, the smell of brimstone, the cracking of the ice as a section suddenly yields to the heat.

'Well, what are we waiting for?' Lundager asks, and slowly peels away his trousers. The Icelanders watch as he reveals his Danish underwear: woollen long johns, slightly stained, and matching vest. Now these come away too. The farmer Vigfus Sigurdsson stands.

'You're not going in there,' he says flatly. It is not a question.

'Of course. It's a long time since I had a bath.'

Vigfus shrugs. 'It's not safe, of course.'

Lundager strolls forward, recoils a little as his feet touch the mud, and then wades into the water.

'Ah, it's wonderful. You coming, Wegener?'

I shake my head. The weather is changing. I can feel the uneasiness of an approaching storm.

'Koch?'

'Nah, I don't like smelling of sulphur.'

So Lundager swims alone, up to the mouth of the cave and then inside. Vigfus continues to stand, watching the mouth of the cave until Lundager reappears, caked in mud.

'Not much of a bath,' Koch says as Lundager drips up the bank.

'Nonsense. I am as clean as a blackbird.'

And Vigfus shakes his head and sits.

I was right about the weather. As we climbed down the shoulder of the glacier and on to the lava field beneath a small storm swept up to greet us.

The ground has lifted with the wind and a fine black sand has forced its way in everywhere, even under my goggles, but to remove them would make everything worse. Vigfus is out in front, his head down. He has his pony's stance. They plod along together, a dogged duo, leading the way. After him comes Koch, then another Icelander, then me, and behind me Lundager and then the final Icelander. I look behind me. The gap between us has increased. Lundager sees me turn and waves. I look ahead again. Even Greenland did not seem this barren. There is absolutely nothing here, just black volcanic sand and small pieces of rock. I stoop down. This pebble is far lighter than it should be. When I inspect it, it is easy to see why. It is pumice, a rigid stone sponge. Köppen would be interested, I am sure. I slip it into my pocket. I wait for Lundager to catch up. Even above the wind I can hear his breathing; maybe it is because it is so restricted by the scarf around his face.

'A strange place this, Wegener. Not a single plant all day. Quite astonishing.'

I pick up one of the pieces of pumice and turn it under his nose for him to see the mass of tiny holes.

'I know, I know. And back there, white ones, just the same. And look at this. What do you make of this?'

It is a volcanic bomb, a liquid missile flung into the air where it froze into this curious shape. I tell Lundager that it is a fine specimen. He seems delighted. 'This has been quite a trip, Wegener, don't you think?'

I nod and carry on, but when I turn back again Lundager is where I left him, rolling the bomb around and around in his hand.

When he sees the *Godthaab* Koch forces his pony into a gallop. We clatter along the final stretch and arrive at the quay. After we've all dismounted Koch shakes each man's hand in turn, thanking and congratulating him, then he hands the reins of his pony to Vigfus. 'I'm relying on you to care for them now. We need them healthy, remember, in top form.'

I can't read Vigfus's expression. He says little, but I suspect he feels insulted; caring for ponies is Vigfus's speciality. But Koch shows no sign that he has noticed. Instead he steers Lundager and me to a wall and we all sit.

'A great success, I believe, gentlemen. We've proved what these little animals can do.'

'They can certainly cope with the slopes,' I say.

He turns to look at Lundager. 'And what do you think, Lundager?'

Lundager nudges a daisy with his foot. 'I think I must return home,' he says, then stands and walks alone to the edge of the jetty.

Lundager explained later that he had realised that he was too old in the hot-water river. He had wanted to swim upstream but the water had forced him back. He had tried to coerce his legs into kicking backwards, but they had refused to move. He had felt weak, more weak than he could remember feeling before, and it was then that he realised that if he went with us he might become a liability. It would be better to take someone younger and more capable.

Koch had become indignant then. 'But you're only two years older than me! Are you saying I'm too old as well?'

But Lundager had made comforting sounds. 'I am sure we all age at different rates. Maybe I have not kept myself as fit as I should.'

And so easily had Koch been pacified.

'But there are four bunks in the Borg,' I said.

'So we'll just have to find someone else.'

'Just one?'

'Vigfus has already agreed that he'll come with us to look after the ponies.'

19

It is only the beginning of September, but summer has already ended. At ten o'clock it is too dark to see to write and the air is cold. As if in compensation for its early disappearance the sun brushes the landscape with magnificent colours. It is the last thing I see before sleeping: the sun lighting our untidy encampment strewn with a haphazard mess of containers, the frost adding sparkle, and then, where the land ends, the short sparkling expanse of the fjord. The new ice is so transparent it is difficult to tell whether it is really there. It is only because the ripples become still – became sometimes they stop and then reappear – that I can tell this is no longer all water but something more useful. The small flat areas of land are no longer isolated patches, but linked together with a beautiful shiny matrix. Beyond the fjord is the ice: rising steeply and magnificently in a continuous rippling glacier to the ice sheet above, and then, above this, about twenty kilometres farther distant, the rocks of the vast nunatak of Dronning Louise Land. It is this country that catches the eye and breath: the purples, violets and blues outlined against the rose-red sky, and all this repeated again in a clear reflection on the new sea ice. I never tire of looking. As I perform my tasks I keep checking that the sun is still there, and for an hour maybe it is; but then it sinks too low and the colours fade.

Everything has been landed now. Even the ponies are secure. Naively, after so many weeks at sea, we had thought that they would enjoy the meadow we selected for them at Danmarkshavn, but instead they had immediately run amok over the mountain side. It has been a gruelling task recapturing them. The last to be captured was Koch's horse, Grauni, a particularly ill-tempered specimen. Even now he attempts to bite each hand that feeds him, but he is a strong animal, large, and Vigfus seems confident that he can be tamed.

We have fourteen ponies and one dog, Gloë, to guard the ponies and to warn us of the approach of wolves and bears. I check heads; they are all there. During the night Vigfus and I will check them again; they are so eager to escape. But now, as I re-enter the tent, there is Koch, and from his face I can tell he is going to give me news I will not like. He tells us that we have only enough fodder for ten ponies and so four must be shot. All that chasing around and herding them together for this! How can we decide? He says he will inspect the animals with Vigfus at first light and select the weakest. For once I dread the coming of dawn.

It looks so easy on the map, an insignificant distance west from Danmarkshavn to Cape Stop and then another small hop across a fjord to reach a glacier and the start of the inland ice. A man drawing a small hadn sledge would take just a couple of days, but with ponies dragging a year's worth of supplies it will take considerably longer.

Leaving Vigfus and our new colleague, the sailor Lars Larsen, Koch and I break camp alone. It is like old times. We are happy in our own silences. There are no dogs, no ponies, just two men each pulling his own sledge, enveloped in his own sphere of thoughts. The sea ice is deceptive. In some places it is over half a metre thick, but in others it is just a fragile layer. We have to be careful. Where one thick layer finishes we have to decide either to jump to the next or make a detour. We are like two heavy frogs on lily leaves of varying resilience. But after some hours we reach the other side of the fjord. The sun is setting again, showing off its colours on the ice shapes before us. The ice drops from the high land with a frightening steepness, and from time to time a piece breaks off with a sharp crack; small icebergs calving into the frozen sea. The setting of the sun is slow. We have plenty of time to search the expansive cliff of ice. But it turns out to be so high, so steep, there doesn't seem to be anywhere we could possibly entice a pony to climb. After an hour we begin to feel the task is hopeless; we have wandered around each promontory and cove, but there is nowhere even slightly possible. Koch says nothing. Whenever we stop he is cheerful and determined, urging me around another white cliff, another turquoise berg. Behind one iceberg, sheltered from the sea, we come across a bear clutching a sea lion in a fatal embrace. Koch's gun slithers from his shoulder as we approach, but the bear seems unaware both of us and the uninvited guests by his side: an arctic fox and an arctic rabbit, noses twitching, ready for scraps. We pass by, uncomfortably conscious that we are too close and that the slightest disturbance might cause him to launch himself towards us; but he is too absorbed in his meal, and we pass onwards on our search up the fjord.

By the time we find it the sun has almost gone: a small glacier within the larger one. It is broken up into accessible-looking steps and looks perfect. We make camp on its central flatter portion so as to be ready to investigate the next day.

But this glacier, which we called Breder-Brä, was not as perfect as it appeared. Closer inspection revealed that it was divided into sections by deep wide crevasses, each of which would require extensive engineering for the ponies to cross. It was a strangely clean glacier, with ice the even whiteness of fine bone china. The walls of the crevasses resembled columns of basalt, as if the ice had broken neatly along the planes of a crystal. Around us the ice kept cracking, sudden gunshots I could not get used to, sending hidden fragments into the sea ice below. Although it seemed a dangerous place it appeared to be our only option, so we continued climbing up Breder-Brä from our camp until we reached the pockmarked surface of the start of the inland ice.

How did it happen? I keep asking myself again and again. Why did I carry my equipment just there, on my back? I didn't realise that parts of it were so sharp, so lance-like. I curl up on the snow, waiting for Koch to return. Now that I am alone, the cracking of the ice seems louder and closer. Koch has left a gun but this is no defence against the ice giving way or opening into a crevasse beneath me. I decide to lurch a little forward, careful not to straighten up, for to do so causes such an excruciating pain in my back that I almost lose consciousness. My next movement causes the ground to fade and almost disappear, so I lower myself downwards until my head clears of the faint and I can taste the reassuring bitterness of bile in the back of my mouth.

A sudden loud report, and then another. It is very close, and after a few painful steps I can see how close; a wide break in front of me, becoming wider as I watch. I can't go on. I sink on the snow, but now the snow sears my back. I hear the echo of my scream. For a while it replaces the rumbles and creaks of the ice, and when it finishes, for a few seconds, there is silence, before the icy chorus of rifle fire begins again.

This firing is incessant. Each sound is startling, and tears at my nerves. I start to sing, any tune, my only intention being to cover the battle sounds of the ice. I sing more loudly, more urgently, trying to concentrate on the sound of my voice. Songs come to me one after the other and I grab their tunes, anxious not to stop. My voice enters the fjord below and then echoes back to me in a frantic chorus. What are we singing? A song about gypsies. A song of promises and enticements, and soon it seems to be no longer my voice but a clearer, higher voice I heard long ago in a different world. Don't stop, it tells me, and so I go on until Koch appears with my sleeping bag and sledge. He looks a little surprised at the distance I've moved, but then he loads me on the sledge and pulls me back to our camp ground on the flat portion of the Breder-Brä glacier. There he examines my back, prodding and fingering me until I am trying and failing not to cry out. At last he tells me there is nothing much to see: no big holes or rips. He mutters something about ribs and how easy they are to break and that once he knew someone who broke one by coughing rather too energetically. This does not make me feel better; I thought I was braver than this, and what I feel certainly seems worse than the result of a sudden muscular reflex. He decides to bandage me to restrict movement and then he leaves me again to cross the sea ice to fetch Vigfus and a pony and sledge.

There is little more frustrating than doing nothing. Blank beads fidget on the string. So slowly does one hour follow the next. Every day I tested myself. Was the pain a little less? Could I move a little more today? For two weeks I was an invalid, confined to the tent, first on the camp ground at Cape Stop, and then, after a regal journey by sledge, on the new camp ground on the Breder-Brä. It was so frustrating to do nothing except the small domestic chores around the stove. And there was so much for my friends to do: after the transport of everything to Breder-Brä there was the engineering; crevasses to fill with snow and blocks of ice, and the stables to be cut to shelter the ponies. Every day my comrades returned exhausted, but they also returned a little exhilarated: the passage on to the ice was so beautiful, they said, if only I could see it, everything was now covered by a thin layer of translucent snow, and when the sun set the view was truly magnificent. Soon they had made the first journey with the ponies over the crevasse bridges on to the inland ice, and reported to me that with long ropes to guide them all had gone well.

*   *   *

Again the ice is splintering. I am so used to the sound now it barely rouses me; I turn over, disturbing Gloë at my feet, and drowsily listen to the creaks. But these creaks don't stop, instead they become louder. Then quickly another sound joins in and Gloë leaps up. This sound is coming from somewhere deep within the ice, and it's something I've not heard before, a hissing that hurts the ears. Something massive is moving quickly below us but my movements are slow and awkward as I try to escape from my tight sleeping bag. Meanwhile Gloë is leaping round the tent, whimpering and then barking, working his way to the flaps and nuzzling his way out. He thinks nothing of his friends behind him.

Slowly I ease my body from its sleeping bag, flinching at every move that causes my back to strain. The noise has become louder still. Now there are thuds and more creaks. I feel for my kamiks and call to Larsen next to me. Like me he moves slowly, from exhaustion, I think, rather than pain. The ground is moving. I am sure the ground is moving. I peer out of the tent and see the moon. It is tilting in the sky, and by its light I see two figures fleeing from their tent barefoot, kamiks in their hands: Koch and Vigfus.

I painfully ease my feet into my boots and lace them up. Every movement hurts. I want to hurry but this is the best I can do.

'Larsen,' I shout above the thunder, 'hurry!'

The tent is tipping; some lines are snapping from the ground while others slacken into loops.

'Get out, man, now.'

At last he comes, slack kamiks on his feet, and together we lurch away on the moving ground, dodging bits of ice that are raining down on us like doomsday hail. Even without my broken rib it would be hard to keep balance. With each roar the ground sways and soon we find we are flailing in the semi-darkness, then holding on to each other, rigid arms intertwined around each other's shoulders.

Everything has changed: towards the sea the ice has broken away from the rest of the glacier and tilted. It is an over-hanging colossus of ice, ready to fall, and our footsteps now decorate its diagonal surfaces as if we had previously possessed the ability to walk on walls. Farther down the ice has fallen away completely and is now relocated as an iceberg in the frozen sea where its calving is greeted by a series of splutterings and sighs. Miraculously, it is only the campsite that is relatively untouched. Although new blocks of ice are scattered over the surface, some of them immediately by the tents and stables, nothing has been directly hit.

As we try to follow Koch and Vigfus up the glacier the swaying subsides, but the noise is still there, so we hurry onwards. Koch and Vigfus are now just small figures in the distance. They do not turn round, do not stop, but keep hurrying out of reach of this scraping and shifting ground. Why don't they wait? Why don't they help? Supporting each other, Larsen and I limp towards the first crevasse. The painstakingly engineered bridge has gone; the block of ice, so laboriously cut from the ground, has dropped out of sight as the crevasse has widened. There is no way across. I call out, but Koch doesn't hear me. Larsen and I watch their bodies becoming smaller and more distant and then we turn to regard each other. Our arms are still around each other's shoulders. He is just four years my junior but at the moment he seems little more than a boy. His fleshy face is drawn into an immobile mask of mute terror. He offers nothing: no suggestion, no opinion, not even a voice. He is waiting for me to tell him what to do, but the pain in my back makes it difficult to think.

I call out again to Koch and Vigfus but it is hopeless. I can't even see them any more. I shout again, just Koch's name this time, and my voice returns to me in an angry echo above the softening roar. How dare he desert us like this? How can he run away without considering us? Doesn't he realise we need his help?

Anger is a powerful stimulant. It has come to my aid many times. It is important to value it and direct it so it is of some use. Now I used it to ignore my pain. I gripped Larsen's shoulder and directed him to the northern side of the glacier's valley. We climbed to where the ice seemed more stable and waited there. Still the ice hissed and sighed beneath us. I looked around. This might be our only chance to witness this deadly beauty. I remember remarking on this to Larsen but he just responded with the blankness of his mask. I tried to notice everything: the way one of the stable walls made from crates had dropped away but still contained the ponies; the way a gully had formed immediately adjacent to a tent; the way the ground had subsided under some of the supplies but left them still obviously retrievable. There, in the moonlight, I appreciated the miracle of our survival and tried to replace my feelings of hurt and anger with a sense of wonderment.

Soon the noise died away, and soon Koch and Vigfus returned with bleeding feet, sheepish expressions and kamiks in their hands. We returned to our sleeping bags for warmth, but we couldn't sleep. Time and time again the whisperings of the ice returned and we stiffened, waiting for another calving that this time we would not survive, but it never came.

In the morning we could see more: the sea ice covered by a new layer of icebergs and rubble, a new teetering mass of ice above us, and our campsite, changed overnight into the precarious shoulder of a glacier from which we were now more anxious than ever to escape.

20

The ventilation has made everything comfortable: the lamps burn well with a steady flame and we are gradually mastering the stove. It is a cosy scene; the dog Gloë is on my bunk fast asleep, Vigfus is sorting out the darkroom, Larsen is busy constructing some sort of drying apparatus, and so I have Koch to myself. I have forgiven him for running away. I have told him I would have done the same, probably. I have told him it is a reflex, a survival instinct, to run without thinking when the ground shifts. What would have been the point of waiting for me and getting both of us killed? Maybe I am feeling generous because my back is at last feeling better. It seems that the exercise of that night did it some good, and Koch has since become more attentive over it, rebinding it several times, and not letting me take any part in the building of the Borg. There is still pain, but it is more of a dull ache which I find easier to bear. I am slow, but at least I am moving.

We have built the Borg where we stood, just west of the Breder-Brä, where the ice is stable. We have turned our backs on Dronning Louise Land; for so many weeks it had been our promised land, our winter bunker, enticing us westward, changing the colours of the setting sun into something redder and richer. But it is too far. Only later, when the days are lengthening, will we turn again to these nunataks to the west. We will scour this red land and find a sandstone with ripple marks and fossils, and for a while I will contemplate its significance: this crumpled sandstone, the product of an ancient warm sea now towering above another sea of unimaginably cold ice. How could anyone argue that the continents had not moved? How could anyone argue that such crumpling was due to the earth shrinking?

Koch and I are discussing my moving continents now. He seems particularly interested in the idea of the continents calving away from each other like icebergs. He is drawing a glacier. It started off as another of the analogies, but now he seems to be drawing it for some other purpose. Just a few minutes ago he stopped talking altogether as he concentrated on his drawing. It is a glacier in profile, starting from the ice sheet where the underlying land is almost flat, then through the space between two nunataks to where the land slopes quite steeply.

'Now it is possible for the ice to flow faster,' he says. 'It does so, but only at the surface. Near the bedrock friction prevents it moving much at all.' He draws arrows to show the movement: a big fat line at the top, a small thin one at the bottom.

'Now,' he says, 'the ice changes character. It becomes more like a solid, it cannot deform, it cracks. Great crevasses make steps of ice down the hillside.' He draws how it looks, how it looked at Breder-Brä. But his pen doesn't stop. I watch, fascinated. This could be a model for rocks, for the earth's crust. Instead of crevasses and blocks of ice I see rift valleys and faults.

Now the ground levels out again and the ice slows.

'It is a liquid again,' Koch says, 'it has time to flow.' His pen makes it sag like a loose skin. He draws ripples, insignificant on his paper but insurmountable where we see them on the ice outside. He has forgotten about the calving. I remind him, and at the end of the glacier he draws more crevasses, going deeper and deeper until, at the water's edge, a chunk breaks off and floats away.

'There,' he says, 'the complete story.'

I sit back. We know the complete story of a glacier, but

what is the complete story of the continents? What causes them to break up? Why does it happen? I look through the window of the Borg. Frau Koch has decorated it with artificial flowers. It is a whimsical touch. I think of the time she gave them to us, giggling as usual, and Else silently fingering the too-bright petals.

Koch is engrossed in another diagram. I sit on my bunk and stroke Gloë. Above everyone's bunks, I notice, there are pictures. Only mine is still bare. I think of who should be there: my parents, Kurt, Köppen, Else. I rummage through my belongings for photographs without success. Maybe I didn't pack them. It is stupid to care. They are only photographs, after all, nothing important. I go back to Koch and his glaciers. Now he is sketching the whole ice sheet, a traverse section, from sea to sea, from nunatak to nunatak.

A darkroom in the long arctic night is, I suppose, a bit of an anachronism, but it is still useful to have somewhere dark away from the lamps and the moon for developing film. Of course, a darkroom can also serve as a sanctuary.

It always seems to me to be a small miracle, to see the picture appearing in miniature on the celluloid. A few minutes ago a picture of an ice crystal appeared in the tray before me. It has been difficult to take satisfactory pictures of the ice in the permanent night, but already I have picked out some interesting features: first there are folds, both massive and more miniature, highlighted by the layers of summer dirt; then there are places where the ice has fractured and slipped, the pressure causing melting and a blue line of frozen recrystallised water.

Since I have laboured for so long I have decided to reward myself with my own private project: Else. I have found a film I am sure contains her face, and I am waiting for the film to be fixed.

There is a noise in the living quarters. Vigfus has been quick today, the ponies must be in a cooperative mood, or maybe he has just nipped in quickly to get warm. It is minus thirty degrees Centigrade out there, much too cold to stand still. I take the film from its fixing fluid and wash it to finish the process.

What is wrong with Vigfus? He is tapping at the door. He'll have to wait a few seconds until I finish.

A voice. Not Vigfus, Larsen's. 'Wegener, are you in there? Come quickly, it's Koch!'

I drop the film and open the door. Even the dim light of the lamp makes me squint. Larsen's face is thinner now. It makes him look older but no less frightened.

'What's happened?'

'He's down a crevasse. I couldn't get to him. I didn't know what to do. He said to come and get you.'

'Tell Vigfus. He's with the horses.'

But Vigfus has already heard. He is withdrawing a hawser from one of the cases and winding it around his arm, coil upon coil. I tell him to also find the rope ladder and flashlight, and then order Larsen to fetch Koch's sleeping bag, load it on to the hand sledge and follow us. Grabbing an ice axe, I go with Vigfus to the storage area for our skis. It is hard tying them on, the straps won't thread through, my feet keep slipping, and I can't see. All the time I think of Koch alone at the bottom of a crevasse. He has to be injured. He has to be cold. He has to be freezing to death.

But the snow won't let us hurry. How long has he been lying there now? I count the minutes. I imagine his body. How will we pull something so large and heavy from something so narrow? The thoughts keep going around and around in my head, strangling each other until I can think of nothing coherent at all. I decide to concentrate on my legs. I have to move them faster. I think about their movement: left, right, left, right, a regular beat. Perhaps he is dead. Perhaps he won't be able to hear us call.

We approach the crevasse. It is one we know well, near Breder-Brä. I call out, to let him know we are coming. We trudge up a slope. It is gentle, it shouldn't bother us, but now it seems to go on and on. I call once and then again. Has someone answered between my calls? I listen. Yes, Koch's voice; weak and distant, but it is there.

The crevasse is a black gash in the greyness of the snow. I lie down, my head over the side, peering down. Air, slightly warmer than the air around me, wafts up. It seems wet, smells a little of the sea. I call out, and Koch's voice answers. It is faint and its echoes are even fainter. As they die away I hear the ice shifting; a deep-throated rumble that terrifies me. What if it closes? It shouldn't close, but what if it does?

I turn to Vigfus, tell him to quickly unwind the ladder and lower it into the slit. It falls a few metres, but then catches on something. I shine the flashlight into the space. It is many metres deep. The bottom is just visible, and filled with snow. Koch is more than halfway down on a snow-filled ledge. I can see just small parts of him shining.

'Lower that light down here,' he calls, 'I need to search for something.'

I just want him to come up. His voice has made the ice rumble again. But we do what he says and lower the lamp carefully. As it goes down the walls are lit. They are blue, of a quite stunning intensity, and decorated with so many vicious-looking icicles that I have the fleeting impression of a grotto. The torch stops and the rope is tugged. For a few minutes we see shadows moving below us and then a grunt.

'No, it's no good, I can't see it.'

'What are you looking for?'

For a few seconds there is no reply and then Koch's voice comes quietly back.

'The theodolite, Wegener, it's our only one.'

Vigfus drops the ladder after the torch. After a few minutes it becomes taut. We catch the ends, drive them into the ice and then take the strain, just in case. Koch grunts as he climbs. At first the grunts are strong, but as he climbs nearer they become fainter and then they stop. I edge near the crevasse on my stomach. There is Koch's face, startlingly close. It is drawn and pale, as if he is coming out of a faint, and it is streaked with a blackness that can only be blood. I pass him the rope and ask him whether he can tie it around his waist. He says nothing, but the rope is pulled and then slackens again. Now all three of us pull. It is awkward because the head of the crevasse is so narrow. But he comes slowly. At the surface he gradually straightens and then staggers to his sleeping bag on the sledge. 'You took your time,' he says, and grins, but then his face drops. 'The theodolite . . . you have find it, Wegener. It must be down there somewhere.'

But it wasn't. We spent two days looking, but when a snowstorm struck we finally saw that it was hopeless. The theodolite was our only instrument for accurately measuring angles and Koch had lost it! Why had he brought only one? It was madness! I needed that instrument for so many of my studies: my observation of the northern lights, and the measurement of glacier movement, mirages and hales. We also needed it to navigate across the ice. Without it the expedition seemed impossible. We had endured so much just to be stymied by Koch's uncharacteristic folly. I had never known him before to come away without reserve instruments, and this one was so important. How could we cross the ice blindly, not knowing for certain which way we were going? Once we lost sight of Dronning Louise Land everything would look the same: a flat white sea in all directions. I trudged behind Koch on his sledge, trying but failing not to feel bitter and angry and desperate.

21

Koch lies on his bunk with his foot tightly bandaged. I tell him he has broken a bone, but he insists it is just a sprain. I tell him he must stay off it for months, but he says he'll be fine in a few days. He works from his bunk, demanding readings and observations, so we give him the temperature of the air and the ice like happy minions. In return he allows us to benefit from his opinions: on the ice-drilling (improving), the northern lights observations (satisfactory), my book on the thermodynamics of the atmosphere (fairly good), my photographs (excellent), Larsen's ability at chess (poor) and the Jensen quadrant Vigfus and I have manufactured to replace the theodolite (speechless). The taciturn Icelander is a patient and skilful craftsman. Yesterday we demonstrated the amazing accuracy of our quardrant; we could find the time from the height of the moon to within one minute. So much can be achieved with two pieces of wood, some wax, a small mirror and a photographic yellow disc!

When Koch and I talk, which is frequently, since my meteorological observations do not take up much time, we talk about ice. It is something that fascinates us both. I have managed to take some microphotographs of crystals, and we spend much time examining these. We wonder how these delicate crystals of frost can be converted into the hard blue crystals of the glacial ice.

Snow from the top of the ice sheet is porous. It is packed together very loosely and the cavities between the crystals contain air and water vapour. When the snow is compressed into ice it is called firn. Although it is more dense it is still quite porous; hold a block of firn up to the wind, and the wind whistles through. The ice below the firn is last year's ice. The air has been squeezed out so it becomes more dense and impermeable; a good choice for an igloo. Now, go deeper into the middle of the ice. Here the ice is compressed so much that it melts.

'Melts under pressure': now that is a strange thing. Something that happens only to ice. Squash most solids and they will stay solid, but squeeze ice and it changes to liquid. Water takes up less room than ice. It is the reason ice floats rather than sinks on water. The solid is less dense than the liquid. An auspicious fact. So if you press down hard, the ice takes up as little room as it can, and the way it does this is to turn to water. It allows the skater to glide on a film of water and it allows small ice crystals to reform into larger ones. They grow so big that they form translucent bands and layers that absorb all light except blue. And this blueness allows us to see where the layers have slipped, and where they have bent. Is this all true? It seems to me that it is, but I have so much more to learn and understand.

So our monotonous, dimly lit life continued. In spite of all my declarations about the beneficial effects of seeing scenery on projectors and slides during the *Danmark* expedition, I had not succeeded in bringing any along with me this time. It had been difficult to justify the weight. Everything had had to be whittled down to the minimum. So instead our views of landscape were restricted to the small windows of photographs. But at last I had a picture of Else.

As soon as it has dried I pin it by my bunk. The film has suffered a little on the journey and it is not the best one I have ever taken, but at least it is her face; someone that smiles on me, just me. The photographs beside our bunks are breeding;

each one of us now has a selection. As soon as Larsen notices my new addition he comes over to inspect.

'Very nice,' he says. 'Who is she? Your sister?'

'Fiancée.'

He looks at me, as if he is reassessing me. 'She's a little . . .' He doesn't want to say, so I finish it for him.

'Young? Yes, she was then. She's older now.'

'Of course,' he says, and looks again at the picture. 'She has a determined chin.'

I look closely. What is a determined chin? All I see is Else's chin with its small dent. I keep looking at the shadow on her chin, imagining my finger resting there, stroking its concavity.

'Slavic, is she?'

'She has some Russian blood, I believe, just a little. How can you tell?'

'The eyes. Deep sockets, hidden eyelids. Obvious.'

Else's eyes. I hadn't really thought much about them until now. She always made such a fuss about my eyes, she rather ignored her own. In this photograph she is looking past me into the distance. Lars is right. The eyes are quite deeply set. It gives them a rather pleasing aspect, I think, a little mystery.

'Blue eyes, I suppose?'

I realise, with some embarrassment, that I don't know. It is something I have never noticed. It is impossible to guess the colour from the photograph. Probably they are nondescript, perhaps hazel, perhaps blue, but certainly not as light as mine, and their shape is more elongated.

'It's because of the steppes, of course,' Larsen is saying.

I turn towards him, frowning.

'It's windy, you see.'

'No, Lars, I'm afraid you've lost me there.'

'Well, it's like Darwin says, isn't it?'

Maybe if I wait he'll make more sense, but I doubt it.

'Well, Wegener, I'm surprised you don't know about this.'

Clare Dudman

He speaks more slowly, as if he is explaining something simple to a young child. 'The Slavs, they live on the steppes in Russia, right? So often it's windy, yes? And the wind picks up dirt, and so they have to screw up their eyes like this.' He demonstrates.

'And where does Darwin come into this?'

'Well, it's like he said, isn't it? They screw up their eyes, so their eyes become smaller, and so, when they have kids, their eyes are smaller too.' He sits back on his bench, a small satisfied smile on his face.

'Thought you'd know about that, Wegener, really, you being a scientist.'

He rummages under his bunk for the long pipe he smokes. It is quite an elaborate piece, at least thirty centimetres long with a deep tulip-shaped bowl. Soon the pleasant smell of tobacco fills the room. It won't last long. Even though it looks so pretty the pipe is fairly inefficient and remains alight only for about five minutes. I pull out my own more modest version. It is only half as big, but works twice as well. I fill the bowl with a little of my precious rations and light up. It does no good to argue with Larsen. He has developed his own fixed ideas of the world and won't be swayed. He doesn't seem to care whether they're right or wrong, as long as they make sense to him. I turn back to Else's picture and try to remember the colour of her eyes. I decide on grey-blue. I try to remember times when I stared right into them, but can't. Strangely I can remember plenty of times when she stared into mine, but none when I stared back into hers. Surely that must be impossible. I can't have been paying attention. How hurt she would be if she knew. I resolve to do better, to become more attentive. But there are other things I remember: the way her eyes change shape when they smile. The way the bottom lid curves a little upwards. The way they have another shape when she laughs, how the whole of that bottom eyelid rolls up and laughs too. Then I remember the sound of her laugh; a gentle chuckle

184

with little voice, so different from the rather theatrical giggle of Frau Koch. Then I remember that sometimes, when she starts to laugh, she finds it difficult to stop, and how it embarrasses and yet delights her, and how I can always see the two emotions so clearly fighting on her face.

'Oh, I wish I was like you,' she told me once. 'You never lose control. You laugh but you can always stop it short.'

'Pleasant thoughts, Wegener?' Koch has come in from the stables. His foot is a lot better now, but still has not fully recovered.

'Ha, is that young Else I see before me?'

His laugh has some of his wife's raucous quality.

By Christmas Koch's foot was better. The parcel we had kept for our celebration contained small treats that had been packed for us by our relatives. Better than the food was what was slipped in alongside, like an afterthought: pictures of Else.' Tinted photographs. The colours seemed so bright and alive after staring at my cloudy images for so long. They were images I hadn't seen before, Else with her mouth slightly open, her lips curled, enjoying a joke with the cameraman. I felt jealous. Why wasn't she laughing with me? I had to keep reminding myself that this picture was taken months ago, before I'd left for Greenland, but still I felt I was missing something. What was she doing now? Who was she talking to in Norway? Would she really wait? I examined her eyes; was she enjoying the company of this stranger more than she had ever enjoyed mine? I looked about me, made sure no one was watching, then I traced my finger down her face, as she had once traced her finger down mine. I tried to remember the texture of her skin, the smoothness of her nose, the dry resistance of her cheeks and the heat of her lips. Then I touched her throat. I had seen her put her perfume there, in the hollow between the wings of her collar bones. I tried to remember its smell: was it lavender or something

Clare Dudman

less pungent? My fingers traced the framework of her neck. Could she feel this? Would she gulp? Would she close her eyes and let me touch her?

Someone moved, coughed. It was Vigfus. His quiet, kind eyes held mine and then dropped them again. He stretched over to the stove and stroked Gloë, prone at its base.

'Christmas – it always makes me sad,' he said. 'Maybe we should go and share our joy with the ponies.'

Outside, the weather grew colder still: −45 degrees, then Amundsen's record of −47 degrees and then −50 degrees. Cold, unbelievably cold, even inside the hut away from the stove. Hoar frost decorated the interior walls with delicate crystals, beautiful fronds that grew like brittle, sparkling lichen. We no longer risked baring any part of our bodies to the outside; instead we used the old pemmican cans and the hay; our human smell adding to the ponies' in the stable. Outside, the foxes, which had scavenged at our rubbish heap, disappeared; perhaps they returned to their own Borg nearer the sea. We felt more isolated than ever. The cold sank down around us, hemming us in. We were reluctant to emerge. The preparations for each meteorological reading became longer and more arduous as our movements became slower and more clumsy. After Koch had painstakingly constructed a rota, he insisted on a rigid adherence. Our brains and voices slowed. It was difficult to think and harder still to argue. The cold and the struggle to keep it at bay preoccupied us.

I suppose it makes sense that the most frigid part of the year is just before the sun reappears. The ground has time to forget its warmth. Gradually all the remaining reservoirs of heat are used up and there is nothing left. Snow buried the Borg, adding to its insulation, so each morning we had to dig our way out. It was difficult to move. Even inside the Borg our layers made us so bulky that we lumbered around like old polar bears. The room seemed to shrink so that each movement ended in collision. I became desperate to go out and then, once out, desperate to go in again. The air outside was too cold and the air inside too stale.

On the fourteenth of February the sun came back. We could see the upper edge of its disc edging along the horizon to the south. We crept outside, and we could feel its faint radiation. Larsen threatened to remove his shirt to celebrate, but instead we persuaded him to make do with a cigar. The next day was cloudy, but the day after, at noon, each living thing acquired long-legged shadows, and this time we celebrated with exercise: a two-hour ski trip for us and an outing for the ponies. Now I became more adventurous with my meteorological efforts. I attached a camera to a balloon and obtained wonderful pictures of mirages: Gundahls Knoll, a nearby nunatak, sprouted peaks, lost its summit, and then inverted itself, just for my satisfaction.

Soon we began to make journeys out from the Borg to establish depots to the west in readiness for our great journey across the ice. We wanted to be ready for the season of the midnight sun and make the most of its beguiling light.

22

Why do Europeans like to leave their mark on the land, as if to declare ownership? The Inuit would regard it as a perversity: they would say that the land belongs to no one in particular, it belongs to us all. The Inuit place names evoke memories and serve as warnings: this is the valley where one man starved to death, and this is where another died from cold. Beware.

How would the Inuit describe the place we entered that spring of 1912? Surely not Dronning Louise Land or Achton Friis Cape or Lindhards Island. Sometimes it seemed to me that everyone on that 1908 expedition had claimed a piece of the landscape: so before we reached Gundahls Knoll we had to first pass through Aage Bertelsen Cape. Since the ice rose steeply towards the ice sheet, we made each journey twice so as not to overload the ponies. Once we reached Gundahls Knoll we doubled back on ourselves to begin our journey again and finally say goodbye to the Borg.

So long have these walls kept us safe and dry. It is familiar now, and even though it is so primitive, it feels like home. I think we are more sad to leave this place than we would be to leave a more comfortable structure in our homeland. From now on we will be desert nomads, travelling with our tents, but instead of camels we have ponies, instead of sand, snow, and instead of a lifeless heat, a lifeless cold. We pack carefully and regretfully, leaving the precious small things until last; Larsen's pipe, Vigfus's whip, Koch's maps and my photographs. I hide my favourite photograph of Else under my coat. I am a little embarrassed to be so sentimental. Koch,

I notice, has left a rather fine picture of his own woman pinned above his bunk, but he is sentimental in other ways. For instance, after he has finally looked around the place and said goodbye, he refuses to go in again, even to leave a report on the desk. He asks me to do it, so I am the one who finally smells the place, who looks around and realises that even now it is not quite silent. There are rustles and scratchings and sighs as the temperature changes and the timbers shift. I look around at all the things we are leaving: a chessboard, a set of spoons in a canvas holder, a landscape painted by Friis, and, finally, not so regretfully, Koch's picture of the King of Denmark, which has glared at me through the whole winter from his desk.

Then, as I shut the door, I feel I am not me at all but someone else. I am someone from the future arriving at this place, opening this door that I now seal shut, and then finding everything as we left it; the bunks, the photographs faded on the walls, the coffee mugs hanging from hooks, and the novels on the shelves above. What will I smell? Maybe a bottle containing developing fluid will crack, allowing its odour to trail along the floor. Or maybe there will be that strange stale smell, peculiar to a place where the cold precludes decay, of something old and rancid. Then I will overcome my trepidation and enter, begin to pick through things, lift them up, inspect: a mixture of intense curiosity and nostalgia. Why am I here? Have I heard reports from whalers or is it just that years have passed without news? Am I on some rescue mission, or am I just here to find out what happened? Whatever the reason, I feel sure that the men who lived here are now quite dead.

Outside, Koch unfurls the Borg's flag. It is easy to reach now that the snow has risen to the level of the roof, where we haven't dug it away. He spreads it out on the snow and we all sign the faded canvas and then let it fly again.

Now we are anxious to be off. Koch has the ponies in place:

Lady, Cavalier, Fox, Polaris and the ill-tempered Grauni. They drag the Nansen sledges with their beautiful polished wood, masts, canvas sails and zipped canvas covers. And so, without looking back, we set off, a final time, a disconsolate ambiguous caravan, heading west under a grey sky heavy with clouds.

How can I describe this place? How can I tell you what I see? It is such an alien world, quite unlike anything I used to know, except in small ways. For instance, after trudging through snow, deeper than anything you could imagine, we reach a lake. But, except for its flatness, there is little to distinguish the lake ice from the ice of the glacier. Both are covered with snow and both seem to resist our passage with intent. Then, ahead of us, beyond the lake, there are the mountains, some days looking a little like an Alpine scene, but on other days wavering and shimmering, as if unsure of their shape. Through all this strangeness we march, sometimes sweating with effort and then a little later freezing with cold, until after fifteen hours we reach camp, eat a little, stable the ponies, and then wriggle into our sleeping bags with undisguised relief.

I look no farther than the pony's hindquarters. To look any farther would be to see the bank of snow, appearing almost vertically in front of me. I don't want to see. I don't want to know. If I can just travel as far as the pony, if I can just do that. I look no farther. I celebrate each one of these small victories in silence, and then go on again. Sometimes I tell myself that when I reach that point just a little ahead of me we will stop and rest, or stop and make camp. But we don't. We go on, no one wanting to be the man to demand a rest. Sometimes I tell myself that we are just a few steps from the top. From the top, I decide, we will be able to see the start of the great inland sea. We will be able to see it stretching ahead of us in easy undulations. If we just go a little farther. If we just climb over this ridge of firn, then we will see what we are aching to see. But we never do. There is just more and more snow, more and more ice, and the only thing that changes is that sometimes it is deeper, sometimes softer, sometimes breaks away in pieces, and sometimes groans a little under foot or crunches. But it is all just snow. Or ice. Part of a slope that doesn't seem to end, just goes on and on, until my clothes are wet with effort.

But at last it did end and we could see what lay ahead; not the expected easy flat land of the ice sheet but the complicated scenery of Dronning Louise Land, free of ice and impossible to cross with sledges. Somehow we would have to find a way through. So disconsolately we made camp, and disconsolately we waited while a storm of violent winds swept over and through us.

Everyone is in my way. Every time I move there is someone's elbow, someone's foot or someone's cup of coffee. Sometimes I long so much for solitude that I consider venturing out into the white swirling air and just walking away as far as I can go without considering the consequence. I try to write my diary. I try to formulate the most basic thought but someone is there preventing me.

'Wegener, how long do you think this'll last?'

'I don't know.'

'But you're the meteorologist.'

'It's not that easy.'

'But when do you think we might be able to risk moving?'

'When the winds die down.'

'And when might that be?'

'I told you, Lars, I don't know.'

The edge of irritation in my voice finally silences him.

'I was just asking,' he says a few minutes later with childish petulance.

'And I was just telling you.'

There is an uncomfortable silence. I don't care. It is not only

Larsen who has asked, but Vigfus, sometimes, even Koch. I feel as though I am to blame. Just because I study the weather it doesn't mean that I'm responsible for its bad behaviour.

'I think we can expect change any time now.' It is Koch. As usual he sounds as if he knows.

'Thank you. That's all I wanted to know.'

Koch used to fool me with his confident voice. Now he just fools Larsen. Vigfus, I notice, never asks Koch anything.

'You can't tell,' I point out. 'This could go on for days and days.'

'But it has already,' comes Larsen's whine.

The voice of reason replies: 'They never last for longer than a week.'

It is a law of meteorology I have not come across before.

'What makes you say that?' I ask.

But Koch does not reply; he just swipes me on the head with the side of his kamik.

And, just as Koch had decreed, the winds briefly died away, and we were able to make a reconnoitre. From high up on an adjacent nunatak we could see our way forward; northwards up the westward arm of a glacier and then west over the sea of gleaming ice.

It was not until the seventh of May that our journey on to the inland ice began in earnest. We discarded everything that was not essential: from now on we would eat only pemmican, the stables would be roofless and we would lead a life of absolute frugality.

The snow dunes line up in front us in an endless army. Their surface is smooth, hard, all loose snow swept away by a recent wind, and so the ponies tread easily, their sledges bouncing along behind them, as if they are small boats on waves. The sun shines so brightly that we squint, even through our goggles, and our eyes burn with tears. The snow is painfully white, too white to see, so I look away, up to the perfect blue cloudless sky, and after a while I feel so peaceful that I forget where I am. I am aware only of contentment. We are moving so quickly. Surely the whole journey will be like this. It is as we thought. The inland ice is calm, without weather. At last I feel I am on my way home.

Now the wind builds a little and causes snakes to grow in the snow. They burrow beneath us, just a little below the surface, slithering patterns racing ahead, as if they are mocking us. Is this all you can do? Look at us. We are as free as the wind and as fast. Where it goes, we must follow.

Where does the snow come from? Certainly not from clouds. The sky is still clear. But the snow is there; scurrying above the snow snakes, shaking them free, then tumbling higher and higher until it reaches our faces and makes our eyes sting in a different way. All the items of clothing we had discarded in the sun are retrieved and the snow gets into every layer. It is a different animal that inhabits this place now. Something smaller, something that squirms and burrows more effectively than the snakes. Something that pinches and stings. An insect. A stinging insect that can bite again and again without losing any of its poison.

We look up and they are there: clouds, stratus clouds; layers and layers of snow-laden promises. They do not promise for long. They droop lower and lower until they meet the snow driven up by the winds and there is just snow; no ground, no air, just a mixture of the two driving us downwards.

Polaris stumbles first. We pull him upwards, coax him forward with threats and then the stick, but after a few more steps he goes down again. This time his head is lowered and there is no persuading him onwards. Koch gives him an experimental kick on his flanks then shrugs. He orders us to make camp. We dig for three hours and, when we have per-suaded the ponies down into their icy home, we erect another for ourselves: a three-man tent with no home comforts.

In the morning the tent is smaller. Hoar frost is an irritating travelling companion, greedy for space. Snow has crept into everything; every article of clothing, every sleeping bag, even into the Primus stove and pots and pans. There is little prospect of removing it because the wind blows still. It is the tenth of May and we are 2,200 metres above the sea. Already the ponies are looking weaker and more bedraggled. When we try to march forward again Polaris collapses into the snow. His body heaves against it, his white fur almost indistinguishable from the whiteness of the snow. Vigfus wades over to him, strokes and then lifts the pony's head, and calls for Koch to come close. He points to the animal's right eye. It is so red and swollen his eyelids are sealed together. We inspect the others. They are all suffering from the effects of the prevailing wind. We lighten Polaris's load, but of course that means increasing the load of the rest. As I strap more luggage onto Grauni's sledge he looks at me in that ill-tempered, accusing way of his, and gives me a little grunt as if in warning.

We gather around Polaris and watch Vigfus try to coax him into life. Polaris moves slowly forward. Reluctantly the caravan moves behind him.

The land has disappeared now, even at the horizon. I feel a little anxious at its disappearance. I feel we are so much like ships at sea and already I long for port. The snow has become looser, and gusts sweep it up. The ponies are stumbling more often and Polaris's good eye seems to plead with me when I help him up: make it stop, make it stop, make it stop.

We decide on a change of plan; instead of going for as long as we possibly can we will make do with two short marches with a long lunch in between. Maybe, says Koch, the ponies will bear this better. I look at Vigfus, but he is looking eastwards and his face says nothing.

At noon Koch makes measurements with the sextant I've converted from the quadrant. Everyone awaits the results of his calculations with eagerness. Our height is 2,287 metres, he says. We grab each figure and try to make it make sense: 2,287 metres above the sea, a long way up. No wonder we all feel short of breath. Then he tells us our latitude and longitude and we try and imagine those. It is hard to imagine where we are: in every direction there is just the undulating snow and above it an intensely blue sky.

Larsen produces a mirror from his bag. He smiles when I question its necessity and says he is sure I also have some extraneous material about my person: so he has seen Else's photograph. We take it in turns to admire our faces. I see the face of an old man. The skin on his nose is dead and droops. Beneath his beard there is another patch of skin, also raw, also dead. Would Else love me now? I wonder. Would she admire this decaying face, these eyes swollen with tears?

We have established a new routine when we make camp. The digging was hurting my back, and so it was agreed (or mainly decreed again by Koch) that Vigfus and Larsen should dig out the stable while he and I erect the tent, cook the meal and deal with the ponies. As soon as they become still the ponies begin to shiver. They are a pitiful sight, their grey and honey-coloured backs streaked with snow, their long manes matted, their ears wilting and their eyes half closed. Even Grauni has become dumb now, and there is no longer any danger of my hand being nipped when I attach his nosebag. While we are waiting for the stable to be finished Koch and I make a windshield from a pair of skis and a sail and the ponies shelter behind this, chewing the contents of their nosebags until the stable is finished. We have little trouble enticing them down into their temporary home. They have learnt it is more comfortable for them there, and Vigfus always makes sure that the cribs are filled with hay.

Then we feed ourselves and Gloë, a predictable meal of pemmican soup, and then we sleep in the cold, cold daylight.

A single gunshot. Vigfus can look no one in the eye. When he walks alone across the ice no one follows. He eats the evening meal in silence; a fresh meat none of us savours. In the morning we will have to redistribute the load between the four horses that remain.

'He was a good horse, willing,' Vigfus says suddenly.

We all loudly agree, glad to have the silence broken.

'Loved his food,' says Koch meaningfully.

Vigfus is unaware, because he usually leads the caravan, that for days Koch had mesmerised the poor animal with a bag of hay held just in front of his nose. It had walked towards it trustingly until it could walk no longer. Larsen and I say nothing.

The next day it is snowing heavily. We shouldn't attempt to break camp but we do. No one argues. We want to leave this place. We can still see the red patch of snow under Polaris's head, even though fresh snow covers it. Cavalier carries little. Koch has his eye on him. He has already let it be known that he thinks he will not last much longer, and it is as if the animal knows. He stops frequently, as if waiting for something, and then moves forward slowly again. Again and again we have to wait, and while we wait we shiver. We cover only eight kilometres before we make camp.

For a few seconds I am alone with little to do. The stove is lit; all I have to do now is make sure that it burns correctly and that our water boils. I open my coat and take Else's picture from its special place. The paper is a little bent, and there is a diagonal crease almost dividing the picture in two, but it doesn't matter. She is there in front of me, smiling past my shoulder. I try to decide which part of her I like the best and conclude that I can't. Each part of her has an attraction: the gentle curves of her eyes and mouth, the softness of her hair, her delicate nose, and that chin, which may be determined but may also be cupped in my hand. Her face, I decide, is like a precious bud on the verge of flowering.

The tent flaps move and I put the photograph away. It is Koch.

'Still foul out there,' he says. 'I think we may be forced again into doing a little detention.'

I smile. It is a joke we pass between us: sometimes we are schoolboys, sometimes servants, sometimes soldiers, but in each reincarnation we are being punished.

'How's that coffee coming on?'

'It'll be a little while yet.'

He groans and flops down on his sleeping bag and I return to Else's picture. I don't need to see it to know how it looks. I can travel over it just by shutting my eyes. I can rearrange the hair, tilt her chin, make her laugh.

'Vigfus says Cavalier is ailing, but I say he's faking it.'

When I get back I am not going to stop looking at her. All the time I've wasted, when I could have been looking at her face.

'He's always been a strong animal, don't you agree, Wegener? But always the sly one.'

And I'm going to make her smile that smile at me. Whatever she wants, whenever she wants it, if only she will smile that smile.

'I can see it in his eyes. I told Vigfus. It's not as if he's collapsing like Polaris, merely standing still.'

We'll need a house in Marburg. It'll have to be a small one, of course. Maybe a flat.

'But Vigfus is too soft. He won't hear anything against the animal.'

And we'll need furniture: a desk, a table, chairs, book-shelves, maybe a dresser, and a bed, of course.

'I sometimes think Vigfus regards his horses more highly than humans. It's strange the way he talks to them, don't you think? Whispering like that. It's odd, isn't it? I mean, it's not as if they understand.'

A big bed with a soft mattress and a heavy quilt.

'Well, I think he's being too soft.'

Outside we can hear Vigfus and Larsen thumping snow off their kamiks. The tent flaps rises and Vigfus and Koch regard each other briefly.

'The horses are eating well,' Vigfus says. '*All* of them.'

We wait for the snow to stop. For four days we, and the ponies, munch on pemmican, fuelling ourselves only to sleep. The tent is either too warm or too cold and always too smelly. Coffee goes in and then comes out again with disgusting efficacy. The sound of urine filling an empty can sings louder than the storm. There is nowhere to turn, nowhere to look, and we have come to know each other with an undesirable intimacy. Vigfus makes himself comfortable without warning but with little fuss, Larsen apparently tries to hold off for as long as possible, while Koch urinates frequently and loudly, sighing as he finishes, as if an empty bladder is one of the most blissful experiences of his life.

At last the weather clears. The ponies are released from their torture of immobility and into another one in which they are moving.

A rumble starts in the distance. I imagine the ice-quake approaching; the firn ice settling, wave after wave; the crystals of snow flattening themselves against each other; the air expelled, each molecule finding a new place to live as the firn above collapses. Then I imagine the gradual shift outwards from this icy dome: the creep, the flow of ice, one grain displacing another. The sound of settling approaches us quickly. Soon it is beneath us and the ground is shaking. We stop in a rigid tableau. At the sound of a loud crack Lady's legs buckle with shock. As she collapses into the snow Gloë yelps and dashes round our legs, desperately seeking the safety of something solid: my ski and then one of the sledge skids, where he cowers, shaking.

But it is not Lady who hears Koch's gun tonight, not yet.

It is Cavalier who hears his final thunder. How can we redistribute his load among just the three that remain?

Every half-hour Koch takes a reading with the quadrant at the front of our caravan. Slowly the degrees of longitude acquire minutes. While we glide along on skis the ponies trudge thigh deep in snow. While our eyes are protected by goggles theirs are sealed shut with pus. While we freeze-dry our sleeping bags and knock away the ice, they have only an icy hole to enjoy. It is a poor reward. But we breathe the same air, and this has become thin and sparse. It is an effort to dig, an effort to pull up the tent, even the Primus struggles for breath, and the ponies pant and struggle forward, quite blindly now. Our journeys are becoming shorter and shorter. I see Koch making calculations in his head. How far have we gone, how much farther can we go? How much food? How much petrol? But the barometer and our straining lungs tell us we are still rising. Maybe the highest point, the blunt summit, is not midway, but lies somewhat to the west of this. The ponies are moving so slowly through the snow it sometimes appears they are not moving at all.

Vigfus and I have harnessed ourselves to the sledges instead of the ponies. They can pull no more. We trudge almost as slowly as the ponies' hooves do behind us, our skis scraping away the snow. We keep our eyes on the horizon, where the sky meets the flatness of the snow. Over there is a promise of home. Over there is food, warmth, a shelter from this wind. Is it too far away? Are we too late already to catch the last ship of summer? I have only to shut my eyes to see Else's face, not smiling, each part of it drawn away from the rest with concern. What will she think when there is no news? Will she hold on and wait even though her face is bursting into bloom? Beside me Vigfus grunts and points. We both stop. Above us is a small bird hovering and then darting downwards. Where has it come from? From the east coast or the west?

When we stop I can hardly find the energy to prevent myself

collapsing, but the ponies seem a little better for their stroll behind the sledge. Koch has calculated that they can have extra hay. As he says this he is careful not to look at anyone. I pat Vigfus on the back; he looks at me, and even though his face looks desperately exhausted he seems to appreciate the gesture. Koch is acknowledging what we all know now: the ponies will not last much longer, we may as well help them go as far as they can.

It is the second day of June. A bright morning, but a little too crisp: minus thirty degrees.

We rest, hoping the ponies will recover. While we wait Koch and I dig into the ground.

'I think that's it,' Koch says. He looks at me and smiles. 'Some hole, eh, Wegener?'

Now that we reckon ourselves to be at the centre of the ice sheet we have decided to conduct a small investigation. It is seven metres deep and the digging has been difficult, especially the last two metres where the ice was particularly hard and compacted. But now we can see the layering quite clearly when I brush away the snow. We insert the thermometer at different depths and then extract samples of ice and measure their density. It is so cold here, so desolate, even in the height of summer the temperature doesn't get close to melting point. Yet even here we see snow being converted into ice, just as it is in other, less extreme places. Koch makes notes and sketches while I take photographs.

Lady stops and refuses to go farther. Now we make a sad caravan: only two sledges but still the Danish flag flutters on the mast. We leave a trail behind us; there are more and more things we are discovering we don't need.

Vigfus produces snowshoes for the ponies. The man is like a magician, suddenly making things appear before us. We attach them to Grauni's feet. I think I see him smile.

In the morning Larsen reads the temperature. On the ninth of June it is minus thirty-four degrees. We all have frostbite.

Koch's toe frightens me. He mutters darkly about amputation and it does look as if the flesh is dying. In the fog we see a white rainbow and then a big bird. For several moments we stare at it, hoping it is a promise of green land and the end of this winter. But then it twitters a small-bird sound and we can see it is just the light playing tricks. It is just the small snow sparrow again.

In the afternoon our faces blister in the sun. I cover mine with a handkerchief.

Koch has made more calculations. This time he confers with me. Are we really running out of pony fodder? Together with Vigfus and Larsen we inspect the two ponies that remain. They are both ill and blind; they huddle together in their small stable, as if they are bringing each other comfort. Then Koch strokes Fox's russet skin, takes him by the lead and coaxes him out, whispers into his ear and leads him away, waits for Vigfus to turn and then presses his gun against the pony's head.

There are six of us pulling the sledge: four men, one pony and the wind. Still the Danish flag flies. I see Koch looking at it. He likes the red, he tells me. He likes the way it looks against the snow. Maybe it inspires him, but this party is only half Danish, and, to me, this small red-and-white flag only emphasises our puniness in this vast white landscape.

It is the twelfth of June and we are at almost three thousand metres, and yet all around us it looks flat. It is difficult to believe, except by virtue of the way my lungs have to labour for every scrap of air, that I am as high as the mountains around Innsbruck. But we are going down. It is even more difficult to believe this, as there is no apparent slope, just the readings on the barometer, but we celebrate anxiously with sardines and a little porridge cooked in milk.

There are footprints in the snow. They are fresh, uncovered by any firm. We examine them eagerly. We can only guess at what has made them, but it is certainly something with four feet, something that has ventured out on to the ice from its home in the west. We look out west, straining to see signs of distant mountain tops.

Grauni is weakening. We and the wind do his work, pulling alongside him, battling to keep the sledge upright. When we make camp Vigfus conducts an anxious inspection. Now that the wind has changed direction his other eye has become blind. We decide to take a day's rest at camp to allow him time to recover.

But still he weakens. Even though the weather is much warmer it makes no difference to the poor animal. He struggles onwards until he can go no farther, and when he throws himself into the snow we make camp where he lies. We are determined now to save him. It doesn't seem fair that he should come so far to be abandoned so close to green fields and pasture.

Grauni trails behind the sledge while we pull along with the wind. We make good speed, but then again Grauni throws himself down and we stop.

Now Grauni is packed upon the sledge. His legs are tied, and we have covered him with our tent and sleeping bags to keep him warm. From time to time he nibbles from his fodder bag. When the wind is strong we hardly notice his weight. We cannot give him up now. We are only three days from the depot. A seagull cries above us, telling us stories about the sea.

When the wind drops the tent becomes like an oven. There is a strong smell of decaying caribou.

The ice is changing into soft snow, and ridges are appearing, heralding the edge of the ice sheet. Grauni sleeps on his sledge. We do not shift him. If he is undisturbed he might last. We have little food. Koch thinks he can see the coastal mountains, but they are just clouds.

We career downhill on skis, ignoring small crevasses. Grauni weighs little, but is an effective ballast on the sledge.

We can finally see mountains. Ahead of us is the nunatak that signals our depot. But now there are surface brooks and we have to wait for the night to freeze the water away to a trickle so we can cross, and when we do so Grauni falls, and even though we do our best to make him dry he continues to shiver.

It is impossible to continue with the horse. We make camp and dig a stable. Still Grauni shivers. But the depot is in sight now. If we go without our luggage we can make it there and back in a day. We try to stir Grauni but he will not come. I whisper to him, tell him about sweet grass that lies just beyond his nose, but he will not listen. He squeezes his swollen eyelids together and lets his head sink into the snow. Vigfus fetches water from a brook and leaves it by the bag of fodder. The edge of the ice is just a mile away, but the pony is too tired to smell it.

There are flowers beneath my feet. They seem like small miracles; small heads of flowers like cotton bolls, and springy clumps of purple vegetation clinging to the ground. And grass, enough for an army of Graunis. We stop as if on a signal, listening and smelling, marvelling at the rapid transformation from desert to Eden: bees are humming, mosquitoes are playing zithers and the birds' songs seem to be the most complicated chorus I have ever heard. The smell of herbs crushed beneath my feet mingles with that of grass.

We find the depot easily and celebrate with a cold breakfast and cigars. There is just enough here to sustain us until we manage to reach a settlement on the coast. While Koch and Vigfus go towards the coast to look for human help, Larsen and I go back for Grauni.

The grey mound of fur hardly moves. When we touch him we can feel that his breathing is weak. He is dying. It is cruel to keep him going any longer. We offer him food and water but he will take nothing. Before I can think too much about it I take out the gun. It is my last ball cartridge. Larsen is angry.

Why now? he asks. Why can I not wait just a little longer? I tell him the animal is suffering, and he asks, what's new? The animal has been suffering for months. We have all been suffering for months. Then he grabs the gun from me and pulls the trigger. Grauni's legs twitch and then he is still.

Larsen is still angry. Because of that, he says, kicking the carcass, we have had to go slowly, we have had to wait while it recovered. We even carried it, for God's sake. We even gave it our bread. Why did we have to shoot it now?

I tell him that even a healthy horse would have struggled over the terrain to the depot, and Grauni was by no means healthy.

Larsen sits down in the snow, shaking. 'Why did we bother?' he asks between sobs. 'What was the point?'

He is not talking just about the pony any longer, but I pretend that he is.

'Because he deserved our help,' I say, sitting beside him. 'Because he always took the largest load, because he tried, because he never gave up, and because he was a vicious little brute that would have buried his teeth into our behind if he'd ever had the chance.'

Larsen looks up. 'He went for you too, then?'

I nod.

'But Vigfus always makes out he's such a little angel.'

'I think he was afraid of Grauni too.'

23

The edge of the ice is always difficult to transverse but this edge was more difficult than most. Besides the deep crevasses there were large midday potholes caused by the ice melting beneath. Again and again our feet plunged inside and we would trip and fall and cause the sledge to lurch. But it was downhill, and so we pulled and the sledge followed, and soon we came to where the ice ended and we were once again on rock.

It was impossible to make camp without any soil so Larsen lit a fire and we sat around it for some time talking. Koch was confident that we could reach Prøven in six days. It wasn't far, we just had to follow the bank of the Lax fjord to the bulging outcrop of Kangek and then go south to the sea. If we didn't then attract attention with our flags, we could paddle our way to Prøven Island with an improvised raft. We had two tins of pemmican, and some bread and milk; enough food for five days if we were careful. We set out in the evening.

The weather is wonderful. It is the sort of bright clear day that brings out old men to sit and children to play. Unfortunately, in Greenland, it also brings out the insects. The mosquitoes never give up. Even Gloë is sent into small frenzies. As soon as one is smashed against my neck another buzzes at my head. They bite incessantly, creeping beneath my clothes to find a new part of me to poison. And then they itch; an itching that cannot be relieved no matter how much I scratch. We snarl, we swear; the insects are achieving what the snow and cold could never achieve; it is making us into monsters. I scratch and scratch again. No one talks unless they have to. Even Gloë is silent. We make camp. Koch opens another tin, carefully extracts exactly half of the contents and returns it to his luggage. The meaty smell makes Gloë whimper. Only half a tin left now, but we can hear the sea.

The map is wrong. It leads us down ravines with steep cliffs that go nowhere, forcing us to retrace our steps upwards. Then it leads us into marshes. So, in order to see where we are, we begin to climb. The weather worsens. The clouds hide cliffs and mountain sides, making Koch uncertain. We stop while we are still on relatively low ground and search for vegetation that is still dry enough to make a fire. We have no stove. We shelter by mounds of rocks. We have no tent. We cook our pemmican. Now we have no meat. Just milk and bread. I am too hungry to sleep.

We begin to climb again. It is a strange feeling to climb into a cloud. I feel unsettled, as if I am somehow climbing into nothing but air. Now that the pemmican is gone I dream of meat. I think of thick cuts frying in a pan, shrinking as they cook, and a hand turning them, a small hand that flinches as the fat spatters up. I think about this so hard I can smell the grease. I think about all the the things I would like to fry in the pan: potato, eggs and wurst. I mix them all together and throw them into a heap on my plate. It steams and smokes; a vapour that causes my stomach to ache. I want so much to sit at a table and eat with the owner of that small hand. I want it so much that my chest throbs with pain. But I can't stop. I have to keep climbing. It is only by climbing that the pain will go.

As soon as the sun disappears it becomes cold. I'd forgotten it could rain. Every step is heavy. When we reach the summit we find there is another. This is not the simple mountain of the map but a complicated plateau; another Dronning Louise Land. There is no shelter and no possibility of making a fire. Gloë gives a small howl. Larsen sinks to his knees and demands rest, but Koch urges him upwards. If we stop here, he says, we will never move again, and anyway he has seen a fjord he thinks he recognises on the map. From the end of that fjord, he says, we should be able to see Prøven Island.

At the bottom Koch says nothing. He just looks from fjord to map and then down at the fjord again. At last he says the map is wrong. The scale is too large. The fjord we need is farther west, behind the hard black basaltic cliff that projects from the ground behind us like an enormous closed door.

Again we are walking in a cloud. When I turn to look at Vigfus his face is grey. It is becoming hard to move. Above me Koch seems to be still and yet I am not getting any closer to him. I look behind me again. Vigfus is still there, but his face seems faded. When I try to stare through the fog he seems to disappear altogether. I can't see Larsen.

'Wegener?' Vigfus's voice is a whisper.

'Yes?'

'I have to stop. Now.'

'Where's Larsen?'

'I don't know.'

I call to Koch and he lumbers down towards us. Then we wait until Larsen's shadow appears from the whiteness behind us. We need heat, so I walk farther along the rock, tearing out clumps of woody vegetation. When I come back they are slumped together, Gloë curled into a ball at Vigfus's feet. I start to assemble the fire and Koch stirs himself to help.

'We can't stop here,' he says.

'But Vigfus can't go on. Maybe if we eat.'

We drink the last of our milk, and eat the last of our bread.

The rain turns to snow. The track we were following has gone. We continue upwards to where there is a small overhang. There is just enough room underneath for us to curl up and sleep. Four men and one dog.

But I do not sleep. Even though Gloë provides a living

blanket I am too cold to sleep. So instead I watch the snow fall while the light fades, grows bright, and then fades again.

Even though I am surrounded by their warm bodies I feel alone. Sometimes I am so convinced that life has left them that I squirm and nudge them until a cough or a shove back reassures me that they are with me still. But we should be moving. It is stupid to hide here. It is as if we have given up.

The snow stops. I sit up. Lack of sleep has not dulled my senses; instead it seems to have heightened them. My head is clear, more clear than it has been for days: we have to move, we have to move now. The thought is urgent and impossible to ignore. I shake Larsen first, then Koch and then Vigfus. Gloë leaps up, barking, helping the process.

'Hurry, grab your bags, the snow has stopped.'

They move as if they are still asleep. I shake them alive.

'Come on, now, quickly.'

They shuffle into their rucksacks. They stagger from the shelter, walking unevenly. This time, the only time, it is Koch who falls. He falls face downwards into the snow, arms outspread, the impression of an angel. I grab him quickly, force his face to look at mine, but his eyes are shut.

'Koch,' I yell at him. 'Look at me.'

His eyelids pulse and then lift.

'Sit up.'

He tries to move, slowly rolls over and raises himself on his elbows. Then his face pales and he sinks again.

'I can't, Wegener. You'll have to go on without me. Take the others.'

But I am not strong enough to go on alone and this sleep-deprived mania will leave me soon. Vigfus manages to pull out the water from his pack, but is unable to open the bottle. I open it and pass it around, but no one can drink. I have to squat beside each one and pour it carefully on to their lips.

Anger murmurs inside me. I encourage its growth. We can't die now. All that we have endured, all these months of cold and hunger, of digging holes and making notes, will be for nothing. I think of Else's face. I think of her turning away and bestowing that smile on another. I shut my eyes and take hold of her chin. Tears are collecting at the corners of her eyes. She will not look up. You are mine, I tell her. Her eyes lift a little. You are mine and I'm coming back. She blinks. One tear is held briefly in her eyelashes and then falls on to her cheek. I lift it away with my finger. I look into her eyes but I can't see their colour.

I stand up and look around. Our only hope is food, but all I have is a gun and a lifeless hillside. Already I can feel the anger dying away and losing power. We have to live. We have to eat. Gloë whimpers and collapses on my feet. He doesn't see me lower the gun.

No one asks where the meat comes from. I try to light a fire from the scraps of heather around me, but it is too wet. Instead of burning it just gives off a thin trail of smoke. I bury the pan in its small heat and then drop the roughly cut pieces of meat into the water. It is a long time since I have felt hungry but I know we must eat. The water warms a little but fails to boil. When I pass round the cups of broth the meat is still bright red and raw and its smell revolts me. I distract myself by looking outwards towards the fjord. Below us the clouds shift, swirls of white, thicken and then dissipate again. When they clear I can see snapshots of scenery: a patch of beach and a slope of rock above; a small promontory covered in green vegetation; the glint of the sea with a small iceberg. The cloud thickens again, then clears. I look for where the iceberg was but it has gone. I lean forward and look again. The iceberg reappears, a small triangular shape moving too quickly down the fjord. I stand up, carefully, in order not to spill my soup. Beneath the iceberg is the hull of a boat and the shadow of a man. I yell for the telescope and it is handed to me quickly.

I can hold it with one hand. The iceberg is an umiak with a sail. Now Koch and the others are standing. They look to where my telescope points and begin to shout. The clouds are clearing. The boat is coming round. Has he heard us?

Koch grabs the rifle and fires a shot above its sail. Now it moves towards us as if it is searching for something. We begin shouting; voices that we have hardly used for months suddenly regain their power. Then we hear a voice answering ours. We shout again, any sound just so long as the umiak keeps coming. Then Koch, the man who couldn't move without fainting just a few minutes ago, throws down his cup and starts to slither down the slope towards the boat.

I watch as the boat comes to rest by the bank below and the shadow of a man throws his anchor into the water. His iceberg sail flops a little and then is fastened upright. After placing my cup carefully on a nearby ledge, I follow Koch, Larsen and Vigfus on to the deck of an itinerant Inuit minister.

Part III
Die Methode

24

So many faces. I want to hide and not be seen. The noise is overpowering. So many people talking at once, their mouths moving, their heads wagging. Too many. I look from one to another, trying to decide what to do next. Koch seems at ease. I can hear his voice welcoming the attention with a laugh. I walk forwards and the bodies crowd closer. I feel a little trapped; all I want to do is go. But now the living wall is shifting. Someone is making a space for me to walk through, someone small but very determined.

Is there a silence around her? It seems to me that she has made the air around her hold its breath and watch. When I step closer I breathe in her peace with long, slow expansions of my lungs. Her eyes smile.

'You waited?'

She nods. The sun catches her face, lights up the platforms of her cheeks. My eyes travel down from her head to her dark high-necked blouse and black skirt. She is smaller than I remember. Her head is tipped to one side, examining my face.

'Did you find out about the ice?' she asks.

I nod back. I think about her waist, the way my arm could so easily encircle it.

'And your meteorological work – it was satisfactory?'

'Yes, it was, very, thank you.'

'And your photographs?'

But I do not answer. Instead I lunge forward and pull her to me. I think I speak. I think I say that I've missed her, but all I really want to do is look at that face I have examined so often. But now we are so close she has to tilt back her head. The sun lightens shadows. I stare without stopping.

'Your eyes,' I say, 'I've been wondering what colour they are.'

'Oh, they're hazel, I suppose, boring, neither one thing nor the other.'

I shake my head. In her eyes I see ice: turquoise, pure, perfect.

In spite of the lulling of the sea I had not slept for nights. I had been so impatient for the air to become warm, for the icebergs to become smaller and then melt away to nothing. And then, at last, I was in a Copenhagen hotel room with Else, vowing all sorts of things, promises I intended, just then, to keep. I remember telling her we would never part again, that I would keep holding her for ever, that I had so much to tell her it would take my whole life, and for a short time she had laughed, a breathless, delighted sort of giggle, but then she had lifted her hand and covered my mouth. She had just returned from Zechlinerhütte, she told me, as soon as I was silent. I drew in breath. I wanted to ask about Tony, my father, my mother, but her hand would not let me speak. Then, when she saw that I was ready to listen, she took both of my hands in hers and began quietly to talk. First of all she told me that my mother was all right, that the doctors said she would probably recover, but only very slowly. I took another breath but she squeezed my hand, a reminder to be quiet. A stroke, she said, on the worse side, the side that controls speech.

I remember then an interruption. Who was it? It's hard to remember now. A young man. A light jacket. A straw hat. Smiling. Confident. Just a few questions, he'd said. A loud, clear voice, but I had been louder, ordering him out, pushing him a little to add emphasis. Then I had shut the door. It had been difficult to force his foot away, but I had. I had slammed the door so hard he could not mistake my intention. And then, when I was sitting again by Else, I remember watching a hand that didn't belong to me. This hand was shaking so hard that Else took it and held it tightly in hers. Then she took my head and held that too. She became old and I became young. She became strong so I could be weak.

Else says I was given a medal, some sort of cross, by the Danish king, but it was of little interest to me. I remember halls with lots of people and then, at last, Köppen and then the peace of Zechlinerhütte.

How wonderful it is to see trees. How wonderful to see the colours of their leaves, to shelter under their quickly diminishing canopy, to hear my voice muffled in their swishing and stirring. There are no trees in Greenland, I tell my mute mother. When she smiles only the left side of her mouth moves. Only dwarf bushes, and they are only in the south. But there are the same colours, I tell her, oranges and russets, just like these, on small plants that clutch the land with determined roots. But their autumn is in early September, and the leaves don't fall, they just seem to wither away. Is she listening? I think I can tell by her eyes. Sometimes they seem to be the only part of her that still lives. I think she likes to feel the wind and sun on her face and watch the trees and small ripples on the lakes. So I take her out in her chair and wheel her around so that she is immersed in this living world.

Sometimes Else comes with me. We talk in whispers. It seems cruel to let my mother hear our words now that we are planning a future so full of excitement. Maybe I will get a professorship this time, I tell Else. It is something I have applied for before, but Berlin does not seem to regard meteorology or cosmic physics with sufficiently high regard and I am afraid that I shall again be rejected. Maybe it will be better for us to wait until I have a permanent position with more money before we marry. I pause. I give her space to disagree, and she doesn't disappoint me.

'I'm very good at being economical. You'll see.'

We stop and look down at my mother in her chair. Half her face is smiling.

We found a large but cheap flat on the corner of a street in the old part of Marburg. From there we could look out at the half-timbered houses of the city and on to the hills beyond.

I am standing in an empty room, listening. There is little noise, just the distant murmurings of human life outside the window.

'Everything's perfect,' Else is saying, hugging herself, 'just perfect.'

I am behind her, my chin resting on her head, my arms around her waist, and from here it seems to me I can see everything. It will be just as she says: in front of me a desk covered in papers, and beside it, where the sun and the windows are making rainbows on the wall, a bookshelf.

'Just there,' she says, spreading out her fingers, 'a rug, with lots of colours, and on the wall there, covering where the paper's faded, your bear skin, and through there' – she points into the room at the back – 'our bedroom. And there, tables and chairs, maybe a best room for visitors, and then . . .' She stops. Her head twists under my chin. 'You are happy, aren't you, Alfred?'

My eyes are closed. I can do nothing but smile and nod. It has been just as I imagined it would be: a small wedding with few people and little fuss, a quiet journey back to Marburg, and now this flat and Else. And now just Else. At last. I rock her in my arms. At last. Just Else.

I had missed the snow, but here it is again. Of course, it is just a temporary covering in Sauerland, but it is enough to allow

Else and me to ski. We set off confidently. Else declares herself a veteran – it is another one of her experiences in Norway – but she tires quickly. Soon she has slowed down so much that it is hard for me to keep going. I have to keep doubling back just to keep warm. But at last we reach the south slopes where there is little snow and we have to remove our skis and carry them.

She sits suddenly. Her clothes subside around her. We look at each other.

'Not another step farther,' she says, 'until I've had some food.'

I remove my rucksack and we devour our small feast. I am hungry but it appears that Else is hungrier still. She searches out the scraps from the bottom of the bag until every morsel is gone, then she sits back. I move beside her, letting her head drop on to my chest. I look around. Every time I see these snow-covered hills I am reminded of the peaks of Dronning Louise Land. But here, when the sun is low, it means that it is about to set.

'Come on,' I say, 'we'd better go back.'

I try to pull her up but she won't come.

I laugh. 'I do believe you're putting on weight, Else.'

'Maybe I am.'

'You're eating too much.'

'Well, I'm very hungry.'

'You'll get fat.'

'I certainly hope so.'

'I'll have a round little hausfrau that waddles down the street!'

'For a couple of months maybe.'

I look at her, a slow realisation filling me with alarm.

'Aren't you pleased, Alfred?' Her smile has disappeared.

I reach down and this time succeed in pulling her up towards me. I try to smile.

'When?' I ask.

'The end of August.'

Exactly nine months after our marriage. My smile broadens. Köppen will be delighted.

What next? Thin Else becomes fat Else. I shut my eyes and there she is: small, round, a little out of breath.

'But there's no room, Alfred.'

I am trying to find a place for my papers.

'There will be if you get out of the way, o fat one.'

'Where's it going, then? Come on, tell me that.'

'In there.'

I shove the box into the spare room. The door is a little difficult to shut.

'I'll see to that tomorrow, it just needs a little sorting.'

'But you've got all this to do first.' She indicates the study floor with her arm and together we survey the problem. It is rather disheartening. In fact, if I am honest, I know she is right; I'm never going to have time to catalogue everything before the baby comes.

'Oh, just get me some water.' She sinks on to a seat, her face red, loose curls of hair sticking in whorls to her forehead. 'I'm so hot.'

In the kitchen it occurs to me that I could surprise her. It is such a hot day I am sure that she would appreciate some ice. I make sure she is comfortable with her glass and then hurry down the steps into the sun.

It is Saturday. I think it is Saturday. I guess it must be the last day of July, but really I am not sure. Ever since the end of term I have been so busy writing my reports that I have not stepped out of the flat at all.

I look around. Usually the street is bustling with people at this time of day. Instead the place looks as if everyone has followed a carnival out of town: flags hang at windows, flyers and pages from newspapers litter the pavement. It looks so untidy; usually the street is clean, even horse manure is not allowed to remain here for long.

The shop I want is at the corner of the market square with its ancient timbered buildings and backdrop of the Landgrafenschloss towers high on the hill above. It is a view I usually enjoy but today, as I emerge on to the plaza, I am distracted. In front of me there is a parade of students chanting and singing, obviously a little drunk, and along the pavement edges are the townspeople with their children waving flags and cheering. I recognise the man in front of me; the seller of pots and pans in the shop below our flat.

'What's going on?' I ask him.

He turns to look at me. 'Haven't you heard?'

A shout from the head of the parade interrupts us. A man at the nearby kiosk is changing the announcement on his board. The news travels backwards along the street like fire through paper. 'Russia mobilised. Declaration of war imminent.'

The students are whooping, running around and shaking hands with everyone they meet.

'Well, that's it, then,' says my friend, slapping me on the back and grinning. 'Looks like we're both going to be heroes.'

25

It is just dawn. There are no birds, just a ringing silence because the artillery have finished their chorus. We scurry, like crabs or spiders, limbs holding us just slightly above ground until we feel the earth loosen. Rocks and stones shift upon each other, long-buried subsoil releases its unique smell of mould, and then we are there. A sharp drop, a slither and then the feeling of being enclosed in something damp; the trench.

It is newly dug, just a long slit in the earth, a crumbling crevasse. It is our job to make bunkers, deep places where men can wait out a bombardment, and so we start to dig out hard pieces of limestone to form a hollow. Before we finally become subterranean we take a final glance outside: in the distance is Rheims cathedral, a Red Cross flag flying from its mast, around it the warm colours of roofs, then just across a large battered field is the French front, a reflection of ours, a grey-brown mud wall.

Soon the hollow has been enlarged so that two of us can dig side by side. I close my eyes. It is quite possible to keep on digging with them shut, the action is so familiar: the chipping away at the sides, the small pieces coming away, and the almost impossibly slow progress. Did I really once dig into snow?

'Are you all right, sir?'

I open my eyes, nod. It is easy to imagine I am back there, happy and at peace.

'Have we finished here, then, sir?'

I look around. Maybe it will do. I ask the private to lie down in order that I may guess at the dimensions, but as soon as he is lying there I ask him sharply to rise. He looks at me, puzzled, but I don't want to explain. His motionless horizontal body had converted this place into a palely lined mausoleum.

We move off down the trench, past a pit that has become a primitive latrine and already stinks so much that my stomach gives an involuntary heave as I pass, on to another embryonic bunker that must be enlarged into a mausoleum. Already there are rats; clods of mud detach themselves from the walls and scurry ahead of us in the shadows.

A sudden hissing. Like steam escaping. Louder and louder until all I want to do is tuck my head away. Then, just as I think I cannot bear it any more, it ends. Now a metallic explosion. A sound I feel on my face. At first the grenades hit a little left of the trench but then they hit us full on. The sound is so loud I think I can see the air distorting with the waves. I bury my head as much as I can, pull cotton wool from my pack and insert great wads into my ears, but still the wall of sound comes, instantaneous, awful, crashing at the ground beneath my feet, each roar making my nerves raw. Even though I know that each hiss will end with thunder, I twitch at each one. I look around at my comrades. Incredibly, they talk quietly through the blasts as if everyone can hear what they say. They emphasise their words with their hands while mine remain firmly over my ears; if I were to remove them everyone would see how they shake. Eventually it stops. But we do not trust the lull. We strain our ears to hear more but there is nothing. When at last we are convinced we reach for our spades again and begin to dig.

The sun is hot. This is no weather for marching. It seems to me I can hear the pulse of my heart in time with my boots. Each fifty minutes of marching is stretching out longer than the last. Gradually the thumpings in my head overtake the thumpings of my boots and, just before the order comes to halt, the world becomes liquid. All I can think about is the order to rest and that five minutes and the next and the next.

The stars are out. Everything is peaceful. After sleep the world seems different. I notice that our billet is a barn with a broken wall at its entrance, that there are bullet marks on posts, that the air is still warm, and that there is no moon. Our orders are to take the village ahead of us.

We follow the railway line. It has a clear track, easy to follow in the darkness. Although I have the same boots, the same rucksack on my back, I feel none of the discomfort of the day. The air has cooled now and dawn is breaking. A bird sings near by in a tree and another answers. As I walk I can see farther and farther between the trunks. There are just fields, barns and then isolated houses, each one dark and broken. The track is leading us through a cutting to the west of the village and then down a wooded slope. There are not many trees and through them we can see our comrades huddled together on the ground. If they turn round they will see us, but they do not, they seem to be embroiled in some sort of skirmish that keeps their attention on the ground ahead of them. On this side of the hill I feel uncomfortably exposed. The village is in clear view, its shuttered windows like sleeping eyes.

I give the order to move. If we retreat a little, if we press ourselves against the opposite side of the cutting, we will be safe from view. We move carefully, following the railway sleepers and tracks, but even so twigs snap under foot and the noise quickly carries to the east. Have they heard? The answer comes quickly.

Missiles slam into the trees, brutally pollarding them at the crown. The sound of the splintering and cracking is paralysing. Every explosion lights up the faces of my men, each one pale and frozen against the earth. The dawn light catches the white cloud of shrapnel that bursts from each impact. There is nothing we can do but watch it fall; a prolonged spatter of metallic rain, scorching the ground, making it desert. The outburst stops briefly and then starts again. Now a cold realisation wakes me; their guns have an altered trajectory, they are coming closer. We must move. I decide to spread the men over to the left, it will be dangerous but the trees will provide some cover and our grey uniforms are almost invisible against the earth.

We move in small groups, one pocket of men and then another, like a many-footed animal, each foot occupying the same secure enclave again and again. Very soon we arrive behind our friends and their skirmish. Now it is fully daylight and we can see their battle quite clearly from our position on the hill. The French have entrenched themselves behind hedges. It is a clever piece of work. Under the cover of the hedge they can shoot with accuracy, but we outnumber them and are slowly gaining an advantage.

Barren ground, the life beaten from it with shells. Corpses, mutilated and broken apart, bright French colours and dull grey German; irrelevant differences in death. And I'm looking, looking. My eyes are drawn towards them by a macabre fascination I cannot resist. They're not real. They can't be real. These objects are so covered by mud that they must be part of the ground, maybe mute vegetation, or maybe something that has never lived. Is this how I manage to continue, by pretending they are something else? Is this how, when the guns start firing again from the village ahead, I manage to fling myself down into one of the French trenches and ensure that my men do likewise?

The first thing I notice are the butt-ends. There must be hundreds of them, all in one place, as if someone were making a collection. The next thing I notice is the smell; a complicated mixture of mud, old cigarette smoke and the latrine. I breathe through my mouth. The trench seems a very temporary structure and not well built. The sandbags have been piled up rather carelessly, and there is no obvious dugout, nowhere to hide. But there are fire steps and, at the bottom, platforms of wood so our feet are kept dry. I lean back. I am so tired. In spite of the gunfire I shut my eyes. I wonder whether, if I try hard enough, I can think about something else, something complicated, a plan maybe, or an idea. I imagine the ground beneath my feet shifting slowly. What is the point in fighting for territory if that territory moves? The thought makes me smile. Beside me is a ledge of mud. It is sheltered, and surprisingly comfortable. The ground is soft and forms a pillow at my head. The sounds become more distant and easier to bear. I think of the earth gently drifting. But the gentle drift suddenly turns into something more violent. The soft ground beneath my head falls away and squeals. By my nose are the remnants of his dinner. As I march I looked ahead. I try not to see the human-sized lumps that are there. Beyond them are the things that have always been there: the lower branches of trees, a bush, a bird, a blade of grass. And by my side is a single flower and on one petal a polished black ant.

The enamel dish is burning through my trousers. Have the kitchens come to us or have we retreated to the kitchens? There is still enough light to make out fibres of meat and small lumps of potato. I should be hungry, I should be able to smell pepper, maybe onion, maybe pork, but all I can smell is dog. I should be plunging in my spoon but my hand is still on my lap. How can I eat when my heart is hammering? How can I eat when there is such loud gunfire in my head and with each double thud someone falls, and falls again. At the first thump he is hit backwards through the air and on the second he drops. As he falls his hand stretches out and his eyes meet mine. If I close my eyes I can see his face: from a distance he is Willy, closer he becomes Kurt, closer still and he is sometimes Koch, sometimes Köppen. But when I stoop to look in his face, the eyes I see are mine.

26

A miracle. I had forgotten there could still be miracles. Amongst all this hatred, there is still something that can demand unconditional love.

I can't hold her. Else offers her out to me, but even if my arm were not still wrapped in bandages, I would be unable to take her. She looks so vulnerable and small. Maybe I would crush or drop her. I shake my head, and Else smiles and places her back in her crib.

I look at her face. It is not how I thought it would be – it is a little too pink, and the head is slightly pointed with too much hair. I had not expected hair. It comes right down her forehead, almost reaching her eyebrows, and it is long. I stroke it gently with my fingertips.

Ever since the first few days of the war there have been no letters, Else says, so they weren't expecting me. And I was expecting just two of them. Not three.

I had let myself in with my key and crept up the stairs. The door had banged against my arm, making it throb again. It had throbbed all the way up the stairs and then I had seen them. Three of them: two on a rocking chair and the third with her pencils and paints making a record on canvas. It was completely quiet, I remember, a tableau I couldn't disturb.

Else had seen me first. She had cried out, tipped herself off the chair, knocked her mother's easel out of the way, and slammed herself into me, ignoring the child. So I had felt Hilde first rather than seen her; a small soft lump between her mother's chest and mine. Of course, then she had woken, and her mewing had been the background to what came next: the exclamations of delight, the questions, the hugs, the tears. But at last everything was quiet, Frau Köppen had gone to make coffee, and I was able to examine my daughter in peace. I had never seen a baby being fed before and I watched the process with interest: the small head bobbing, the tiny outstretched arm, the legs kicking its blanket, everything so perfect but in miniature. It was difficult to believe that a small part of me was in there. Then, seeing the two of them together, I also felt something else, something I am ashamed to admit: a feeling of exclusion, and a little jealousy. They seemed to need just each other and me not at all.

But then Else had turned to me and begun to talk. She had talked without stopping, describing how life had been; the change in the town now the men had gone, the way women were doing things they'd never done before, the price rises and shortages, the news that they'd had, and the news that they hadn't, and then the backache that had begun five days earlier and grown worse, changed position, and grown again until she had thought she would surely split apart, but she hadn't.

Three days old. What is it like to be three days old? It seems to be a tiring business. Hilde cries to be lifted from her crib, but before she finishes feeding she is asleep again, and Else has to wake her, tapping her softly on the cheek. Then Else detaches her and turns her around so that she can suckle again. How does she know how to do all this? I ask her, and she smiles and shrugs, then reaches out with her hand to touch mine.

The thought of my impending return depressed me, but Else said not to think of it, to think just of now, to enjoy every moment so we could both remember it later. Eventually she made me take my child in my arms, sitting down so it wouldn't matter if I dropped her. I still tell Hilde how she felt that first time. It is something she likes to hear, even now that she is more woman than girl. You weighed nothing, I tell her – no, honestly, it seemed to me you weighed nothing at all. If I had shut my eyes I would have sworn that the blanket was empty, you were so still. Then, as soon as I had taken you in my arms, you had opened your eyes. It was the first time I'd seen them open, and it seemed to me you were looking at me, inspecting my face. Then I had smiled down at you, my best smile to show how much I approved, and you, not liking what you saw, had cried your first proper baby cry, not a mew, but a cry with a voice, a cry that didn't stop until your mother had taken you back again. It is a tale they all like to hear: Hilde's first frightening encounter with her father's face.

Then I had to go back, to continue, I suppose, what I'd started.

It is our turn to be the front line. Our comrades who led the advance yesterday are to pull back and allow us to lead. The generals think that this way they are preserving our sanity; no one can stand the pressure of being continually under fire. But we are going too slowly. From behind us comes a message brought by a sheepish runner on a motorbike: we must proceed, why are we holding back?

Above our heads, since daybreak, snipers have been firing. The bullets have been so high above our heads we have concluded that they must be warning shots; their tone is pure, unchanging, a high-pitched singing that we listen to with interest rather than with alarm. They are simply reminding us that they are there. It seems quite amiable, considerate of our safety. But now, as we begin our march down the lane, the firing changes. The high wail becomes a buzz, and the shots are no longer aimless but turned specifically on us. We have become a threat. Why are we advancing into this angry swarm? It is madness. We should be waiting for our artillery to dampen them with their rain. We watch our comrades in the open field to our right, their heads down, as if they are fighting their way through a heavy storm, as if the bullets are an inconvenience, as if by bending your head and taking a firm stance it is possible to stride through anything. But they don't stride through. They fall. They fall faster than any men I have seen falling before. They fall like the last wasps of summer in a sudden autumnal frost, until the only thing left to do is to retreat.

But now our artillery catches fire. Shells howl over our heads and down on to the enemy half a kilometre ahead of us. I shake with every impact, follow each missile's path, waiting for the roar I can do nothing to avoid. Now another runner appears, launches himself from his motorcycle with careless ease and rams the instruction into my hand. It is an insistent repetition of what has been said before: 'Attack.'

I look before us. There is a field of carrots, but their frond-like leaves can barely be seen below the white haze of smoke. I indicate to the men what we are about to do and take the lead, scurrying forward, bent at the waist and knees, an awkward low-level run. I look behind. They follow slowly. Every time there is a missile, I motion for them to fall, and we all dive, faces plunged into the wet cold earth between the carrot heads, and stay there until the ground stops shaking. We have formed ourselves, quite naturally, into compact groups that move together, zigzagging across the field. Everyone is most careful to use small steps, to creep, to keep as low as possible below the level of the smoke.

Barbed wire. I see now, too late, at the end of the field, there is barbed wire. But I have already careered into it, entangling my uniform, ripping out great chunks of cloth in my struggle to be free. I whistle a quiet warning to the men, and they approach more furtively. We creep along the edge of the field, trying to find a gap, gingerly feeling forward with a gloved hand. The smoke is choking us now, and it is an effort not to cough. My eyes sting. Surely somewhere our mortars have made a gap in this lethal tangle. In front of me a private suddenly drops from view. I creep closer. He is squirming in a crater and beyond it the route to the village is clear.

Now the men hold their bayonets up high. They are running, and working themselves up into a frenzy. They rush forward and I find myself following rather than leading them. I try to run too, I go forward a few paces but then have to stop. My chest hurts. I try to run again. I force myself forward, but the pain returns. I stop, throw myself down and allow a minute's rest. Behind my eyelids the falling man falls and falls again. Ahead of me there are shouts in German and French. There are thuds, bangs, shots being fired. I lift myself up. It seems the French are still here in the village. One of our privates falls to the side with a shout. I go to him; a bullet wound to his calf has lamed him for now but he is not seriously injured. Where has the shot come from?

A bush. Red, brown, blue, green. The red and blue parts move. Red trousers, blue jacket, easy to see. A gunshot and the colours tip sideways. My injured companion lies back, a satisfied smile on his face.

'Now I can die happy,' he says, and promptly falls into a contented sleep.

Now that the smoke has cleared I can see French soldiers everywhere. Their uniform is from another era, a time when it was useful to recognise who was your enemy and who was your friend on the smoke-filled battlefield. In this modern war of snipers and trenches it is more advantageous to be disguised with grey or khaki. Some of them come forward, their hands held high, some of them jabber, some of them plead in French for their lives. I look around. My men are wild eyed, their breath panting from their lips. They seem frenzied, and as the French come forward they approach too, their bayonets ready for action. One of them aims a rifle. I can see his finger hover over the trigger. When I tell him to hold his fire he looks at me with contempt and snarls something about his brother. But his fire is held.

We found few corpses; most of the French had managed to retreat to a new position. But now we needed to find their new entrenchment. I took three men with hand weapons and followed their route out of the village to the south. The lanes were surrounded by hedges that were so high their branches met at the top, and it was a little like walking through a tunnel. We walked confidently, certain that by now the French were far ahead of us in another battle.

The first bullet causes us to scurry for shelter, back the way we have come, behind a clump of trees. For a few seconds we stay there, waiting. Then there is another bullet, out of the hedge we have just passed. We dive into the ditch on the other side of the road and creep forward. From here we have a good view of the hedge. If he is French he is not wearing his brightly coloured uniform. We wait. There is no sound. We wait a little longer. Maybe he has managed to sneak away. I raise my head slowly above the ditch. Another shot and I am hit forward, a sharp pain at my neck. My fingers feel for the wound. There is little blood. I breathe my relief out slowly; just a glancing shot.

There is a rustle and the man besides me sends a bullet into the trunk of a tree. The rustling in the bushes moves farther away and then I can hear the sound of feet running in the distance. One of my men scrambles out of the ditch, and begins to give chase, but it is futile. He returns almost immediately.

'Too late, sir, sorry, sir.'

I ask him to examine my neck. I gasp as his fingers probe into the flesh. He apologises, squeezes a little harder, pulls something sharply away and then turns to face me. Between his thumb and forefinger he holds a bullet.

27

When I wake he is still there; the man who falls with every beat of my heart. Even when I open my eyes he is still there, his back arching backwards, a tumbling black image with a changing face, falling in time with each thunder-thud in my ear. Each time he falls I feel it too: a throbbing in my chest, a desperate attempt to draw in breath, and then a feeling of panic as my lungs deflate. I reach out but I can't touch him. If I could touch him I am sure he would be safe, but he draws away from me, disappears; the more I try to see the less I can tell. Then it begins again. He is closer this time and the banging is louder. Each shot makes my body stiffen. Each time I glimpse his face I think I know who he is.

'Willy?'

How can it be Willy? The face turns, the hand reaches out and I am reaching out too.

'I am coming, hold on, I won't let you die again.'

But he is too old to be Willy. Now his mouth is opening. Above his mouth is a blond moustache. A Danish accent.

'So you're just leaving me, eh? Why don't you come looking?'

'But we tried.'

'But not you, eh? Not you, my German friend.'

I reach out. But he is disappearing. 'Come back!'

But he goes, and this time, in his place, a pair of small hands reach out and touch mine.

'I am here, Alfred.'

And now, as the figure starts to fall again, I see another face in front of mine; a smaller face with hair trickling alongside, and this face doesn't move, doesn't fall, doesn't disappear but stays exactly still, her eyes immobile, staring into mine.

Sometimes I think that every wound changes us for ever; every grazed knee, every insect bite, every insult, every injustice. They can make us stronger or weaker, more defiant or more vulnerable, but we are always changed. Perhaps the longer they take to heal the more they change us: the hole in my neck, for instance, closed in a few months, but the falling man still haunts me. He has become a barometer for my state of mind; sometimes he is just a suggestion of a hazy image but sometimes, on days when every thought I have is black, he is there – clear and cold, falling, reaching out, demanding and yet contemptuous of my help. I have to fight to be rid of him. It was a fight I started in Hamburg in the Köppens' house and at first it was the hardest battle I had had to face.

When the light comes I know I must rise. So I struggle from my bed, wince at my throbbing neck and lurch towards the seat at the window. The light will burn away the pain and the noise. But for now, and until I can make him go, the man will fall. I try to look through his moving shadow, notice everything I can see beyond and tell it to myself. So here is Köppen's garden, over there the hedge and the grass, there the leafless trees, and there along the top caught in the branches are flags, drooping and melancholy in this windless morning of winter. All this is real, the rest is not. I repeat this thought again and again, trying to make it true.

Now a warmth at my shoulder. A hand there, gripping tight. A quick touch of her lips at my face.

'The flags are for you, Alfred. Papa was so delighted at your homecoming.'

We look at them silently together, then Else giggles.

'Frau Braun thought the war had been won. Silly woman.

As if only Papa'd know that! As if there wouldn't be marching in the streets!'

'And the men returning.'

'And bands playing.'

'And laying down their guns.'

'And children singing.'

'Without wounds, without memories . . .'

And her hands reach out, take the weight of my head and allow it to sink towards her.

I remember the mornings were the worst; hideous times of trembling and weeping. I felt so weak and angry at myself, each evening I would resolve to start afresh the next day only to be defeated again at dawn. Eventually the military doctor examined me and diagnosed a weak heart which had been weakened further by the march across Belgium and the nervous strain of warfare. At least, that is what I reported back to Else. He had also blamed my trek across Greenland, but I discounted that. Greenland had just made me tired. Anyway, the diagnosis meant that for the time being I was unsuitable for active service, and Else smothered my announcement of six months' sick leave with a whoop of delight.

It was only after we had returned to Marburg that I realised the extent of my freedom: for the first time in my life I could devote my time to anything I pleased.

I write without stopping. Sometimes I feel it is some other mind directing my hand over the paper. Fifty pages in two weeks! The ideas surface easily, there is no need to search for them. I need no papers, no references, just my pen, my paper and a lamp by my desk.

That first book, it was so small, just ninety-four pages long, not really a book at all, just a summary of my ideas, and yet it contained my entire theory.

*   *   *

Ideas come to me in the night. I wake and they are there. I stare for a few moments into the darkness and know they will not wait. How can I sleep with this idea inside me? So I turn back the quilt. I wait for the bed to creak and for Else to grumble and turn in her sleep. If I write it now it will be safe. It will be there when I wake. The European geologists want their land bridge and the Americans want a permanent ocean bed. I can give them both. I reach my study and coax on the light.

Before Hilde wakes she gives a warning: it is a hiccuping cough. I put her lamp on low. Her head is turning from side to side, searching for and then rejecting her fist. The dark long hair has fallen out now and a fine blonde down has taken its place.

Else groans herself awake: 'Not again.' Then gives me a quick glare. 'You haven't woken her, have you?'

I shake my head. 'She was starting to cry.'

'You were up?'

'Yes.'

Her eyes soften. 'That man again?'

'No, not him. Other men: Bacon, von Humbolt, Pellegrini . . .'

'Oh, those.' She looks down at Hilde and Hilde gazes back.

She's heard it before, of course. It is another accusation from my critics: my idea is not only wrong, it is unoriginal; people have been noticing my jigsaw for centuries, ever since the Atlantic was mapped.

'Maybe I should acknowledge them.'

She nods but she is still looking at Hilde. They seem completely absorbed in each other.

'At least I should mention that American, Taylor.'

She nods again but I don't think she's listening. I lean against them both. Hilde's head is hot against my side.

'But remember, Alfred, only you have followed the idea through.'

She is right, of course. Only my ideas explain the landscape of the whole world: mountains, volcanoes, islands, even the way the tips of continents trail behind the rest.

'Can you take her?'

How quickly the child falls asleep. Her mouth is open. A dribble of milk falls from the corner. I lift her without disturbing her and lay her down in her crib.

A chapter on isostasy was followed by a chapter on the composition of the earth. There were pictures of floating continents, and diagrams to show structure. I included Trabert's graph showing the two average levels of the earth's surface; a giant's step up on to the land just above sea level, and another step down again to each ocean floor: a step so consistent it could be called a law. So strange to think that most land and most ocean floor should be close to just these two different levels, stranger still that no one had ever before thought to explain why. It was easy using my theory, of course; just my iceberg continents again, floating in the viscous sea of the mantle.

Else is tired. She says everyone is tired. She is tired of being told there is no coal or wood or milk or cheese, tired of slippery farmers charging too much, tired of children coming to the door selling war bonds and tired of this stupid war. It should be over by now, she says, that's what they said. Why isn't it over? Today she has to queue for eggs and she is determined not to take Hilde. If Hilde comes she will cry, she always cries, so she is leaving Hilde in her crib, with me.

'What if she wakes?' I ask.

'She won't.' Else stands by the door with her hat. 'She's been fed, changed and so she should sleep.'

But as soon as the door shuts Hilde wakes, and the only way I can hush her is to walk with her over my shoulder. Maybe she wants to see or listen, maybe I should tell her a story. I decide to tell her about the earth and about time. I will tell it in a soft voice so that maybe she will listen.

There is a time, I tell her, that takes so long that only the land can understand. It is the land's time, with land-seconds, land-minutes and land-hours. In this time there are different rules; substances change character, even the most brittle solid can become liquid enough to flow. A land-second is long enough for an icicle to bend, and for a glacier to creep downwards to the sea. In a land-minute rocks can be pushed into mountains and they can curve and fold like baker's dough. But during a land-hour the solid-liquid continents have time to float by in the liquid-solid mantle; they fracture, they rift, they form valleys and then they float away. They push their way through the sima-mantle that has now become a liquid sea. Imagine the hours creaking by, Hilde, imagine continents colliding, earthquakes making the whole globe shake, and a mountain chain rising in a colossal wave.

Her head is sinking on to my shoulder. But when I shift she wakes and whimpers so I talk again.

Ah, such mountains, my little one, if only we could see them: one continent nudging another, India against Asia, buckling up the land between to form a plateau in the clouds. Or the Andes, ribbing the earth like your curled-up backbone, such a colossal chain, arching backwards as it encounters the chilled Pacific. So many land-hours have passed. The sima-surface of the ocean floor has set quite hard and the westward drift of the Americas has become a push. The leading edges buckle, the sial splinters, and from these rents volcanoes quietly exude a runny lava.

I stop. By my neck there is a wet patch of dribble. When we pass a mirror I see that her eyes are shutting and then being forced open again, and so I continue.

A land-day has passed and what do we see? Behind the estately-moving continent are a dozen islands, sloughed off in its wake, and in front of each island, at the cold bottom of an old ocean, the sima has become brittle enough to fracture and form a trench. So deep, Hilde. Imagine the blackness, imagine the cold. Every movement is sudden and ferocious: earthquakes, great tidal waves, and before each shift a mighty swelling up of sima. Imagine a volcano, all that fire, all that heat.

She whimpers a little then sucks her fist.

But this is so far away, little one, or so long ago. Even the land does not remember when the sial of Marburg last swept through oceans. There is nothing to fear. The only earthquakes here, my love, are the ones we make ourselves.

I listen. All I can hear is Hilde; her mouth is open from where her fist has fallen. Else says that sometimes, when the wind blows from the west, she can hear the faint boom of gunfire, but all I hear now is the breath of my sleeping child. Now that she is soundly asleep she seems more heavy on my shoulder. I unpeel her gently from me and lay her in her cot.

And then there was chapter eight. Ah yes, chapter eight; it was short, a little tentative, some have called it weak. I described forces – the earth's spin and the attraction of the sun and moon – and suggested that these may be strong enough to cause my iceberg-continents to drift. Both ideas have been derided, of course. Stupidly my detractors think that by contesting these ideas they undermine the rest. They do not realise that it is quite possible to be certain that something is true without knowing *why* it is true. Did Copernicus need to know *why* the earth went round the sun? Did men need to know *why* an apple falls to the ground in order to believe that it always would? No, the reasons were found later. The Newton of Continental Drift has yet to appear, but that should not prevent anyone from accepting the truth.

I finished with a flourish. It was my most important piece of evidence and I kept it until last: the actual measurement of the drift from various determinations of longitude, including of course the measurements Koch and I made on Sabine Island.

At first it does not seem an idea at all but a memory. I shut my eyes and I am there with Koch. Our figures are wrong. We remeasure but still it doesn't come right. We are too far west. Then, when I feel the wind blow, I know. We are moving; and it is not just the ice, not just the sea, but the land. The land is moving westwards, away from Europe.

I write to Koch. I ask him about the accuracy of our measurements. His letter takes weeks to come back. I read it rapidly: he sympathises over my injury; expresses his relief at my survival; asks after Else and the child; hopes that my experiences have not been too traumatising. I turn over the paper with impatience. Has he done what I asked? There, at the bottom of the second page, are his calculations. Even though we have used the notoriously inaccurate lunar method to calculate our longitude he considers our differences to be significantly greater than the error. In the eighty-four years between the discovery of Sabine Island in 1823 and our measurements in 1907, he agrees that it looks as if Greenland moved almost a thousand metres west.

28

Else says there is a statue in the market square. It is wooden, she says, an effigy, man shaped, wide, with the kind eyes of a grandfather, and people are taking it in turns to hammer nails into his sides. When she had asked an old woman what she was doing she had explained that she had bought the nails for 'our Hindenburg', and every tap bought aid for our troops, victory a little closer, and provided the old man with one more link in his already invincible armour.

'Can you believe it?' Else asks. 'Surely it is a graven image? How can we worship the god of war during the week and then pay homage to the God of peace on a Sunday?'

But the ministers at the church just repeated the speeches of everyone else: God will look after His holy empire and punish our enemies.

'Turnips!' Else says. 'That's all there was, no potatoes, no swedes, just these pale miserable things . . . again.'

We look at where she has thrown them down on the table. They are small, white with a withered cap of purple.

'I am so sick of turnips. You know, the farmer had the cheek to say that if I baked them they'd taste like potatoes?' She sighs and looks dismally at me across the table. 'All I've got for tonight are eggs . . . and turnips. If you've any suggestion as to what I can do with those I'd be interested to hear it.'

She folds her arms and waits for my reply, but I haven't one. My arm is aching and my neck throbs.

As soon as I had finished my book I began to work again at

the university. Professor Richarz was short of staff. The pay, of course, was poor.

'Do you know how much these cost?'

Else opens her hands. Inside there are two eggs. They are small, dark brown, and one of them has a crack along its length.

A thud and then a cry from Hilde in the next room causes Else to drop the eggs too quickly on the table. The cracked egg falls open. There is a choking smell from its orange yolk.

A letter on the door mat with a government stamp. We both look at it in silence. We know what it means: my sick leave is over.

When I kiss Hilde goodbye I notice with satisfaction that her cheek has a plump resilience. How long will you be gone? Else asks. Have they told you yet? But I shake my head. This war has so many secrets. All I know is that I have been commanded once again to work for my country. I wave from the window. I watch Else pick up Hilde's hand and wave it frantically until I am out of sight. As soon as they are gone the numbness returns. If I allow myself to think then the falling man will appear in front of me, reaching out for help. I am killing him again: my navigation methods direct the mortar that throws him up; while the prevailing wind, which I have used all my knowledge to predict, will send a green gas to drown him when he is down. To remain numb is better. To think of nothing is more comforting.

How can we be winning, Else writes, when every day she sees a wagon full of wounded soldiers, and the cemeteries are overflowing? And what can she say to Frau Wagner, who has lost all her sons, three of them, within two months, now that her husband is missing too? Is it best to say that he will come back? Or just to say nothing, and listen?

She will meet me in the Rhineland; a few hours is better than nothing at all.

Alexis is missing, she says, as soon as she catches my hand. As we push our way through the crowds at the station she talks without stopping. I can't bear it, Alfred, this not knowing, it's worse than . . . and her voice trails off, and she hugs Hilde to her.

Hilde is walking well now: Else's writing is careful, evenly spaced along the page. Our daughter's legs are good and straight, but there are children down the street with rickets. And have I noticed that all the old people have gone? When I come home I will see; the market square is quite deserted, no one sitting there at all, even when the sun is shining.

'Alexis is safe!' It is Else's voice. I turn without believing. Somehow she has found the location of my barracks, just outside Berlin, and is calling through the railings.

'He's all right, Alfred. Can't you come closer?'

'But he's not well,' she says more quietly, reaching for my hand through the railings. 'No one will say what's wrong and they won't let my parents see him. But at least he's safe.'

Alexis is being kept in a room with one other man. Even though her words are written I know they are rushed. But it is as if he is alone. He says nothing, does nothing, just sits there for hours, staring at the floor. Nothing helps: we tried holding his hands, his head, whispering, shouting, hugging him close, Papa even tried slapping him, once, a half-hearted stroke against his cheek. But it was as if we weren't there. Then, just as we were going, someone in the corridor dropped a tray. It was such a small, sweet sound, Alfred, a little like the bell a calf would wear, but Alexis had leapt up and tried to scramble under his bed. It had taken a long time to pull him on to his bed again and then he had just sat there, his legs shaking and tears running down his face. What will happen to him? Mamma has not stopped crying since we left and Papa refuses to come out of his room.

I have no answer. I allow the letter to flutter to my desk. The falling man lands beside it and both of them stare up at me, demanding my attention. But *I* don't have to look. *I* can turn away. I can make the falling man's voice fade away and replace it with something else. Maybe Alexis cannot.

I pick up the letter again. Just the letter, nothing else. There is another sentence, a postscript, as if it is an afterthought but I know it is not: Is that day's leave in Berlin definite?

Here is a memory I have; it is one of my wartime beads, but this one is bright and cold in the hand. I am in Berlin, on one of the busy streets of Charlottenburg, rushing to meet Else. It is winter, and the night has come early. There are lamps, but they are not brightly lit. They exude a sort of dimness, lighting only the space immediately around them, yellow, hazy globes of half-light. It is difficult to see people approach. I hear them rather than see them; a clip-clop of wooden clogs, a sound that used to belong to horses, but now belongs to the feet of the poor, then, just before they pass, there is a sudden cutting out of light and a sour smell of human dirt. Maybe we are all a little unclean. The winter has been a cold one, colder than anyone can remember, and there is no coal. The lack of coal is the reason why the lights are low and the trams are silent. It has also closed the bath-houses, which had anyway run out of soap some time ago. Of course, I grew used to the smell of unclean bodies in Greenland; it is a complicated mixture unique to each individual and now it has become a game I play, matching the smell to the person, guessing who they are. It is necessary for us all to play such games, to keep an interest, no matter how bizarre, otherwise there is a danger of being worn down. The brutality of this life equalises us. Each one of us is cold, each one of us dirty and hungry. Hindenburg's machine is in charge of us now, dictating how we will work, where we will work, what we will read, what we will see on the screen of the cinema, even what food will be presented to us on the kitchen table. As the bent bodies clatter past I hear murmurings in their wake. No one is happy. The whiff of rebellion is pungent.

And now, in the middle of all this, another bead: short, sharp, black edged. 'Alfred: Father dangerously ill. Come at once. Tony.'

The hill to the church is steeper today and the church is taller, the redness of its brickwork a startling purple against the winter sky. I used to feel a warmth here, a comfort, but today that is difficult to remember.

We stand quietly in the graveyard behind the church listening to the minister rumble out blessings. Kurt stands stiffly by my mother's chair, his face matching the paralysed half of hers, while Tony weeps silent tears for them all. Hilde moans softly against her mother. I stroke her face. My daughter. His son. One generation following another. In spite of the trees I feel exposed. There is someone making models. Someone making choices. Someone replacing old figures with the new. Someone deciding who is too old, gradually supplanting one generation with the next, and I do not like my place in his queue. There is so much more left to do. If only this futile war would end. I have so little time and I am impatient to start.

Then, in 1918, it seemed that the war would end: I had been posted to a position at the old German university of Dorput in the Baltic, and every newspaper report was bringing news of a new German victory. Everything would soon be well. I looked forward to bringing Else and Hilde and our new little one to this quiet old town. My temporary title of professor would be made permanent, and we could live in one of the lovely old buildings by the river.

At the end of September, however, the reports suddenly changed: we were not winning after all, but retreating. It took just days to convert impending victory to defeat. The great Hindenburg machine was in terminal decline. Later I learnt that we retreated with dignity; there was little desertion and no unorganised running. We were disciplined. Even then the motions of the machine were too well ordered for chaos. My colleagues and I read each report in silent disbelief. Our men were demobbing quietly. The machine was being dismantled at its edges and now only the control room remained, relaying orders into empty space. Even though we read all this, Ludendorff's announcement of defeat on the twenty-ninth of September was still unexpected. How could everything change so soon? But it had. Everything was lost, including, eventually, for me, the university at Dorput.

Later, when Hindenburg described how the army had been stabbed in the back, I would feel that I had been stabbed in the back too; yet again I had lost my chance to become a permanent academic with a title. Instead I had to return to Marburg, to a new flat, with one heated, barely lit room which now contained a toddler in a high chair, a baby in a playpen, one maid, one wife and a lodger. I was bewildered by it all. I had returned to an uncertain future. Again my faculty petitioned for a professorship on my behalf and again it was refused. The only academic posting for meteorology in Germany was Köppen's in Hamburg, but Hamburg had no university. I had no option but to stay in my unsalaried post, dependent on a small income from my lecturing. But at least the library at Marburg was just as warm and quiet as it ever was, and soon I found something to preoccupy me in one of the university laboratories.

29

When did men first notice that the moon has a face? Is it always the same face? I wonder. Or does it look different to different people? to me the moon always looks surprised. He seems to look down on us all with astonishment, as though he can't believe our foolishness.

It is 1609 and Galileo is experimenting with his new toy. He has already inspected the surrounding buildings and has made a rather interesting observation on the extramarital affairs of one of his neighbours, but now it is night, the shutters have been drawn and there is little to see except the stars and the moon. Since the moon is bigger and seems more interesting he swings it into view. What he sees causes him to look and look again: without the telescope there is the familiar face, but with the telescope he can see mountains – judging by the shadows, they are huge – and between these mountains, spots. For a few hours they glare at each other; one surprised face looking at the other. But it is Galileo who looks away first, and once he has looked away his attention drifts. One of the shutters has opened near by, and the light sears the darkness with a perfect square. Inside, he can see a woman's arm, and fabric dropping from it suddenly, like a drop of water grown too large. His telescope quivers. This is far more interesting than mountains and moons. Quickly he jots in his notebook a few observations about the moon's spots, then follows the arm up to the body of its owner.

Now, almost a hundred years later, another man looks at the moon. This man is less easily distracted because, for one thing, his telescope is somewhat less discreet. Being ten metres long, it is not the sort of instrument you can idly train from your bedroom window without attracting attention. This man, Hooke, looks at the moon with dogged attentiveness. He has read about Galileo's spots and wants to find out more. With his enhanced magnification he can see that Galileo's spots are, in fact, dishes. He draws them carefully. In a place called Mons Olympus he can see several dishes, one inside the other. It reminds him of something, something he has recently seen, and later he retires to his work room to experiment. He acquires some clay from the man who makes his tobacco pipes and moistens it to make it soft. Then, allowing this soft solid to settle in a bowl, he bombards it with various missiles. He is impressed with the results: there are many circular bowls, one inside the other, just like the moon. He makes more drawings and notes, becomes a little excited at his discovery, and then he stops. What could possibly fall from the sky like a bullet? The Academy of Science has recently discounted meteors and meteorites as the superstitious ramblings of the ignorant, so how can Hooke justify these missiles falling on to the moon? If he continues with this maybe he and all of the rest of his ideas will be discounted too. Scientists have to be so careful these days; the price of publication of new ideas could be something more dangerous than ridicule. So he looks again at his dishes and another thought enters his mind; the thought of food in pans, the thought of porridge boiling. So the next time his cook makes porridge he looks in the pot. He notices the way the bubbles form, collapsing and fleetingly forming a crater. Maybe this could be a more acceptable answer: a thicker porridge, the bubbles forming and setting hard, a boiling rock, perhaps, suddenly gone cold.

There have been other theories since then, of course; von Humbolt, for instance, advocated volcanism, and Darwin's relative, George, insisted that the moon's surface is a layer of slag that is spasmodically punctured by the tides of a liquid beneath. Later, a man called Gilbert would have ideas that were as bizarre as they were creative and brilliant. The moon was an amalgamation of debris, maybe from a ring like Saturn's, and the craters were the remains of the bombardment by the final fragments.

Gilbert had been right, but he had made things too complicated. My experiment was quite simple. I have proved to my absolute satisfaction that the moon's craters were formed by meteorite impact. It is as irrefutably true as the fact that the continents have drifted. So why is the truth ignored? Sometimes it seems to me that the moon looks more than surprised, it looks shocked. How can men know so much and yet refuse to accept the obvious?

Professor Richarz has given me a fine work space at the university. I think maybe he feels a little sorry for me; a fine way to reward my efforts, he says, why can they not grant a professorship to one who has done so much for his country? When I am there I am happy. My stomach doesn't grumble and, even though my fingers sometimes stiffen, I do not feel cold.

It is important to have two colours; one for the meteorite and one for the lunar surface. It is also important that this surface should be weak. No matter how strong the surface of the moon, compared with the force of the impact it will be weak, and so to mimic this I have used cement powder; grey for the surface, and then whiter stuff for the missile itself. It works well.

First of all I arrange the tank. I take the bag of cement and carefully shake the contents so that a large area is covered. Then, with a broad flat piece of wood, I smooth the surface of all irregularities. I stand back. It has a smooth blankness that pleases me. It is a little inviting, like a new slate or a clean piece of paper . . . or a wet field before battle. Now I form my meteorite. It is necessary to do this by hand. I have to plunge my hands into the white cement and shape it into a small soft ball. I have done this so much recently that my hands have become dry and cracked. Else doesn't like to look at them. She urges me to stop. But I have almost all the results I need now, I tell her, it would be stupid to give up now. Köppen, of course, does not approve. He says that once again I am trespassing into fields that do not concern me. But he will come round, he always does. He did with Continental Drift and he will with this.

As soon as the meteorite is adequately spherical I launch it into the concrete. This is the part I enjoy. Each time I throw I feel I am hurling something of me away, something I don't like any more. I enjoy the sound of the motion through the air, and then the welcoming squelch as the meteorite hits home. Then I inspect the result, examining the juxtaposition of white and grey. The grey is flung outwards by the white, and the two of them together form the rim of the crater.

I take measurements, I jot down the result, I race to finish before he comes: the man who falls. Sometimes, after he has fallen, a piece of shell lands beside him and throws up the mud. The clay flows over him and my fallen man becomes a statue, smooth and quite still.

It was only when my concentration lapsed that he came. It was as if he needed an empty place to fall. So I strove to become engrossed. I asked myself questions: what would happen if the layer of grey cement were thin? Or if the layer immediately beneath were hard? Or if I replaced the powder with a viscous slurry? I made craters with central peaks, craters with double ring walls, even chains of peaks, and for each example I could find a match on the lunar surface itself. To check I measured ratios of heights and widths and depths and compared them with what we knew about the craters on the moon. They matched. I came home triumphant, telling

Else all about the results. She listened and then demanded to see my hands. As she turned them over, inspecting them for cuts and cracks, I continued to talk. The evidence was conclusive. I would publish it in a paper as soon as possible. Once people saw my results it would be impossible for anyone to believe anything else. But Else said nothing. She just pursed her lips and picked up baby Käte from her cot. We both knew people would believe what they wished.

What are the signs of happiness? A smile maybe? A laugh? I cannot remember my mother ever laughing, and yet I am sure she spent most of her life content.

Alexis has brought his violin; although he has recaptured his tongue he says little, preferring notes of music to words. He is sitting on the deck playing something French, something sad, and the music swirls languidly among the mosquitoes over the water. As he plays he looks at me. It is a little unnerving, a little unfriendly. But how can I complain? What should I say? But when he looks at me it is as if he can see what I see. So I look away. I watch the mosquitoes spin in time, I smile at my mother slumped in her chair, I wrap my arm round Else. Am I happy? I think I am. At last I have a permanent academic post. When we arrive back from this little holiday in Zechlinerhütte we will take up residence with the Köppens in Hamburg.

As I lift my mother from the boat she smiles her half-smile and pats my hand. When she looks over the water, when she suddenly starts, when her good eye widens, I do not notice. She tells only Tony, later, when she is lying in bed: as she looks back across the lake she notices someone on a nearby bank. It is someone she recognises, someone she has been waiting for. When he sees her he waves and then he beckons. And that beckoning, she tells Tony, means that it is at last her time to go. But just as my mother is being startled by this apparition

I am watching Alexis. He is sitting with his legs dangling in the water, his trousers, shoes and socks still in place. When I call him he lurches so quickly backwards that the boat rocks. Only then does he notice his feet and begin to laugh. He laughs until the sun has set and the stars are fully out.

It is cold and I am tired. I have been in Hamburg for only seven months but it feels like seven years. I am so tired of the journeys: west to give lectures at the university, to the port for the marine observatory, to the east for my own private research, as well as two days in the local meteorological station at Grossborstel. This city is so large and so busy, my two days a week at Grossborstel in the suburbs seem like a peaceful paradise. I turn the corner into Violastrasse. Each house has a garden, and the trees lend the street a countrified grace. Even in winter the conifers retain their elegance with a white-green symmetry while the deciduous ones show off their lack of restraint with a wild array of disordered branches. Else says the trees have been fruitful; sometimes she says we would not have survived healthily without them. But we are healthy, in fact we are multiplying; already Else is expecting another child and even Köppen is impressed at our fertility.

As I approach the house, a quick movement causes me to look up. It is Köppen waiting at his first-floor window. His white beard shines quite distinctly from the darkness of the room. When he sees me he waves and disappears. I smile but hold myself ready; no doubt he has had an idea. It is just a few short paces through the garden to the front door of the house, but even so it is Köppen who opens it. He wastes no time bothering with the formalities of greeting.

'Look,' he says immediately, producing his small globe from his pocket, 'if we move the pole again, just there, south of the cape, it all fits. What do you think?'

There is no time to answer. Else's voice calls from the living room.

'Is that Alfred, Papa? Are you bothering him again?'

'I'm not bothering him. He likes it. Ask him.'

We hear Else's footsteps approach. She is wearing the grey of a Prussian soldier; my old jacket altered to fit her minuscule frame. It looks ridiculous, but, as she says, this one garment now provides warmth for two.

There is a wail from the living room: 'Uncle Kurt, give it back, at once. It's mine, not Käte's.'

I look at Else. We don't need words. How long has he been here?

'Since about four,' she says. 'But I don't mind, truly I don't, he helps with the children.'

'Yes, we're always happy to see Uncle Kurt,' chips in Köppen. 'The more the merrier.'

All three of us enter the living room. Whatever it was Hilde was moaning about has been forgotten already. She has placed Käte in front of her on Kurt's back and he is crawling around on his hands and knees making rather humiliating neighing sounds.

'Ha, another pony,' he says as soon as I enter the room.

'Oh, don't bother asking him, he won't play,' Hilde says, dismissively waving an arm.

Else and Köppen laugh together. It is the same laugh, one a higher-pitched version of the other, and usually I find it infectious, but today I find it irritating. Why are there always so many people in my house? But it's not my house, I quickly remind myself, it is Köppen's, and I really should be grateful that he and Marie have migrated to the first floor, but just at the moment I'm not.

'It seems the daughter knows the father,' Köppen says.

'Indeed she does.'

Maybe my voice is little too cold. There is a short silence in which everyone, including Hilde and even Käte, seems to be looking at me. Else is the one who breaks it. 'Are you staying to dinner?' she asks Kurt.

'Oh yes, a nice big family get-together,' says Köppen. 'I have something I want to discuss with your brother, but I'd value your views enormously.'

Else sighs. 'So that's decided, then. I just hope there're enough potatoes.'

Köppen makes sure that Else is out of the way before he reveals his globe. He compares it with my bigger one, which has been placed carefully on a high shelf out of the reach of the children. My globe, with its jigsaw continent, is covered with coloured pieces of paper. I have found out so much so quickly. Hans Cloos, a geologist from Marburg, although not a convert, has always been happy to support my quest with information whenever he can. I am still working from his notes. Each piece of fossil evidence has its own colour. For example, the mesosaur, a small swamp-dwelling dinosaur of streamlined appearance, is assigned a singular scarlet. These red patches match on either side of the Atlantic. With help my jigsaw pieces have become decorated with a spectrum, the colours matching again and again on adjacent pieces. There are lines and patterns too: mountain chains that are truncated on one side of the ocean only to continue on the other; coal seams that start in North America and continue in Europe; and ancient lava flows that are snapped in two by the little matter of an ocean. It is easy to match the pieces with so many clues.

Köppen's small globe, in contrast, is wooden, and the outlines of the continents, all displaced and crowded together to depict Pangaea, are augmented with a series of crosses.

'You see, Wegener, if the pole is here,' he says, pointing out one of the crosses, 'then it all matches. The ice cap would extend over South Africa, South America, southern India, and Antarctica . . .'

'Yes, yes.' I pause and take a deep breath. It is so hard not to be irritable when I am tired. I think about how things used to be and how long it has taken to persuade him. But now he has the zeal of the recently converted, and is my staunchest defender. Remembering this calms me enough to continue. 'So that all the real tillites are accounted for.'

'Real tillites?'

I'd forgotten about the hovering Kurt.

'Material we know for certain has been swept down from a glacier,' Köppen says quickly.

'So there are unreal tillites too?' Kurt smirks.

'Yes, yes, sometimes material from desert floods can look somewhat the same.' I wish Kurt would go home. It is so irritating having to explain everything to him like this. I turn back to Köppen. 'And something else fits too. With the pole just there, the equator must be . . .'

'Where the coal deposits are.'

'Exactly.'

We exchange a pleased grin.

'Will someone please explain to me why finding coal deposits under where you predict the equator to have been can make both of you so happy?'

'What is coal, Kurt?'

'Fossilised something?'

'Yes, fossilised tropical swamp in this case.'

'And how do you know it's tropical, for heaven's sake?'

'No rings on the trees.'

'Amongst other things.'

'So no season of slow growth.'

'So no cold season.'

'Even Professor P. couldn't argue with that!'

'Yes he will.'

Köppen and I exchange a smile.

'He's determined to remain ignorant,' Köppen says. 'Some people are like that, you know. And that man is worse than most. Have you noticed he's always on the attack? Never offers anything in its place, of course. Just likes to pick holes in everybody else's work, no matter how worthy.'

'Who's Professor P.?' asks Kurt.

'Pea brain.'

'Pig ignorant.'

Kurt sighs. 'You two are quite the little double act,' he says.

I think he is a little jealous of our closeness. I regard him and he looks away. There was a time when we would talk like this, when it would be the Wegener brothers who were united against the world, but since the war Kurt has become distant. The fighting has changed him. Everyone can see it. He is more bitter and more pessimistic. Köppen says that like Alexis he was too sensitive to be involved in such a thing. At one stage Kurt had taken to writing to him from the front and Köppen has shown me the letters. He shared things that should not have been shared: the smell, the sounds, the taste of fear. Since then he has become lonely and miserable, frequently exchanging the room Else found for him for ours. He should have friends of his own, I tell Else. I'm worried about him and I'm worried about Tony. She too seems friendless and isolated whenever I visit her in Zechlinerhütte. Else says I should invite her to live with us, but it wouldn't work; we have too little room as it is, and anyway Tony says that she prefers the peace of Zechlinerhütte.

Our house in the suburbs of Hamburg was never quiet. Often it was a relief to retreat to my study and work. I was always busy; one paper seemed to generate more. It was an effort to find enough fuel for the lamps and stove, so I could stay at my desk and write. Apart from reports on Greenland, meteorites and meteorology, I now had enough information to refine my theory on the drifting of the continents. Instead of just dealing with the opening of the Atlantic I decided I was now confident enough to show the whole of Pangaea. The jigsaw pieces fitted together so well that I could now, with Köppen's help, indicate the ancient positions of the poles. With the poles in place the coalfields occupied the equator, the salt-laden sandstones indicated the desert-forming horse latitudes, and the tillites marked out the area around these poles. There were other matches as well: instead of just aligning the Appalachians with the Hercynians of Europe, and the sierras of South America with the cape mountains of Africa, I could now pick out extensions of the Caledonians in Newfoundland and Norway, and link the ancient Precambrian rocks of South America and Africa. The jigsaw was becoming complete and obvious. No one could argue with it. It was time to write a second edition of *The Origins of Continents and Oceans*. This time surely there would be converts.

30

Whose idea was it to print so many unsupported banknotes? I hear it started during the war; no one would lend the German government any money, so we just printed some more of our own. And then, after the war, we had to pay reparations, but still we had no reserves and so we printed yet more. Day by day those printed pieces of paper became worth less and less. I remember feeling that I was standing on a sandy beach and the tide was on the turn. On pay day the waves washed over my feet and I would feel temporarily rich, but as soon as I tried to spend this money the tide went out and the ground underneath my feet was sucked away. We needed more and more to buy less and less.

I suppose the only good thing that anyone could say about the whole business was that this national debt equalised everyone. We became equally poor. Equality is something Köppen had always said he wanted. It was part of an eccentricity which endeared him to all the visiting academics. But it is easy to be magnanimous when you don't have to be, quite pleasant to travel third class when you know you can afford to travel first: but when you have no choice it is another thing entirely.

We kept chickens, dug in allotments, harvested fruit, and made do. But it wore us out, and it made us old. I suppose, at forty, a certain dying down of enthusiasm is to be expected, but Else had not yet reached thirty. It was Kurt, of all people, who found a remedy.

Else is a little reluctant at first.

'What about Hilde and Käte?'

'Marie says she'll take them for the day. I've asked her.'
'And Lotte?'
'Well, she's not going to run around too much just yet.'
'No, but . . . Oh, I don't know, Alfred. It just seems so . . . frivolous.' She looks down at her writhing hands. I take the top one and hold it still.
'Oh, just come, will you, woman. The change'll do you good.'

When we are out on the Elbe she is quiet. This place affects us all. Even though it is a miserable day, with the sky hidden in a continuous bank of uniformly dark cloud that threatens rain, it has a peaceful splendour. The water is opaque too, its surface shimmering with a rainbow film of oil. It does not seem possible that anything could live in this mass of heavy coldness, but from time to time we spot the balloons of jellyfish floating languidly in the water, and occasionally the metallic flash of a fish's back. Else trails her hand then quickly draws it in and gives a small laugh. There is little other sound, just the lapping of water against the wood, the whistling of the wind, the lines of the sails slapping gently against the mast, and then the cry of seagulls and distant bellow of a steamer.

That laugh. I realise how rare it is these days and now I want to hear it again. I look at her and smile and she smiles back. No laugh, perhaps, but an expression of intense pleasure.

The cold is pleasant, real, touches the skin and holds its hand there. Kurt turns the boat and the wind turns too. It is in our faces now, glorious, catching our breath. Else's hat blows from her head but is held by the string under her chin. That laugh again. She pulls the hat on to her head and checks the cradle on the floor beside her.

'Asleep,' she mouths to me, and looks down again. Her expression is so tender as she rearranges the blanket around the baby that my heart hurts. Last for ever. If only I could command time. Stay still. Just as you are now.

* * *

But time did move. After two years it took Kurt away and when he had gone I missed him. I missed his complaints as we travelled together into town, his irritating presence in my house, and his unbearable ability to play for hours with my children. I missed his boat and his hand at my rudder. But Kurt was happy, I consoled myself. He was making progress, doing what I often said I wished he would do; now he would be alone in Berlin he would have to make friends. Maybe he would meet his Else and maybe even he too would one day admit to happiness.

In the meantime I was busy with travels of my own. The second edition of *The Origins of the Continents and Oceans* was reaching a wider audience and I was invited to explain myself in person. Invitations came from Berlin and Leipzig, and in each place there were wolves smiling, licking their lips and waiting.

They do not need to be pointed out to me. They are at the front, sombre suited, and when I enter they separate reluctantly, still whispering intensely, and smile. Penck, the one in the middle, does not use his eyes to grin. It is a strictly local affair involving just the lower part of his face. His co-conspirators are equally mirthless: Schweydar, the geophysicist, doesn't bother shifting his face much at all, while the geologist, Kossmat, allows a quickly fading glimmer of his teeth.

When I start to speak they listen intently, especially Penck, who is sitting upright, as if a napkin is fastened around his neck. They eat my words in different ways: Penck's note-taking is calm and efficient, Kossmat's is more of a scurrying shorthand, while Schweydar waits until a morsel catches his eye and then swoops down with his pen to spear it.

Even though the theatre is filled almost to capacity I notice there is a space around these three, and when I finish it is to this island of men that everyone glances. We do not have to wait for long. When Penck wishes to speak he does not stand; instead he sits back, allowing his legs to stretch out beneath the desk in front of him, almost touching the lectern. He grins and waits for me to smile back before he starts. At first he fools me into thinking that I have won a convert. He compliments me on the clarity of my lecture and thanks me for taking the trouble to communicate my ideas so quickly. He even agrees with me that the mountains on either side of the Atlantic match. His voice is slow, lulling, and I relax a little, my shoulders slumping downwards towards my chest. Maybe the rumour I had heard was wrong, maybe he has not completely rejected the idea of Continental Drift after all, and now that he has been presented with all the evidence he cannot help but agree. I glance around the rest of the audience. They are all looking attentively at their chief, some making notes but most of them poised in anticipation. Now, as his voice continues in the same neutral drawl, some of them glance quickly at me. Why? I try to listen past the soporific tone of his voice. It is hard to take in.

'But this theory is totally unbelievable,' he is saying. 'The idea that masses of land can move . . . it is totally preposterous. As I believe a colleague has said, these proposals, they seem like the delirious ravings of an unbalanced mind . . . A simple matching of land form is by no means proof, how can it be? . . . After all, there are many mountain chains throughout the world, many massifs that could be matched . . . all of this can be explained by the well-founded idea of land bridges . . . so why invent another?'

All that he has said has been said before. I thought I had argued quite categorically against each of these well-rehearsed points. He can't have been listening. I rise to reply but I am uncertain how to begin. All I do is repeat what I've said before.

Now Kossmat the geologist stands. He peers around nervously, coughs, and also begins with an agreement. The continental shelves may certainly have moved, he says. But only vertically and only in relation to the level of the sea. Indeed, he says, the proof is undeniable – everyone has seen fossils of marine animals thrust high above the waterline. But deep-sea sediments, that is something else again. He cannot believe that the deep seabed can be thrust up.

I look up. Surely he is disagreeing with Penck and agreeing with me. All that he has said so far fits the theory of Continental Drift and refutes the idea of land bridges. Maybe I have at least converted one. But now his voice fades, and then stops. He clears his throat. He glances towards Penck and then at his notes.

'But continents cannot move,' he continues. No, he cannot believe that. He looks at Penck again and his voice becomes stronger. The transformations involved would be impossibly large. And what could cause such a process? His voice becomes more confident now. Dr Wegener has provided no real answer to that question, as far as he can tell.

He sits suddenly, pretends to scribble on the paper in front of him and then hangs his head. I have no answer. How can I answer something he admits is only a belief? I might as well tell him that there is no Santa Claus, no golden egg-laying goose, no God.

Schweydar, the final member of the trio, stands deliberately and makes sure that everyone's face is turned towards him before he begins. He wastes no words. He looks at me coldly, with not even an attempt at a smile. I look at my hand, wondering how a geophysicist will explain the contradiction of land bridges and isostasy. He does not.

'The fundamental prerequisite of Wegener's theory, that the sialic continents drift through a sea of sima, seems to be entirely justified by geodesy,' he says, just that, and sits down.

There is a short silence and then a rush of exclamations and questions. Schweydar and I gaze at each other in silence. Is he converted? His face gives no sign. It is impassive and impenetrable. What he has said was too short for me to be sure. But he made no obvious disagreement. I think he is enjoying my disquiet.

At the end of the discussion I find little else to encourage me. But I decide to talk positively, reiterating my certainty that I am right.

'The major barrier to the acceptance of my theory is merely a psychological one,' I tell them. 'As Kossmat says, it is a question of belief. Once it is accepted that such a thing can happen, that continents can move and drift thousands of miles away from each other, then we will wonder how we could ever have looked for another explanation.'

They are silent now, looking from my face to the back of Penck's head and then back to my face again. Penck says nothing, just shakes his head; a weary motion, false and affected.

'But I am grateful to you all for listening to me now,' I continue, 'for asking questions, for showing me how I must continue.'

I pause again, and look directly at the three in the front row.

'Your reaction today has shown me that I must investigate for more evidence, for better proof, for a clearer explanation, and, above all' – and now I look at Kossmat and smile so broadly he is forced to give a tight smile back – 'the reason why all of this happens.'

So there was nothing new to say. I had finished one battle only to fight another, and this one too was full of fronts and trenches, and people staking their place and digging in. Very few dared to climb out and listen to the gunfire, but there were one or two. Milankovitch, for instance, wrote to tell me that he had been overwhelmed by my lecture and my evidence. But these were brave souls. Even in my new university, in Hamburg, minds were closed and frightened. I had hoped to cultivate a palaeontologist there, another Hans Cloos, but there was no one who would dare to help. Without a geologist to guide me I was a blind man; all my evidence had to be found alone with an outstretched hand. But gradually I found it, rather more than I thought, as if by reaching out I had discovered a loose bottom brick and everything else had come falling down around me.

Sometimes I stretch black on my chair and just look. The piles of papers are circling the room now, and above this room there is another, Köppen's, with piles even higher. There will have to be two books, we have decided, with two different approaches. One I shall write alone, a third edition of *The Origins of Continents and Oceans*, and another will look at the whole theory in a different way. It will be the biography of our planet showing how the continents and climates have changed and will offer reasons and evidence. This book, which we have decided will probably be called *The Climates of the Geological Past*, will be the joint effort of Köppen and myself.

My third edition is on the floor around me. I keep it locked away in this small room at the back of the house. No doubt Hilde, Käte and Lotte would love to play in here. Sometimes I see their small faces pressed against the window; a shadow of their exhaled breath left behind when they run away pretending to be frightened. Maybe they'd like to hide behind the columns of paper, or make dens. Hilde, I think, would like to look at the maps, while Käte would want to hear about the dinosaurs, her particular passion, but Lotte would be the most destructive. She loves to throw paper, loves to demolish towers, and here there are a lot of towers. No, they must not be allowed in. The towers are critical and must only be dismantled with care. Each collection of papers is a careful argument. It has taken hours of work to find and categorise each piece but it has been worth it. Even though these towers look flimsy they are strong and represent fine arguments that no one can fault. There is one for the Geology, another for the Geophysics, another on the Palaeontology and Biology, a section on the Palaeoclimatology and another on Geodetics. After I have introduced my theory of Continental Drift and demolished the alternatives, these chapters will follow. They will be the most important section, my pillars, my strength. There will be a hundred pages of irrefutable evidence that will impress even my most vociferous doubter. It is difficult to begin, difficult to summon up enough courage to make the first mark on the page.

I sit back, knock out the contents of my pipe into the bin beside my desk and then open my tobacco tin. The contents are so moist looking and dark they seem like something I should be eating rather than something I merely set alight. I take several fat pinches of the stuff and press them into the tulip-shaped bowl. I am concentrating so hard on this task that I do not hear Hilde enter. She waits until she is right beside me before she speaks, then laughs when I jump.

'Mamma says to come at once. There is someone here to see you.'

Her blonde hair is smooth under my hand. As the strands escape they fight to be away from each other. She shakes me free.

'Don't do that, Papa!'

She marches towards the door but is distracted by the topmost sheet of an adjacent pillar.

'What is the name of that place again?'

'Pangaea.'

She skips through the door, singing, 'Pangaea, Pangaea, Pangaea . . .'

There is something familiar about how this man clicks his

heels and salutes me in greeting. Something familiar too about the shape of his chin and the intense expression in his eyes.

'Professor Wegener, I am so glad to meet you again.'

Again? I really can't remember. Obviously he sees that I am struggling.

'Johannes Georgi, sir, a student of yours from Marburg. Remember, I used to help man the observatory.'

Ah yes, an image comes back to me now: a man who clicked his heels together as this one does now, a man who listened so intently to my adventures with Mylius-Erichsen. The man who asked about the cold, who seemed so curious to find out how it felt. He has followed me to Hamburg, he says, and has just started work in the Grossborstel weather station this morning. He has found a house just around the corner, and has a wife and a boy about the same age as Lotte. Maybe they could play together. He is, he says, particularly interested in the upper atmosphere. For a while I listen to him talk, but I am anxious to return to my work. Happily, when I tell him that I am looking forward to working with him again, he takes this as his cue to stand.

'Well, you have certainly had an excellent education,' I say as he takes his hat. 'My compliments to your teachers, especially your mentors in applied physics and cosmology.'

For a second he stands a little awkwardly, his mouth opening and closing.

'But that was you, sir!' he says at last.

'Exactly,' I say, grinning.

It is only then that he realises. His guffaw is a little forced.

'Yes, excellent teaching,' he says. 'People are always telling me so.'

I remember he always did tend to take things a little too far. I am relieved to return to my study and the almost blank paper.

I take up my pen. I write down the words 'Australian

Wegener's Jigsaw

biological and palaeontological evidence' and then I shut my eyes. I lean back and listen. I hear cries and calls; not the cries of children playing in a Hamburg garden, but something more exotic and primitive. The air is wet, warm and sticky; a rainforest with ferns that stroke the back of my hand. I am not of this time. I am spectating. I am walking through and not touching. I tread without making a mark, down to the river where small reptiles grin contentedly in the mud, where they nose at the banks and uncover an ancient stink of rotting wood, where they fight for small fish and then stop to sniff for enemies. This is a warm land. A lizard licks the air. Beside the reptiles there are worms. Roundworms. They eat the soil with a joyous zeal, squirming quickly through the continent.

What is this place? I borrow the name of one of Suess's land bridges: Gondwanaland, a southern part of Pangaea. The land that will one day be India, Madagascar, Australia, Antarctica, South America and South Africa is now, at the end of the Permian, joined to form one continent. Some parts of it are covered in ice, but here it is warm. The earthworms wriggle and enjoy the heat.

I open my eyes and shut them again. In the blink of an eye the Jurassic has passed. Something has changed. It is not just that the land is cooler, it is smaller too. The country to the north, the land that will one day be India, Madagascar and Africa, is now separate and warm. What is left, the land that will one day be Australia, Antarctica and South America, is quiet, and less lush. The continually growing trees have been replaced with others that can sleep in winter, and there are strange new animals that have fur to keep out the cold. Listen: there is a quiet grunting and then the sudden whiff of the newly born. It is difficult to see. This animal, with her long nose, continues to nuzzle the ground for food while she defecates a soft-shelled egg. Nonchalantly she pauses, feels among the leaves below her and then manipulates the egg into a shallow pouch. She is not alone. Now that my eyes are accustomed to this dim light I can see a colony of these creatures inspecting the ground. I creep forward; they cannot see or feel me, so I creep up close. I gently lift and inspect pouches until I find what I seek: a recent hatchling. It is as raw and bleary as a bird. It squirms and licks the skin surrounding it until it is rewarded by the taste of milk. This monotreme does not provide nipples. Instead its Cleopatra young are bathed in milk until they are ready to leave. It seems to be a sticky existence, but a pleasant one.

What else is in this quiet, cool place that smells of change? Apart from the small spiny creatures there is something large, leaning over, licking a track through her fur. Another mother giving birth. Is this all the creatures of this place do? This large animal does not squeeze out an egg but rather a foetus squeezes out from her, and then another and another. They are small, pink, the blueness of blood vessels showing clearly through the transparent skin. Their eyes are sealed shut. There is no afterbirth, just a completely deflated yolk sac, and it is this sudden famine which causes these barely alive grubs to paddle their way through the tongue-flattened fur towards the pouch. What drives them forward? Maybe it is the smell of milk, or maybe it is the knowledge that there is not enough room for them all. So they move quickly, mouths open, sniffing the air, searching for something to fill their stomachs. At last it comes. They suck and a small teat swells. It grows to accommodate each mouth until the foetus is anchored to its mother in a happy dependence.

What else is here? Very little except the trees and this collection of primitive mammals. The only worms here are the flat ones that the marsupials carry. The round ones of the earth have been discouraged by the frozen soil, have migrated northwards and left with India.

I blink and it is different again. Now Australia is alone. Its peculiar creatures are marooned and free to develop their own idiosyncrasies: its deer jump on large hind legs;

its ducks have fur; its rabbits and mice hop; and its small bears climb as freely as monkeys. Around the rest of the world there are higher mammals with bigger brains, thinking things out and taking over, but in the drifting Australia there is no interference. The marsupials develop at their own leisurely pace.

Another blink and Australia is caught in a hook of islands. Now the rest of the world can enter in a trickle: island-hopping rats, and dogs and humans. Nothing will ever be the same again.

I open my eyes. I stand and move quickly to one of the pillars and search through the pile. Then I walk back to my desk and dip my pen in the ink. I am anxious to start.

After the publication of the third edition of *The Origins of Continents and Oceans* there was an explosion in interest. I was asked to give talks to a wider audience and to present my ideas in other languages. These, in turn, generated more requests for reviews, and soon I was on a lecture circuit that included Holland, Sweden and Denmark.

The children have been allowed to stay up late for my return. Hilde has a map of a land she has invented to show me, Käte has a piece of pointed flint which she is convinced is a dinosaur's tooth, and Lotte has a new song about chickens which she has made up with her mother in honour of tonight's stew. Else looks tired. In the shade of the lamp her face is divided into softly sided triangles. When I tell her I will take them to bed she shakes her head.

'They never settle with you. Why don't you start opening all those letters on your desk? I caught Father holding one of them up to the light yesterday.'

My study is cold after the warmth of our living room. As I turn up the lamp I see that my room has been decorated for me in my absence. On pieces of paper around the room are pictures of monsters. There are monsters with large heads and black open mouths lined with teeth; I guess these must be Käte's. The next one is Hilde's: a monster dressed impeccably in a suit but with a head like a cauliflower erupting from its collar, and then there is Lotte's. She has drawn the monsters that children her age always draw: a monster that has just a face and legs. I hear the children pass now. They are complaining about the touch of the tiles on their feet. I consider thanking them for their pictures but then Else tells them to be quiet and to go quickly to bed. After a few minutes I hear Lotte start to whimper about the chickens. Soon they are all back down in the kitchen again waiting for Else to warm bottles for their beds.

The letters are in a bundle on my desk. Some are routine: reminders about articles I have to write and notes from publishers. Then there is business to do with the bank, the university and the meteorological station: my application for more funds to finance the replacement building for the kite station has finally been approved, but the grant is worth so little now that I shall have to begin the whole application process again. Such a waste of time. I store the letter in the box at the end of my desk but crunch the envelope into the smallest ball I can make and throw it into the bin. I sit back and take out my pipe. But my tobacco tin is empty. Now I remember; I used up the last scrap on the ship homewards and Else has been unable to get more. There is a temporary shortage, she says, another one. If I had known I could have begged a little from Koch before departing. I collect my pipes together and knock out their contents into a heap on the desk, then throw them down in frustration. Why is everything like this? Why is everything so much effort?

Else opens the door. A draught of cold air enters with her. She sits beside me, balancing on the arm of my chair. Her chin rests on my shoulder.

'Sorry about the tobacco,' she says, looking at the cinders on my desk.

I squeeze her hand. 'It's not your fault. Thank you for my pictures.'

She gives a short laugh. 'It was Käte's idea. She called them Papa's little monsters. My mother let them borrow some of her paints to keep them amused while I was in the allotment.'

I turn her hands over on my lap, inspecting them. The backs are scratched, old scars ripped open by new, and her palms feel as if they are scuffed too, with hard calluses and bumps.

'You work too hard.'

'Oh, open the letters, Alfred, the ones from America and England. I want to know what they say.'

I open the American letter first. It contains, as I expected, a review of *The Origins of Continents and Oceans*. Only the second edition has been translated. The review is three pages long and is written by an American geologist called Reid. Three pages is all he needs apparently to dismiss both my theory and also a couple of papers of Köppen's.

'Is it good?'

I shake my head. Reid is like the rest. I had hoped that the Americans with their lack of tradition and dogma might have been more receptive but they are not.

'It is not just my theory that he is attacking, Else, but my method.'

I hand the letter to her, watch her as she reads the words: apparently I have been too anxious to stride forwards. My observations lack care, my theories are guesswork and my deductions are wild.

For a second she is silent, then she says, 'I don't think he fully understands what you've done, Alfred. How can he possibly know about all this?' She kicks a pile of papers with the tip of her foot.

'I've provided references.'

Again there are a few moments of silence before she replies: 'Well then, he's stupid, Alfred, or a monster.' She looks up at the pictures on the wall. 'Maybe like that one of Hilde's, the man with the suit and the large empty head.'

I reach for the English letter; maybe this one will be better. It is another review, this time by Lake. Like Penck he draws me in and gives me hope before turning around and lashing out. It hurts more. It hurts too much to read it out. I hand it silently to Else. He has picked out details, the way the continents do not exactly fit, the way there are gaps. He also picks out isolated pieces of glacial tills and fossils, which as far as he is concerned fail to fit like the rest. He concludes that I have proved nothing.

When Else has finished reading she slides on to my lap, drops the letter then reaches up to throw her arms around my neck. 'Oh, Alfred, I'm just so glad to have you back.'

I smile at her, kiss her quickly on the head. The letter is on my desk. I can see the words. I follow them down the page again.

Else reaches out and turns the letter over. 'Enough,' she says softly. 'Don't let them haunt you.'

Then she turns again to me, draws my head towards hers so our noses touch. 'None of them matter,' Else whispers. 'You know that.'

But behind her I can still see them on the wall: monsters with teeth, monsters with large open mouths.

She kisses me then rests her head on my shoulder. She is heavy, warm; I can smell chicken fat in her hair. How good it feels to have her lie against me. I clutch her closer and she makes a soft, small murmur. 'I'm so tired, Alfred. Let's go to bed.'

But there is just one more letter, from Denmark this time, I tear it open: Copenhagen University regrets that it is unable to offer me a position as professor.

'Good,' says Else, kissing me again and slowly slipping from my lap. 'You're needed here.' She reaches out, takes my hand, pulls me from my chair and smiles.

'To clean out the hens,' she says, turning off the lamp, 'and dig a new potato patch.'

In the dying glow of the gas mantle the monsters leer.

31

The rain has cleared and some of the trees along Violastrasse have managed to hold on to their blossom. The red brick seems warm and cheerful in the sun, and as I pass through the gate I think I hear Käte's voice in the garden. But there is no one. For a while I look around, enjoying the early summer sun. I investigate the children's den, Marie's little summer house, the chicken run, the neatly trimmed fruit bushes and trees. I test out the swing someone has hung under a tree and then notice something in the corner beside the back door. A fish tank. That hadn't been there this morning. It doesn't seem to be filled with anything very much, just a lot of mud and then above it some very green water.

'Leave that alone!'

I swing around.

'Alexis! What are you doing here?'

'It seems I live here now. The same as you.'

I remember the cuff of his sleeve, white and then grey as it shook under the dappled shade of the tree, and both of us watching this arm as if it belonged to neither of us, smacking the air with a spasm until he held it down with his other hand. Then, laughing too loudly, he came towards me.

The sound of the violin carries down through the floors, past Köppen's quarters and into our own. With it comes his laughter, thin, strange, the sound of a spectre.

'A ghost,' says Hilde, looking at Käte.

'But a ghost has to be dead and Uncle Alexis is alive.'

'No, some ghosts are alive, aren't they, Grandpa?'

And Köppen nods as he passes, handing a letter to me.

An invitation to Tauern in the Austrian Alps! I leap around the kitchen with it pressed to my forehead.

'You're too old to do that,' Else says, dragging a bucket of water across the room to the sink.

'We're going to Austria.'

'You are, I'm not.'

'Yes you are. Look: Swiss francs, not marks, enough for us both.'

'Enough for you.'

'No, both of us, Else. A holiday.'

'Really?'

'Yes . . . really.' I prise the bucket from her fingers.

'But what about . . . ?'

'What about nothing.'

'Some holiday,' she says, struggling up behind me. But she is grinning.

'Some rest,' she says but the little snorts she is making are snatches of laughter. Even though she is dressed in bits of my old uniform and suiting she is beautiful. The jacket strains over parts it wasn't designed to cover, and I am looking forward to our night alone in the Inn keeper's cabin.

'It's wonderful!' she says as she gazes down into the valley of the Inn.

'Better than Norway?'

'Better than anything.'

But when we arrive at the cabin the innkeeper's son is not there to greet us and let us in. The sun is setting and already it is cold.

'Up there,' says Else, pointing to a window.

On the first floor there is a broken pane.

Then, before I can say anything, she is climbing up. My old uniform trousers stretch and then give as she reaches above her.

'Good job we can only afford to eat once a day,' she calls, and slips inside the narrow gap.

Soon the window opens and a rope dangles beside me.

'Where did you learn to do that?'

'In Norway,' I reply with her.

The bedroom is locked but at least we have shelter. It is not quite what I had in mind, but we make ourselves as comfortable as possible on the wooden floor.

'Do you think there'll be smugglers?'

'Maybe.'

'What do you think they'll do?'

'Eat us alive.'

A quiet tut.

'Alfred?'

'What?'

'Is this like it was in the Borg?'

'No.'

'Why?'

'It was quieter.'

Another tut.

'And a lot less dangerous.'

'Why, what might happen?'

'This.'

Ah. One of my private beads. I keep the pattern turned in so it is close to my skin. How I miss Else. But I mustn't think of it; to dwell on it and yearn after her is a useless distraction. There are more important things to tell.

The weather was stranger that year. It was as if we were in communication with the god of rain and he was on our side. For the weeks we hiked along the Alps the sun shone. As soon as we reached Gastein for the conference a gentle rain started. After all our days without calendars and clocks we arrived a day too early. The only other delegates there were the organisers: Professor Ficker from the University of Graz and Professor Exner from Vienna; my old enemy.

Maybe it is because Else is here that the conversation is easy. There are no awkward pauses. Each time anyone stops Else finds something else to say, something someone has to reply to, and I have to say very little.

I am tired, but it is a comfortable, welcome tiredness, a reward for physical exercise, rather than the mental exhaustion that is my constant companion in Hamburg. Tonight we shall sleep in a bed, and that thought in itself causes me to close my eyes a little and sit back. The voices belong to another world; only odd words register and then float away. It is strange that Exner is sitting beside me, strange that he should be laughing. Is he my friend now? It seems so long ago. So much has happened since. Would he still malign my book on the Thermodynamics of the atmosphere, if I asked him now? I open my eyes. Maybe I should mention it. I wait for an opportunity to speak but there isn't one. Words trip so easily from Else. As soon as one topic ends she thinks of another. She is telling them little bits of gossip, harmless stuff, about people we all know; this world of meteorology is still so small and all of the Scandinavian branch are frequent visitors at Grossborstel. She tells them about the way the Bjerkes make their beds, the Scandinavian way, the quilts turned upwards at the edges, she tells them of Köppen's current obsession with ice ages and how he seems to be preparing for another one, then she tells them about our adventures in the mountains, about the cabin, and how our rucksacks seemed too heavy to carry all the way up and how we had hidden them under some rocks and she had spent all day not enjoying the view but worrying about whether we'd ever be able to find them again.

'And did you?' asks Exner.

'Oh yes, Alfred seemed to know exactly.'

So they all look at me, but I can't think of anything to say, so I just shrug and smile.

'And do you like Austria, Frau Wegener?'

'Oh yes, I think it's wonderful. So quiet after Hamburg.'

'Then you wouldn't mind living here perhaps?'

'Somewhere quiet,' Ficker adds. 'A small university town, maybe. Somewhere like Graz?'

Now Else is quiet. She looks at me: Graz is where Ficker holds his chair.

'I don't know,' she says at last.

'Is there likely to be a vacancy?' I ask Ficker.

'Yes. I've decided to take up an offer from Berlin.'

'You're the obvious choice as successor,' says Exner.

In spite of my book? Maybe the fact that it has gone to several editions now has swayed him. They are looking at me.

'I think Schmauss is quite keen to get you. I think you could choose your terms.'

I held out for the best possible.

No one is speaking to me. It is quite amusing. At last I have been offered a purely academic post as professor of meteorology and geophysics at a university small enough to be ideal, but I not taking it yet. I am waiting them out. The Austrian ministry has offered me a grade that is too low and I have no intention of reducing my income. There are also problems with my pension. The ministry has referred my case to the treasury, and Else has referred my case to Köppen. So none of them is talking to me. Exner is of the opinion that I should accept now, that my salary will increase once I am in tenure, and Else thinks that my chances are diminishing the longer I wait. Even though she is not speaking to me she is saying a lot. She says that I am obstinate and that her father and mother agree. She says that Exner is right; if I don't accept soon I will lose everything. But I know that if

I agreed to work under their conditions it would rankle, and I hate feeling bitter.

There was, after all, enough to feel bitter about already. Now that the second edition of *The Origins of Continents and Oceans* had been translated into five other languages it was becoming even more widely read and the rhetoric was growing.

When I am alone I open the report of the meeting of the Royal Geographical Society in London. I want no one to witness my sighs and tuts and the childish slamming down of anything that comes to hand. It is Lake again. The monster with the wide open mouth who begins each review with a smile and ends with a bite. He says that I am not looking for the truth, that I am merely promoting my own cause, and that I refuse to see or listen to any fact or argument that tells against it.

His arguments are petty. He picks out my diagrams and pretends that they are supposed to represent mathematical models when they are not. He accuses me of fabricating my diagram showing the two different average levels for the land and sea floor, and yet agrees with the concept of isostasy. But then he says he is quite 'certain' that the sial has sunk beneath the sea and risen again many times. How can both isostasy and sial-sinking be true? He cannot seem to accept the inconsistency.

But he reserves his greatest relish for my jigsaw. He picks it up and throws it down again, trying to make the pieces fall apart. But they do not. Can he not see that they do not? He says that I have distorted shapes, that the pieces belong to different puzzles, that my flattening of the Alps and Himalayas does not make sense. He questions my matches, refuses to accept corresponding dates, even though they are not my own. The strikes of the mountains in the Hebrides are slightly out of line with those in Labrador, he says, the gneisses of

Africa and South America are not well enough mapped, the Caledonians do not have a counterpart in America, the distribution of the *Glossopteris* fossil is too wide. His petty list goes on and on. But it is just detail: just because a ball bounces, does it mean that the theory of gravity is wrong?

He ends with a flourish. He plucks up Australia and dumps it down nonsensically into the Arabian Sea just for the general amusement of his audience.

I lean back. There is a quick knock at the door and someone enters. I hear Hilde's voice, staccatoed, a pant between each word. 'Papa, you're to come upstairs at once.'

I look at the place where I expect her face to be but her voice comes from somewhere higher.

'Why, what's happened?'

'I don't know. Something to do with Uncle Alexis.'

And she is gone.

I don't very often go up to the Köppen quarters, but now I enter running behind Hilde.

Marie has the letter. It is a small thing with not many words but she is turning it over again and again.

'I don't believe a word,' Köppen says. 'It's all rubbish, you'll see.'

'Well, we can't go after him,' says Else. She is sitting on the arm of her mother's chair, watching the revolving paper. 'He could be anywhere by now.'

'Yes, all we can do is wait,' Köppen says, beginning to pace up and down, up and down.

Sometimes Alexis is the falling man. Sometimes as he lands his face turns and looks accusingly into mine. 'You didn't try,' he says, and I know he is right. I was so busy with my own petty worries that I ignored him. But there was another reason too: he disturbed me. His tremor, his arm displacing air, his silences, his sudden bursts of laughter, all worried me.

He knew too much. He could see my falling man and he could see him clearly.

Did I see Alexis leave? Did I see him walk away, his violin case protruding from his rucksack? For three weeks I tried to remember. When had I seen him sitting alone on the steps of the Rathaus? When had I seen him standing in the shadow of a bridge staring into the water? Was it yesterday or was it last month? Had the sun been shining? What had he done next?

While Else went around the neighbourhood asking friends, I went to the university. Yes, he had finished his written papers but had been marked absent from the oral. When was he likely to reappear? I said that he wasn't well and that I'd let them know.

Then, in the post, a letter. Detailed instructions, a map, a time. I went alone.

The road passes over a bridge. It is a fine bridge, with grey stone and gentle arches. Beside it, just as he says, is a place to park the car. The car skids on the gravel, shakes me over a large rock and stops. Beside the stopping place there is a path. A white path, picked out with stones leading through trees and along the river. The river is quiet. There has not been much rain. The trees thin. There is a field. Bright yellow. Ripe wheat. Above the field a solitary bird of prey. It is too far away to say what it is, but it hovers as if it is held there by a wire, completely without motion. The path leads down a little. Follows a curve in the bank. There is a place where there should be a waterfall but the river is too low. Instead there is a trickle. The sound of water breaking. Beside me the bank divides. It is not a bank at all, I now see, but a wall. A wall so old, so laden down with damp-loving vegetation, that it has become something living, something that will always be here. Through the opening another path. At the end of the path a broken-down house. Someone lived here once. Someone grew a garden, planted the herbs that have now turned to wood. Under foot wild garlic oozes too strong a smell. The door is open. It has not been shut for decades. Inside, the timbers of the upper floor have fallen and there is a complicated array of triangles and lines. I feel forward. Everything is damp. My hand comes away from every touch greener and more slippery. The holes where the windows have been are closed by creepers and trees. Roots climb the skeleton of the stairs. I stop. A smell. A smell I remember. Someone unscrewing a bottle once then withdrawing it quickly. Almonds. Squashed apple pips. Marzipan from Lübeck. Cyanide.

'Alexis?'

Something falling. A man. His arm loose, describing eccentric circles. Something splintering. Something scattering around me like shrapnel. I bend down. His face. Alexis's face. Staring. Too white. And a man screaming. My voice. Screaming, running, out of the smell of prussic acid and garlic and decay. Into the light where the bird still hovers.

32

Köppen is a man who likes to classify things. The classification of climates is his most famous venture: it was his idea to group regions that had never been grouped before in terms of how much rain, how warm the summer, how cold the winter. It was his idea to identify them, to colour them in on the map and to see the pattern reflected both sides of the equator: Tropical, Temperate, Mediterranean, Arctic. Having classified the climates he traced them back through time and found journeys: where England changed from tropical to desert, where Spitzbergen changed from temperate to the arctic it is today. It is now an important piece of my puzzle, another piece that locks in with the rest: as the continents shifted about the globe so their climates changed, giving rise to different fossils and different soils. Dig down and you will see their recorded journey.

Köppen has also attempted to classify men. He has taken the shapes of our noses, the texture of our hair, the colour of our eyes, and attempted to classify us into another set of climates. This, he says, is not so easy. Freckles are a problem: should they count as broken-up areas of brown skin or are they a feature on their own? But the main difficulty, he says, is our tendency to interbreed. We so often give rise to misfits, he says, to people in between who are awkward to classify: the individual who is tall and white, for instance, but whose yellow hair is as crinkly as a bush man's.

But it is this problem of misfits which interests me the most. The things that refuse to be classified fascinate me: the edge of a desert with a sudden freak rainfall, the side of the tropical mountain that is covered in snow, the blonde-haired woman with the black eyes, that piece of graphite, the one so black and matt it could never be metal, and yet it conducts electricity so efficiently . . . So many things refuse to belong. So many things can happen in the wrong order. A spring flood can come after the summer drought, flowers can erupt from the branch before the leaf, and sons can die before their fathers.

'Alfred, Vladimir has asked to see you.'

Marie. In my study. Entering my thoughts. Sitting in amongst it all. The tiny woman with her round glasses and high voice. Her face familiar in the crowd of imagined people. Something ordinary and drab in among the glamour I have invented for the Philosophical Society of Philadelphia. 'Utter damned rot,' the man at the front is saying of my map of Pangaea, and Marie's face is smiling, agreeing with them all.

'Alfred?'

I shake my head. Of course she would not agree. She is as big a supporter as the rest of them, it is just that she is more quiet, and more uncertain.

'He's just woken, and says he needs to see you.'

Köppen has flu. It is not the virulent flu that wiped out so many at the end of the war, but in Köppen it is bad.

'I don't know whether or not to open the window,' Marie says as she opens the door.

The room smells of sickness. A syrupy sort of smell, as though the air is thick. I find myself labouring slightly to breathe it in.

'Maybe a little fresh air wouldn't hurt.' I reach forward and pull the window down. Even though it is late December it is not cold, and across the street the houses are lit with a pale winter sun. Someone has pasted a Christmas decoration on the window and I am reminded that it will be here soon, all of us forcing out smiles for the children.

'Ah, air, I told the woman I needed air,' Köppen warbles from his bed, then interrupts himself with a long fit of coughing. 'Come and sit down, I need to tell you something.'

His face looks small among his pillows. His whiskers, usually so white, now appear to be a combination of grey and yellow.

'Would you like to sit up a little, Vladimir?'

'No, no.' He ushers Marie away with his hand. 'Go away now, woman, and find out what your grandchildren are up to.'

'Still the awkward old fool,' Marie whispers to me loudly so he can hear, then drops her voice a little so he cannot. 'I'll be just outside if you need me.'

'She fusses too much,' he says as she closes the door. 'Always been the same. Last time I had flu she took advantage of me, you know.'

Marie pauses by the door, listening.

'Because I couldn't move she drew me. Such opportunism! And what a picture! So ugly, so old. I was depressed for months.'

'And so realistic,' she says just before the door closes.

'But a good woman,' he whispers, 'on the whole . . . A good mother to . . .'

His voice trails off. He pretends that another cough has interrupted him, but it is a forced sound, covering up a voice that has broken.

'Shall I sit here?'

He nods. I draw up a stool so I am close to his bed.

'I've heard from the publishers,' I say. 'They want the manuscript for the *Climates* as soon as possible. So you'd better hurry up and get out of this bed.'

'Your wife doesn't think I will.'

'Rubbish.'

'She doesn't. I heard them talking. They thought I was asleep. I snored, like this.' He demonstrates a snort. 'And they fell for it. They were talking about measuring me up before the new year.'

'You were dreaming.'

'I was not.'

'Well, you sound strong enough to me.'

Now. At this moment. But not yesterday. Not this morning. Maybe not tonight.

'Exactly.' He pauses. His eyes shut and his breathing deepens. I wonder what it is like to be him. So weak. So apparently near to death. I wonder how he feels. Whether he senses his strength seeping away, whether the world is becoming more distant, as if he is drifting into unconsciousness.

His eyes open. 'You're still there? Good. I wanted to ask if you'd heard from Philadelphia.'

I tell him about the report. It is just like the rest. He reaches out. His hand, small, curled up a little at the joints, touches mine. It is cold, dry. A rash of goose pimples brushes my arm from hand to shoulder.

'One day they will feel so stupid. You must keep going, Alfred.'

'*We* will, together.'

He smiles and shuts his eyes again. Now his chest rattles as he breathes. He coughs deliberately. His hand reaches out for a handkerchief and I press one into it. He clears his mouth. He doesn't open his eyes. It is as though he is talking in his sleep.

'You are my son now, Alfred.'

I can't say anything. My breath too is caught. Trapped inside. Struggling to break free.

'I had three sons, you know.' He sounds as though he is starting to tell himself a long tale. 'Three sons – Otto, Max and Alexis. All ghosts now, one way or another.'

He pauses. A drop of saliva nestles at the corner of his mouth. When he talks it grows. 'We buried Otto under flowers. Spring flowers. So many. They dropped all around us that day. Petals like rain. As though the trees were weeping. And then I had to collect his brother from the station. Max'd been away when it had started, you see. Camping with his cousin Waldemar. When he'd left he'd had a brother. When he came back he . . . I didn't tell him. Not straight away. I wanted him to sleep first. He looked so tired. I remember he had bruises under his eyes.' His voice fades. The saliva has bubbles, lots of tiny bubbles making it white.

'But Max always looked tired. Always tired as if he lived too hard. Always a bit nervous and moody too. I suppose that's why we didn't notice at first. After Otto it was hard to notice anything much.'

He seems to be forcing himself to go on. The words are coming slowly, as if each one has to be persuaded outwards.

'Otto was my favourite, you see. I know it's wrong, but I couldn't help it. Always so joyful, and so happy. I used to watch him with Else. She was just a baby, but he had such patience, singing the same song to her again and again just so she could learn it.'

He doesn't require me to speak, doesn't even seem to require my presence. If I crept away now, would he notice? But I don't want to creep away. I want to hear what comes next.

'But Max was different. Erratic. Forever making decisions and then changing his mind again. History at Leipzig or maybe philosophy at Dorput. I refused to listen. Eventually he appeared settled. We waved goodbye. Economics at Jena. He seemed to be so interested in money, after all. Ways of making it. Ways of making more because he never had enough. He spent all I could give him and then demanded more. Where was it going? Marie and I kept asking ourselves: where was it going?'

Köppen opens his eyes, looks for my face. Searches for my eyes. What for? Reaction? Sympathy? Or maybe just to check I am listening.

'We should have guessed, Alfred. We were so innocent. When he came home that first Christmas. The morose silences. The snorts of contempt when I refused to give him money to tide him over. Then the inexplicable cheeriness. The laughing at nothing. Irritating, incomprehensible. Then the hidden bottles.'

He pauses, lies back, takes a deep breath that sucks the spittle in.

'There's no cure, you know. It's hopeless. And Max didn't want to be cured. But I blamed myself. Instead of sleeping I went through his life. What had I done wrong? How could I have made things better? But I found no answer. There is no answer, Alfred. I believe people are born already addicted. It is just a matter of time, of opportunity. We sent him to Leipzig, we thought maybe in a big city . . . oh, I don't know what we were thinking, but it didn't help. He just gave up the pretence of studying. In the end it was all we could think about, the only topic that moved us to talk. We went over it again and again. We could see him shrivelling, changing from something fine and new into something old and useless, and we could do nothing. Nothing at all about any of it.'

Köppen stops, lies back. For a few seconds he is silent, and then he takes a great breath in. It comes out as a sob. He turns his head away from me, but still I can see his face, crumpled, hurting with uncried tears. When he speaks again his voice is controlled.

'It was so much worse, Alfred, so much worse than even hearing Otto scream out with his poisoned appendix. With Otto we had memories, beautiful memories of laughter and happiness, but with Max there was nothing. What he became wiped everything else away.'

He stops again. I don't know what to say. Even after all

these years I am afraid to intrude. I pat his hand. He gulps quietly and continues.

'I remember seeing a poster. Start a new life in Baltimore, it said. And next door was the ticket office. So I bought one. An impulse. Second class, one way. And when he came in that night I presented it to him. A second chance, I told him. Kill or cure.'

His face turns towards me now. It seems more at ease. From one eye there is a wet trail leading into his hair.

He wants me to ask a question.

'And did he go?'

'Oh yes, he went. We had a few letters. One from Philadelphia in 1915. I suppose this conference report has made me think of it, made me think of him. He was still the same. That was the last. Do you think I've done wrong, Alfred? Do you think losing Alexis was a punishment?'

'No, I'm certain you did everything right. You did everything you could for Alexis, I'm sure you did the same for Max. They were lucky to have you. We all are.'

He smiles weakly and then coughs again.

'Would you like to rest now?'

He nods.

When I reach the door it opens easily. Marie is there, listening at the crack.

'How is he?'

'Better, I think.'

'He's told you about the ghosts?'

I nod.

'Sometimes I wonder. You see, my father died in an asylum . . . Do you think it's me?'

She blinks up at me, her eyes magnified into those of an owl's by her glasses.

'You mean you think you've passed a sort of madness on to them?'

'Yes, I suppose that's it.'

'No, I believe that is completely impossible.'
'Oh.' She crumples a little.
'A totally barmy idea. Utterly insane.'
She smiles. 'Thank you, Alfred.'

By the end of February 1924 the Austrian treasury had agreed to my demands on pension and salary and I became an Austrian citizen.

How is being an Austrian different from being a German? I wonder. We both speak German. We both remember a grandeur lost and we are both smarting in defeat. But there are differences too. On a Sunday I notice the mass: sometimes little girls dress up as brides and there is a whiff of incense as I walk past. On a weekday I notice the accent. It incorporates a little from its neighbours; a little Slav, a little French, a little Italian, and sometimes I am lost. But mostly I feel at home. It is just a short step to the Physical Institute at the university. With Else and the children it will be perfect. A small university, and more chance to lecture and do my own work. I lean back in my chair, shut my eyes in a smile that must be smug. Graz: small and beautiful. It is all I could ever wish.

Before she leaves the North, Else says, she needs a holiday. She wants to make one last trip to the lakes, like we did before, she says, in 1919, with Alexis and your mother. She wants to say good-bye, she says, and looks at me so long I have to agree.

Tony is already packed when we reach the house in Zechlinerhütte. She keeps the house with a spartan neatness. The rooms are empty of everything except that which is too heavy to easily be removed. The curtains are drawn back emphatically, every scrap of frame visible, and the sideboards are bare and shine with a furious burnish.

'Where is everything?'

Tony shrugs.

'You haven't thrown it all away?'

My mother loved her clutter; every surface had an embroidered cloth, every picture an elaborate frame, every wall was decorated with hanging plates and clocks.

'No! Of course I haven't. It's . . . around.'

She leads me through to the corridor and opens a door towards the back of the house. The door opens only a little so we peer in. It is dark with furniture. One item and then another shoved inside with obviously no thought of arrangement. It smells faintly of rotting wood.

'There're a few more rooms like that, so don't worry. I'm not depriving anyone of their birthright.'

She closes the door and follows me out into the light.

'Auntie Tony!' Hilde rushes up to her and the two exchange hugs. Käte and Lotte hang back a little, waiting to be invited forward, and their hugs are not as warm. Else receives a smiling nod and I have received a curt 'Hello'.

No one can understand why Hilde and Tony have developed such a close relationship but they have.

Hilde leads Tony down to the barge. Even from a distance and from her back it is possible to see she is irritated and disappointed.

'I thought it would have a cabin,' she calls back.

'It has.'

'But we can't all sleep in that. It's too small.'

'That's why we've got a tent, Auntie Tony,' says Hilde.

And because it's Hilde who says it, it is all right. She steps aboard with her bag and sits erectly at the back. 'You may proceed now, Alfred,' she says, and raises a black umbrella over her head.

The bow of the barge became her territory, marked out by the shadow of her umbrella. It seemed like an isolated storm cloud, rain falling from underneath it, rather than being held away. Only Hilde went close when the umbrella was up, the rest of us keeping to the more sunny climate of the stern. She said little, and when she did talk it was mainly to complain or to give us poisonous little anecdotes about people we didn't know.

We have pitched the tents. Inside one I can see the silhouettes of Käte and Lotte. Inside another are Tony and Hilde. This tent is in darkness, but Else has allowed the two younger girls a light for a short time as long as they promise to be quiet: an empty hope.

'Where is Auntie Tony's husband?' Lotte's voice, too loud.

The other tent listens.

'Dead,' says Käte with certainty.

'In the war?'

'No, she killed him.'

'How?'

'Don't know. Poison, I expect.'

Else seems to be attempting to stuff her entire hand into her mouth so it is up to me to speak.

'Quiet now, girls. Go to sleep. Or I'll remove the light.'

Else sighs, leans against me. In the distance we can hear a gramophone playing and a woman's song floats over the water.

'It's not the same, is it?'

'No.'

'Too many people.'

In 1919 there had been no gramophones. My mother and Alexis had been watching angels; angels waiting in the shadows of the trees, hanging on branches, waiting for us to pass. Alexis had reached up and brought them closer; while my mother had brushed away their wings with her good hand and told them not just yet.

Now I must start to describe last times. Of course, there have been many already: the last time I saw Mylius-Erichsen, the last time I saw my father, my mother, Willy and Alexis. This is the last time I saw Tony. Sometimes I think that the Tony beads are part of a pattern that is already finished; grey opaque beads that I tried to see inside so many times.

Only Hilde follows me inside. The rest of them wait, pretending to unpack and pack again for our journey to Hamburg. I take Tony's bag, it is not heavy, and put it on a chair in her kitchen.

'I suppose you'd all like some coffee,' she says.

'No, we'd better get going.'

She sits at her table, looking at her hands.

'You're glad you came?'

'It made a change.'

There is too much to say, too much to ask, and I can't start now. With Tony it has always been too late.

'Well, I'd better go.'

'Yes.'

Hilde dives forward, throws her arms around Tony's neck, forces her to raise her head.

'Goodbye, Auntie Tony. I love you.'

And even though Tony smiles, I cannot see inside. What is there?

'Come on, Hilde, we'd better go.'

I disentangle their arms. My final touch, my final interaction.

Tony stands and Hilde falls from her. A single unguarded moment. In that final shedding I glimpse her interior; it contains so much painful disappointment I have to look away.

'Goodbye, Tony.'

'Goodbye. I'll wave from the window.'

'I'll write from Graz.'

'Yes.'

There are some things you can do nothing about. There

are problems that cannot be solved. It is useless to try. Other problems are less intractable. The problem of what to do with Else's parents, for instance, had an obvious solution that suited everyone.

Even though everyone knows already, Köppen insists on listing the reasons why they are coming with us to Graz. We are all sitting in the garden enjoying the summer sun.

'There's Aline,' he tells Marie.

'Yes, I know.'

'Our eldest daughter.'

'Oh, that one.'

'Moving to Sofia.'

'Is she? Now how did you find that out? Ah yes, it must've been in that letter I read to you last week.'

'Which would be easier to visit from Graz. And the grand-children – we'd miss them.'

'I wouldn't.'

'Grandma!'

'Well, maybe just a little.'

'And you'd miss Mamma and Papa too, wouldn't you?'

'Sometimes, I suppose.'

'And you'd have to take lodgers if you stayed, wouldn't you?'

'They might like to play the trumpet.'

'Or the drums.'

'Or have a terrible voice.'

'Or argue after ten o'clock.'

'Well, I'm used to that.'

'Who argues?'

'You do.'

'With whom?'

'Me.'

'So you've decided, then,' I say.

'Well, we might.'

'Yes, we will.'

'Ah well, it seems that Marie's made up her mind. I suppose I'll just have to come as well.'

'But you said you'd decided last night.'

'I said I'd *almost* decided, if you'd been listening properly.'

'You're the one that's deaf, not me.'

'I'm not deaf.'

'And awkward.'

It is Else's turn to make a cake. It is a concoction of pastry and apples and spices that she always does so well. She has also made something with chocolate and cherry jam. She says that since it is her first time in Graz she wants to do it well.

Victor Hess, one my colleagues at the Physical Institute, is holding forth. As usual he has everyone's attention. Else and Benndorf's secretary are listening too, rather though they are trespassing, but later I know Else will remember each word and ask me to expand.

'Of course, it is easy to make an electroscope,' Hess is saying. 'Two squares of the thinnest gold leaf you can lay your hands on, attached to a rod and the rod to a plate.' He draws a picture and holds it up. The students peer round to examine it.

'Of course, I needed to protect it from the wind up there. So I used a box, insulated from the rod, of course, with transparent windows.'

'How far did you go up, sir?'

Hess smiles; it is, no doubt, a question he has been waiting for. 'Over five thousand metres.'

I whistle.

'Without oxygen,' he continues smugly, then turns to me. 'How far have you been up, Wegener?'

'Oh, nowhere near as far as that. What was it like up there?'

'Cold. Difficult . . . you know . . .' He smiles at Benndorf and then at me. We are experimental scientists together, conspirators; any danger is worth the risk.

'And what happened to the electroscope up there, sir?'

'It's well recorded. I charged them up, you know, the usual way, rubbing the plate with a cloth until the gold leaves drew away from each other, and then timed how long it took for them to discharge, for the leaves to come together again. The higher I went, the shorter time it took. Not as you'd expect at all, if it was only radiation from the ground that was causing the air to conduct.'

'So there is something up there, sir? Something bombarding us all the time with radiation?'

'Looks like it.'

'Where does it come from?'

'The sun maybe, I don't really know. All I know is it is up there. It's a bit like Wegener's theory, I suppose. It is there, I don't know why it's there. I just know that it is.'

Now they turn to me. They want to know more. What is this theory, will I explain it, when will I explain it? After I have promised them a lecture they want to know about Greenland and Mylius-Erichsen and Koch. They want to know everything, they say, so I promise a lecture on that too.

'And can we then have more discussions like this one?' asks Benndorf, smiling. He is a handsome man, so Else says. Even though he is only ten years my senior he has assumed the role of a fond uncle.

'If you wish. I'd be delighted.' I smile back.

It is so good to be surrounded by friends, but in truth I am already feeling a little isolated here in southern Austria. I am aware of the Alps, rising up so close to the north of us. Even though I know it is perfectly possible to journey through them in a day, I still feel there is a barrier separating me from Germany and Berlin. What are they talking about up there without me? What new discoveries are they making? I feel a little excluded. But there are compensations, of course. I glance towards Else and she smiles back. In a few minutes we will be home. In half an hour I can begin my work in my study. There is so much I want to do. I plan to start with my promised lecture on Continental Drift, because once again I have begun to accumulate papers.

Since the publication of the third edition the information has grown enormously. Now almost every scientist seems to have a view, and, very obligingly, each one sends me papers of items they regard as the definitive proof for or against my theory. I am no longer a lonely voice, but part of an argument with men shouting their views across the moving continents. Harold Jeffreys, for instance, an eminent professor of geophysics in England, still advocates a shrinking earth that is solid and rings like a bell whenever an earthquake strikes. We can see it quite clearly on our seismographs, his supporters say, the waves are so strong they could only have been transmitted by something as truly solid and reverberant as steel. So there is no liquid and so there can be no drifting.

A voice from across the Atlantic answers. Daly, a geologist, has taken my side; like me he says that it is quite possible for something to be solid and yet not rigid at the same time.

Imagine the small stage of a village theatre. I am a magician, dressed in black and white, the sort that plays tricks and deceives the eye, but what I will show you is the truth. From the hat in front of me I have taken a long piece of sealing wax. Examine it, and tell me what you see. Well, it is red, you might say, and shiny. Now I take the wax from you. I hold it up. With a roll of the drum I let it fall. What happens? Kneel down and tell me what you see. Broken pieces, you might tell me, sharp and jagged. Exactly what you'd expect if you dropped something solid and brittle on to the hard floor of the stage. I gather the pieces together. I am not going to hide them away. Instead I produce from my hat a new piece. It is long and thin and red like the other. Would you like to examine it, to make sure I'm not cheating? Now I am going to balance that long, thin piece of wax between two matchboxes and I am going to just leave it there. Now here comes the magic – maybe it's not the sort of magic you expect: with a wave of my wand I can make time pass quickly. Although we seem to come back immediately but somehow we know that days have passed. We look at the wax. Something has changed. It is no longer straight but droops between the matchboxes. Even though it looks like something soft when I ask you to pick it up, you will tell us it is still hard, still rigid, still brittle. But little by little, over the days we have left it, the molecules have moved – flowed, you might say – as directed by gravity. Like glass, wax is merely a frozen liquid, non-crystalline, but still solid. Do you remember entropy? I suppose it has lots of entropy: like Tony's room full of furniture, the molecules have been thrown together without order, and, if they are left, they will settle into a more stable arrangement. No doubt Tony sometimes hears this settling; a creak and a thud in the forgotten room as the minute movements caused by the cold and heat allow the furniture to find a more favourable resting place. Yet a sudden shove, the door opening too quickly, perhaps, would cause the whole lot to tumble as in an earthquake.

But for Jeffreys, our English geophysicist, solids are not like this. They consist of crystals in which the particles are as ordered as a stack of neatly interlocking chairs. Maybe they will settle a little, but there are none of the sudden thuds of Tony's furniture. Jeffreys' earth is similar to Suess's in that they are both shrinking and continuing to cool. Around the only part that is still hot enough to be liquid, the core, there is a cooling and contracting mantle, and around this the fragile crust. The crust collapses into the newly created voids in the solid mantle below, and where it tumbles, one layer upon another, are the mountains.

So the voices grow. Sometimes they become so deafening and so numerous I cannot pick them out. There is Argand, a faithful disciple since the early days, even voicing his opinion during the war in neutral Switzerland when any German theory was automatically disregarded. He specialises in applying my ideas to the folding of the Alps. Then there are the voices from South Africa: Molengraaf and du Toit. Maybe it is not surprising that they should support my views with such vehemence. The evidence there is overwhelming: here there are the tillites, here are the scratches of moraine-filled ice on land that is now baked in the heat of the veld, here are the fossils of the *Glossopteris* fern, identical to the fossils found in the same aged rock of Australia and India. Just recently du Toit has compiled a summary of similarities between the geological formations of South Africa and South America. It is hailed by some as a breakthrough, and I suppose it answers those who questioned the adequacy of my own matching across the South Atlantic, but really it is just support for what I already knew all those years ago in Marburg library. The match was then, and is now, overwhelming.

Yet another voice is Joly, an Irishman who is both a poet and a scientist of repute. It is so important for me to hear these voices from the North. Although he purports to attack my theory he is in fact supporting it with new views of his own. Instead of constantly drifting continents, Joly's continents move erratically. Outpourings of heat from the radioactive interior periodically melt the the mantle beneath the continents and dislocate them. He says that since the continents are now lubricated by something so liquid they can move freely under all the influences I have postulated. The effect of the Eötvös force, where the continents are attracted to the equator by gravity, and the effect of the moon causing tides, are now plausibly large enough to cause the movement. But this movement is a sporadic thing, happening only when the convection currents in the mantle cause sufficient upsurge. So his continents move in bursts, and eastwards, in the opposite direction from mine. He is wrong only in detail. I am happy to accept him as one of my supporters, one of the few.

So many voices. I was anxious to hear them all. I needed to travel. I needed to listen. I needed to escape the barrier of the Alps for a short time and absorb the sounds of the North.

33

One day, when the sun dies, she will lie here. She has dug her grave already, an almost perfect circle blasted from the pale limestone, now filled with water. It is a beautiful place for a grave, somewhere her children will like to visit; a glade of trees, a quiet road passing by, isolated, alone, on an island in the east Baltic sea. They will have to sail from Riga in Latvia or Reval in Estonia, Hanseatic ports on the Baltic coast, old, proud places at last independent of the empires that once swept over and enslaved them.

The old gods and old religions hold out here, hidden among the forests and islands. In Latvia, Saule, the sun goddess, is watched with careful appreciation. The night of midsummer, when she barely rests, is celebrated with enthusiasm. For the Estonians, descended from an earlier, different race, midsummer is when witches shed their clothes and their magic becomes more powerful. The sun sinks and then immediately rises up. Maybe she touches this bed. Frantically the Baltic people entice her back. It is their perennial fear. At the end of each year the sun disappears for longer and longer. One day she may never come back. One day she will find this grave on the island of Östel and sink into it for ever.

But at the moment the sun is in the sky and we are at liberty to explore.

'Well, what do you think?' asks Meyer.

I look from the small lake to his face. It has changed little since our days together at Dorput; maybe a little more sagging around the mouth, a few more toes on the crow's-feet around his eyes. 'You're right.'

He smiles. 'I knew it. There are lots of theories, you know. People hold them quite strongly. There's one man at Riga who is adamant that it is the caldera of a volcano. Then someone else, at Dorput, I think, maintains that there has been some sort of underground explosion.'

I shake my head. 'Who at Dorput?'

'Oh, no one we know. Someone new.'

I lean back. For a while I am again in Dorput. If only Dorput could have remained ours they could have had another German renaissance. I shake myself. This is a worthless regret. I am happy in Graz.

I look back at this lake in front of me. The rims are high, just as I'd expect them to be, maybe a little distorted by fortifications at the top but otherwise exactly right. It is not big, maybe just a hundred metres across, but it is perfect.

The cement bomb of gypsum is held directly overhead. I let it go. It falls in the dark; a bright light in the sky, its tail blazing behind. The ground shakes and then there is a perfect circle in the grey concrete beneath. The gypsum and the concrete have been swept up into the grey-white walls of a crater: a sun's grave.

Meyer lifts a pale, flat piece of limestone and skims it across the water.

'You know what this means?' I ask him.

'What?'

'The first meteorite crater positively identified in Europe.'

'Surely not.'

He stands still, looking at the pond.

'Are you sure?'

'Yes.'

After a week of surveys and investigations we crept quietly away. We had enough for a paper. Maybe this one would cause some sort of reaction, or maybe it would be ignored and forgotten as my lunar one had.

The weather was fine. I leant against the rails of the ferry, looking back as we steamed away back to Riga. Above the shore line, too far up, I saw the crumbling remains of old buildings. Like Scandinavia and Finland, this land is rising from the sea. It is an effect of isostasy. If only Jeffreys could see this, surely even he would be convinced. The land is still recovering its equilibrium. Lighthouses on Östel are now behind beaches. Shore-line animals struggle to keep pace. Gradually they find their homes drying out more profoundly each year until they have to migrate or die.

I remember stretching upwards. From that small steamer in the Baltic I remember rising until I could see the whole of Östel and the lobes of Scandinavia behind. Then I made the sun move more quickly. It dipped to the east and rose from the west. I was going backwards. From high on the land between Norway and Sweden the ice cap grew. I moved a little higher, shifting position slightly I could see to the west. At the edge of the world was another glittering shape: Greenland. Farther west again and another mountain of ice grew on the continent of North America, heavier, more massive, weighing down the land, diverting rivers at the edges, choking them with moraine and boulders. And as the ice grew, freezing and holding the water, the sea began to shrink. It moved away so quickly from the land it seemed that it was being sucked away. At last I could see the edges of the continental shelves: a perfect match across the shrunken ocean.

For a while it stays like this. The sun rises and sets in the wrong direction and we travel back in time again. Now the land sinks beneath the weight of the ice, it responds slowly, but soon the shelves are lowered beneath the water again and the world waits. We do not wait long. Something is happening. It is the ice retreating. It is too soon. The ice age has not passed, but still the ice retreats. It is something that my opponents Penck and Bruckner have found in their study of the Alps; the ice age is not just one big freeze but several. There are periods of intense cold and warmer times between. So the seas rise as the ice melts and after a time the land begins to rise too. Where there was just the glaring whiteness of ice there is a darkening and then a hint of green.

The sun moves more quickly now, up and down, longer days and then shorter ones, and the ice is on the move again. White mountains creep forward towards the equator from both sides, and once again the sea begins to disappear.

But why is all this happening? Short periods of cold can be explained by the dust of meteorites or volcanoes blocking out the sun, but what causes these longer cycles of warm and cold? If I examine the sun in this time of ice I can see that it has become dimmer. Of course, with a dimmer sun the earth becomes cooler and the ice will grow. But why has the sun become dimmer? It is because the earth spins around the sun in an orbit that changes with time. For instance, its path can become slightly elongated into the shape of an oval so that the sun is no longer at the centre of a circle but a little to the side of an ellipse. This causes our winters to become cooler. Also the earth can tip. It can tilt more and it can tilt less. When it tilts less the summers are cooler. This is important. During the cold summers the ice caps cannot melt. They reflect more of the sun's heat and everything becomes colder still. Also the earth's spin can change. Each of these changes is inevitable, predicted by rules and the effects described by formulae.

Some people love formulae. They like taking them and plotting graphs. It is a source of pleasure to them to make curves, to compare one with the other. A man called Milankovitch took all these rules that describe the changes in the way the earth orbits the sun and used them to find out what effect they would have on the temperature of the earth. He had an idea that the times of low temperatures could correspond to ice ages. But it was not that simple. Different latitudes and the different hemispheres gave different results. Which latitude was the most important? Köppen and I conferred: sixty-five degrees north, we decided, through the middle of Iceland, the place where glaciers can grow or melt. Now Köppen encouraged Milankovitch to calculate back – maybe we could find a link with the ice ages of Penck and Bruckner. It formed the final chapter in our book. The cool parts of Milankovitch's curves corresponded exactly with the ages of Penck's glaciations. It completed the biography. Even the minutiae of ice ages are nicely explained in this biography of our planet's climate. Milankovitch announced he could die happy. But not yet, I said, we are both too young, we are just starting, there is so much more to do.

But after a few months back at Graz I had lost my enthusiasm.

My writing is bland and hesitant. Something has changed and I can't understand why. Surely I am happy now: I have a wife, children, a house, work I enjoy in a place I love – why am I not greeting each new day with enthusiasm? Maybe I have too much time. Or maybe it is because I know that whatever I write no one will listen. Everything I do seems to be either vilified or, worse, cast into some sort of scientific oblivion. Or maybe it is just this place. Maybe its cosiness makes me feel trapped and restless. It is too warm, too comfortable. I need to find something real and raw.

The start of the Dachstein glacier is close to the top of the peak. The rock is a pale grey and the arêtes cut the air with the sharpened edges of a caveman's flint tool. Between them the ice makes its sedate progress downhill. Even though Kurt and I have started out early it is now late morning and we still have a little way to climb. The snow is deep and we have to hold our skis high above our heads. My arms are aching. From time to time we stop and look back. It is a view I never tire of seeing: the sudden change from rock to forest and then from forest to patches of meadow, then the small lakes, sometimes green, sometimes a dark turquoise, and the concentrated colour of the villages beside them, a sudden burst of sunlight making them appear warm and welcoming. This view plays tricks on the eyes. Everything seems close and yet too small to be near. The odd sound carries, a solitary dog or the bell of a church, but mostly there is nothing but the hiss of the wind, spliced by the arêtes and curling back to form eddies, and Kurt's voice talking about the bureaucracy of Brazil. His voice is in turn irritating and comforting. When the walk is hard, when my legs ache, when I feel sweat begin to chafe my back, I just want him to be quiet. But when we stop I want him to share the view and admire. I want him to tell me I'm lucky to live here, lucky to have both this world and my more comfortable world below. It is as if only his presence can make me appreciate my good fortune.

We eat before we begin the descent. We sink into the snow and munch bread and cheese and drink a little wine. I lie back. The sky is empty of cloud and is a uniform blue. Kurt's full mouth ensures the quiet. We are in a wide gully of snow between two high walls of rock. Here and there pinnacles of rock break through like miniature nunataks, their surfaces glittering with chunks of quartz and odd flakes of mica. Where we are sitting now, at the top, the gully is fairly flat, but below us it slopes downwards quite steeply. I look around us, deciding on a path. I am anxious to start, but Kurt is still finishing his bread.

At last he packs his flask away in his rucksack and looks at me.

'Ready?' I ask.

He grins.

We clamber to our feet and fasten on our skis. Now we are standing the slope looks even steeper. My legs are trembling a little, I hope with anticipation.

Kurt starts first. It is like the old days: it is the older brother's privilege to lead. He begins cautiously, leaning back as far as possible, and rotating his feet one way and then the other so he makes small, short swings from side to side. Now he gathers speed, gives one jubilant cry for me to follow, and he is out of sight. I am careful not to follow in his tracks. I want to make my own. There is something satisfying, even to a forty-seven-year-old, to be the first to mark this new white paper. The snow is deeper than I thought, and softer, but still it lets me through. Like Kurt I pick up speed. I breathe in. There is nothing to think about but my speed, nothing to feel but my feet sliding away beneath me. I go faster still. The mountain side glides away around me. I could out-ski an avalanche. I could ride the collapsing mountain side it as if it were a wave. A whoop rolls down the hillside in front of me. It is mine. It is the euphoria of the professor of meteorology and geophysics at Graz University, and he doesn't care who hears. He is out of control and he wants to scream out his joy. To swerve is an ecstasy, to steer, lifting one foot and leaning outwards, the purest intoxication. I am senselessly happy. I know it must end but I want it to go on for ever. The snow becomes deeper. Towards the bottom of the incline it bulges out. We sink deeper and deeper. I can barely see to the side. Around me is a gorge of snow, and when I slow and eventually stop, there is no sound at all.

'Kurt?' I call.

'Here.' He is very close.

I remove my skis and plunge through the snow. Our faces meet. We are like two basking seals both deciding to take a wallow. We blink. His eyes reflect mine.

This is the moment that I remember now; my last real bead with Kurt, undiluted by the company of others. The moment when Kurt and I lay side by side after that glorious descent in the silence of the snow. We lay there for several minutes. The sun was strong. I remember I could feel it touching my face. I remember wondering whether he was remembering too: that time we found the badger near Zechlinerhütte, that time we shivered in a balloon over Jutland, that time we scaled a rock face not far from this one now. I tried to follow stories in the movements of his eyes.

'How long did we take?'

'About ten minutes.'

I look up. The slope is almost a wall beside me. Half a day to go up, but only ten minutes to come down. The route in front is more gentle and leads, in the distance, through trees.

'Are you ready?' he asks.

'Yes.'

I reattach my skis and we begin the glide towards the wood.

And now another moment, another last bead, another time I became so restless that I looked for an excuse to escape.

Koch lives in a pretty house near Copenhagen. It has bright yellow rendered walls and a roof the colour of plums. An elderly maid answers the door and shows me into the room at the front of the house. Mrs Koch sits there alone, disconsolately embroidering a tired-looking piece of cloth.

'Ah, Alfred, I'm so glad to see you.'

I am shocked at her appearance. So quickly she has become old and worn. And she wears a black silk dress, longer than is fashionable now, as if she is in mourning. She throws down the cloth as though she is grateful to give it up and indicates a chair opposite hers. A necklace of big amber beads sways over her chest, and from her sleeve a patch of broken lace trails. 'He's been asking when you'll be here.'

'How is he?'

'Good days, bad days . . .'

'I'm sorry.'

A mirthless giggle; inappropriate and slightly shocking, and something I remember from long ago.

'He's been worried about the results. It was very kind of you to suggest that you work on them together. It had upset him so much to contemplate giving them up completely.'

'I'm sure it would.'

We sit for a few minutes in silence, and then she giggles again.

'Oh, I'm sorry, Alfred. I've forgotten my manners. Would you like some coffee? A little cake perhaps? No? I'll see if he's awake, then.'

She rises from her chair. The amber swings downwards. It really is a very long and large necklace. She steadies it with a hand. She notices my eyes.

'He likes to see me wearing this. Baltic gold, he calls it. He remembers buying it for me, you see.'

This time the giggle ends in a choke. She hurries from the room. She is wearing slippers, they creak a little as she walks. Underneath, the soles have been worn through in patches. The creaks fade away up a corridor and then disappear altogether when she shuts a door.

I take out my case and leaf through the report on the ice. It is almost finished now. There are just one or two places where I would like Koch's opinion. All this work should have been finished long ago. The war interrupted things, and then there was Koch's work as the head of Danish military aviation, which kept him too busy, and now there was this illness.

The creaking returns. 'I think he's ready for you.'

Some things frighten me more than others. Physical danger has never affected me much, and of course I have become quite used to standing up in front of hundreds of people and giving speeches. But now, when Mrs Koch tells me to come with her to meet my old friend, I am filled with such apprehension that I have to fight an impulse to run away through the front door. I stand still in the middle of the room. I am aware that my breath is noisy.

She turns around, walks back towards me and lays a hand on my shoulder.

'My dear Alfred, are you quite well? Have you risen a little too quickly?'

For once her giggle is welcome. It gives me a reason to smile back.

'I think that must be it. I'm fine now. Please let's go and see him.'

He is sitting on a chaise longue. I can see that his feet are up in front of him and that they are covered with a blanket, but I can't see his face. He is sitting in front of a large picture window and the sun is blazing in. I walk up to the couch and press my hand in his. There is no response.

His wife leans forward and shakes him gently.

'It's Alfred, Johan, he's come to show you what he's done. I think he has a few questions.'

Beside the chaise longue is another chair. I sit down on that and remove my folder from the bag. I turn to where I have a question: a detail on the depth of a reading. When I look up I can see his face. It is thin, clean shaven. He wears a small circular cap, but beneath that he appears to be completely bald. His wife shakes him again. His head moves. His face turns to mine. It is too still.

'It's Alfred, my love, remember?'

His eyes travel over my face. His eyes lock on to mine.

'Are you the man selling amber?' he asks.

34

'Of course,' says a voice, 'he's completely wrong.'

'Who is?'

'Wegener, of course, our so-called professor of meterology and geophysics that everybody thinks is so wonderful.'

What do I do now? To get up, to bow, to smile the meaningless smile of a crocodile, would be embarrassing for all concerned. Of course, whoever it is, and I do not recognise his voice, has no idea I'm here. Anyway, I'm curious. So I stay almost completely still and pretend to read the book that lies open in front of me. Libraries are such strange, secretive places; all these desks screened off from one another, like small cells in an insect's colony, each one nurturing a brain before it takes flight. But this brain of mine has taken flight already, and that apparently is the problem.

'Why? I thought you were in full agreement that the continents could move.'

'Ye-e-es, but . . .'

So he is an ally, but he doesn't sound like a very encouraging one.

'It's what he proposes as the forces pushing the whole thing along that I take issue with. That stuff about tides and that idea that the continents slide to the equator under gravity . . .'

'And precession comes into it too, I think . . .'

'Well, whatever. It's all rubbish. None of it is anywhere strong enough to push up mountains. Anyone with any intelligence would see that right away.'

I turn a page. I cannot resist gulping.

'I can't believe he's got away with printing such rubbish.'

'I suppose you've got a better idea?'

'As a matter of fact, I have. Undercurrents. Wegener knows about them, I'm sure of it, but . . .'

I have to cough. When I can hear again their voices have moved away.

'Why don't you mention it to him? I hear he's very approachable.'

The other man snorts. 'I told you, he knows already. I'm not about to rub his nose in it . . .'

'But really, Schwinner . . .'

'No. My mind's made up.'

Later that day I found out from my good friend Benndorf that Schwinner is in the geology department; a place I tend to avoid. It's not really intentional, it's just worked out that way. The Physical Institute has always been so welcoming that there really wasn't any need to go elsewhere. But after overhearing that little outburst in the library I investigated Schwinner's ideas again, and found that maybe they had more credibility than I had first supposed. It is something I intend to study further as soon as I return to Graz from this last expedition. Maybe I shall make a fresh start with the department of geology. Maybe I could offer them some choice specimens from my expanding collection of rocks. The idea is really just an elaboration of Joly's: that radiation heats the sima underneath the continents which causes convection currents. In some places the currents rise, breaking up the continents, then dragging them apart before sinking downwards again under the oceans. It is an interesting idea, my only objection being that it implies that a sima that has rather more liquidity than can be justified from our knowledge of seismology. I have decided to include it anyway in the fourth edition of *The Origins of the Continents and Oceans*.

So is Schwinner a friend or an enemy? I suppose he is a

friend. At least he accepts that the continents drift; which is still an unusual stance for a German-speaking professor of geology. Hans Cloos, I am very sorry to say, remains charmingly but obstinately unconvinced, as does his equally influential colleague, Hans Stille. The rest of them are like mice: shout 'Continental Drift' and they scuttle away, following Stille and Cloos into the comforting burrow of Fixism.

So many enemies. For a short time they just mumbled their disapproval from a distance. Then one of my supporters decided it was time to flush them into the open, and out they came, blinking and rather irritated.

I take the papers from the envelope. I should be used to this by now, but I am not. Somehow my stomach has shifted upwards and I have run out of breath. The report is thick, the papers heavy. Is that good or very bad? I flick through: van der Gracht's speech has taken up more than half the proceedings, so at least I have been strongly represented. I put it down. If van der Gracht has said so much then that must mean that the rest of them have said very little; has he silenced them, has he demolished all their arguments before they had a chance to present them? I breathe in deeply, take out my favourite pipe and fill it to the top of the bowl with my newest tobacco. I light it and draw on it a few times until the nicotine takes hold. I feel a little calmer now. So much depends on this conference in New York. It is the first time the international world of science has examined my theory and attempted to assess its worth.

Köppen knocks on the door as he has been trained to do by Else.

'Well,' he says, 'what's the verdict?'

'I don't know yet.'

'Is that it, there?'

Perhaps I need to be bullied. Perhaps I need to be made to read. I pick it up and skim through it enough to know.

'Well?'

I hand it to Köppen without a word. It is worse, much worse, than I anticipated. After van der Gracht their replies are short, succinct and completely contradictory.

For a while Köppen reads. I can see exactly where he has reached by the motions of his head. He nods with van der Gracht but tuts and sighs at the rest. At last it seems he can restrain himself no longer.

'No match! No match!' I can see particles of his spit in the light from the window. 'Hasn't that fool Chamberlain even looked at our maps?'

He reads on, shaking his head and tutting. 'Footloose? Awkward facts? How dare he! He's implying that you're deliberately ignoring evidence, Alfred. Hasn't he bothered to read all your lists?'

I pull him towards a chair and he takes it without lifting his eyes from the page.

'Ah, here's what's rankled him, the little idiot! He thinks they're ignoring his father's precious theory in favour of yours. That's why there's so much pontificating about the lack of the Precambrian . . .'

I sit opposite him. This is cheering me a little. Köppen can always be relied upon to give his opinion and it nearly always matches mine.

'Ah, Professor Schuchert, another one of these Yale professors, now what does he make of it all?'

I shift forwards, stretch out my legs and lean back so that only the base and the top of my shoulders make contact with the chair. A bad posture, Else would say, bad for my back, but it means I'm almost horizontal. I shut my eyes.

Schuchert illustrates his lecture with pictures of an eight-inch globe. Like me he has cut out the continents and moved them around. But where I used paper, he has used plasticine; where I found a good fit, he has found none. He says it is

impossible to match the continents without taking uncon-
scionable liberties. He points to a gap and pulls a face.

The laughing starts at the back.

'Look, he says the Bering Strait bridge has completely
vanished, poof!' He looks incredulously at the slide and
scratches his head.

The laughing travels forward, each row infecting the one
in front.

'Anyway, why should the continents retain their shape? We
are all aware, as geologists, that the shape of the coast is in a
state of continual flux: waves pound at cliffs, currents deposit
beaches and take them away, and yet Wegener expects us to
believe that these shapes have been retained over a hundred
and twenty million years. But then Wegener is not a geologist.
How can we expect him to know about the little details, those
things of no importance, gentlemen, inconveniences such as
erosion, deposition or even rocks!'

There is uproar now. There are men in the middle theatri-
cally pounding the desks in front of them with tears running
down their faces.

He goes on to give his own account of the evolution of the
earth, which involves land bridges and which he says explains
everything quite satisfactorily. He finishes with that mocking
quote from the director of the Geological Survey of France.
It is the one I have heard so often before: when Termier calls
me a poet he is not intending to admire but condemn; and
when he describes my theories as beautiful and as alluring as
dreams it is because, of course, they are completely without
substance.

The applause is rapturous. There has not been such geological entertainment for years. They retire for refreshments,
wiping away their tears.

No doubt the afternoon brought more entertainment.
Willis, from Stanford University, questioned my mechanism
of mountain formation along the western sides of continents;

while Bowie of the US Coast and Geodetic Survey could not understand why there are oceanic ridges and trenches on something so soft and yielding, or why there are violent earthquakes under the oceanic floor. The next speaker, Gregory, a Scot, declared himself to be a supporter and then promptly proceeded to prove himself an enemy. He had made a list of all sorts of biological anomalies that are in direct conflict with the theory: alligators that live only in America and China; and earthworms that are at the same time American, Indian and Australian.

The ball goes back and forth. Some things I can answer, some things I cannot, but one day the answers to all these questions will be found.

For Chamberlain I shall extend the drifting as far back in time as he desires; to the very start of the geological record, to the Precambrian and beyond.

Schuchert I shall take by the hand and show him how to move the continents, correctly, rotating them around where the pole was then, rather than where it is now, so the Bering Strait remains intact. Then I shall ask him to choose: would he expect the coastlines to fit or not? If, as he says, he would expect the coastlines to be too worn to fit after millions of years, then why has he given up so many hours to shifting pieces of plasticine around on his schoolchild's globe?

To Willis and Bowie I would point out that the bottoms of the oceans are cold. This converts the sima into something strong at its surface. It is strong enough to resist the sial, to make the sial buckle and form mountains, strong enough to maintain ridges, and to propagate earthquake waves.

For Gregory I have no specific answers yet. I am sure they will come along. I shall leave it to the biologists. Although it was nature which started me along this tract, it is something I have never pretended to master. It is wonderful and mysterious, that is part of its attraction, and I am sure it will continue to produce anomalies for as long as it exists. It is as hard to pin down as the races of man, I tell Köppen, and he nods and smiles. Yes, he agrees, nowhere as easy as climates, or mountain chains or oceans or continents.

I see now how much it affected me. The unease that had started to grip me during my work on the Baltic crater grew. I began to question the point of it all. Often I would sit on my own, contemplating the walls. Else would come and go, demanding that I should eat, join them in the garden, or at least go out with them for a walk. But I was not interested. I pretended I had work. The falling man returned, at first at the edge of my vision and then directly in front of me, where I could see each flailing arm and each sudden jerking back of his head. He began to accompany me to work, straying into my sight whenever a lecture finished, whenever I worked in my office or was left on my own.

'What's up?' It is Benndorf's voice. I hear it vaguely, as if from behind a heavy curtain. It must be time for our habitual morning coffee.

The falling man turns his head, reaches out.

'Oh, nothing.'

'What you need, my friend, is a bit of a change. A party would do the trick, I think. I'll get Hess to think of some ideas.'

'No, no. Let me assure you, Benndorf, a party is the very last thing I need.'

'What is it, then?'

I give him the piece of paper from Denmark.

'Well, this is great, Wegener, aren't you pleased?'

I look up at him. He is smiling widely, trying to encourage a smile in me. But all I can do is shrug. I can't seem to feel anything any more.

'But surely this is a vindication of everything you've said?'

'I suppose.'

'Greenland is moving westwards?'

'Yes.'

'And this rate – isn't it very close to what you've always said?'

'Yes.'

'Well, why aren't you excited, man? Why aren't you hopping up and down?' He slaps me on the back. 'Come on, what's wrong?'

He stops. He looks at me. 'These radio transmission measurements can't be wrong, can they?'

'They're the best that we have.'

'Well, come on, then. Let's celebrate. I insist. A great mug of beer and a whopping new Cuban cigar I've been saving for a special occasion.'

I look at Benndorf and smile.

The fallen man fades.

'Thank you, Benndorf. I don't know what we'd all do without you.'

For a short while the arguments continued; a man called von Ihering finished a book on the Atlantic Ocean with a chapter describing two world views; the wrong one (mine) and the right one (his). Continental Drift, apparently, was my fantasy that would one day pop like a soap bubble.

And suddenly it seemed that it had. No one spoke of it at all. It was as if that conference in New York had persuaded geologists everywhere that the idea was too ridiculous to be even contemplated. I became aware that there was something even worse than vitriolic rhetoric, and that was being the object of an embarrassed silence.

People wrote to me about other things. Koch, in a shaky hand that gave up halfway through and was continued by his wife, expressed his pleasure that I had finally managed to write up the mapping and glaciology so well. Then Georgi, my colleague from Hamburg, wrote to tell me of some very strong and very high winds he had noticed in north-west Iceland. They seemed to be coming from Greenland, and in order to investigate them further he had secured funds to make year-long observations in the middle of the ice sheet.

I am jealous. I can't deny it. Ridiculously I feel that Georgi is stealing something from me. Overwintering in the middle of the ice sheet was something Koch and I had always intended to do. It was something we had discussed with Freuchen in 1908. No doubt it was something we would have done already if the war hadn't interfered. But I write back to Georgi, congratulating him on his idea and asking him to keep me informed.

Koch is dead. A black-edged letter falls from my hand. The falling man falls, again and again. Sometimes he becomes so large he blocks out the light.

Else knocks at my door. Why does she still do that? I don't need to look up. I just transfer my gaze from the wall to the door.

'Alfred, Professor Meinardus is here to see you.'

Professor Meinardus from Göttingen; I had forgotten. He'd sent me a letter. Something about passing through Austria and would I do him the honour of meeting him? I think I'd replied, I think I'd have said yes. Anyway, here he is: a small man of about sixty, peering through a pair of round glasses, making short, quick steps across the room to my desk. I stand up. We shake hands. He begins what he has to say immediately with a nervy impetuousness.

'We have developed an instrument at Göttingen,' he says, swaying slightly backwards and forwards, 'that is capable of measuring the thickness of an ice sheet.'

I take advantage of his slight pause: 'Won't you sit down?' I indicate a seat.

'Thank you. Yes. It works using reflected sound waves.'

'Ah yes, I've heard about it: an explosion that sets the ice shaking in all directions.'

'Exactly, an artificial earthquake. After the explosion you wait and listen. Some of the shocks just travel along the surface. They'll hit you first. We register them on a seismometer . . .'

The wall in front of me disappears. In its place a sudden fountain of ice.

'And some of the waves travel downwards through the ice, hit the rock floor and then bounce back up again.'

'And because they've travelled farther they'll take longer. Yes, I see. It all sounds most interesting.'

'Everything's been worked out. We know how fast the waves should travel. We've tested the whole apparatus out in the Alps and everything seems to be fine.'

Now he pauses. He twitches a little nervously.

'We've been awarded funding by the German emergency committee. You see, what we are hoping is that someone will agree to use this method in Greenland.'

Greenland! The room fades away completely. The wind howls and I am walking alone in a vast white emptiness.

'And we were wondering if you, Professor Wegener, would feel disposed towards making a short trip. After all, you are familiar with the place, I believe. It would be just during the summer, so there would be minimum disruption to your teaching commitments . . .'

He stops. He looks at my face and smiles.

'So you would be willing to consider the idea?'

Sometimes I would like to rid myself of my Northern restraint. Sometimes I would like to do whatever comes into my head, no matter how inappropriate. Just at the moment what I would really like to do is to kiss Professor Meinardus on his almost hairless head.

After Meinardus had departed I made plans. I was not, I

decided, going all the way to Greenland just for one short summer. At last I could finish what Koch and I had started in 1912. It would be an expedition in his memory. If he knew, I was sure he would be smiling. I sat back, and another thought occurred to me: I could incorporate Georgi's work as well. I felt sure he would be pleased. His letter had seemed a little uncertain. Spending a winter in Iceland is an entirely different matter from spending a winter in the middle of the Greenlandic ice sheet three hundred miles away from anywhere. He would need guidance from a seasoned arctic traveller, and what better guidance could I give than to be there, organising the arrangements?

I realise now that it was then that I last saw the falling man. He fell just before Meinardus entered the room and then he disappeared. Two years ago now: perhaps he has disappeared for good. I remember dancing into the kitchen after I had shown Meinardus out. Else was at the stove, and the girls were at the big table in the middle, all busy with their respective projects. It had been quiet until I had entered.

'Greenland! I'm going to Greenland!'

Four pairs of eyes blink silently.

'I'm going back there. At least for a summer, longer if I can persuade them.'

Why are they not smiling too? Why are they not laughing and congratulating me?

I sit back to front on a chair by the table, rocking in the way that usually makes Lotte laugh, but now she just looks at me as seriously as the rest.

'Just think, Else, I can do all those things I didn't manage to do in 1912.'

'Like get yourself killed, you mean? Like wait until the glacier is just ready to calve and make camp upon it? Like fall down a crevasse? Like starve yourself to death? Well, make sure you do it properly this time, Alfred. No half-measures.

Kill yourself good and proper, and please don't think of us waiting here for you . . .'

She stops suddenly. Lotte gives a loud sob and Käte puts her arm around her. All of them are glaring at me as though they hate me.

Else lets the metal spoon she is holding clang on to the metal top of the stove. 'You're too old, stupid! And you've got us now!'

'But it's the chance I've been waiting for!'

She turns, wipes her hands on her apron and then shoves back her fringe from her forehead with the back of her hand. She gulps and speaks in a measured cool voice. 'If you go I'll never forgive you, never.'

It took me some time to convince them. I gave them articles to show how Greenland and arctic technology had changed. I told them about motor sledges, and caterpillar tractors. Then I told them that, as expedition leader, I would not have to put myself through particularly strenuous physical exertions. My role would be to command, and that wouldn't necessarily have to be by example.

Hilde was the first to be convinced. At fourteen she already had the poise of a young woman.

'You're going to have to let him go, Mamma. He won't be happy unless you do.'

She sounded so resigned, so adult. I leant forward and kissed her hair.

Else looked at me as if she was calculating something, or as if she was trying to see inside my head. 'You promise you won't take risks?'

I nod.

'And this place, Umanak – you say it's populated?'

'Yes, lots and lots of people. Quite safe.'

'And you'll be staying fairly close?'

'Yes, just a boat journey away.'

'Well, I suppose I'll have to say yes, but on one condition.'

'What?'

'That I come too.'

It took even longer to persuade her that this was a bad idea. In the end we reached a compromise. I would send for her once we were established and we could come home together.

Now I could make plans. The first thing I would need to do would be to convince the German committee that such an expedition would be worthwhile. I wrote carefully, outlining my scientific objectives and requirements. I gave them two options: an expensive one which would be supported from the air, and a cheaper alternative which would be supported by a combination of motor boat, pony, dog and motor sledge. I knew that providing a cheaper option would make them bite; they would think they were obtaining a bargain.

Imagine I could take a slice through Greenland. I would go as far north as I could before hitting the region of pack ice on the east coast: seventy-one degrees north. Imagine I could slice through everything here and make a profile. What would I see? At the bottom would be the bedrock, high at the edges, forming mountains and ridges, lower towards the centre. The next layer would be the ice: from the mountains at the edges it would rise either side to form a flattish dome about three thousand metres above sea level. On top of the ice would be the air. Maybe this would be the most interesting of all: at the edges there would be storms and great winds, rolling off the ice to the sea, but in the middle there would be calm, the well-known anticyclone of the ice sheet.

In order to make this profile, I proposed that we would establish three meteorological and glaciological stations on the ice which would maintain readings for an entire year. One would be at the western margin, just north of Umanak, one would be at the centre, and one would be established independently on the east coast at the western edge of the Scoresby Sound.

I decided I would need to make a short preliminary expedition as soon as possible the following summer. The main problem of the expedition proper would be that of transportation, especially up on to the inland ice itself. The preliminary expedition could determine a suitable place at which to ascend and would also serve to test out equipment and begin some of our scientific experiments. I proposed to take just three men: Georgi, and two other men I knew who were interested in glaciology: Dr Fritz Löwe, of the Aviation Institute in Berlin, and a secondary schoolteacher, Dr Ernst Sorge.

It seems so easy now, so clear cut and neat. Plans are always like this: precise, ordered, untouched by reality. If only I could have followed it, even a little. But at least the plan worked well in one regard: the German committee were most interested and granted the money immediately. Now I could work out the details. I decided to start from scratch, designing as much as possible myself.

A company in Munich agreed to make up the tents as well as some of the clothes. I decided that since the Inuit had had thousands of years to perfect their clothing for their climate, I would use this as a model for our own. So I sent them an anorak from the 1912 expedition and asked them to duplicate this for my men in wind-resistant material. It worked so well that the company made more than we needed and sold them to people in the fashionable winter resorts. I remember Else smirking when she found out. 'Maybe you should forget Greenland and take up residence in Paris,' she said, holding one against her.

Now I realise she was suffering. Sometimes I'd catch her alone, stirring something on the stove that didn't need stirring, and looking at nothing. Only once, after that initial outcry, did she ask me whether I really had to go. I was explaining to her my new design for the sledges, in bamboo, so they would be strong and yet light enough to carry over difficult ground, when she came over to me, pressed two fingers over my lips, and dropped herself on to my lap.

'Do you really feel you can do this? It sounds so difficult and hard. Is it worth it?'

'It'll be fine. Don't worry.'

She lowered her head, and when she raised it again two brimming ponds searched my face.

'Why do you want to leave us, Alfred? Is life so unbearable here?'

She blinked and her eyelashes caught the drops. Still her face searched mine. Frantically I reached out and hugged her close. I couldn't bear her to see. I couldn't bear for her to know. I loved her but I needed something else too.

'I'll be back, and when I am I'll never go away again, I promise.'

'That I don't believe.'

'Well, unless you come with me.'

She came with me this time as far as Stockholm. We kissed the children and the Köppens good-bye outside our house in Blumengasse. I remember that the street was crowded; members of the institute had come to see us off and there were a lot of tears and promises.

Just as we reach the end of the street, Lotte catches us up.

'Papa, I've just remembered there's something I wanted to ask you.'

'What is it, my little one?'

'Will you name a bit of Greenland after me? Käte says that you can. She says to name a bit after her too. I suppose you'd better find something for Hilde as well.'

Else laughs.

'I will.'

'And can mine be a bigger bit than Käte's?'

'Yes, all right, since you're the one that remembered.'

'Thank you, Papa. I love you.'

'I love you too, Lotte.'

On the journey to Stockholm Else agreed with everything and seemed endlessly cheerful. When it was time to separate she kissed me lightly on the cheek and bade me farewell as if I were just leaving for the day, not for six months. Then she walked away, a little quickly, up the gang plank for her ship to Oslo, and disappeared into the hull. For some time I gazed at the ship, hoping she would reappear on the deck or at the window, but she did not. I felt cheated. Eventually I turned away and began my own journey to Copenhagen, where my travelling companions awaited me aboard the *Disko*.

Part IV
Der Schluss

35

At the captain's table I inspect them. Do they notice my eyes travelling over them, taking note, guessing at their character? Georgi, of course, is familiar to me: maturity seems to suit him; exposure to the elements has made his face look more rugged and less peevish. He smiles more than I remembered, and seems calmer and less anxious to please; an encouraging metamorphosis. Löwe, at thirty-four, is five years younger. He is tall, a good few centimetres taller than me and Georgi, and his limbs have a tall man's stiffness. His face has an eager, intelligent look about it that encourages me, and he seems the most quiet and thoughtful of the three. He is a war hero, and I try to imagine him in the trenches, leading and shouting to his men. I fail. He seems too gentle, too dignified. Sorge is young, still in his twenties, but he is the sort of person who is born middle aged. His round glasses give him a priggish expression, and his chin recedes to nothingness below. He is as tall as Löwe, but thinner and more delicate looking; not a good characteristic for an arctic explorer. I imagine that during term time he practises aloofness and severity, but now he is excited and animated. In fact his chattiness borders on the irritating. Maybe he is apprehensive, that would be quite understandable; he is new to this, after all.

In less than a month we reached Holsteinsborg on the south-west coast of Greenland, transferred our provisions from the *Disko* to our small ship the *Krabbe*, and hopped up the coast from one settlement to another until we arrived at Jacobshavn.

*　　*　　*

There have always been people here, it seems. At the southern end of the town are the remains of a village, Sermermiut, rings of stone four thousand years old. Maybe I see their descendants now; faces representing this race and the remnants of others: the friends and relatives of Jorgen Brønlund and Tobias Gabrielsen. Tobias Gabrielsen! A face detaches itself from the crowd, a figure walks forward and clutches his warm, wide body to mine. I'd forgotten the smell of fish and sweat; it's been over twenty years and so much has changed.

Tobias guided as farther north to Quervainshavn. Quervainshavn, at seventy degrees north, was one degree south of where we planned to build our stations the following summer. The Swiss explorer de Quervain had used this fjord to start his crossing of the ice in 1912. If it proved possible to travel north-east from here it would serve as a reserve route if we failed to find suitable access on to the ice farther north. Leaving Tobias alone on the Krabbe, we rowed ashore in our small rowing boat, the *Moses*.

I look around. It is so familiar: the smell of the wind, the crunch of moraine under foot, the overpowering feeling of desolation and abandonment that thrills me like no other. Nothing lives; just a few sparse bits of plants between the rubble. I stoop down and inspect one. I admire the way it swirls from the ground, its small fleshy red leaves sheltered by stones, but reaching out, grasping for what? Moisture? Warmth? Georgi turns away and urinates on to the ground. Even this sound is loud, swirled around our ears by the wind. I hug myself. The memory of this wilderness has haunted me for so long. Koch should be here. The thought of him hurts and then worries me. I am in charge now. There is no one to consult, no one to blame. I am the expert, the one expected to provide the answers. I walk over to the supplies in silence. We are alone, isolated, no one can help us but ourselves.

I look at the hand sledges and the tents with their bamboo poles and take a breath; every part of them has been made as light as possible so that they will be easy to carry. We will succeed, I say out loud, and touch the box carrying the flag. I think of the black, red and golden flag flying over the ice; at last another German expedition to the Arctic. Then I kneel down and inspect another box. It is strange how making something smaller makes it seem more perfect; this sextant, for instance, so small and light and yet so perfect in detail.

A crash, near by, too close. I had forgotten that sound.

'Quick, pull the *Moses* up the beach.'

Löwe is just in time. He catches hold of the line holding the anchor and pulls. A large wave from the calving glacier submerges everything up to the moraine. Sorge and Georgi run to help him. The *Moses* bobs and tugs but they pull back. They keep pulling until the *Moses* is safely on the beach, and then they carry it inward a little more.

'Can we just leave it here?' Sorge asks.

'Well, I don't think anyone's going to steal it, do you?' Georgi replies.

We are interrupted by the seagulls. They are suddenly here, as if the ice has made them from its splinters, wheeling and crying out above the new icebergs.

'Fish,' says Georgi. 'They're after the fish.'

And a seagull swoops downwards into the water and its newly churned mud.

It took six days to transport all our belongings on to the edge of the ice, and then another two days to transfer it twelve kilometres inland to the depot we called Koncordia. Here Löwe drilled out the ice and sank a bamboo rod. We intended to come back on our way to the main expedition the following year to see how far the level of the ice had fallen. We knew the ice was in retreat; even since 1912 this much was obvious. Already I had seen glaciers smaller and farther up the mountain than they had been then. We wanted to find the speed of this retreat in Quervainshavn.

While Löwe drills we build a snowman. That is what we call it. Of course, it's not really a snowman at all but a rather carefully engineered pyramid made from blocks of ice. Inside I have put a piece of red paper so it is more easily seen. We are anxious to be off but we are waiting for the sun to drop. It will not set. It is the season of the midnight sun and already we feel exhausted by its constant light. Last night, as it nearly set, it made a pillar; a piece of the sun pulled out until it was a long beam of light catching the clouds. We are waiting for it to happen again but it doesn't. When the sun is at its lowest point we set off, making the most of the cooler temperature and the firmer ice.

Already we have found out a lot. We have discovered what doesn't work: the tents are too delicate and rip when pulled from the ice; and the automatic step counter is unreliable. Instead we have to use a more traditional means: Löwe. Every time he counts to two thousand we stop and build a small snow pyramid.

I remember my promise. The next camp is Hilde, the next Käte, and by the time we reach Camp Lotte we have crossed the crevasses, potholes and lakes of the ice margin, and have reached the outer part of the ice sheet proper. There is no longer any need to plant rods. From here on the ice does not sink away but accumulates. Ahead of us now, for as far as we can see, are the long ridges of snow that form in the wind. The Russians have a name for them: zastrugi.

We carried on. At the next camp Georgi's son Hans was honoured, while at the next we immortalised a storm. At Gerda we conferred. Now that we had established that this was a viable way on to the ice sheet we could go back. It could be our reserve route if we failed to find an entrance on to the ice farther north. But if we were all willing to survive just on Amundsen's pemmican we could make a further two-day advance into the interior. I looked around. It was immediately obvious that Sorge wanted to continue. He had removed his hood and revealed his face. The low sun reflected from his glasses, making him look a little mysterious and sinister. 'I think we should, definitely,' he said, but didn't give a reason.

'We might as well if everyone feels fit,' Georgi said. He too had looked around at the rest of us.

'How about you, Löwe?'

Löwe was more careful. 'As long as everyone is sure.'

So we continued. But now we plunged into storms and temperatures above freezing. The warmth made things difficult: rainy sleet fell on to the snow, and the snow softened. Frieda followed Gerda; fifteen kilometres and then over twenty. Now we lightened our load still further and decided to make a final dash to the east: the camp ground Else, a particularly demanding one, I noted in my diary, knowing that she would read it later, was 150 kilometres from the edge of the ice and over two thousand metres above the sea.

I have found out something else, something rather vital: the Amundsen pemmican is inedible. Each time I swallow a mouthful my stomach fills with bile and I am sick into the snow. Is it because I am older than the rest that my digestive system rejects so much fat? I simply cannot keep it down. It has taken such a small thing to completely incapacitate me, and now I find I am hardly able to walk, let alone pull my sledge. My comrades are taking turns to pull it for me, and I am feeling so wretched I have to let them.

'One thousand. One thousand and one, two, three . . .' Still Löwe counts, a clock I only hear now when I listen.

After resting for a day and watching the German flag droop and then billow out at Else, we are making our way back.

'. . . twenty-one, twenty-two, twenty-three . . .' Something else we have learnt: not all steps are the same. With a lighter load we step out farther: twenty-nine kilometres becomes thirty-one.

'. . . forty-three, forty-four, forty-five . . .'

The sky is covered with cloud and the light causes the layer of wind-swept snow and the sky to be an indistinguishable grey. It is as if we are marching in nothingness; there is no ground, no air, no solid surface. I have the sensation that I am balancing on something that is not here, or curves away from me so sharply that I am bound to fall.

'. . . fifty-six, fifty-seven . . .'

Horizontal could so easily be vertical, it is difficult to tell. What I know to be smooth grey ground now appears to rise up in front of me as if it is a wall. If we take another step forward it seems we will collide with it, and it takes all my determination to keep up the same steady pace.

'Sixty-nine, seventy . . .'

My stomach heaves again. They stop, waiting for me to finish. Georgi approaches but I wave him away. I cannot help but splash my furs in the process and there is no way of cleaning them. I rub in snow but of course the stink persists. The thought that this sour smell will now accompany me for the next three months depresses me.

'One thousand two hundred, one, two, three . . .'

It is still too warm. I can see where the snow has melted; temporary streams have snaked through the surface. If the ice has melted this much here, farther down it must have melted more. What if the snowman has completely melted away there? How will we find our way back? We will be like Hansel and Gretel, their trail of grain eaten by the birds.

'One thousand seven hundred . . .'

When we make camp again, the smell from this fur will be overwhelming. I shall have to leave it outside. Maybe I could cover it on a sledge.

'One thousand eight hundred . . .'

I look into the distance. Is that our track leading between those two dunes or does it continue more towards the north?

'. . . ninety-five, ninety-six . . .'

The sun breaks through. The sky is covered loosely with cloud and we can see the shadow of each one as a moving blue-grey patch upon the rippled surface around us.

'One thousand nine hundred . . .'

We should be almost there. We should be able to see the snowman if we have followed our own trail and not one made by the wind. Sorge checks his compass.

'Two thousand and three, two thousand and four . . .'

Löwe can't seem to stop counting.

'Two thousand steps there, two thousand and twelve steps back,' he says. 'We must be getting tired.'

We have come too far. Surely we must have come too far. We stop then spread out across the ice, each man searching his area methodically. If we do not find Gerda's snowman soon we will have to make camp and start again after we have rested, but the thought worries me. We have no food and very little fuel.

There it is! A long shadow in the low sun. Around it the scattered objects of our depot. Our pace quickens.

36

Greenland is a place most people never notice. It is on the outskirts of the globe, too far to the north to be of any consequence, and of course most of it is covered in ice. But the shape of Greenland amazes me. I love to look at it, examining the parts: the jutting in and out; the southern tip gently curving backwards to the east; and the flat wide top splayed out with fjords. I suppose if I had to describe the shape of Greenland I would say it was like a tear drop. I would say that it was as if someone had made a tear drop of pastry and thrown it on the board, and then had pressed downwards until the edges frayed.

This is one of my most ignored theories: my theory of fjord formation. I believe that the ice causes fjords by pressing down on the land, forcing it to crack at the edges under stress. Of course, the fjords are drowned and eroded by the ice too, but that is just part of the story.

I saw so many of these fjords last summer, but I never tired of them. We explored a region of two bays. The bays are so enclosed and sheltered by islands and promontories that sometimes it is difficult to believe you are still on the ocean and not in some landlocked lake. The most southern bay, Disko, is named after the island: a high patch of land, whose topmost snow remains frozen, even in summer. Jacobshavn, Tobias's town, is in the middle of the mainland coast of Disko bay. If you stand at Jacobshavn and watch the sun sink, it will sink over Disko Island, a smear of land beyond the icebergs. Quervainshavn is at the northern end of the bay. North of Quervainshavn the land begins to jut out west and form the promontory of Nuussuaq.

North of Nuussuaq there is another bay, just as sheltered as the last, but with bigger icebergs and with cliffs that rise magnificently from the sea in a colourful contortion of stripes and recumbent folds. These rocks predate Pangaea. Their whirls of orange, black and white decorate both the towering cliffs and the sharp little island that gives the bay its name. Umanak: the heart of the land at the top of the world.

We began at the southern end of Umanak bay, systematically investigating each narrow fjord for a way on to the ice.

The low cloud makes the top of the cliffs part of the sky: invisible and yet too close. It is as if it is pressing down on us and no wind escapes. The water is still, and, when Tobias stops the engine, perfectly quiet. From time to time a seabird wheels overhead and calls, but it is a solitary creature, black feathered, using the wind with a masterly confidence. We have seen no one since the morning when we passed the settlement of Uvkusigsut with its small collection of huts and houses vying for space beneath the cliffs. I sit back and allow Sorge to row. In spite of his apparent fragility he is strong. I have a map in my head. We have very few places left to try; just a couple more fjords at the top of the bay and we have tried everywhere.

It is Georgi who points it out as we pass: the Ingnerit fjord has a side arm heading to the north-east. I look on the map. No glaciers are marked but we know already that this map is not particularly accurate. We peer down as we approach. There are certainly glaciers but they all look too small and steep.

I am woken by shouting. I turn over irritably. Why can they not allow me to sleep? But now I hear Löwe's voice joining Georgi's. I have never heard him like this; Georgi can become excited over a good hand in cards but Löwe is usually calm and reticent. I throw my rancid fur over my shoulders and step out on deck.

'It's perfect,' Löwe is saying, 'just perfect. Close to the sea, just a small break, nothing to bother us.'

'Kamarajuk,' murmurs Tobias suddenly. 'That's what we call it. Light bay.'

Are my beads becoming a little jumbled? I have tried so hard to keep them in order on the string, but now I am finding it a little difficult to separate the images of last summer from the one that has just passed.

There is no one here to welcome us. The old fishermen look only slightly curious as the *Krabbe* approaches. They sit by the warehouse huts along the quayside, silently smoking in the sun. When we are almost alongside, one of them rises casually to his feet and helps to pull us to shore. There is little space, but we manoeuvre the rest of the boats to make room. We have to step from boat to boat to get ashore. But now there are more people, blinking and screwing up their eyes as if they have been sitting in the dark. They inspect us silently, talk in quiet voices to Tobias then divide for us to continue up the track to the top of the village. The smell of fish is overpowering. There is not much here, just the huts, the drying racks, and the dogs. It ends suddenly with a graveyard.

This is Uvkusigsut: a collection of sod houses and huts, squeezed on to the small patch of flat land beside the cliffs, the nearest settlement to Kamarajuk, our way on to the ice.

A man emerges from his hut and immediately he is surrounded by dogs, straining towards him from their chains and howling. A couple of puppies, unrestrained, chew at his trousers. He casts a weary eye in our direction and reaches up to where the yellow flattened carcasses of fish hang with a jagged stiffness.

From Uvkusigsut we eventually acquired twenty-three dogs and seven men, both species apparently equally idle in the summer. They would work alongside us as navvies as we made our first attempt to convert the Kamarajuk glacier into a highway on to the ice in preparation for next year.

But first a funny little bead, one that Else likes to hear again and again. I am at a glacier north of Kamarajuk, searching, I think, for yet another way on to the ice, when we find a group of Greenlanders fishing from a beach. One of them, a pregnant woman, asks me for my name.

'Alfred,' she repeats, rolling the sounds carefully along her tongue. 'Alfred,' she says, and pats her belly. She is pretty, with large round cheeks and wide laughing eyes. She speaks a few words to Tobias.

'What did she say?'

'You've been honoured. Inside there is little Alfred. Boy or girl – she says it doesn't matter.'

All I can think of saying is thank you and, as an after-thought, I give her a quick small bow.

It is this which amuses Else; somewhere soon, near Umanak, a baby girl could be born named Alfred.

When I told Else, the tale ended here. I suppose it was stupid not to tell her the rest; after all, it means nothing, just the superstition of an old culture.

'You're not expected to be a godparent or something, are you?' asks Georgi. 'Sending regular gifts and tips for guid-ance?'

'I don't think so.'

The woman is still watching me.

'It doesn't mean anything, does it, Tobias? All that stuff about the name being part of the soul – they don't still believe that round here, do they?'

'The old ways, well, they're still important to some,' Tobias says carefully. 'After death the old soul . . . they say it can't rest until a newborn takes its name. Then that newborn, the one who takes the name . . . well, it's partly a new person but it's partly the person who's died, partly someone else.'

Georgi shivers. 'But this Alfred is not dead yet. It's a bit ghoulish, isn't it, all this business? I'm glad she didn't pick me.'

The woman is still watching, not smiling now, just watching me. All this talk of souls and intense looking is making me uneasy. I bow again, wish her good luck with her hunting, and walk back towards the *Krabbe*.

And that is it: a strange little bead with two colours of no consequence.

Is it this year or last? I am watching Löwe through binoculars: with a few swift turns he has drilled a hole into the ice and then he inserts the rod. Ah, it must be last year, we are quite alone. He attaches the charge and steps back, trailing a wire along the snow, letting it out slowly from the spool, and then attaches it to his box. Then he squats on his haunches and looks at his watch.

Now I am with Sorge and Georgi inside the tent. Sorge is kneeling before a single beam of light directed on to a mirror. This mirror is sensitive; it trembles as we enter the tent and close the flap. As we watch, Sorge feeds the end of a roll of light-sensitive paper into place. Ten seconds before ten o'clock he starts the small motor that feeds the paper from the roll into the path of the reflected light. Where the beam lands on the paper, the paper darkens so that at first there is a smooth line down the centre. We feel the explosion first.

The light wobbles as the ground shakes: this is the surface wave that has moved quickly along the top of the ice. Soon afterwards, the light wobbles again; this is another wave, the one that has travelled downwards through the ice, has been reflected by the bedrock and travelled back through the snow to greet us. Eventually, when the experiment has almost finished, we finally hear it; a crack and a rumble as a slower wave has completed its journey through the air.

Now, at last, the final bead of last summer: we have transported enough of our supplies up our rudimentary track to begin our first journey on to the ice with the dogs from Kamarajuk.

Twenty-one years since I did this last, and yet it comes back. Once again I am listening to the gentle trot of the dogs on the snow and enjoying every minute. The day is clear, just a haze near the ground, with little wind. In front of me Johan Davidson, our Inuit dog handler, whistles at the animals in front of him. It is morning and the low light paints long shadows on the snow. And now a strange thing happens: I become young. I know that this is a ridiculous thing to say, but that is really how it feels. As we travel across the ice with the dogs I can feel myself becoming more and more youthful until, halfway to the centre of the ice sheet, I am the same young man I was in Danmarkshavn.

Our last bamboo: the quick thrust downwards, the slight resistance of the ice and then the crunch as a million crystals are displaced. One hundred and twenty-five miles inland, halfway to where we plan to establish our central station. It can be done. It will be done. I shut my eyes.

Is it possible for the legs to regain old movement, for the heart to recall an old vigour? You see, as I plunged that bamboo down I really believed, for a few seconds, that I was twenty-six. My future seemed as endless as this ice sheet and I was quite certain that it was possible for me to do anything I wished. There were no constraints. I was independent and alone; middle age and death were just alien things that happened to older men, like the one I had been nine days ago.

Now I knew why I had come, now I knew why I would come back. Along with the overwhelming feelings of accomplishment and satisfaction, there was something else: an unexpected sense of rejuvenation. As I slapped Johan Davidson and Georgi on the back, as we saluted the flag, I wanted just one thing – to go on towards the east.

The next day we would discover more. We would dig a deep hole and make some preliminary measurements on the temperature and density of the ice at depth. We would determine our position with the help of my miniature sextant, and all the time I would be feeling so happy and triumphant that my words would escape on their own. Even though I knew that Köppen and Marie and Else were right, that it was ridiculous of me to come, that it would have made far more sense for me to have stayed at Graz and lectured and written books and entertained my children, I would be glad that I came.

We were there. There was no argument, no controversy; just a pure, simple accomplishment that no one could take away.

37

Why are the German people still being punished? We were, after all, just protecting what was ours. So what did we do that was so wrong? No more, no less, it seems to me, than any of the other countries around us, but because we lost it seems that all of us, no matter how innocent, are having to pay the price. After the Treaty of Versailles came the bill for reparations, and after that outrage, inspections, strikes, investigations, a putsch, a local uprising, and so many changes of government I stopped taking notice many years ago. For most of us this long decade has meant just two things: food has been scarce and our money has become worthless. How did this happen? We are the German people, cultured, knowledgeable, inventive. How can we have been driven down like this?

Last year I came back to a Germany in catastrophe: unemployment was rising, the finances were becoming even more chaotic, and in the short while I had been away there had been a communist uprising in Berlin, and bombings in the North. The government was a coalition of changing colours and voices. Only one thing remained constant: there was not enough money.

His Excellency Schmidt-Ott will not meet my eye. He listens with his face averted as I answer his question in full: so tell me, how was your expedition in Greenland? When I stop talking he turns a little to face the window. He is powerfully built with a rather splendid but old-fashioned full moustache, and a monocle. I have never understood this fashion for a

Clare Dudman

monocle; are there really so many people that have just one defective eye?

At last he clears his massive throat and speaks. It is a small voice, incongruous in such a large man. 'The thing is, Wegener, my friend, things have changed since we last spoke.'

This is not going to be good news. I wait for him to continue.

'The way things are now . . . the mark, of course, is worth much less now than when you started out . . . maybe if we wait a year or so . . .'

I can't wait. I am forty-nine years old. At the moment I am fit, but who knows what the next few years may bring?

'But surely, sir, things are not likely to improve in the foreseeable future? In fact could they not become worse?'

He turns to sit at his desk and then glances at my face. 'You are right, of course. Heaven knows what will happen.'

'And it will be a complete waste of the committee's money, if you don't mind my saying so, if we leave it now. Everything is ready, everything.'

This last is an exaggeration, but I need to make my point.

'Well, I'll put your case to the committee. As you must be aware by now, Wegener, I am your staunchest ally in all this.'

I mutter my thanks.

He seems to be considering something. He picks up a pen and passes it between his fingers then examines my face.

'Wegener, I've just had a thought. Maybe you could persuade them of the soundness of their investment. A talk perhaps, illustrated with slides, of course, on the economic advantages to Germany of such an expedition.'

It would do no good to balk at such a thing in this distinguished company.

'Of course,' I say, hating the idea, 'I'd be delighted.'

* * *

342

The farewell of the members of the preliminary German expedition to Greenland, then, was not a happy one. Until then we had been joking, planning and, whenever anybody thought about it, congratulating ourselves yet again on the success of the mission. Now we were all subdued.

'But what am I going to tell my school?' asks Sorge.

'Just what you know. I'm sure they'll be anxious to have you back whatever happens.'

'More important, what am I going to tell Frieda? When you get married, Sorge, you'll realise that this is a far more frightening prospect.'

We try to laugh.

'You'll keep us informed, eh, Wegener?' asks Löwe.

'Of course.'

And so we separated. I had not expected to be travelling south to Graz with such despondency.

They are there at the station to greet me, lined up in order of size along the platform. I don't know which one to greet first, so I gather them up, as if they are flower stems, and bunch their heads together into one magnificent display. My Else, my Lotte, my Käte, my Hilde – so often I have dreamt of this moment when I have them all in my arms again. I look at their faces. They look so much like flower heads, reaching up towards me. But what is wrong with Hilde? I kiss each face, leaning over to catch the tip of a nose, a forehead, a cheek. Why is Hilde's face so cold? When I let them go they fall apart laughing.

'Well, did you do it, Papa?' Lotte asks. The first person to speak.

'Yes, my little one, we got there, halfway to the middle of Greenland, just as we . . .'

'No, not that, Papa, did you find a piece of land for me?'

Hilde leans against her mother as if she is finding it difficult to stand. She looks so pale, and her face has become so thin. I look over her head to Else and ask a question with my face.

'Kidney inflammation,' she says. 'She's been bad for weeks.'

'Papa! Did you, Papa?'

'What?'

'Find me some land?'

'Yes, and some for your sisters.' I lean down to her and whisper, 'But yours was the highest.'

'Thank you, Papa, I knew you would.' She hops away up the platform singing.

The Köppens do not stay long. Else ushers them away. Käte and Lotte busy themselves searching through my belongings, and for a while Hilde kneels beside them, watching as they withdraw my little souvenirs and make noises of disgust. Each of them has a piece of walrus tusk carved into a tupilaq to bring bad luck to their enemies, as well as a selection of knives and combs. But eventually Hilde heaves herself up and announces that she will go to bed. She takes her tupilaq with her; a particularly virulent figure with an open, gap-toothed mouth and webbed feet.

'I think she'll need it,' Else says. She leans heavily against me. 'She's been so ill, Alfred. I don't think anyone really knows what's wrong.' She pauses, then adds quietly, 'Sometimes I thought I'd lost both of you.'

But Hilde was getting better. Even to me it was obvious. The next day she woke and ate breakfast, something, apparently, she had not done willingly for weeks, and even managed a little pancake for lunch. Else was delighted and hugged me.

'You're our remedy,' she said, 'you're all we need.'

Then she glanced at me and said, 'You're not really going to go back again, are you?'

'It doesn't look like it.'

Her joyous eyes irritate me. 'Oh, Alfred! I'm so pleased. Thank you, thank you.'

I say nothing. Perhaps I am a little stiff. She looks at me as if she is wondering.

'It's not your choice, though, is it?'

I cannot speak. Suddenly I am so tired of it all. It seems that everything I touch is destined to be rejected. I shake my head.

'Why, what's happened?'

Wearily I explain: the money, the false assurance, the lecture. She listens as she always does, drinking it in with her eyes, and now I can't stop. I tell her about the cold, the days of toil and searching, the joy at finding Kamarajuk, the triumph of our journeys, our discoveries, our plans, even about the bamboo canes still lying in a line across the snow waiting for us to pluck them out and inspect them. Now, as she listens, her face changes. It is no longer just sympathetic; there is a set look about her mouth as if she is forcing it into shape. It is something I have seen before. It is Else's face showing me that she is making a decision. I think she is deciding to be strong.

'It's very important for you to go back, isn't it?'

I have almost run out of words. 'It's my last chance, Else. Another year and I'll be too old.'

'I think, Alfred, that at the moment it is the only thing that is going to make you happy. I don't understand why, but I believe that it's so.'

I look at my hands. How can I do this to her and to the children?

'And your being happy is all I want, all I've ever wanted, you know that?'

I nod, slightly. Her selflessness makes me wither.

'So, I've decided. I'll work with you. You'll never be able to do it all alone. We'll work together and we'll make it happen. Now . . .'

I squeeze the rest of her words from her.

*   *   *

'What's that smell?' Else says. 'I think it's coming from your study.'

We go in together. On the floor is the pile of objects the girls have unpacked from my bag. 'I think it might be these,' I say.

Just before we'd left Jacobshavn Tobias Gabrielesen had given me souvenirs for my wife: a pair of slippers made from the skin of a polar bear, and a cushion made from the beautiful skin of the bearded seal, the top decorated with a careful appliqué of different-coloured leathers. I had been delighted with them; there had been little opportunity for me to find or even think of buying gifts.

'They are pretty,' Else says, turning the slippers over in her hands. 'But they're too small for me. Maybe they'll fit Lotte.'

But the slippers were too small even for Lotte, and the cushion smelt of fish. For two days we put up with it in the kitchen before transferring them, and my whip and kamiks, to the shed in the garden.

Tobias had hung around a little after giving them to me and then presented me with a piece of paper with writing on it. Apparently he had had a cultural exchange in mind. In return for these gifts from Greenland he had a specific request for some things that had taken his fancy: a pair of European cloth trousers and a pair of lace-up boots, and these were his measurements on the paper. Köppen inspected them with interest: the measurements for the soles of the feet were very short and almost square, while the trouser legs were shorter than Else's, with the waist measurement wider than the leg.

'It's as I thought,' he said, 'short and squat – the greater insulation keeps out the cold, and there is less wind near the ground. Don't know how you're going to find anything around here to fit, though.'

I handed the task over to Else. Suddenly I was busy again, and, now I had Else's support, happy.

I can't remember the Berlin lecture now, I can only remember the preparation. It was hard, I suppose because the whole concept was abhorrent to me. How can anyone say which research will turn out to be economically valuable? The purpose of the investigation of the weather system over Greenland, of course, was obvious: it would provide information for a successful German air company. But how could I justify my investigations of the thickness of the ice? In the end I had to invent: from a knowledge of how the ice is changing we may discover if the earth's climate is changing; and if it is we might be able to decide which crops to grow; and from the right choice of crops, of course, there would be a profit for Germany's farmers. And there I stopped. That would have to do.

I have a vague memory of applause and smiling faces. They seemed enthusiastic, but they had seemed enthusiastic before. I told them that I had to know soon, that it was imperative we were ready for the spring, but before I could explain more His Excellency Schmidt-Ott's cough stopped me. I had said enough, it was time to go.

'A couple of weeks,' he whispered to me, 'before Christmas at the latest. And don't worry, Wegener, you've done well.'

There is a small stout man waiting outside the lecture theatre. He is pretending to read the notices in the corridor but this is just a front, because as soon as I close the door he approaches. I back away; he looks determined enough to be a reporter and I am determined enough not to give interviews, especially now.

'Professor Wegener?'

'I'm sorry, I'm in a hurry. If you have any questions please send them to me at the university in Graz.'

'I'm not a reporter, Professor.' He removes his hat – he has little hair and what there is is grey and wispy.

'I'm Weiken, Dr Karl Weiken, from the Geodetic Institute

in Potsdam. I'd heard you were in town. I was wondering, are you still planning on doing a gravity survey in Greenland?'

'What of it?' I am interested now. I like the look of this man. As Köppen would say, his build would be ideal for the arctic climate.

'Well, I'd be interested in coming along. I may not look athletic but, well, I can keep going, and I'm not as old as I look.'

I laugh.

'If the glasses are a problem, I could take them off, if necessary. I can still see . . . well, a little, anyway.' He has removed his glasses now and is screwing up his eyes in my direction.

'And what would you expect to see, Dr Weiken, with your gravity measurements?'

'Well, evidence of isostasy, of course, but under the ice, I'm not quite sure . . . has the ice pushed down a big block of sial, do you think, so it's thicker than we suppose? I'm sure it would be quite fascinating to find out.'

'Put your glasses back on, Dr Weiken. Have you eaten? Please come to lunch with me. I have just been through a most gruelling experience and now I want to celebrate. There'll be some company: my wife, my brother . . . I'm sure they'll be pleased to meet you.'

'Are you going to make any measurements for your theory of Continental Movement on Greenland, Professor?'

'You've heard of it, then?'

'Oh yes, I'm an enthusiastic supporter.'

In the end the committee were as quick as Schmidt-Ott said: I received my reply before Christmas and the verdict was yes.

Ah, last Christmas. A most joyous bead, covered in all the usual colours of green and red and gold. The details are still quite clear to me: Hilde was completely well again and becoming a handsome fifteen-year-old, Käte had just sprained her ankle jumping from a wall, and Lotte was inconsolable because a dog hadn't arrived for Christmas.

'But if you have a dog, who will look after it when you come with me to Greenland?' For a moment the room was completely quiet.

Later I had to agree with Else that it was a bad idea, and an even worse idea to announce it to the children before discussing it with her. She had more reasons for them not to go than I could count, the most obvious one being that Hilde had only just recovered from her illness, and was north-west Greenland the most sensible place to go for someone so vulnerable? The children, of course, held a completely contrary view; they were most pleased to be asked, and now most indignant at the offer being withdrawn. There were tears from all quarters, and for a time it looked as if I had ruined our last Christmas together, but eventually we agreed on a compromise: they would all come to Greenland, together, for a month in the second summer. By then my work would be finished and I would be able to devote some of my time to a tour.

From now on Else and I devoted ourselves to the organisation of the expedition. I soon came to realise that I would need a bigger scientific team than I had at first anticipated. Word had spread and I received many applications, but I had to choose carefully.

Such a warm room. And once it has been occupied for an hour it becomes warmer still, and stuffy. I can see that the fifth applicant notices it as he enters: he sniffs the air, and then his shoulders droop, just a little, and he sets his face.

'Please sit,' I say, and he does, stiffly.

'Your name?' I ask, and he tells me: Rupert Holzapfel, a name I recognise, a local meteorologist.

'So tell me why you want to come.'

There is a short silence. As I examine him he seems to be

examining me. He is balding, bespectacled, unremarkable. Yet I have heard good reports about this young man.

'Come, Dr Holzapfel, there must be some reason you want to come on my expedition.'

'Because I like the cold?' He grins and his face is transformed into something mischievous. I smile back. I can't help it.

'And I enjoy being uncomfortable, bored, cooped up for months in small places, irritating my fellow man, and besides . . .' He pauses, examines my face, which is now grinning broadly. 'I have women from every state in Europe after me.'

I laugh out loud, which seems to encourage him. He leans forward and motions with his finger for me to lean forward too. 'Although, on the minus side, I am quite good with kites, and I can assemble an anemometer in a force nine gale.'

'In that case, Dr Holzapfel, I'm afraid I'm going to have to enlist you immediately. I'll send you notification in the post.'

We stand, bow, he leaves the room. And that is it. Not very rigorous, but under such artificial circumstances what else could I do?

The Göttingen scientists want to know how our ice thickness measurements have gone, and they want a demonstration rather than a paper or a lecture, so we have all retired to the Ötzalter Alps in order to go over the technique together. It is really, of course, just an excuse to blow up some ice with two kilograms of explosive, a bit of a change from the rarefied rooms of the institute. I show them how Sorge has modified the technique in the Arctic: the dish for the developing paper was an inconvenient shape, so he has found a better one; and it was important to eradicate all light coming into the tent, a difficult task sometimes in the Arctic where the sun, if it is up, is always low. They all nod and take notes, and then, fairly soon, someone proposes that we adjourn our meeting to a nearby inn. This is agreed unanimously and the researchers begin to squeeze out of the tent. One of the last to leave is a slight young man with blond hair and small features. He stands back to let me pass. He seems a little self-conscious, a little shy, and I have the impression that he is clenching every muscle in his body taut. I tip my head to him and duck under the tent flaps. As he emerges behind me Meinardus comes over.

'Ah, Wegener, I was hoping you two would meet. Allow me to introduce Dr Kurt Wölcken.'

The young man bows his head.

'I was hoping that you might be able to find a place for him on your expedition. He really is an outstanding geophysicist.'

Wölcken and I regard each other. Some people I can't imagine in a sleeping bag, and he is one of them. He looks a little too neat. Even the clothes he has chosen to wear on the trek up this mountain look as if they have been freshly laundered. I think I can still see creases in his trousers.

'Perhaps you would like to see me later in the hotel,' I say, and he smiles slightly and says, obviously without conviction, that he would be honoured.

As he retreats carefully down the slope in front of me I watch him move. He is careful, considerate, he seems to be fit and he seems to fit in. But I still can't see him in an old raggedy sleeping bag made from smelly caribou, and, as if to confirm this, before we enter the inn, he carefully removes a needle of a pine tree that has somehow lodged itself in the immaculate turn-up of his trousers.

I took Dr Wölcken anyway, and by the early spring I had enlisted six scientists: Dr Johannes Georgi, Dr Ernst Sorge, Dr Fritz Löwe, Dr Karl Weiken, Dr Kurt Wölcken, and Dr Rupert Holzapfel, together with six technicians.

After the men came the organisation of supplies. Now Else renewed her expertise of 1912. Every day now, when I came home, she would be at the kitchen table making calculations: how much hay, how many luggage saddles, what sort of sleeping bags? There were ponies and dogs as well as men to consider. So much had to be ordered well in advance so it could be packed conveniently in Copenhagen. That was another thing: we had to ensure that everything was packed in the correct order so it was easy to transport immediately by pony once we got to Greenland. The motor sledges had to be safely encased in crates; the winter station had to be packed in easily carried portions; supplies for the central station had to be kept separate from supplies for the western station; and all the time we had to ensure that the weight was kept as low as possible. There were many crises and many trips to Copenhagen and Berlin, and once, I remember, a trip to Vienna.

My train is a few minutes late. I rush to the waiting room. Else is there, sitting on a bench, just as we arranged. She doesn't hear me enter so for a few seconds I just look at her. It is still early in the morning and cold. She has a hat, the sort that has a name, I can't remember what it is, but it comes low over the sides of her face so she looks sweetly protected.

How old was she then? Thirty-seven, the same age as she is now.

What is she doing? I remember now: a book. There is a book on her lap and she is reading it, the tip of the forefinger of her left hand in her mouth.

She had travelled from Graz to Vienna early in the morning while I completed my journey from Berlin so that we could meet and be together for part of a day.

*　　*　　*

I am waiting for that moment. That moment when she notices I am looking. That moment when something intrudes into her peripheral vision and she turns her head to see what it is. That moment when her eyes widen. That moment when her lips part to release the smallest gasp: 'Alfred!' That moment when my name passes across the room in a whisper.

The book closing with a snap, her page lost, a standing and revolving and plunging that is just one movement. We are alone. That moment when she presses herself so close I feel as if we're merging.

What was I doing in Vienna? I have been so many times. Else would know. I think I was arranging my replacement for the year at Graz. I had to see Professor Exner: the enemy that had become a friend. Was it the last time I saw him? What did we talk about? The qualities we should look for in my temporary replacement? He had looked quite healthy, maybe a little tired.

'Only fifty-three,' Else says, when she hears. 'That's too young to have a heart attack.' But that was another time, a little later.

At last everything seemed almost ready. Else and I said goodbye to the Köppens and the children and travelled to Copenhagen. Stables had been constructed from old railway carriages for the ponies on board our ship, the *Disko*, and all we needed to do now was to pick them and their handlers up from Iceland. Vigfus had agreed to come and I was looking forward to seeing him again.

But I was not ready. There were things that I still needed to do. I wrote letters, lots of letters: letters to the men, letters to their wives, which I hoped would be reassuring, letters to Kurt, Tony, Köppen, Marie, the children. Then, at the last minute, there were irritating things to sort out: there were small but essential supplies that had still not arrived, there were men to see and reporters to avoid, and there was Georgi, who was refusing to sign an agreement with the German Committee because he wanted more control over the pictures he took.

Else is standing at the dockside inspecting a crate. She leans over it while a sailor from the *Disko* stands impatiently by, his hands on his hips.

'No, that's not right,' she says. 'It's something they'll need first, so it must be packed at the top. Put it over there with those others.'

She moves to the next. 'This one can go on now. But be careful, some of it is a little fragile.'

I glance over at her, catch her eye. She smiles back: confident, competent, strong.

Else is sitting in the meeting room of the German Committee. She is listening to Sorge's new wife ask a question about the mail. When she answers her voice is clear. The women sit forward to listen.

'During the winter I doubt we'll hear much at all. It is better not to expect to hear anything, I think, and then be surprised when we do.'

'What about the wireless?'

'Well, they'll have that too, of course. But remember, things might be difficult. Greenland is very mountainous, and of course weather may be a problem. Expect little, that is my motto. It saves worry.'

The women sit back with a murmur. Else looks around her, her eyes settling briefly on each face.

'Don't worry,' she says, 'they're in the safest possible hands. Remember, my husband is most experienced, and he has a motto too: The men come first. He has always told me that that is the order; the safety of his men comes before everything else, before science and before discovery. He doesn't believe in taking unnecessary risks. Your men simply couldn't be in safer hands.'

Our eyes meet. I don't think anyone else has noticed me at the side of the room. Our gaze is held for several seconds but her face doesn't change, then she looks away.

'Are there any more questions?'

Now Else is sitting at the dressing table in our hotel room in Copenhagen, listening while I talk. She has reassured me so many times before: she is sure that I will be able to lead by example, she is convinced that the men will pick up the necessary skills in time, she is quite certain that my choice of transport is the correct one and that it will work, she is completely certain that I will make a good leader, she is positive that the men will work together and that I have chosen well. She rests her head on her hand as I talk again.

'Why is Georgi being so obstinate?' I ask her. 'He knows it is imperative that we leave soon. Why is he making things so awkward?'

'He's just prevaricating, you'll see.'

'But what if it's a sign of things to come? What if he refuses to listen and he takes Sorge and the rest of them along with him?'

'A mutiny, you mean?' She laughs. 'I'm sure it won't come to that.'

'What if they're not strong enough to resist? What if they crumple at the first sign of difficulty?'

'I'm sure they won't, Alfred, I've told you that already.'

'What if . . . ?' Now I see the ice sheet in front of me. One second it is there, a silky layer of loose snow obscuring the surface, and then it is gone. I am in the thick haze of a snowstorm battling my way forward, whipping the dogs, taking steps and yet not moving anywhere. I shout commands to the men but they are gone.

'I don't know, Alfred. I don't know anything any more.' A small, flat voice.

Have I been talking? What have I been saying?

The hand holding her head has given way and she has buried her face in her hands. Her voice is muffled. 'The only thing I do know is that I wish, with all my heart, that you weren't going, but you are. The only thing I know is that I shall hate every minute that you're gone.'

I touch her shoulder but she flicks me off. 'Don't do that. I can't be strong if you do that.'

Her shoulders rise slowly then fall with an exhalation of air. She looks up and glares at me with her father's eyes. 'Just come back, will you?'

'I promise.'

38

The last time I saw Europe it was from the *Disko* at the very start of April. Else was there, with the other wives, waving from the dock. She had found a handkerchief especially for the occasion, she'd said, but she wasn't going to show it to me, I'd have to look. So I did: white, a lot of lace, just a flurry in her hand. But I didn't want to look at a piece of cloth, I wanted to see her face. It was hidden beneath the shadow of that hat-with-a-name. But I saw teeth, I'm fairly sure I saw teeth, so I expect that then, at least, she was smiling.

So soon the noise dies away. So soon the stillness of the Baltic gives way to the ferocity of the North Atlantic. In the heavy seas even the steady little *Disko* rocked. After we had taken on board the ponies, my old friend Vigfus and two other farmers at Reykjavik, the storm continued. The ponies were stabled on deck.

There are twenty-five of them, in a space so tight they have to huddle. There is no room for them to thrash, to slide or to fall over. When the *Disko* lurches so do they, and when the ocean tips in they shiver and wait nonchalantly for it to tip back out again. I pat the nearest flank: a mottled grey. It is dry, the film of sweat from yesterday has gone; a good sign. When I scatter more hay in the trough in front of them they nuzzle it curiously before reaching forward with their lips. It is important they remain healthy because so much depends on them. The ripple of a shiver passes over the back of the nearest pony and then passes over me too. A drenching from the sea has revived me. As I lurch away from them back into my cabin, I hear the grey pony snort. Another Grauni is showing his impatience.

On the fifteenth of April we arrived at Holsteinsborg. In a few weeks we had sailed from a warm spring into a cold midwinter. When we had left Holsteinsborg the previous year a thick mist had covered everything, but now the air was clear and snow was showing off the bright colours of the houses and the relief of the mountains behind. It was still and hushed as the *Disko* slid into harbour, and the townsfolk emerged sleepily on to the dockside. We unloaded our cargo. The ponies came first, tugged along gang planks, fished from the water, persuaded with sticks on to the land and then into a storehouse that had been prepared for them. They have a little donkey in them, I think: there is something mulish in the way they try to resist anything that is required of them. Vigfus locked them in and kept the key in his pocket; we both remembered the ponies' tendency to run wildly away given the opportunity, and we were taking no chances.

Four days later the *Gustav Holm* arrived. A rugged explorer's ship with thick ice sheathing and a crow's-nest, she was designed to sail the waters of the west Greenland coast and was small enough to sail right up to the Kamarajuk glacier with our belongings.

Everything is wedged in. There are not enough cabins, but there is plenty of hay in the saloon. Drums of paraffin are in the coal bunkers, while beneath the ponies' hay there is dynamite with boxes of provisions beneath. On deck there are ponies to one side, and crates containing the motor sledges to the other. Everything just fits. It is as if every nook has been measured and filled. Even the lifeboat is filled with petrol cans and boxes of detonators. Of course, we are a potential inferno; one spark in the wrong place would cause an impressive display of bangs and flashes and then, no doubt, an imposing island of fire among the icebergs. We wouldn't stand a chance but we'd go out with the splendour of Viking warriors.

A boat pulls up alongside. A man sits upright at the back surrounded by a group of giggling women. His Inuit oarsmen secure the boat and then the governor, his wife and daughters clamber aboard. He is expecting to be entertained. These people have been thrust from a life of middle-class anonymity in Denmark into the positions of royalty in Greenland, and they have taken to their new life with alacrity. I think the governor would like his food to be eaten for him to save him the bother. He and his women pick at everything we supply with apparent suspicion, pausing between each bite to ask whether it has been cooked and for how long. It is only after we distribute the rum toddy that they begin to mellow. The daughters start to laugh and flirt with some of the younger members of my staff, while the wife sits back and shuts her eyes. At the sound of a guitar she opens them with curiosity and looks around. With astonishment I see that the player is Holzapfel, our meteorologist from Austria. How could he have hidden a guitar among his belongings? He is picking out notes without any apparent enjoyment and breathing heavily as his fingers stretch over the fingerboard of his instrument. It is a pretty song, one we all recognise, about a woman who is waiting for her lover to come back to her from across the ocean, and a few of the younger ones snigger at the choice. Suddenly a mouth organ joins in the melody. It is expertly played and adds to the air of sentimental melancholy. But the player is another surprise: it is Kurt Wölcken, drying the instrument carefully with a pristinely white handkerchief as soon as each tune has finished.

The afternoon became more noisy. Holzapfel and Wölcken continued to play and, instead of listening, the men began to talk over them. Lissey, one of our assistant surveyors, a young engineering student, slipped his arm around one of the governor's daughters and she giggled more than ever. It grew warmer and more smoky, but no one wanted to let the cold winter day in through the hatches. The governor started to laugh and, just as suddenly, stopped as he saw his daughter. Lissey was leading her out of the saloon into one of the cabins in the stern. It was time to stop. I clapped my hands and called on Lissey, as one of the younger members of the party, to propose the first toast. Under the scrutiny of the entire expedition he blushingly dropped the governor's daughter's hand and mumbled a few indiscernible words.

'Well, thank you, Mr Lissey, I'm so sorry to have interrupted you.'

His blush deepened as the rest of the men hooted and whistled. The girl's sister pulled her away and Lissey sat down where he was. A couple of the others gave speeches and the governor replied. The totty had worn off now and he had become more sombre. From time to time he exchanged glances with his errant daughter, and I exchanged glances with Mr Lissey.

'What did you think you were doing?' I asked him once the governor had disembarked.

'She just wanted to see around the rest of the ship.'

'With just you as escort? Do you think that was wise? I want to bring back just as many men as I brought, Mr Lissey. No less and certainly no more. Do you understand?'

'Yes, sir.' He examined the table in front of him.

Now we started to sail up the coast. At Godhavn, on the southern tip of Disko Island, we helped slither the *Krabbe* into the sea from its winter housing. It was colder now and the snow fell thickly. I changed from my European clothes into my Greenland furs and went up on deck to greet the governors of the settlement. They brought bad news. Umanak was still icebound, and since we only had charter of the *Gustav Holm* for a limited time, it was unlikely that we would be able to reach the Kamarajuk fjord in her as I had planned. We would have to unload our luggage on to the ice and transport it to Kamarajuk by some other means.

It is May. Who would guess that it is May? To one side of us is the iceberg-laden, choppy ocean, while to the other is the motionless sea; a solid continuous whiteness to the Umanak mountain. From this distance, and in this light, the mountain looks like just another iceberg, pointed and enormous, and indeed between us and it there is another iceberg, just as huge, with its platform top decorated with hundreds of seagulls. Both are immobile. The ice is set solid; when we try to barge it with the strong keel of the *Gustav Holm* she just thuds against it ineffectively. Maybe the people in Umanak hear us, maybe their lookout to the west sees us, because now across the ice comes a a team of dogs. They have been waiting for us. They have been doing a lot of waiting this year. Spring is very late, they tell us. The ice is still strong and shows no sign of breaking up.

We crawl forward along the ice edge, parallel with the coast, until, to the east, we can see our goal: the mouth of the Ingnerit fjord in the distance with the settlement of Uvkusigsut on the southern side, and behind that the mouth of the Kamarajuk fjord. The inland ice is teetering on the tops of the mountains; so tantalisingly close and yet impossible to feel. I send out Georgi and Sorge on a sledge to Kamarajuk. If the ice is firm all may yet be well. Here is another plan: instead of taking the *Gustav Holm* right into shore we will transfer our equipment and supplies to Kamarajuk by sledge. It should be possible, if the ice is firm.

But the ice is not firm. Georgi and Sorge come back with despondent faces. The word they use is 'rotten'. A good word to describe something so decayed and useless. In the Kamarajuk fjord itself they could put a stick right through it; a pony's hoof would penetrate just as easily. There is nothing we can do now but transfer our luggage to Uvkusigsut and wait for the ice to melt.

Our friends from Uvkusigsut come streaming out to greet us; each dot turning into a streak of dogs and sledge as they approach. The Greenlanders welcome us eagerly. I recognise their faces, but their names, for now, are still deeply buried. News has spread quickly. We pay for each kilogram they will transport to the shore, so they try to pile on as many kilograms as possible. Loads teeter, so I have to specify that the load must also arrive intact. We winch the ponies on to the ice. They cringe in the air and then wobble as they alight. So many days at sea and now this: something that is too slippery to be land. The dogs are close to wolves. It is not just their howls which give their ancestry away but their tendency to sniff at anything around them for their next meal. They are less discriminating than goats. Anything that moves has the added enticement of being fresh. They look at the ponies with greedy eyes.

The *Gustav Holm* escapes; a noisy salute, a waving of flags, and she is gone. We are alone at Uvkusigsut with a mountain of supplies, a couple of small boats and two tents.

Now we waited; it was not unpleasant in our two well-made tents, down bags, wire mattresses and wooden floors. We played chess, we cooked food and we waited. The weather remained cold and calm. The snow piled up around us. We ate, and our ponies ate, and we waited. We counted our diminishing bales of hay and made new calculations. We listened for the drip of melting water or the sound of a wind to drive out the ice but everything was quiet. When we used up the last of our milk I boarded the *Krabbe* with relief. At last there was something I could do: a return trip to Umanak with Lissey, Tobias and Friedrichs, our expert engineer from Hamburg, for supplies.

* * *

'Look!' Friedrichs points in front of us and stops the engine.

Tobias comes to stand beside him and yells over the side of the ship in Greenlandic. From the back Tobias and Friedrichs look identical: I could have saved Else a lot of bother by just asking Friedrichs for a spare pair of trousers and boots.

'There're some hunters down here,' Friedrichs says over his shoulder, 'stranded. It's a good thing we came by.'

The three Greenlanders seem unperturbed. When they hear Tobias they smile and wave back. Have they not noticed that the ice floe they are on is drifting out to sea? They seem more concerned with their catch, and point out the glittering carcasses of fish piled up beside them with hoots and calls. How would they get back? Tobias points out the kayaks strapped on to the sledges. Apparently they came prepared. Would the dogs have been abandoned or would they have been forced to come too, swimming in the colder-than-ice water behind them? Friedrichs manoeuvres us alongside and they and their dogs scramble aboard. They have been out for a couple of days and they smell so strongly of fish I have to move upwind of them on the deck.

The *Krabbe* went as close to land as it could, and, just as we touched the edge of the ice opposite the mouth of the Ingnerit, Lissey, the three Greenlanders and I disembarked and hared along the ice with the dogs.

The föhn is strong and great gusts of it are blowing into our faces. Gradually our warmth is driven out. Lissey says nothing. His young, sensitive face seems vulnerable. He sets his jaw and looks forward. His beard is unformed, and anyway is so fair that it is hardly visible.

'All right?' I ask.

He nods, curtly. Has he forgiven me yet for embarrassing him in Holsteinsborg?

The sound of the dogs' paws changes. It is no longer a crisp trit-trot but something softer.

'We're sinking!' Lissey is looking at me, his mouth and eyes wide with panic.

I remember that sudden realisation and terror: we are on the ice in the middle of a bay and it is sinking beneath our feet. We will either drown or freeze to death.

'Keep going!' I shout it, as loud as I can. He must not stop.

He searches my face for traces of alarm but he will find none. We will survive, I am quite certain. I know the distance, the depth, the texture of the ice and the speed of the dogs. We will reach the shore. I have the deepest conviction. He looks away again. He is calmer now. He looks forward not down.

'Yes,' he calls back, looking towards the mountains, 'I will.'

We follow the Inuit to shore: a band of hard ice and then a softer band loosened by the tide, and then, at last, the foot-ice itself, adhering to the land, leading upwards on to the beach, a steady incline changing imperceptibly from solid ice to solid rock.

Still we waited. At Uvkusigsut the two wireless technicians, Kraus and Kelbl, had succeeded in establishing a time signal for Weiken to start his measurements.

I creep into the tent. Weiken is sitting on a small canvas stool. It is low and so his legs are folded up either side of him, a little like a frog on a river bank. He is crouching behind his pendulum: a shiny piece of brass threaded on to a piece of line, which he is holding up, ready to drop. Are his eyes closed? It is difficult to tell. His glasses reflect the light. All I can see where his eyes should be are two reflections of the overhanging lamp. He is wearing the headphones, and he listens without moving, like the frog waiting for his chance.

There it is. A sound. A bleep. Even I can hear it. And the frog flicks out his tongue and catches the moment: he lets the pendulum go. Weiken's head tips. The reflection of the lamp disappears and I can see his eyes following the brass as it sweeps slowly across the space between us. Every time it returns to where it started he makes a mark in the book on his knee. He does not look up, he looks only at the piece of shiny metal disappearing into darkness and then emerging again into light. Yesterday Weiken told me that this pendulum was his best friend. He said that her name is Gerda and that at home he lets her sleep beneath his bed. Did I not agree she was rather beautiful? Would I like to feel her weight? To make a good gravity measurement, he said, you need to be tranquil. You must allow nothing to disturb you. You must watch only the brass and count its swings. It becomes mesmerising. He has had such clear thoughts under its influence: he has solved problems, completed poems, and painted the most wonderful pictures in his head. It is the most compelling experience, Wegener, he said, you should try it.

I take a stool and sit opposite him. I try to imitate Weiken's eyes. I follow the swing. What does it show, this shining piece of metal? The longer it takes to swing back into position, the lower the force of gravity beneath us. Will it be slower or faster than we expect? Will it show us that the mountains surrounding Greenland have deep roots, deeper than we thought?

I have forgotten to blink. My eyes are dry. Weiken is still watching Gerda. I tip my head towards him and slowly rise. Gerda must have her favourites because I cannot hold her attention for long.

Still we waited. But the ice held fast. My daily calculations became more frantic; we were using up too much oil, food and petrol. I chewed my pipe and made splinters in my mouth. I needed somewhere else to pace.

*   *   *

I am alone, completely alone. I know that if I were to slip
and fall through the ice there would be no one to grab my
hand, no one to pull me to safety. Yet I find myself looking for
Koch . . . Sometimes, for a few seconds, I am quite certain he
is there, just behind me, his step in my step and his tall figure
in the shadows I have just passed. I turn round suddenly to
catch him. But it is just a bird or a seal slipping into the sea.
Such foolishness to be haunted by ghosts.

At last I enter the Ingnerit fjord. Now I have company.
In the middle of the ice there are two fishermen dropping
lines for sharks. They call to me and then come towards me.
Who are they? Why do I trust every man I see in Greenland?
Why do I expect each stranger to help, to share what he
has? But he always does. Now, in broken Danish, these
men offer to take me back to Uvkusigsut and my ghost is
banished.

Still we wait. Under the midnight sun the air is still. There is
a wily little weather clerk, Löwe says, playing games with us:
too much snow, too much ice, not enough wind, not enough
sun. I tell Löwe that this little clerk is killing the expedition.
He is allowing time to slip away through our fingers and we
can do nothing.

It is the sixteenth of June, almost midsummer, and we have
been waiting thirty-eight days for the ice to break. Thirty-
eight days of doing so little and with so much to be done. In
a few days the sun will start dipping nearer to the horizon
and we have still not reached Kamarajuk with supplies. A
motor schooner has arrived at Uvkusigust from Umanak and
I think her captain, Olsen, can see desperation in my eyes.
He takes me to where the ice looks most rotten. Across the
short stretch of the Ingnerit I can see the Kamarajuk fjord.
It is now completely clear, but closer to us there is still a
barrier: icebergs and their fragments in a matrix of thin
sea ice. Without changing gear Olsen begins to ram his way
forward. The pieces break, drift and then fuse together again

to form an even more solid barrier. Olsen curses, puts his motor in reverse and charges again. This time we penetrate a little farther but when the ice fuses together this time we are completely stuck. We look around desperately. There is little we can do.

'I suppose we'll just have to wait,' Olsen says. He looks over the side nervously, inspecting his hull for signs of damage. 'You might as well go and rest.'

There is a sound, a voice, crying above me. 'The ice is on the move!'

I rush up to the deck. Olsen starts the engine. The ice is moving in a mass thanks to a strong föhn, coming from the south-east. Now there is only about half a kilometre separating us from the clear waters of the Kamarajuk, but the ice is so thick that Olsen will not consider driving at it. So instead I decide to use dynamite.

Löwe and Wölcken drop stealthily on to the ice with the explosives.

The holes are small, but they are enough. The schooner pulls them apart like perforations. At last we are making progress, but it is slow and we are using up a lot of explosive. After eleven hours we are almost there.

It is five in the morning and Löwe and I are again surveying our progress.

Löwe points out a black seabird and we follow it to where it lands, a little to south.

'Why?' he says flatly, and points to where the bird has landed. Beside it the ice has broken. There is a wide rift leading through to the Kamarajuk fjord. At last, after over five weeks of waiting, we were about to start our expedition on to the great ice.

39

Can it be just four months ago we collapsed briefly on to the beach at the bottom of Kamarajuk? The sun was hot, sometimes so hot that some of my party shed their shirts and still drew sweat while they worked. Such a short time ago, and so close to where I am now. It is difficult to believe.

If I shut my eyes I can still see it: our crates lying in confused heaps, filling the entire width of the beach, ponies trying out their hooves on a new piece of gravel, Vigfus and the other two Icelanders constructing hasty enclosures for their charges, another group erecting a makeshift tent, and our two wireless experts, Kelbl and Kraus, running around with their aerial looking for a place to lead it upwards into the air.

We could not afford to rest. That evening, after everything had become a little more ordered, I called a meeting and detailed work.

They were so eager, and so willing. All they had done for six weeks was wait and now they longed to start. I gave them all tasks: Kelbl and Kraus should continue trying to establish contact on the wireless with Godhavn, the Icelanders should shoe their ponies, and everyone else was to begin excavation work, or navvying, as Georgi said, with a cheery sigh. It was something I had made sure they all knew they would have to do: there was to be hard, back-breaking work that could go on for weeks. The next day we would all go up to the break in the glacier and start. There had to be a road wide enough for the laden ponies, and another passageway, to be blown out by dynamite, that was wide enough for the motor sledges to be dragged or winched up by rope.

After the meeting I went back up to the break to remind myself of the task. I clambered between the uneven blocks, and examined the crevasses and surface streams. It would be hard work but it was feasible. There were obvious places for bridges and hairpin bends. There were walls that could be widened and places that formed natural tracks which needed just a little smoothing. But it would be soul-breaking, it would drive us all to despair. The sun would be a constant enemy, melting away the previous evening's work and then creating a little more: widening crevasses, converting snow sheltered by the planks of bridges into pedestals, deepening the channels of streams, and, at the bottom, making the ice shrink back, so that a fresh morass of mud would be sent each morning on to the beach.

The sun is sinking and Lissey is emerging from the tent. He looks towards the sea and then stretches. He doesn't turn and so he doesn't see me sitting on one of the massive rocks above him. Now he looks at his watch, smiles, turns and opens the flap of the tent. 'Get up, you stinkers, and let some air in. A man could suffocate to death in there.'

'Had a good night, Mr Lissey?' I ask.

He turns, his mouth open. Now he sees me. It is difficult to distinguish colour in this light, so his face seems merely to darken.

Now there are voices from the tent. Friedrichs: 'Lissey, you lazy dog, just shut the flaps and get some coffee going. It's your turn.'

And then Wölcken: 'And don't let it scorch this time, will you. I could hardly force it down yesterday.'

'Looks like you'd better get busy, Mr Lissey.'

I continue smoking my pipe as Lissey busies himself with the stove and the pots. On the top of a nearby cliff I have noticed a large round boulder. It is balanced there. It looks as if the merest wind would send it down to crush us. Yet it has probably been there since the last ice age. Is it an erratic brought by the ice, or merely a piece of bedrock whittled into this shape?

The smell of coffee draws the men from their tent. Little Friedrichs, bending slightly at the waist, emerges, looking scruffy and dishevelled. Wölcken, however, crawls through carefully on his hands and knees, stands, and then brushes down a pair of impeccable sealskin trousers.

We start work immediately after the porridge. It is Friedrich's turn to be cook while the rest of us have to harness fifteen ponies. Lissey does this quickly, while Wölcken is more careful. In fact he is too careful and too slow. After his second pony I cannot bear to watch and concentrate on my own task. After the saddles come the crates. While Wölcken holds the pony's head and tries to distract him, Lissey and I approach the pony's saddle from either side and try to hook the two crates simultaneously on to the harness. We step back. It is too heavy. I know it is too heavy but there is nothing we can do: there is so much equipment and so little time. The pony's legs tremble, his head twitches behind him, he neighs once, but he remains upright. So Lissey and I move on to the next.

Eventually we have loaded three trains of ponies, each with five ponies apiece. We lead them slowly towards the glacier. Every sunlit night is precious. There is so much to do.

The glacier was now alive with sound. At the bottom there was the clang of pots, the clattering of hoof against pebble, laughter, wails and whistles. In the middle section Icelandic voices mingled with the gentle rasp of ponies' teeth tearing at grass and the jangle of a harness. While at the top, above the howls of dogs, human voices interlocked, rose up and down in pitch with excitement. Isolated words would catch in the ice, and echo around the crevasses: pressure, inversion, depth, velocity, anomaly, temperature, gravity.

How I longed to stay and listen, but there was too much to do.

Johan Davidson's nickname, Kasak, means good-natured rascal, and now at last I see how the name is earned. When I tell him the payment will be the same as last year he tips his head to the side and smiles.

'Like last year?'

'Just like last year, three kroner a day, an extra kroner on the ice, another still if things get bad.'

'And the extra?'

'What extra?'

His smile becomes a line stretching across his face. How can a smile look so mirthless, so sly?

'Two sleeping bags I got, also a tent I got, and a crate . . . with food, and another crate . . .'

Is he bargaining? I am sure this list is a complete invention.

'Maybe this time, also, something else . . .' He opens his eyes slightly to examine my face. 'A little bottle, like this.' He holds up his hands. 'Aquavit. Is good. Warms Johan when his soul is cold.'

My laugh is as humourless as his smile.

'Ah, Johan, Johan, what beautiful stories you tell. I think you had just one sleeping bag, a spoilt one, of Sorge's . . . no crates.'

He waits, still smiling expectantly.

'How about if I give you another bag this time, on top of the Kamarajuk?'

He nods his head and holds out his hand.

'*Ap.*'

It is agreed.

Kasak was important to me, worth more than a sleeping bag or a crate of food or even a bottle of aquavit. Johan had been on the ice and had come back again. He had encountered the spirits, the Quivitoq, which everyone can hear, screaming in the wind. He had encountered the restless souls of those who had died and not found a newborn to take their name, he had heard the voices of the unavenged murdered, he had, no doubt, even seen the souls of hill-men possessed by the Devil. He had encountered all this but had not become possessed himself. He was still the same Johan Kasak, still as wily, but richer now and wanting more. I intended to use him as evidence. The spirits were old ideas but among some of the people they still held sway. Christianity and the old taboos lay side by side in a comfortable partnership. I needed to show them that the great ice was quite safe; we had ways of conquering it, we could lay out flags and snowmen and, like Johan Kasak, we would come back.

At every small settlement I would gather an audience and speak, Johan Davidson or Tobias Gabrielsen translating my words into Greenlandic. I showed them what I could offer and what I would ask them to do and they would finger their amulets and listen. If they were to go, what would keep them safe? Maybe the roof of a bear's mouth or the dung of a fox. It was the older men who were tempted the most, those married with children, those a little slower and less useful on the hunt. They gathered together their dogs and sledges and offered them for hire too. They looked at me with a weary expectation and followed me on to the *Krabbe*. They were not looking for adventure. They were looking for an easier life.

'I still need more kite wire,' Georgi says, and looks at me as if it is my fault.

'Haven't you any at all?'

'Oh, I've got some, just not enough.'

He checks through his list again. He is nervous. It is a long way to the middle of the ice. I have tried to reassure him, we've gone through the list he's made, and it seems to me that he has all the essentials for now, but still he worries. I have suggested that he pack the sledges a little higher, but he has rejected that idea, insisting that the dogs are overloaded already. Now he gives me another list.

'Stuff I've left out,' he says. I give it a quick glance and nod. It is, as I expect, just more of everything, and the hut, but he won't need that just yet; all of this can be brought later.

'Maybe the motor sledges could bring them,' he says, but I say nothing. They are untried and so I feel wary of depending upon them.

Ignoring my silence, he nods towards the Greenlanders' tent. 'Our new friends are being a little awkward,' he says. 'To be honest I've just about had enough. They're just trying it on, you know: first of all it's their knees, then their eyes, then they say they haven't got enough stockings or anoraks . . .'

'It's a great terror to them, all of this, the Sermerssuak.' I mouth the word carefully, proud of its acquisition, and look towards where the great ice begins its upward curve in front of us.

'I know, I know . . . they're being very brave and all that, but it just gets a little tedious, you know.'

I pat his shoulder. 'It'll be fine, Johannes, you'll see, once you start.'

'I suppose.'

'Anyway, I have something for you.'

It is the reason I am here. Besides just saying goodbye I wanted to give him this: his mail, which had just arrived on the *Krabbe*.

He looks at me. His face adjusts, the tension above his eyes slips.

'Thank you, Wegener.'

'I'll wait for you to reply, if you wish.'

It will be his last chance for some time; his final opportunity to tell his wife all the things I tell Else. He sits in his tent and removes some paper and carbon paper from his kit. Every letter we write, every list we make, is duplicated, just in case, except for our diaries – with those we take a chance.

The sledges are ready, eleven of them, the big sledges with the high curved backs, typical of west Greenland, and each one is strapped with a small mountain of luggage. So many packages! The Greenlanders have been reluctant to load their sledges so high, but Georgi has pointed out to them that the polar Inuit take far more on their sledges quite successfully. Even so I think they could have taken just a little more. The dogs howl. There is a great colony of them, almost a hundred; soon they will have to be separated into teams. Everything looks ready. I am quite envious. I wanted to go but everyone here was dead against it. Some leader, some authority! I click my fingers and everyone tells me to be quiet. But there were so many loud voices claiming that I would be more useful at Kamarajuk that I had to take notice. Only I can speak Danish, only I have the authority to negotiate with the Greenlanders; it seemed that everyone had a reason why I should stay.

Löwe and Weiken are checking their rucksacks. Löwe, as usual, is calm, but then he is only going halfway, making a depot and returning again with five of the Greenlanders; Weiken, however, will see the centre. He and his three Inuit companions will see the flat expanse, help Georgi to unpack and then return. They will know the place, they will pick the spot and give it a name: Eismitte. Now Weiken is going through each item in his pack in turn, asking Löwe whether he thinks it is essential. I clap him on the back, wish him good luck and tell him I will look after Gerda for him.

'Not too well,' he says, smiling. 'I want her to miss me.'

If only I could go there too.

By the time Löwe and his Greenlanders have come back from the midway point on the twenty-seventh of July, I have thirty-five Greenlanders working on the glacier. I am worried about our progress.

The sun darkens everyone, even me, even Löwe. He greets me on the moraine, where I am still helping to broaden the track.

'Three days to come back!' he says. 'The weather was wonderful. No wind. Blue sky. Cold. Idyllic.'

'Lucky man. Three days on a sledge with the scenery flowing past you, instead of this.'

He smiles.

We stand back to let the ponies pass. From here we have a good view. Twelve ponies in a line pass over the bridge that Lissey has made from the beach on to the glacier. Then farther up the seven ponies that have just passed us are transporting supplies from the Icelanders' depot at the break to the scientists' base above. From here the dogs scramble up to the station at the edge of the ice sheet. It is a little like a machine, one part transferring the load on to the next until it has been moved from the bottom of the glacier to the top.

'It's going well,' says Löwe.

'Yes, today I believe it is.'

Today I can admit to feeling some measure of success. If I think of all the things we have already accomplished I feel a little happier. We may yet succeed.

Such a small thing can cause my mood to change. A single louse, for instance. It can change everything. A single louse and it reminds me of so much: guns, trenches, disease. At the corner of my eye a man hovers, in the balance. Will he fall?

An exclamation mark travels up my shirt. For a while I watch. It is an idle moment, a moment while nothing happens, a moment before I know what it is. A louse. I pinch it away. But now I cannot rest. How many of its neighbours wait in the seams of my shirt? I spend the whole day washing, cleaning, treating my clothes with benzene and

Flit. It is to be expected, of course; living in close proximity to the Greenlanders makes an infestation almost a certainty. How long have the Inuit had these most intimate of friends? It is the reason that they used to go naked in their homes while the winter raged outside; they would rather be a little cool, they'd say, but alone in their clothes.

But by the time I have finished with my disinfection the day has gone and I have done nothing useful. I sit down where I am at the bottom of the Kamarajuk glacier and look around me. A telegram has come from the eastern coast, where they are attempting to set up a station to match the ones we have here and at Eismitte. I suppose I should not be surprised that spring was late there too. They are, like us, fighting to succeed.

The sun dips below the horizon with my mood. It is a relief to have a little darkness but it reminds me that winter is on its way. We have so much to do, so little time, and everyone is already exhausted. The ponies are slowing down, the moraine work has stopped, Georgi's journey on to the ice was too late and he took too little, the motor sledges are proving as problematical as I thought they would be, and the engineer Schif declares there is little likelihood of them starting soon. We are running out of supplies again and I shall have to beg for more. We never seem to have enough of anything: enough men, enough hay or enough dogs. My days are a constant battle to find more, and of course I have to accept any that will be lent, so now we have a collection of the mangiest, most ill-tempered animals that have ever been called dog. Success is slipping away with the last of the light. The summer will end soon and we have not accomplished enough.

I try to sleep but that louse is crawling on me still. I can feel where he has been and where he is about to go.

On the seventh of August Weiken returned from the centre of the Greenland ice cap with his four Greenlandic heroes.

They had left Georgi in fine spirits. They had taken fifteen days to reach Eismitte but only six to get back with the wind behind them.

They look now as if what they did was nothing. This was not just a step on to the ice but a great long stride. The big ice has been conquered absolutely this time, and there was nothing to fear: the shadows and the voices are just the wind. All the ideas that haunted them until now have surely been banished: they have not been suffocated, the dogs have not died, they have not starved and they are not possessed. But their smiles are unsure, even Johan Davidson's. Even if the spirits didn't come this time they may come the next.

40

The hum of an aircraft engine. The smell of aviation fuel. Greenlanders creeping up to Schif's great green tent.

'*Kamasuit.*' A sound, hushed but loud. '*Kamasuit.*'

I stop, relishing the word. The big sledge. Red-painted metal noses out of the tent flaps on four hickory skids. A visor looks down. A roar and then a louder one. The Greenlanders squeal, chase after hats and hoods while Schif, Kraus and Kelbl nudge each other and laugh.

'Well, what's your verdict, Wegener?' Schif says, catching sight of me.

'Good, yes, very good,' I say, nodding. I shut my eyes and listen. At last the sound of success.

One day maybe all arctic travel will be like this: hovering with the snow, lulled by a constantly roaring engine, sitting back on a padded seat, warm, safe, fast. I can smoke. I can talk. I can think about all we can do, how much we can move, how Georgi will soon have his hut at Eismitte and all the supplies he wants. We pass Sorge and Wölcken's dog sledges with ease. Schif sniggers at the oval mouths and widened eyes.

'Wave,' he tells me, 'it's only polite.' So we wave, one either side, and the Greenlanders wave back.

I say goodbye to Sorge and Wölcken and their team of Greenlanders at the margin of the ice sheet. Sorge seems to be looking forward to his winter of isolation with Georgi. I count the sledges, one trailing behidn the other to Eismitte. There are too few and each one is stashed too low.

I make calculations. I examine lists. We practise loading the motor sledges to determine their capacity. So much is needed to maintain two men for eight months in an arctic station: fuel, shelter, clothing, medical supplies and preferably a wireless. We haven't even succeeded in transporting all of the housing yet. There will have to be a final dog sledge party as well as the motor sledges, and I shall take it. This time there will be no argument.

The twenty-first of September: four days since the two motor sledges, *Eisbär* and *Schneespatz*, set off for Eismitte. Maybe they are already there. Now it is our turn. One by one the Greenlanders whoop and slash at their dogs. The crunch of sledge. The patter of the dogs' claws. The smell of the cold. At last. The start of the ice is flattened by tracks. There is little need for the black flags and the snowmen but they are there anyway. It is a fine day. Perfect sledging weather. I settle on my perch, relax against the upright bars. How Else would love this. The wind, the sound of the dogs. How often she has asked me how it feels. Maybe next summer I shall take her.

A cry ahead. Something has happened. My sledge catches up with Löwe's and then with the Greenlanders' at the front. One of the Greenlanders, Nikola, points into the distance. A streak is separating into separate pieces. It's Wölcken. Of course, it's Wölcken and his Inuit companions returning from Eismitte.

The dogs howl. Traces intertwine. We stop. There are the usual slaps on the back all round.

Wölcken is looking scruffy. At last he is looking scruffy. There is a hint of frostbite on his nose, a large bloodstain smearing the front of his fur, and when I come close I notice that he has the smell of a man who has not washed for several days. But he is happy, happier than I've ever seen him before. There is a certain bounciness about his eyes, and, when he speaks, his words stream from him.

'Well, Wölcken, how's the hermit?'

'Fit and stupidly cheerful, as usual, especially now Sorge

has joined him. You should see what he's accomplished there. The instruments . . . it's truly amazing . . . They said . . . Well, it's all in here.'

He hands me their letter. I read quickly: a list that turns into an ultimatum. I hand it to Löwe.

'We were expecting the motor sledges to overtake us,' Wölcken says.

'Ah yes, the motor sledges . . . You must have seen them.'

'Only on the way back. Halfway. They were waiting for the snow to clear.'

I turn to Löwe, I point to the piece of paper. 'Well, what do you make of that, my friend? Do we go back?'

Löwe reads from the letter. 'Seventeen large cans of petroleum, snow bucket and rucksack with contents, one box (red) marked Sorge . . . They've been rather specific.'

'Look at the end.'

'If these necessities are not here . . . by October twentieth, we shall start out on hand sledges . . .' Löwe stops, and looks at me. 'They can't do that!'

'No, it would be quite suicidal.' I am careful to keep my voice steady.

There is a short silence.

'Well, do we go back?' Löwe asks.

I look to the west. 'I rather think we should.'

How I hate false starts. When the children were small we had so many of them, we seemed to be always forgetting something. The goodbyes have to be said all over again, and then, of course, in Greenland there is all the unharnessing and reharnessing. But by the next day we were ready to go again. Everything on Georgi's list was packed, and we were sledging in our own tracks. The going was so easy that by the end of the second day we were already twenty-five miles towards our destination.

* * *

Of course, the Greenlanders hear them first.

'*Kamasuit, Kamasuit!*' One of them, Nikola, I think, comes running back, shouting, from where he was unharnessing his dogs. I stare out east, hoping he is wrong.

But I can't hear or see anything except the sky and the dunes of snow darkening. I look at Löwe and he shrugs back. The Greenlanders are still talking excitedly.

It is becoming quite dark now. If the motor sledges are indeed returning it would be quite possible for them to miss us in this gloomy twilight. We organise the Greenlanders into a chain across the snow. If the motor sledges are coming, this way there will be more chance of their seeing us. But nothing comes. We wait while the sky changes from one indigo to a darker one, but there is nothing: no hum of engine, no lights, no sound of voices, nothing. Maybe the Greenlanders, in their nervousness of the interior, are seeing spirits after all. We go back to camp, convinced that the Greenlanders have been mistaken.

But they are not. In the morning it is quite obvious; just a mile or two ahead of us are the outlines of a couple of tents and a single motor sledge. Just one sledge. As I walk forward I forget to breathe. Something is wrong. Just one sledge. What has happened to the other?

'Damned thing,' Schif says, as soon as he sees me. He gives the sledge a vindictive little kick on its paintwork. 'The piston's worn out. The same thing happened to *Schneespatz*, five miles back.'

As the rest of the dog sledge party draw up we continue to look at the motor sledge in silence.

'I don't think they're up to it,' he says, 'especially in these conditions. They overheat. They need to be bigger, more powerful.'

We all crouch inside a tent made for two while Schif relates the whole miserable tale. At the halfway point a blizzard had started up. The driving snow and wind had kept them in their tents for two days and, when conditions eventually improved, the *Schneespatz* had refused to start. It had taken an entire day of the most dangerous measures, including heating the engine with a Primus and soldering lamp, to get the engine started, and then another two days to dig out both sledges and get them moving. After this they had made one final attempt to move eastwards. They had all agreed that this was proving impossible. So they had made a depot of what they had been carrying and returned.

I can't speak. Haven't I learnt yet not to count on anything? Not on people, not on ideas, especially not on machines. But I have to speak, they are waiting for me. I remember it is important to be encouraging, but it takes me some time to think of anything encouraging to say.

'At least the load is halfway there,' I say desperately. But what good is halfway there? What good is a side of a hut 125 miles from where it should be?

'It's not your fault, you did your best,' I say, but I don't even believe that. How hard had they really tried to drive the sledges onwards?

Now we have to redistribute the loads. Such a depressing task. And we are not as organised as we should be. If only Else were here I am sure everything would be accomplished so much more quickly. I decide to help the process along. I grab hold of a petrol can, clutch it firmly around its waist and lift. It is heavier than I thought, more bulky than I remember. Just as I think it is on the sledge it begins to roll off. I try to stop it falling but it's too heavy. I push against it frantically, then, just as I am about to admit defeat and let it roll, another pair of hands appears next to mine and together we secure the can on the sledge. I look from the hands to his face. It is the young Inuit Rasmus, and when he catches my eye he smiles. I am too tired to smile back. Instead I pat him on the shoulder.

The twenty-seventh of September, six days into our journey. After saying goodbye to Schif and his team we have made little progress, and the going has been particularly difficult with snowstorms, cold winds and a steep gradient. If I look back I can still see the mountains of the western coast; the shimmering deceit of a mirage. In front of me is our small encampment. A few minutes ago all the Greenlanders crammed themselves into one of their tents for a meeting; not a good sign. They are obviously unhappy. The only thing I can do now is wait to see what they have to say.

One by one they enter. How can fourteen men fit inside a two-man tent? But they do. They sit in silence. They look at the ground. They smoke their pipes, and soon Löwe is driven outside by the stench. At last the oldest man speaks.

'We go home now. We cold.' Now he searches for words in Danish. 'We have not enough . . . skins. We . . .'

'We've given you clothes. Surely you have enough clothes.'

'When we sleep . . . is cold. The . . .' He asks behind him, receives a word and continues. '. . . dogs die. They go too long. They die.'

Has he stopped? He has not. he decides to give up on Danish and says a few words to me in Greenlandic. Such a hard, incomprehensible language. All the words sound the same and yet I understand nothing. Short vowels and strange consonants that come quickly, one after the other. I call for Löwe; he has picked up more of the language than I.

'What is it?' I ask him after they have gabbled at him again.

'I think they want some sleeping bags.'

'But they have them all.'

'I know.'

'Offer them more money.'

They shake their heads.

'Tell them they'll have to go back alone.'

But they don't seem to care. The old man looks up at me with his calm eyes and I can see I am defeated.

'Ask them if anyone is prepared to go on.'

'I can't, I don't know how.'

I point to a young man at the corner.

'You come with us?'

He hunches his shoulders and shakes his head.

'You?'

Again another shake. This is useless. I take out my pipe and add a thin trail of blue smoke to the haze of theirs.

Eventually four of the Inuit agree to continue, while eight Greenlandic cowards head back towards the west. I know I'm being harsh, I know I'm being unfair, but I keep looking at what we're having to leave behind and what we're taking and I know it's not enough. And while we weigh and repack we are wasting time. It is nearly the end of September and we are not moving one metre closer to Eismitte.

And now it snows. We watch them behind our tent flaps; mesmerising, slowly falling flakes that make my head ache. Löwe and I make calculations. Already it is the start of October and we have only reached the 75 miles cairn. This snow will make our progress even slower. The sledges will sink farther down, making it difficult for the dogs to pull, and we will run out of food. Already Detlev, the leading Greenlander, has tried a weak revolt. We decide to unload the sledges, take only what we need ourselves, and pick up the paraffin the motor sledges have depoted farther on.

So slow. Just one mile in one hour. We wade, we stagger, we get nowhere. Why do I keep fighting? Why do I not give up? But how can I give up when I know I'm right?

'We go back. Now.' Detlev faces me in the snow. His legs planted wide apart.

There is no arguing with him. Exhaustion is pulling at his face.

'All of you?' I ask, and they all nod, quietly, a little sorrowfully.

Two sledges, then. I pull at the ropes tying on my load.

There is little now to unpack but every movement hurts, and seems slower than the one before.

A hand on mine. A small face looking into mine. His eyes watching my eyes. Rasmus Villumsen. You can still go away. You needn't tell me that you will come. You needn't look for my smile, my gratitude. But he does.

Now Rasmus takes the lead. He finds the flags hidden in the snow and the twilight. It is the end of the first week of October and sun is showing little of her face. He forms a track so that Löwe and I can follow. He forces his dogs onwards and onwards again.

The snow deepens. Now the dogs are wading in it up to their bellies. There is no sound of paws, just the slow slithering of the sledges. I imagine Georgi and Sorge leaving Eismitte with just their bamboo sledge. I see them stumbling, slowing, becoming weaker and weaker. Then I watch myself coming across them, two small mounds in the snow, barely visible. Their wives are grieving and someone is comforting them. Else. The thought of her face makes me want to bury my head in the furs in front of me. What would I leave for her if I too became a snowy mound on a sledge? A house, I suppose, a pension, three children, of course. What else? Just a theory that no one mentions any more, and a book or two ... Would she be proud of me? I wonder. Would she think any of this worth it? Suddenly I want to stop. I want to turn round, go home, beg her forgiveness. What have I done to them all? When have I had enough time to really love them? I have devoted myself to so many other things, some of them so irrelevant, so stupid, when the only truly important things were my Else, my Hilde, my Käte and my Lotte.

The halfway depot, 125 miles inland. Löwe confirms the date: The thirteenth of October. We have taken twenty-two days to come just this far! We look around. How strange to suddenly come across all these objects in the snow. We think carefully and select. How little we will have to show for our efforts: one drum of petrol, one canvas bucket, a two-man tent, a shovel and a lantern.

Why do our dogs fail when they are adequately fed? Rasmus has all our load and yet his dogs are all sound. Maybe we have acquired just the ill and the old of the dog population, or maybe it is exhaustion or the cold. Every gunshot sickens me.

Rasmus has lost hope. He looks at the two dog carcasses and then looks at me.

'I go home now.'

I touch the boy on his arm and shake my head.

'We'll meet friends soon, you'll see.'

He nods and walks away.

At four o'clock dusk falls. Still Georgi and Sorge have not arrived. If they came now they would seem like ghosts. Leaving Rasmus in the tent, Löwe and I take a walk to the east. There is nothing there, no specks becoming larger, no dots moving, only the shadow of the earth falling gradually over the snow.

The dusk becomes black and then a small green glow appears on the horizon. What had we been saying? Now it seems unimportant. We are silent, waiting. From the glow a plume of light leaks into the air above us and then wafts from one side to the other. Where it passes it leaves impressions of itself in the night around us: glowing colours, reds, greens, pinks, each one gradually acquiring life and wafting too. The colours brighten, pass overhead and begin to fade.

'Do you ever hear them?' Löwe whispers. 'I did once. But then I shut my eyes and it was gone.'

'What did it sound like?'

'Like this. Listen.'

I think I hear something, a rustling that can't be here.

If I could have seen the sun's image reflected on to paper from a telescope two days ago then I would have seen a plume of light erupting from its surface. If I could have followed it, if I could have been swept along in its wind, I would have seen the earth becoming bigger and brighter. And now the wind hits the edge of our atmosphere. It takes just a single electron to feel it. A single electron to hurtle towards the magnetic poles of the earth, to crash into the gases there and light them with its energy. Which gas could cause a green light? I asked this so long ago now. Not anything we knew then. I decide to call it geocoronium.

I shut my eyes. All is quiet. The aurora borealis is fading. It is the twenty-fifth of October. If Georgi and Sorge had decided to leave Eismitte when they said they would be here by now. We are so close. All we have to do is go on.

Now winter begins to bite. It bites our faces, it even bites our breath and it bites Löwe's toes.

My hands move slowly. Every touch hurts. But sometimes it is necessary to remove my gloves, necessary to touch with my flesh. But I don't feel, I burn, everything burns: the tent poles, the dogs' traces, the pemmican cans, the cups, the stove ... We are satisfied now with half-measures. The tent is almost up. We crawl inside. A third of the dogs are separated, we crawl inside. The pemmican can is opened, the last one. We crawl inside. Inside, the hoar frost doesn't melt, even above the stove. It is cold, but it is not as cold as outside. The dogs' pemmican is so hard it can only just be broken with an axe. One blow downwards with the axe. We come inside. We must go out again but we do not, we cannot. The dogs butt at the walls with their noses. I take a breath. I plunge outwards before I can think. My breath freezes before it leaves my nose. Those tiny crystals seed others. A cascade of crystals grows around me in the air and follows me out to the dogs and back again. I scatter the hard, broken chunks of pemmican on the ground. They melt it slowly with their tongues. They are too weak to howl.

Löwe cannot feel his toes. It is something he says casually, as if it doesn't matter. I grab his feet and begin to massage.

We move forward. Rasmus is in front. Only he can stir his dogs into life. Only he can keep his sledge moving. Two hundred and thirty four miles inland. I take hold of Löwe's toes and move them around and around in my hand.

The dogs eat the last of their food. A little ahead of us Rasmus picks up a black flag and puts it back into the ice a little higher. Two hundred and forty-six miles inland.

There are no flags. There must be flags. We make camp, painfully, and wait for morning. I reach for Löwe's feet, roll them around and around inside their kamiks.

We abandon our load. It makes a pitiful pile. We lurch forward. We use the last of our paraffin. We heat our final morsel of food, a little black pudding, on the our remaining scrap of solid fuel. Löwe's toes are cold. I massage them anyway.

Outside, there is a mist. A strange mist coming from a castle. We stagger. We crawl. We hear voices. Rasmus first, then me, then Löwe. It is light then dark. White then blue. The smell of human excrement. The smell of a sooty flame. The sound of my feet on something softer then harder. And warmth.

41

So the famous meteorologist Hobbs is wrong. There is no glacial anticyclone. The air over the centre of the ice is not still, clear and cold as he claimed but is as turbulent as it is elsewhere. It snows, ferocious winds blow drifts, there are storms, heavy clouds, and days of fog. He is right about one thing, though: it is cold. Unimaginably cold. Lower than minus fifty degrees Centigrade. To go from this into an ice cave that has been heated to minus five, then, is stupefying.

Rasmus sways, clutching his head. He sits suddenly. He groans and drops his head into his hands. I would like to remove my clothes but my hands are still too clumsy. Instead I sink beside Rasmus. I look around but see nothing. Nothing I remember now. Just a space. A warm space.

'Thank you.' My breath hardly makes a mark any more in the air. 'Both of you. Thank you for staying.'

They have Löwe between them. The end of his journey has caused him suddenly to become aware of his feet. As he comes near the lamplight I see that his face is drawn in pain. He sits, clumsily, next to me, from time to time surfacing from some place to embellish the story of our journey. Finally he allows himself to be tipped backwards. The three of us are sitting on some sort of raised platform of ice, and on it are strewn furs and sleeping bags. Georgi removes his kamiks and inspects his toes. I do not need to look. I know every ridge of nail, every wrinkle of skin, and I know they are cold, white, dead.

'They need to come off,' Löwe says. 'Someone better do it soon before my entire foot goes.'

We look at each other.

'Maybe there's no need, Löwe.'

'You know that's not true. There's no point in waiting. You have a knife?'

'Of course I've got a knife. But it's too early. You must wait. There's still a chance.'

Löwe groans and throws himself back. 'You're wrong this time, Wegener. It's too late.'

We cover him up and amazingly he immediately falls asleep. Now I remove my furs. Underneath them all I can feel rivulets of sweat trickling and then being soaked up in my underwear. I can't believe it is below freezing, but Sorge assures me that it is and that they have deliberately kept it so, otherwise the ice melts and drips upon them when they are sleeping and working. I look around. There are two icy platforms here. When Rasmus is led to the other he sleeps too.

Now it is Georgi's turn to talk. He tells me how it began, how he began to dig almost as soon as he had got here to make a place for his fragile mercury barometer which had arrived at the station miraculously unbroken. The tent was no good, too small, so he dug a cave, three metres below the ice. Then he needed a place to make the hydrogen for the balloons and then a sheltered place to fill them, so he dug again. Two more caves. Then when Sorge came, he started to dig too; he needed a place to store his seismological equipment.

'We both started work immediately, Wegener, look.' He shows me his books. 'We haven't missed a day – wind velocity, pressure, temperature, the lot. Look.'

I whistle appreciatively.

'But then it got colder,' Sorge says.

'Yes, minus thirty-five in August, minus forty in September, minus forty-five degrees Centigrade in October.'

'So we took this kerosene lamp Georgi made' – Sorge holds up a jam pot with a sardine-can handle and four glass photograph plates above – 'and decided to become troglodytes.'

'Every time we fancy another room we just dig out a little more and add the ice to the surface. Did you notice the tower?'

'I'd like to see it again.'

I've said the right thing. Georgi is delighted. The three of us head to the surface. Georgi shows me around: a proprietorial estate agent.

'Up here, the tower, with the theodolite in position, as you see, for following the balloons. Notice the attention to detail, gentlemen, the fine craftsmanship of the balustrade, for example, and the built-in seat. Now, if you follow me down . . .' We descend a spiral stair, and encounter a corridor leading underground.

'Avoiding the shovel just there, if you don't mind. Yes, another spadeful would not go amiss, Dr Sorge.'

Sorge shovels a small mound of drifted snow out of the way of the entrance.

'To the right, the balloon cavern; open, of course, to the atmosphere. We call it our terrace. We like to take the occasional aperitif here, don't we, Dr Sorge? Just before dinner, underneath the stars.' He gives a quick snigger.

'Now through the double door, if you please – best reindeer skin, you'll notice, no compromises in this establishment, of course . . .'

It is dark now and the wind has disappeared. The skins make an astonishingly effective seal. Georgi lights his lamp and flashes it into the opening on the right.

'Here we have the hydrogen-making room, replete, of course, but not replete enough, with calcium hydride and a little acid. Notice the highly ingenious tube leading from this room to the balloon-filling room next door.'

We move quickly on. Even in the cold, the smell of excrement carries.

'This, gentlemen, is the stores, such as they are. A little more work needed here perhaps for it to match the high standards of the rest of our little fortress . . .'

We go out into the corridor again. Ahead of us is another skin door. Georgi pushes it aside.

'And in front of us, Dr Sorge's pet project . . . After some thought he decided to go for the staircase prototype rather than the vertical shaft. We thought it would comply more closely with health and safety regulations.' He stops to share a smirk with Sorge. 'Notice the complete mastery of the ice chisel, if you would, and the ruler. Each step is precisely twenty centimetres below the one above . . . is that not so, Dr Sorge? Notice the skilful carving of handholds and recesses for lamps. Still in its preliminary stages perhaps . . . but quite impressive nevertheless.'

'How far down have you got?' I ask Sorge.

'Just a couple of metres so far – the ice getting colder and denser all the time.'

'And now, of course, the central hub of the establishment, the living quarters. Notice the extensive use of built-in furniture: beds, chairs, cupboards, hooks for clothes . . .'

'The marble-effect decor.'

'Ah yes, a little problem with one of the stoves.'

'The descending ceiling.'

'Maybe a little attention needed there from one of our resident engineers . . .'

Georgi gives up. We sit around the stove.

'Well, what can I say, you two. I'm impressed, very impressed. You're so comfortable here. I'd never have believed it possible.'

'Of course, we had to . . . If we'd stayed out there . . .' Georgi gestures upwards with his hand. 'We'd never have survived.'

'And you've accomplished so much work. So many measurements, every day. It really is most impressive.'

'Of course, we wished to do more.'

'Yes, I know.'

'I'm not going to have the chance to do much that I planned.' Georgi looks at me. Is he complaining? Is he blaming me that the supplies haven't come? Maybe he thinks that if he had come out alone, as part of a much smaller expedition, he would have accomplished more.

'If you manage to just stay here the whole year and take the measurements you're doing now it will be a great thing. Something the world will acknowledge and celebrate.'

Georgi grunts. 'When is any German celebrated these days?'

'They will, you'll see. One day everyone will know what you've been through here and will appreciate your dedication. Both of you.'

Sorge smiles. 'I could have done with that rope ladder,' he says wistfully.

'And gloves and torches and candles and clothes and bandages.'

'And a wireless.'

'And batteries, a few drilling tools . . .'

'And a little matter of a hut.'

'And a gramophone. Oh, what I'd do for a little music.'

'I could sing a little.'

'Your Brünnhilde is too high, Sorge.'

It was important to plan what we would do next. I was anxious for Rasmus and I to go. Every hour we were here we were wasting time. We discussed ideas in a council of war. There was certainly enough food for two men. Obviously Löwe was not fit to return, and Georgi had to stay, but what about Sorge? Löwe would be an invalid, unable to produce any of the glaciological measurements. Another able man would be needed; so it would be better if Sorge stayed too. But could the food be stretched to feed three? We checked supplies. It was just possible with the strictest economy. Sorge would stay.

That Friday, the last day of October, I rested. It was my last day of being forty-nine. After midnight we celebrated my birthday with a defrosted apple apiece.

Some images you know you will carry in your head for ever. They are the treasured beads you would like to pick out from the string and carry alone on a chain.

Georgi and I are lying on our ice beds in our sleeping bags. We are warm, happy, we have just finished telling Sorge a little anecdote about our time together in Hamburg: and Sorge is hobbling around in his bag, feeding sandwiches to anyone who is still awake.

We slept and then it was time to go. Georgi packed us food and organised the dogs. We had seventeen animals and two sledges. Around us swirled the frozen mist from the cavern's vent. It was daylight but it wouldn't last long. We posed for pictures. Sorge's moving-picture camera turned.

Sorge and then Georgi hugs Rasmus's fur and then mine. We shake hands. No one can find anything to say. We mount the sledges. The dogs are lively after their rest.

I look back. Two figures are waving after us. Behind them the fairy castle, a wall, a tower, complete with crenellations. Some people would call it a folly.

42

What can I tell you about the first days of this last journey? It was cold, of course, and the going was good. The snow had a hard crisp surface that the dogs' legs barely dented. The wind was at our backs. I felt happy. I was going home. I had made the worst journey anyone had ever made on Greenland and I had survived. Sorge and Georgi and Löwe were safe at Eismitte and were working well. When we returned to Germany we would have a treasure trove of results. I kept thinking about Köppen's face when he saw them, how he'd be astounded at the temperature and the force of the wind, how he'd laugh at the lack of an anticyclone.

Of course, the days were short. The sun had hardly shown itself above the horizon before it sank again, and for the first two days it was anyway completely obscured by fog. Rasmus and I worked well together. He was almost silent, answering questions in single words of Danish. He showed the same efficiency at finding the flags, and at camp we divided the tasks between us much as before; he dealt with the dogs while I dealt with the tent. But the nights were cold, even colder than they had been a few days earlier. We huddled together, but it was impossible to get warm. We woke early, decamped slowly by torchlight, tripped over the dogs and their traces in the darkness, and went on.

Four days passed before the dogs showed signs of weakening, and six days before they started collapsing as they ran.

It is snowing. There is no point in moving. Around us the dogs emit the piteous wail of the newborn. They are too weak to throw back their heads. Too weak to rise from the burrow that their bodies have made. When I break up their pemmican with an axe only a few manage to stand, only a few career towards it in their old way. The rest creep, making the sad, slow walk of the very old. Rasmus looks at me. They are not going to last.

In the night a dog creeps in. He lurches towards my bag and lays his warm head on my knees. In the morning he is cold. When I gather up the dogs I count. Two more mounds of snow-covered fur that do not move. Another has to be shot. Thirteen dogs that will not last. I throw a can of their meat into the snow. We have too much. We need to lighten the load. We are still 177 miles from the western coast.

The air warmed but the snow deepened. We had reached the edge of the plateau and were slowly coming down. The ice became textured with wide, deep ripples. At the crest of each ripple the snow was solid. In the troughs it was not. We shoved our way through the troughs, dogs and men both sweating with effort. Once my feet became wet they never became dry.

After ten days the snow deepened even further. There were no ridges. There was just the snow, sharp like sand. Every movement forward a bitter struggle. The dogs fought and lost. At last there were too few for two sledges. We were 158 miles from the western coast. We stopped, we camped, we repacked. We left one sledge by a broken cairn. We continued, Rasmus on his sledge, and I following. One ski in each track.

The ski will not glide. All I can hope for is that the grains will move apart and let me through.

I tried to keep up. At the beginning of the journey I did keep up. After I had slept it was just possible. One foot pushed forward and then the other. A rhythm I could not afford to let go.

I slip. My ski is slightly out of line and I stumble. I lurch forward with my sticks, saving myself. I stop. I watch my breath clouding the air in front of me. Rasmus is fading. I try again. One step. The effort is huge. Another. How can I forget what to do in seconds? Another. Another. I am determined to make them move. Levers: they should work like levers. Rasmus has gone. Fog swirls around where he was. I try to keep to his track.

That first time, yesterday, he was waiting for me. We made camp when I caught up with him. We rested when we shouldn't have rested and this morning I was determined we should make up time. There was a fine snow, not enough to hinder us, and just a scrap of a breeze. 'Keep going,' I told him. But he shook his head. 'You must. I'll catch you up.' And at first I had.

It is strange the way the snow swirls. I have never noticed this before but sometimes you can make out shapes. You can see things you know are not there. In the last few minutes I have seen spirits, wolves, polar bears and people I know. Am I going forward? It is difficult to tell. I can't see enough to take a bearing. Sometimes I think I have missed Rasmus's tracks altogether and I am simply following my own, around and around.

A rock. My face hitting snow, air, ground, cold.

How does he know where to find me? the dogs are breathing in my face. A smell of rotting fish. His hand reaches down. He indicates for me to remove my skis and I do. We are too much for the dogs, but we do not go far. The 125-mile depot. Already. Is it a mirage? No, it is real. Great cans of petrol. Crates of food. Even the sides of a house. An oasis in the desert.

Have I told you about my beads? Well, here is a little one. Rasmus putting up a tent by lamplight.

Here is another: a small red wooden box, half submerged in snow.

Here is another: the same small red box on the kitchen table at 9 Blumengasse Graz, and Else, packing it with straw.

'You should forget them,' she is saying. 'They don't matter.'

But I walk away.

'Alfred!'

I do not turn. She overtakes and stops me.

'It doesn't matter what they think, what they say, anything. You have us and we have you. It's the only thing that matters.'

When I go back it will still be there: my fairy tale. What will make it true?

'Forget them, Alfred.'

The box is sitting on the quay side. Else is looking, inspecting its contents. When she sees me she chalks its side quickly.

'When you see this again, remember your promise.'

A promise. I can't remember what it was.

We sleep. We wake. When he mounts his sledge, Rasmus looks at me with a question.

'Keep going. Don't slow down.' I clap him on the shoulder.

The snow is thicker today. It hides the ground in a heavy dry mire. My legs are pistons, like Kurt's legs, a long time ago, on a frozen river. The arms join in. I am a machine. Nothing more. A machine following Rasmus and his sledge and his dogs. A gentle snow is falling. Adding to the ground. The wind driving it forwards, with me. Snow on the ground. Snow in the air. None of it melts. My skis push through it like the western side of a continent. To watch it is mesmerising. One foot, then another. One hand out and then the next . . . One continent forcing its way through a white sima. What could make it move? What could make it crumple? If I could answer this, would they listen? Rasmus fades. Comes into view. Fades again. I have the sensation that I am walking in nothing. I look ahead. Like the fog, the snow forms shapes. In front of me a man, falling.

A hand. Whose hand? A hand reaching down. A hand reaching down towards me through the ice. Willy's? Kurt's? I don't remember falling.

A hand, pulling, pulling me up. Köppen? The smell and sound of dogs. Koch?

My feet beneath me, not mine, dragging through the snow. How are they being dragged? By whom? It doesn't matter. All that matters is that they are moving. There is no one to convince. It is true, and that is the only thing that matters.

The smell of a sledge. A bear skin, oily on my face. A jolt and I move again. The sweeping sound of the skids. The muffled ticking of the dogs' paws. They are slow now and becoming slower. The snow has stopped falling. If I move my eyes I can see the ice. Oh, if you could see it as I see it now – a sweeping, glistening carpet, hovering, and above it the sun stretching as it sets – your heart would hurt too.

Extract from *New York Times*, December 12 1931

WEGENER MEN SEEK TO CONTINUE WORK

German Greenland Expedition Balked by
Lack of Funds, Urges Public Interest

MORALE SAID TO BE HIGH

Loss of Leader and Reich's Refusal of Money Failed
to Dampen Ardor

Rockwell Kent reports

Despite lack of money, physical handicaps and the loss of the leader, Dr Alfred Wegener, who perished under tragic circumstances, the members of the German expedition to Greenland have kept up their morale and their eagerness to continue the meteorological and geological observations in the inland ice field of the island continent.

In a letter received here yesterday from Rockwell Kent, artist, author and explorer, public interest in the continuation of the expedition's work is urged. The leading spirit, according to Mr Kent, is Dr Fritz Loewe of the Prussian Aeronautical Observatory, whose appeal for a relatively small amount of money for the upkeep of the expedition was declined by the German Government because of lack of funds . . .

. . . Work Pushed With Ardor

In another part of his letter Mr Kent wrote:
'The death of Wegener appears to have in no way affected the morale of the expedition, and the work that had been planned has been proceeded with all the ardor that good men could bring to it. It had been the hope of some members of the expedition to continue here in Greenland for another year and the request for funds to support it for that time was sent to Germany. It has,

however, been definitely refused, on the ground that German finances were in so critical a situation that not one mark could be spared for any scientific or exploration activities whatever . . .'

. . . Dr Loewe, whose toes were frozen and had to be amputated with a pocketknife, has written to Mr Kent outlining the plans and hope of the members of the German expedition. After declaring that a request for 15,000 marks had been refused in Germany he described the 'modest plans for the future' as follows:

'The work would be mostly of a meteorological nature. In view of the many plans concerning an air route from Europe to America over Greenland I need not point out the importance of the meteorological conditions of the Inland Ice Sea. Particularly important would be an examination of the conditions in the higher strata of the atmosphere . . .

. . . Plan to Use Balloons

'We plan to use balloons in order to measure air currents and also to use captive balloons for measuring temperature and humidity in the higher air strata. Outside of this we plan to make observations on glaciers, which will be very helpful for a proper understanding of the Ice Age. We would also study the origin of glaciers and icebergs, which have such a decided effect on climate and are so important to mariners.'

Dr Loewe added in his letter that he planned to have at least two scientists and a mechanic with him.

'I am willing to work without salary,' he wrote, 'in order to carry on the work of our dead leader Alfred Wegener, with whom I stood on very intimate terms . . .'

Author's Note

In the 1968 Annual General Meeting of the American Philosophical Society the geologist J. Tuzo Wilson described a 'major scientific revolution in our own time' which he proposed should be called the 'Wegenerian revolution' in honour of its chief proponent, Alfred Wegener. By this time it was widely, but not universally, accepted that a geological revolution had taken place.

Wegener's idea, that the continents of the earth are mobile, had been revived in the 1950s. A newly invented instrument, the magnetometer, allowed the study of rock magnetism in various parts of the world, and plotting the results showed that not only do the poles of the earth reverse periodically, they also shift, and this shift appears to be different from place to place; in other words the land masses move independently.

This evidence was supported by studies of the oceanic floor in the 1960s. From studies of gravity, heat flow and magnetism it was proposed that the ocean floor is generated at the mid-oceanic ridges, where rising convection currents in the magma push new material to the surface, and that this continual production of new floor causes the continents to be pushed apart. But instead of the continents behaving like icebergs pushing through a sea of sima, as Wegener had proposed, it was now suggested that the earth's crust consists of a small number of plates which constantly move against each other. These plates are formed at the oceanic ridges and are consumed back into the magma at the oceanic trenches, where one plate sinks below the other. The continents ride on these plates, moving as the plates move. In this way Wegener's theory of Continental Drift evolved into the theory of Plate Tectonics, which is the theory accepted today to explain features on the earth and those on other planets in the solar system.

Wegener's ideas on the formation of raindrops are also now the accepted hypothesis, certainly in cold clouds, although it is usually named after the meteorologists that developed his theory later: Bergeron and Findeison. His work on lunar impact craters was largely forgotten, although the idea that they have been caused by meteorite impact is now undisputed.

I was surprised to find that in spite of the importance of Wegener's ideas his name is little known today. There is little written about him in English for the general reader and most of my information has been pieced together from various German sources; in particular his many papers and the biographies written by his wife, Else Wegener, and Ulrich Wutzke. I have derived Wegener's voice from his expedition diaries, and I have incorporated contemporary recorded comments from the various conferences on Continental Drift.

Although this book is based on real events it is fiction and I have altered a couple of details to give the story a better structure; for example, the location of Sabine Island was found using trigonometric measurements from Danmarkshavn (which in turn was located using the lunar method) rather than the lunar method directly, but the outcome was the same. Incidentally the radio transmission measurements, which Benndorf mentions, turned out to be rather too large; Greenland is moving away from Europe, but just a few centimetres a year.

Further Reading

I have found the following books and papers particularly useful and I am indebted to their authors: Benndorf, Hans. 'Memorial Notice on Alfred Wegener'. *Gerlands Beiträge zur Geophysik*, 31, pp. 337–77 (1931); Brewer, Griffith. *Ballooning and its Application to Kite-Balloons*; Briggs, David; Smithson, Peter; Addison, Kenneth; and Atkinson Ken. *Fundamentals of the Physical Environment*. 2nd ed.; Chickering, Roger. *Imperial Germany and the Great War 1914–1918*; Drake, Ellen T., & Lomar, Paul D. 'Origin of Impact Craters'. *Geology*, 12 (7) pp. 408–11 (1984); Dreyer, J.L.E. 'On the Original Form of the Alfonsine Tables'. *Monthly Notices Royal Astronomical Society*, 80, pp. 243–62 (1920); Freuchen, Peter. *Arctic Adventure: My Life in the Frozen North*; Georgi, Johannes. *Mid-Ice. The Story of the Wegener Expedition to Greenland*. Transl. by F.H. Lyon; Koch, J.P., and Wegener, A.L. *'Die Glaciologischen Beobachtungen der Danmark-Expedition'*. *Meddelelser om Grønland*, 46, pp. 5–77 (1911); Koch, J.P. Trans. E. Wegener. *Durch die weisse Wüste*; Krabbe, Th. N. *Greenland, Its Nature, Inhabitants and History*; Lutgens, Frederick K., & Tarbuck, Edward J. *The Atmosphere: An Introduction to Meteorology*. 7th ed.; Markham, Sir Clements Robert. *The Lands of Silence: A History of Arctic and Antarctic Exploration*; Marvin, Ursula B. *Continental Drift. The Evolution of a Concept*; Miller, Russell. *Continents in Collision*; Reinke-Kunze, Christine. *Alfred Wegener. Polarforscher und Entdecker der Kontinentaldrft*; Schwarzbach, Martin. *Alfred Wegener. The*

Father of Continental Drift. Transl. Carla Love; J.M. Scott. *The Private Life of Polar Exploration;* Smith, Anthony, & Wagner, Mark. *Ballooning;* Wegener, Alfred. *The Origins of Continents and Oceans.* Trans. from the 4th ed.; Wegener, Else. *Alfred Wegener. Tagebuucher, Briefe, Erinnerungen etc.;* Wegener, Else. *Greenland Journey. The Story of Wegener's German Expedition to Greenland in 1930–31;* Wegener-Köppen, Else. *Vladimir Köppen, ein Gelehrtenleben;* Winter, J.W. *The Experience of World War I;* Wutzke, Ulrich. *Durch die Weisse Wüste.*